I0571937

WHAT TIME FORGETS

THE DAUGHTERS OF ARD CREGGAN

K. E. REDMOND

Copyright © 2010 K. E. Redmond

All rights reserved.

ISBN-10: 0615434762
ISBN-13: 978-0615434766 (Tully House)

ACKNOWLEDGMENTS

Cover design by Keith Oberlin, cover photography by K. E. Redmond. With thanks to J.C. Oleson and J. Hind for their generous comments and editorial assistance.

What time forgets,

With longing song

Will swiftly come to mind

—ARD CREGGAN FOLK SONG

CHAPTER ONE

The supply frigate trembled and rolled in the water like a broken toy as each round of missiles tore deeper into her sides. The St. Ares was going down. An explosion aft and the ship listed, spilling cargo, burning spars and seamen's bodies into the sea. The last lifeboat dangling in its lines tore loose and cracked like an egg shell against the hull. Below deck, the cold Galena Sea was rushing in to fill the St. Ares' belly, reaching in to swirl and pull against a man's knees as he struggled to stand upright in the wash. Thankfully, the cold numbed the pain from an ugly gash in his leg. It could do nothing for the man he dragged up the galleyway. From the man's side a long streak of red ran down to mingle with the black water. They halted at the bottom of a ladder leading up to the deck.

"Can you climb?" the younger man shouted over the din of exploding shells and a ship in her death throes. "Jomini, listen to me. Can you climb?"

The wounded man raised his head with effort. "Tiernan. Please. Leave me."

The ship heaved, slamming both men against the metal ladder. Tiernan winced, but Jomini had lapsed into unconsciousness again. Staggering against the water's tow, Tiernan slung his companion over his shoulder and climbed, half in pain, half in panic. The heat from the fires raging above deck scorched his face as they emerged into the open air, but the rising water below was no better alternative.

Rolled out on deck, Jomini groaned and opened his eyes.

"They'll be boarding," he rasped, the smoke deep in his lungs.

There was the splash of oars alongside. A grappling hook flew up to rake across the deck. Tiernan rolled to the deck edge. Below in the water, there was a small boarding party, maybe eight men. There was still a chance. He crawled back to Jomini. The dying man's eyes fluttered open.

"There are things I should have told you."

He fumbled with stiffening fingers to pull a chain from around his neck.

"Take this. For the girl."

A silver pedant dangled at the end of the chain. Jomini pushed it into Tiernan's hand.

"You know a way out? Yes, I knew you would."

His voice was so weak Tiernan barely caught the words.

"You'll need the ring. Return it to Gurama. Zoë must know where it is," he murmured. "I was too blind . . .too sure," he whispered.

He grew heavy in Tiernan's arms, his head lolling now with each roll of the ship. Tiernan slipped the pendant's chain around his neck as another grappling hook flew up and over the side. It caught. He rolled away from Jomini's body and fell down the ladder. Below deck, he retraced his steps up the galleyway, wading through the now waist-deep water. There was a hatch, a tight fit even for his narrow shoulders, but a way out. In the water, he hid among the bodies of the crew as the ship was boarded and the dying screams of those still alive carried to him over the waves. Behind him, the burning hulk of the St. Ares began its descent to the ocean floor. A long time later, the flames sputtered out in the dark water, and the night grew blacker. But by then, he was far away, feeling a rocky beach beneath his feet and the pendant warm against his skin.

4

CHAPTER TWO

"Motley, doesn't it worry you?"

"What's that, my most benevolent lady?"

Motley was feeling agreeable. It wasn't every day a daughter of the Ten Families entered his shop. And Lady Deich, despite her relative youth, was most influential. She was pleasant enough to look at, too. Perhaps a bit on the thin side. He preferred women with a bit of heft. Her hair was short and a most unorthodox red. And she wore pants. He almost shuddered. Still a man might be captivated by those eyes. Green, a rare color for Publicans. But, as always, she was chaperoned.

And by that old relic Aka, too. Now there was a spoilsport. The Lady was a bit old to need a chaperon, or maybe he was her tutor. Such a pity. Learning spoiled a woman. But these old Publican families had peculiar ideas about their females.

Motley smiled. Zoë Lady Deich returned the smile. Fortunately, they could not read each other's thoughts.

"Doesn't it worry you," Zoë repeated innocently, turning the pendant in her hand to read the markings, "that it's a fake?"

Motley opened his mouth and nothing came out. He tried again.

"Lady, I've been called a thief and worse. But no one," he placed a trembling hand over his heart, "no one on eight

5

continents will say that my goods are not genuine. Never. I swear this on my beloved wife's head."

Zoë hid her smile. Everyone knew Motley's talented wife made some of his best forgeries. The shop's door chime announced another customer but Motley was deaf to it. He heard only the sound of a sale going sour.

Motley sold whatever flotsam drifted into the city of Ard Creggan. Crammed into his shop's dusty corners, hanging from its rafters, and wedged somewhere between basement and attic was the trash of untold households, the spoils of several military campaigns, and at least one art movement. Everything could be found at Motley's, providing you looked hard enough. And didn't mind a dubious bill of sale mixed in with the dirt.

"It is a fine pendant, gracious lady," Motley protested, "with engravings by the talented monks of the Island of Gurama. The Publican who sold it to me—and he sold it to me on his deathbed—swore it had been in his family for four generations. He only parted with it to pay the burial fees and," he added matter-of-factly, "because he could not stand his relatives. So you can see it is worth every bit of what I ask."

"I'll give you whatever you're asking," a voice behind them said.

Motley's face brightened. A counter offer was always good for business. The newcomer was taller than Zoë, who was a bit over average height herself. By his bearing, he might have been a military man, but the cane he leaned on, and his grey hair clearly showed the career was in the past. Most interesting of all, he was a stranger. A fact worth noting. In Ard Creggan, all Publicans of a certain class either knew or had heard of each other.

Motley's bow merged apology and encouragement.

"I am afraid the illustrious Lady Deich has expressed an interest in this particular merchandise, but I would be happy to show you others."

At the mention of her name, the stranger's expression quickened into interest. He bowed to Zoë.

"My apologies, Lady. I meant no disrespect."

He continued to look at her so intently Zoë felt the blood rising to her face. "Forgive me for staring," he said kindly enough. "Your father and I are acquainted. I'm afraid I was looking for a resemblance."

"I'm told I look more like my mother," she said inspecting him in turn.

She had the direct gaze of a woman who had been frequently told that looks don't matter.

"Yes," he said, "you have her smile. And her hair. Or was hers auburn? It has been a long time. One forgets."

He plucked the pendant from her palm before she could close her fist around it.

"Are you interested in these?" he asked.

He turned the piece, letting it catch the lamp light. "I understand it is customary for a Publican to receive such a pendant at birth."

"Some wear their pendants from cradle to grave," Zoë replied. "It is a charm. Our shield. Without it, we feel unarmed."

"Pardon me, if this is an unusual request, I am not sure of the etiquette in these matters, but would it be possible to see yours?"

"I don't wear one," she said simply. "I don't believe in them."

Donncha chuckled and dropped the pendant into her expectant palm.

"You are unusual, I think, Lady Deich. Do you get that independence of mind from your father?"

"He taught me there usually is a good explanation for anything we choose to think of as mystical or strange," she replied simply. "He didn't encourage mysticism. He just has a passion for crystals."

Donncha looked thoughtful. "Your father is a collector of some note. And you're right to call it a passion, Lady. Passions consume and collecting is a consuming passion. Some men feel a little of the passion, you might call it warmth. They collect to fill shelf space," he said, "or perhaps to be admired by others. Some,

7

like myself, collect for the love of an object. Ours is a passion, of a kind. But there is another."

"And what would that be?" Zoë asked, reluctantly curious.

His gaze met Zoë's.

"Those who see collecting as a means to an end. Beware of those collectors, Lady Deich. They cannot be trusted."

She shivered despite the closeness of the shop. At that moment the door flew open. There was shouting outside. A man in a high-collared military coat stood in the doorway.

"Captain," he said, "you'd better get out here. We have trouble."

Donncha turned back to Zoë. "I am happy to have met the daughter of an old friend," he said, "and sorry we did not have more time to become better acquainted. Please tell your father Donncha of the Citizen delegation wishes his continued good health."

"Shall I tell my father you will visit us while you are in Ard Creggan?" Zoë's question caught him at the door. Outside, the commotion was growing louder, yet Donncha paused and looked back. His expression, Zoë thought, was one of peculiar sadness.

"It is kind of you, Lady Deich," he said, "But I believe our stay here will not be long."

With that, he was gone. Motley crossed the shop as swiftly as his bulk—and the narrow aisles of his shop—would allow, to lock the door after him.

"Citizens" he hissed.

"You know him?"

"An interfering old man, my most patient Lady. I have had some minor dealings with him before. A meddler. Just the other day he had the audacity to say one of my Boldan sculptures was . . ." Motley caught himself. "But then, my most honored Lady," he continued smoothly, "he is a friend of your renowned father's, who has not visited us in some time. I hope he is well?"

"He is well enough. When he returns to Ard Creggan I am sure he will visit you. But we were discussing the pendant."

"Yes, my most persistent Lady. The pendant. A fine piece. One worthy of your father's collection."

His smile was ingratiating but Zoë discovered her own mood had changed.

"Publicans are using their money to buy food these days, Motley, not pretty rocks. I'll give you half your price. Because sometimes you are an honest dealer."

Not too much later, Zoë emerged from the shop with the price she wanted on the pendant and a tapestry that caught her eye.

Shijian period. Second-rate, but good texture. Aunt Livia will like it. Even Aka was pleased.

"I do not believe your father possesses such a crystal," he said, as they left the shop. "I am familiar with his entire collection and I do not recall such a specimen."

Zoë gave him half her attention. Donncha had been the only interesting thing to happen all day. The shouting they'd heard earlier had stopped, but now an unusually large crowd blocked the street. As her eyes adjusted to the weak afternoon sun, she realized she couldn't move from her spot on the sidewalk outside the store. At her elbow, a dwarf with a monkey on his shoulder pushed by, finding openings in the forest of legs while everyone else was forced to a standstill.

"It must be the Citizen delegation," one Publican said to no one in particular. "Another insult to their dignity and the guard has been called out to get them home all nice and safe."

A man next to him eyed the crowd with distaste. "They're crazy to let these Citizens out on the streets," he complained. "Too many fanatics. There'll be bloodshed one of these times. Then where will their precious peace talks be?"

His neighbor took a lighter view of the trouble. "Well, then we'd be back where we started," he said, "and no one to say we're worse off. Ard Creggan will survive without these beggars."

Another fool, thought Zoë. *He has no idea.*

Some of Ard Creggan's Ten Families encouraged the talk—and the occasional violence against Citizens—as long as their hands were clean. She suspected the key instigator was Sinon Yar, titular head of the Yar Family. He usually found some weak-minded soul to do his dirty work. Zoë saw his hand in this disturbance.

Aka twitched beside her,

"Please, Miss. Your aunt would not like you to be among this rabble."

A Publican within earshot gave him a sour look and Aka became very busy shaking the dust from his robes. Zoë soothed him.

"Let's just see what the excitement is about first. We'll be home in plenty of time." If Donncha was in trouble, perhaps she owed it to her father to see what she could do. What she could see, barely, were the helmet cockades of the Ard Creggan guards, the Counselor's personal troops, making their way through the crowded streets. The people fell away before them, clearing the street. As the Citizen delegation passed, Zoë saw him. But it wasn't Donncha.

It had been nearly ten years since she'd seen Tiernan. He'd been a boy then. Not surprisingly, the years had changed him. He walked with a slight limp now. He was more angular, harder somehow. But the rest was as she remembered. It wasn't his size that set him off from the surrounding Publicans. It was the way he carried himself even in that hostile throng, with an assurance verging on arrogance. Then too, with his dark cropped hair and in the drab clothes all Citizens affected, he stood out in Ard Creggan like an undertaker at a wedding.

It was less than a moment, then the delegation and its guard swept past. The crowd, deprived of its amusement, scattered.

"Did you see them, Lady Zoë? The Citizens?" Aka asked, fanning himself.

Zoë scowled. "They're not animals in an exhibit, Aka."

"Citizens," he sniffed, shutting his fan with a snap. "I've never understood why we let them into the city. A shiftless people. Thieves."

"That's enough, Aka. Come on. We'll be late."

She moved into the press of foot traffic, slowed as much by her thoughts as by Ard Creggan's obstacle course of narrow maze-like streets. Preparations were at full roar for the winter solstice celebration. Booths jostled each other along the streets and carts of all sizes bulged with masks, incense, moon-shaped sweets and, in certain quarters, compounds for celebrants who required a more illicit observance of the holiday. Tonight began the celebration of both the holiest and the most profane of all holidays in Ard Creggan, the winter solstice.

Ard Creggan was a city built atop a pillar of rock in the bowl of a dormant volcano. It was an old city even before the first families staked out their domains within its walls. Digging the foundations for their homes, they came across remnants, a pottery shard, a fragment of a mosaic, left by a more ancient people. The remnants were displayed in museums with very plausible captions, but little was actually known about them— only that they had built the first foundation of Ard Creggan. And that one day they had left.

Now, in the 20th year of the 20th anno cycle, Ard Creggan stood on the eve of the winter solstice. The educational possibilities of the encounter with the Citizens were obviously on Aka's mind as he tried to keep up with Zoë in the holiday crowd.

"There are those, my lady," Aka began, eager to display his scholarship and at the same time improve the mind of his student, "who say the ancestors of the Citizens were the original inhabitants of Ard Creggan. Of course, that's a complete fallacy and not given any real credence by those of us familiar with the historical texts. There are now and ever shall be the Ten Families. And of course, the Counselor." He whispered the name reverently.

Ard Creggan was ruled by the Concordia of Families, headed by the first of the Ten Families, the Deich. They hadn't always been so unified.

Centuries ago, the Ten Families emerged from a jumble of factions. At first, they were little more than well-armed thugs, feuding, making easily broken treaties. Bitter rivalries spawned massacres, double-dealing and generations who lived only to revenge themselves and reclaim whatever fleeting glory they'd heard recounted in family histories. As always, old men planned the battles and young men died. Mothers cried, but only in their sleep. To grieve was to give aid to the enemy. To sue for peace was treason. Then the Counselor appeared.

"We owe the Counselor everything," Aka continued, oblivious to Zoë's bored look. She had heard it all so many times before. "He found the first ore deposits beneath Ard Creggan. And it was he who gave us the means to produce the metal. And fabricate our armaments. Such a wonderful metal. Do you know a single filament of the metal, no thicker than a hair, is strong enough to lift several tons? Oh, it is phenomenal. Nothing like it has ever been seen. The city is famous for it. And so light. We protect our metal, Miss. Our secrets. It is outlawed, punishable by death, for anyone to share the secrets of the ore and metal making."

Zoë gave him only half a mind. *The Counselor.* She was tired of hearing about him. Everyone in Ard Creggan revered — and feared him. It was rumored he knew the sins of the Publicans before they committed them. He used flattery, partnerships and alliances, sometimes treachery, more often blackmail, to control the Ten Families and the rest of Ard Creggan.

"No other people are like Publicans. We are truly blessed, thanks to the Counselor." Aka bowed his head. "Citizens and others like them are fortunate to have our oversight, our favor."

"Except, of course, when they're used to work our mines," Zoë said under her breath.

It was Citizen laborers who sank shaft after shaft into Ard Creggan to wrench out the ore. When the richest seams under the city proper gave out, mining spread into the caldera itself. After that was exhausted, the Publicans moved to claim ore rights on the land beyond. The mining operations rolled outward from Ard Creggan, displacing Citizens and turning acres into wasteland.

The Citizens fought back, of course, disrupting mining where they could, waylaying ore shipments, harassing Publican troops, protecting the land that remained. That was the beginning of the Sequential Wars.

It was in the early days of the wars that the Publicans cast the first of the heavy guns that now stood at each point of the compass on the city's heights. Forged from Ard Creggan ore, the guns were massive and indomitable, with a range well into Citizen territory.

The Citizens were poorly armed. The only thing that saved them, while Ard Creggan's guns pounded away at them day and night, was their ability to run, move their bases, and renew the fight. The two sides fought to a standstill, then held peace talks, failed, and fought again. On the eve of the winter solstice, the old enemies met again to see if peace might trump avarice.

Aka jabbered on, even as a band of minstrels surrounded them. Zoë kept an eye open for pickpockets. In normal times, Ard Creggan with its crowds offered good pickings for the light-fingered. During the solstice celebration, it was a pickpocket's paradise.

"Do you know any Citizens, Aka?" Zoë demanded, trying to keep the irritation from her voice. Her aunt had warned her not to provoke arguments with her tutor. She was doing her best, but her temper was rising.

"What was that, my lady?"

Aka calmly skirted two Publicans coming to blows over a prime stall location. Zoë turned on him as the crowd continuing unchecked around them like a stream flowing around rocks.

"Do you know any Citizens?" she repeated.

Aka blinked in astonishment.

"Certainly not, my Lady. It would not be appropriate."

Zoë heaved a sigh. "Do you know anything at all about their history?"

The tutor was clearly perplexed now.

"Their history? They can't possibly claim to have a history. They're manual workers, no better than vagabonds."

"Vagabonds, because that's what we made them. Do you know that when we wanted to expand mining operations beyond Ard Creggan, we just took the land and threw off any Citizens?"

"That is the law, Lady Deich." Aka continued. "They were adequately recompensed."

They were squeezed to the side of the street as the crowd compressed ahead of them to give wide berth to three figures. Two black robes, one white, in the gaudy holiday crowd. *Two seers and a novice. Now what are they doing here?*

"We offered a fraction of what the land was worth," Zoë retorted mechanically, her mind on the seers. "And if they didn't take that offer, we condemned the land as contaminated—by our own mining operations. We threw them out and tore down their homes. Then when they wouldn't go away quietly—or down into the mines to work for us—we made it a crime to be destitute."

"That's a calumny," Aka said indignantly, regaining her side. "I believe Citizens were always treated with great compassion. But business is business. The ore is necessary."

Zoë dodged a shifting pallet of winter melons two men were attempting to carry through the crowd.

"Compassion. What land we didn't take, we poisoned. Thanks to us, thousands of Citizens starved before the wars, and more have died since the wars began. Do you wonder why they hate us?"

Aka paused, bewildered.

"Why do we care if they hate us, Lady? They disrupt the mining. That cannot be allowed. Really, I have no idea where your ladyship gets these ideas," he said. "I really don't."

"I do," a voice said at her ear.

She spun around.

"Will!" she yelped, loud enough to turn heads in the crowd.

A young man with a wild shock of unnaturally white hair submitted to her hug.

"You're skinnier than ever, Will. What have you done with yourself." Zoë held him at arm's length and looked him over. They'd grown up together, and, until he'd joined the ClearWorlders, they'd been nearly inseparable. His sect's zealotry was a new and uncomfortable development in their relationship.

"Don't worry about me. And, Aka," he said turning to the tutor with a sly smile, "don't worry about the Lady Deich. She's maybe a sympathizer, but she's not a ClearWorlder. Yet. We're working on her. One or two more meetings and maybe we'll have her."

"You look well, Will An," Aka replied stiffly.

"Thank you, Aka. You're a terrible liar."

Will's smile was so infectious, even Aka couldn't be offended. But it was true. He was gaunt, and the hand he extended in greeting to Aka shook.

"Where have you been? I haven't seen you in weeks," Zoë demanded.

"At the moment, I'm trying to track some seers," he replied. "They're been sighted in this area."

"They're not hurting anybody, Will," Zoë scolded. "Leave them alone."

"No one knows the mind of the Divine One. That's what the scriptures tell us," he said harshly. "And yet they pretend to know the future. That is blasphemy."

"There's room enough for all kinds. Who are we to judge?" she offered diplomatically.

"If not us, who?" he retorted. "They must be purged. Scripture demands it."

The abrupt shift from his normal good humor to this fanaticism never failed to startle her. One moment the old Will, the next a true believer.

Zoë riffled the flyers he held under his arm.

"I've been reading about your activities."

The agitated look in his eyes increased.

"It's the only way to get the message out now that the Concordia has closed down the newspaper." He looked around at the people milling past. "Even if the message falls on deaf ears."

"Aunt Livia tried to stop them from closing you down."

"Your aunt was never one of my admirers," Will admitted ruefully. "But whatever she thought of my politics, Livia has her principles. I'd like to think it was my article on the mines that got the Concordia's attention."

"Actually, I think it was the article you wrote about Sinon Yar supporting insurgents in the city. You nearly called him a traitor."

Will suddenly looked haggard.

"Then I didn't write it very well. I meant to be very clear that he is a traitor. And the Concordia still can't see it. They must wake to the truth."

"Well, cousin Samuel is still out looking for the rebel troops you said were out there."

"You sound like you don't believe he'll find them."

"If they're there," Zoë replied. "Samuel will find them. And all hell will break loose if he does."

"Hell, my dear Zoë," Will said, "is already here. And it is my duty to make certain everyone in Ard Creggan knows it. We must eradicate the institutions and trappings that have made us war mongers—more concerned with profit than our own souls. Redemption comes through pain. But first the pain must be made visible."

This rant was too familiar. "And you know I'm happy to talk about it," she interrupted, "but this is no place to debate Ard Creggan's politics. Why don't you come tonight? The least we can do is give you a meal. You look like you could use one."

He looked off over her head, sighting something or someone in the distance.

"Oh, I'll be there tonight. We have a little demonstration planned."

The crowd was pulling them in opposite directions down the street.

"And Zoë," Will shouted back, "don't interfere."

Then he was gone, falling in with the human current and out of sight in no time. Puzzled, Zoë turned back, oblivious to the on-coming traffic.

What is he planning? Redemption through pain? Where does he get these ideas? Whose pain?

But Aka was pressing her to hurry.

"Yes, my Lady, if we keep moving," he urged, "we may be on time."

He groaned audibly when Zoë stopped at a booth selling cakes stamped with red full moons. They were forced to stop again when, in crossing a footbridge into the Old Town, a funeral cortege pushed them to the side of the street. Walking behind the body, a single acolyte swung a censer of burning incense with enthusiasm, imperiling the throng with its arc, while dispensing a pungent cloud that enveloped the pallbearers and swirled around Zoë.

"That's the third today, Aka," she observed, brushing the cake crumbs from her tunic.

"Yes Lady," Aka agreed absent-mindedly. "Mind your package. These people push so."

Feeling a slight pressure on her sleeve, Zoë looked down. From a bundle of filthy blankets at her feet, a hand emerged, wordlessly begging. Zoë dropped a coin into the hand, then followed in the wake of the casket.

"Aka, how many do you suppose there are?"

Aka pulled his robe close.

"How many deaths, Miss? I couldn't say. A few. The winter fevers, you know."

"There are more every day," Zoë said.

She noticed other beggars beyond the footbridge, more human bundles of rags hugging the walls of the plaza. A mother entreated passersby with a sleeping baby across her knees.

"Yes Miss?" Aka was polite, but uninterested. "I believe that beginning next week public funerals are no longer permitted in Ard Creggan."

"I meant the beggars, Aka."

"Certainly the shelters care for them," Aka said. "Please hurry. We are behind schedule and your aunt will be concerned."

They were entering one of the oldest sections of Ard Creggan. For long stretches, tall buildings pressed in on the narrow streets, shutting out the dim afternoon sun. Yellow lamps at the intersections already lit many of the streets. Here the press of bodies, the tangle of legs intensified. Finally, fed up, Zoë elbowed her way into a quiet alley entrance. Her family compound was only a few more blocks and Aka was agitated.

"Your aunt. Your aunt will be seriously displeased. We are late. We are very late. She will hold me responsible. Most certainly responsible."

Zoë had just gathered up her packages again to re-enter the crowd when a man pushed past them into the alley and disappeared around a pile of boxes. She looked after him. His clothes and face had been streaked with dirt. Fresh dirt. The next Aka knew, he had his arms full of packages and Zoë was off down the alley.

"Miss. Miss," Aka wailed, swept off by the crowd. "You cannot be out alone, Miss."

She could barely hear him now.

Odd how the alley changes the acoustics.

A narrow path snaked though debris piled so high the street and Aka were lost from sight within a few feet. A cat sprang to a rocky perch on a mountain of crates, dislodging a box, then a cascade of trash. Leaping out of the way, she nearly fell down a dark hole at her feet.

A hole with a ladder is an awful temptation. And you should always give in to temptation.

••••

Not far from Zoë's alley, another Publican stood before the gated entry of an abandoned mine. He, too, was eager to enter the depths of Ard Creggan. He was irritably aware that the longer he stood, the more notice he drew. But he was stymied by the lack of a guide, a guide who he had been told would take him to a rendezvous. No one braved the labyrinth of Ard Creggan's mines without a good guide or a good map, preferably both.

Not that attention bothered Sinon Yar. It could be said that he had spent his entire career placing himself at the center of attention. But at the moment, a lower profile was preferred, a nearly impossible wish given the familiarity of nearly every man, woman and child in Ard Creggan with his face. Seeing him there, a shopkeeper was bold enough to approach. Business was not so good he could afford to ignore a potential sale, and everyone knew Lord Yar's generosity.

"Excuse me, sir, perhaps you would like to . . ."

A glance sent him scurrying back to his store. Sinon Yar turned back to the mineshaft gate to find a dwarf now stood in front of the gate. Lord Yar deliberately towered over him.

"You've kept me waiting," he growled.

His guide only smiled, slid between the gate's rails and was off down the mine corridor without a backward glance. Silently, the gate swung open. Yar scowled, his interest aroused but his sense of danger tingling. He knew the gate had been locked just a moment before. He'd tried it.

"If this is a trap," he murmured, "it is quite a curious one."

A lamp inside the mine entrance sputtered helpfully to life when he lifted it off its hook.

"Now where has my diminutive guide gone?"

As if in reply, a firefly flickered ahead in the darkness. Negotiating the labyrinth of Ard Creggan's mines, Sinon Yar found himself sometimes walking upright in broad chambers, other times bent nearly double through narrow passageways. Always, the light flitted ahead, leading him on, disappearing around a corner or down a channel if he tried to close the distance. The corridors grew damp, and he splashed through shallow puddles of black water. He shook off the chill.

In the pursuit of his elusive guide, he'd completely lost the way back to the entrance. And he also was aware that any of the myriad corridors slanting off from his path might hide assassins. After all, he had enemies, any of whom would be delighted to find him unguarded and alone.

Let them come. They'll be sorry they ever tried.

There'd be the sudden rush from one of the side corridors, the clash, and the exhilaration of the fight. He would win, of course. Entranced by the vision, Yar didn't immediately realize that the will o'wisp of light had settled down into a glowing yellow rectangle. It was a doorway opening into a rough hewn chamber.

Three figures stood at the far side of the chamber. Three women. Two in the black habits of seers, one stooped and elderly, supported by a ramrod straight but younger companion, and a third, only a girl, in a novice's white dress.

"Good afternoon, ladies. Did I keep you waiting?"

The dwarf was nowhere in sight. He noted with some amusement that the women stood within a few paces of a tunnel opening, a ready exit.

"Really, we should trust each other, don't you think?" he said with his most disarming smile.

The charm was wasted. The elder seer addressed him.

"What is your purpose in requesting this meeting, Lord Yar?"

"If you are truly seers, then you should know what I want," he replied equably.

The elder seer motioned to her companions who turned to the tunnels.

"And that I'd be willing to meet your price," Yar added quickly.

The two seers exchanged glances. Without a word the novice took the elder's arm and they disappeared into the blackness of the tunnels. The remaining seer turned back to Yar.

"I am Eleanor. What do you wish to know?"

There was speculation in Yar's grin.

"You're not what I expected. I didn't realize seers were so attractive."

"Oddly enough," she said impassively, "you're precisely what I expected. Arrogant, over-ambitious, and late."

Yar chuckled.

"I like a woman with a sense of humor." He looked around, for the first time taking note of the room. The walls were pocked with body-size cavities from floor to ceiling.

"What is this place?" he asked.

"I'm surprised you don't recognize it, Lord Yar," Eleanor replied. "Rooms like this were living quarters for miners. As you know, they slept and ate here while working their shifts, sometimes for weeks at a time. Some people have compared it to being buried alive. Your own father, when he worked the mines, probably lived in a room just like this. Or didn't he talk about his time in the mines?"

Yar's face hardened, a smile forced its way to the surface.

"On the contrary, I wouldn't be here today, if not for my late father's occupation. How does the prophecy go? *First born, Digger's son, A son in name, A city won.*"

"So you think you are the digger's son of prophecy?" Eleanor's question held a trace of amusement.

"Let's say I find prophecies enlightening. The lower the rung, the greater the climb. My future has been written in the prophecies."

"Before we begin, Sinon Yar, are you sure you can meet our price?"

Yar dismissed the question; "I can do anything I want," he retorted.

Eleanor's expression was impassive.

"You want to know if you will succeed, if prophecy will become fact."

Yar's hoot of laughter echoed painfully in the chamber.

"Succeed? In the end, I'll rule Ard Creggan. But I want to know what happens then."

Eleanor's smile mocked him.

"Don't tell me the great Yar is afraid of an old prophecy?"

He reddened.

"I only seek clarification. That's little enough, considering the price you're asking. What is the prophecy? *One to rule till Ard Creggan falls.*"

"One of our more succinct prophecies," the seer said dismissively. "I'm surprised you need reassurance on that."

"But still open to misinterpretation," Yar countered.

"You will rule, Basillius," was the response. "And all of Ard Creggan will be at your feet."

"Yes," Yar said with some satisfaction. "I like the sound of that. How long will I rule?"

"Until the very rock of the city tumbles to dust."

"That long? I may have to consider heirs. The greatest deeds die on an empty hearth. And my final question. Because there is a bit more to the prophecy, isn't there, my dear Eleanor?"

Yar was certain the seer tensed.

"That is all that should concern you."

"I have to disagree with you, sweet Eleanor. There was a seer who told me the second part of that particular prophecy."

Eleanor was silent, but her eyes never left Sinon Yar's face.

"*One to rule till Ard Creggan falls*," Yar repeated. "Now here's the interesting part. *Against son's resolve, a daughter's will to end it all.* Now that's what concerns me. That talk of an end, thanks to a son and daughter. Thankfully, I don't have any offspring, bastards or other. Whose son, whose daughter," he demanded, "ends it all?"

Eleanor lowered her eyes. "I knew the seer who told you that prophecy. She died under your protection, didn't she."

"Spare me," Yar sneered. "She was a foolish woman. Much too trusting. But you're not like that, are you Eleanor? I only want a little clarification. And you'll have your price."

"A small price, Sinon Yar. Just the Yar Family key."

"Cheap enough," Yar snorted derisively. "It's not even a key—it's just a ball. A stone. Worse. An antiquated symbol of an doomed and ineffectual ruling class. They're all worthless the day I do away with the Concordia."

"There's no family feeling hobbling you, Sinon Yar. But then you didn't come by your Family key in the usual way, did you?"

"No," Yar admitted, without ill will. "I didn't. Kenon Yar adopted me to pay his debts. You see? There's the prophecy: '*A son in name*'? My adoptive father may have lived to regret it. But he should have had more faith. I will make the Yar Family the greatest in Ard Creggan history."

"You will go far, Lord Yar," Eleanor said without bothering to hide her contempt. "You have none of the usual virtues to hold you back. But what assurance do I have that you'll pay me once you have the information you need?"

Yar drew out a small cloth bag from under his coat.

"I anticipated you might have doubts. So to show my good intentions, I have the Yar key for you now."

He took a step forward but Eleanor backed toward a tunnel exit, keeping the distance between them.

"Throw it there on the floor," she directed. "And be warned. If you have deceived us, you will wander for a very long time down here in Ard Creggan's mines."

Yar chuckled.

"You're fairly ruthless yourself, seer. But I admire that. Now, I've shown my good faith. Tell me about the prophecy."

Almost, he thought she hesitated.

"You are perceptive, Lord Yar. Yes, your rule may be threatened."

"May be threatened. So it's not certain?"

Eleanor smile, heavy with condescension, annoyed him.

"Everyone always thinks prophecies are written in stone," she said. "Think of them as signposts. Indicators of a direction the future may take."

He considered this.

"And knowing the signposts, it becomes easier to alter them and the future?"

"Easier, perhaps. But never certain. You can never be absolutely certain you're altering the right signpost. Misinterpret and you may actually contribute to the prophecy's fulfillment."

"Tell me, Seer Eleanor," Yar asked abruptly, "do prophecies ever come true?"

The look on Eleanor face should have told him this was an all too common question.

"In hindsight, all prophecies are true," she said. "People read into them what they will."

With his boot, Yar nudged the bag he'd dropped on the floor. "I'm paying for certainty."

"Why do men think the future can be bought?" Eleanor returned.

"Because in my experience, it can be," Yar retorted. "We've danced around long enough. Tell me. *The daughter's will.* This is a daughter of one of the Families. Which one?"

"You've spent years looking for her, haven't you, Sinon Yar?" Eleanor mocked him. "A succession of wards, the eldest daughter from nearly every Family. A group of women either singularly susceptible to accident or in exceptionally poor health."

"I was very fond of them all, let me assure you. Their Families welcomed the tie, no matter how fleeting our alliance may have been."

"And, yes, a way to be certain the prophecy does not come true. Who is your next ward, Sinon Yar?"

He looked at her with new respect. "She doesn't know it yet, but the Deich brat. Come now," he wheedled. "We've come this far." He nudged the bag with a toe. "This must be worth something to you." His smile was sly. "It would be a shame if you had to leave Ard Creggan without all the keys. Now, that line about the son. What does that mean?"

"Surely, it's obvious," Eleanor tone mocked him. "Pit the son's resolve against the daughter's will."

"And see who wins?" Yar was thoroughly pleased. "That shouldn't be a question. I am the miner's son, the son in name. If nothing else, I have resolve. Yes, it fits with the daughter's will. The Deich have blocked me at every turn. I would have had a seat on the Concordia if it hadn't been for Livia. Well, my plans will take care of the daughter and her aunt. I assume Livia was someone's daughter, once."

Eleanor's gaze was indifferent. As far as she was concerned, the interview was over.

"I've given you the answers you wanted, miner's son. Your guide will take you back to the surface."

Yar grinned, but it wasn't friendly. "All you did was confirm my own suspicions. I don't think you earned your pay, Seer."

She'd already disappeared into the darkness of the tunnel. Her voice carried back to him.

"Payment in full, Sinon Yar. The future is always changeable to those who see it clearly."

Yar weighed the threat behind the words against the Yar Family key. When a light flickered in the tunnel behind, he followed. But he went empty-handed.

••••

A descent of thirty feet or more brought Zoë to the bottom of the shaft and the entrance to a tunnel. She felt her way as the tunnel sloped steeply downward for what seemed a considerable distance, the blackness lightening to gray. Now she could hear an occasional grating noise. The tunnel widened and the gray light changed to a golden glow. A half-moon stone arch framed the tunnel sides, carved in a pair of undulating serpents, their heads intertwining at the capstone. She passed beneath the arch and entered an area whose circular outline heavy with fantastical carvings was still emerging from the dirt. From where she stood, she could see the chamber was an amazing find, an archaeological treasure. Three men, their clothes stained with dirt and sweat in the dank air, were huddled before a section of the wall. Behind them, the laborer she'd seen in the alley leaned on his shovel and grinned at Zoë.

"Find something interesting, Uncle Eon?"

At the sound of his name, one of the men looked up. He had the look of a terrier, from the close-cropped fringe of hair and stubby legs to the over-bright black eyes that regarded her now.

"You always amaze me, child," he said, as calmly as though he'd been expecting her. "The entire population of Ard Creggan is totally oblivious to our digs. But you find us like a dog on a scent."

"Not a dog, Uncle, a cat. It's cats who are curious."

Eon smiled indulgently. "Then, if you're curious, come look."

His assistants made room for her at the wall. On closer inspection the carvings were even more impressive.

"It's wonderful. Predesarian?" she asked. Eon snorted.

"Much earlier, we think. Some of the glyphs are very intriguing. It's almost as if..." He bent to dislodge a clod of earth from a stone coil. "Well, see here?" he pointed to one long segment of carving. "It's similar to what we've seen of the early Predesarian alphabet. Yet it's sharper, more detailed. Almost as though the Cesarean figures we know were based on a memory of this."

He tapped the wall and under his grimy forefinger a snake sank his fangs into a moon glyph. "I'm betting this is older than anything we've ever found."

Zoë crouched down to get a better view. Up close, the carving did not look like stone. There was a finish to the surface, an exuberance in the carving that reminded her of something.

"It isn't like writing," she thought, "It's like seeing music." She touched the wall—and snatched her hand back.

"Yes," Eon said, making a note on a clipboard. "It's warm. We noticed it too. We think it might be hollow and filled by thermal springs." Zoë looked down the length of the excavated wall. A curve suggested the wall might be part of a circle. Gently, she touched a finger again to the carving.

"It almost feels. . . ."

"Alive?" Eon suggested. "That may have been the original intent. And look at this." He walked down the wall to where the head of the serpent emerged from the damp earth, the nostrils flaring. "Put your hand over the nose. Yes, air. Quite a blast of air. Originally, it must have ventilated this entire space."

"That's a pretty fancy air vent."

"Well, we think they needed it. When we first opened up this dig, my men were falling ill. Headaches, nausea. It wasn't until one digger collapsed over there," Eon pointed to the far wall, the lowest point in the room, "that we figured it out."

"What?"

"A lethal gas. It must occur naturally in this area. And it has a habit of accumulating in low areas. If this was a religious chapel, the priests may have thought the effects of the gas were a visitation from the gods—if they survived. I notice they added our snake for ventilation, so they must have known the gas could kill. I imagine there's a concealed entrance further along that wall where they could enter the room unseen. You know, remove the remains and make the believers think the gods had claimed them. Theatrical, but very effective. Wonderful way to dispose or your enemies or non-believers."

"But these carvings are really remarkable." He moved over to another section. "Now this part we know. It's a calendar. Nearly identical to our own cycles. You see, here is the glyph for each twenty year cycle, and this one indicates twenty cycles. It's probably linked to a prophecy glyph."

Eon leaned forward to inspect the wall.

"The glyphs in this section have been heavily damaged, so we're not quite sure what the message is. It could be symbolic, but then again it might be a historical record. You see, here are ten ships under sail below this arc of six stars. And in this section, they're circled in a harbor. I think that's a wall above them. The glyph indicates some kind of fortress, or more nearly, a place of judgment. Anyway, in this next section, the sea has risen up. Isn't that fascinating? Completely engulfs them. And, look, one ship has survived. Only, it's over a wing glyph which may mean, oh, perhaps the usual flood mythology, who knows."

"What does this mean? The figure over the fortress?" Zoë quizzed him, looking closely at the carving. "It looks like a trident with an arrow through the shaft."

"Yes, yes. Now that's quite common. It refers to a particular fertility goddess. In many cultures, there is a female figure who descends to the underworld to rescue a husband or a brother. This figure persists to this day. In the coastal regions I've seen it carved on a huge scale into the hillsides. A blessing for harvests."

"When did you see those, Uncle?"

"Oh, long before you were born, child. When it was still safe to travel."

"I wish I could see them," Zoë said glumly. "I haven't been out of Ard Creggan in years."

"Well, it is not safe."

"Father travels all the time. Why is it any safer for him?" she retorted.

"Your Father is quite different. He is a man. And he has his work for the Concordia. He's practically a diplomat. Now, we have work to do, so let's get you on your way home."

He drew Zoë away from the wall leading her out to the tunnel where his lantern sent grotesque shadows scurrying, reminding her of the carved figures on the wall. She would have preferred to stay and see more of the dig, but Uncle Eon, whatever his reasons, wanted her gone.

"And which of your chaperons did you lose this time?" Eon asked over his shoulder.

"Aka. He's probably home by now."

Eon chuckled. "Show up without you? Not likely. Your aunt would flay him alive."

"He sneaks in through my father's rooms. She'll never see him."

"Why she doesn't find a chaperon who can actually keep up with you is beyond me," Eon said in exasperation.

Zoë smiled at the suggestion. "I have one. But for obvious reasons Aunt won't let Noor go out in public with me."

"Understandable. The presence of such a creature on the streets of Ard Creggan would cause considerable commotion. I never understood your father's reasoning in bringing her into your household."

"Noor has her own ways of keeping track of me. But you're starting to sound an awful lot like Aunt Livia. All of you seem to think I need watching. I'm not a child."

Eon stopped so suddenly Zoë ran into him.

"For an intelligent young woman," he snapped, "you are, on occasion, willfully ignorant. Your aunt has you chaperoned, not because she doesn't trust you, but because she doesn't trust the rest of Ard Creggan."

"Yes, Uncle," Zoë said meekly, suppressing a smile with effort.

"Don't humor me, girl. I'm too old. These are dangerous times. People disappear. People die. You're not immune, you know." He turned away, muttering under his breath.

She had called him Uncle since she was a child, not because of any blood relationship, but because Eon and her father were as close as brothers. Zoë always thought the two men looked odd together; her father tall and so patrician; Eon short and forever grubby. But he was shrewd. He held his position as head of the An Family, despite talk that too much time in the ground had undermined his judgment.

Eon stopped at the foot of the ladder. "Now what's this, child?" he said and reached behind her ear, drawing out a small silver coin. As always, the simple trick amused her—more for what it said about Eon than its novelty. He was fond of his little sleights of hand and he had a wide repertoire suitable, as he would say, for all occasions.

"Zoë, I need you to keep this dig a secret."

"Certainly, Uncle Eon," she agreed easily and turned to the ladder. He stopped her. "Seriously. Don't tell anyone about our discovery yet. Not even your aunt."

Zoë's interest pricked, but she kept her voice casual.

"I doubt I could interest her if I tried."

"She cares when you come home looking like you've been playing in mud," Eon retorted, "like you do now."

Zoë looked down at her clothes with a sigh of exasperation. *Why is it so hard to stay clean?*

"Well, she'll won't hear about this one from me. To be honest, I didn't expect to find you digging."

"Oh, you mean the tremors. Bah." Eon dismissed them.

"Yes, Uncle, the tremors. And don't act like they're nothing. We've had the seismologists looking at the data. This time we have reliable reports. This part of the city is unstable. You should be careful."

Eon snorted. "Careful? I'm always careful. To a point, anyway."

Zoë was caught between amusement and concern. "You won't stop until we have to dig you out. Will I see you tonight?"

Eon looked blank.

"The solstice, uncle," Zoë reminded him. "You will be expected, you know. If not for the dinner, at least for the Concordia meeting. All the Family heads attend."

"Oh, that nonsense. I don't mind the dinner, of course. I wouldn't miss one of your aunt's dinners. But the Families," he threw up his hands. "And the Concordia. They're so tedious. Of course, I'll attend, of course. I must."

Zoë hesitated. "I saw Will this afternoon."

Eon's frown deepened. "And what was my son doing? Preaching sedition or simply ranting about our morally bankrupt society?"

"He was distributing flyers."

"Ah, then it was probably sedition."

"He didn't look well, Uncle. He worries me."

"You're worried? I've worried about Will every day of his life. But your children reach a certain age and they are strangers. I made a mistake with Will. I encouraged him to find a purpose in life, to work for something in which he believed."

"Well, he's certainly done that," Zoë said dryly.

"Yes," Eon conceded, "he has found purpose in stirring things up."

"Maybe we need stirring up," Zoë said thoughtfully. "Maybe we are too complacent."

"Now you sound like one of Will's ClearWorlders."

"I'm not one of them," Zoë retorted. "They want to shut down the mines. That's simple-minded. Ard Creggan lives and dies by its ore. But I agree with them that we have poisoned the city and everything else for miles around."

"You young people are so quick to see things in black and white," Eon said, sadly. "It's either mine and kill ourselves, or shut down the foundries and be defenseless. It's all misguided. Well-intentioned, but misguided." His sigh was heartfelt. "Oh don't listen to me. I'm an old man. Too old to understand these things. And now I'm losing my boy."

"What do you mean?" Zoë said. "He's OK. He's just a bit obsessed. A lot like his father."

Eon mustered a forlorn smile. "You're a good girl, Zoë. And, yes, I know Will will be fine. I'll see to that. Forget I said anything. Now you'd better be gone." He motioned her up the ladder. "And remember. This is our secret."

Without another word Zoë started climbing. She really was late now, and her aunt, who had not been in a good mood when she had left earlier in the day, would be looking for her. A thought occurred to her halfway up.

"Uncle Eon," she called down.

"What now?"

He was still at the foot of the ladder. She could see his upturned face below her in a pool of yellow light.

"You said the date might be a prophecy glyph. What was the date?"

"The date?" He looked distracted for a moment, figuring it out in his head. Then he chuckled softly.

"How extraordinary. The end of the cycle would be this summer. At the summer solstice. Now, no more questions. Get going."

She finished the last part of the climb in thought. A few moments later, she was back in the alley, and in a few more turning into the street. She may have noticed a small figure dogging her footsteps as she made her way through the crowd, but she had other things on her mind.

••••

The last rays of a blood red sun touched the towers of Ard Creggan as a footsore troop of soldiers entered the eastern gate. A powerfully built man kept pace beside them. Along with his own pack, he carried two others, each with a dangling helmet.

"Samuel! Samuel!"

A man in the gaudy robe of a solstice celebrant pushed through the crowd. It was painful to watch him rock wildly from side to side, one leg obviously shorter than the other. Samuel shortened his own stride to allow him to keep pace.

"I had word from the sentries you were back, Captain Samuel. We've been expecting you for over a week."

"Good day, Pall. Which day, I'm not certain, but good day. There was a lot to see out there, so we stayed for a while."

Pall wrinkled his nose and backed away.

"And did you roll in it when you found it? You're a sight for sore eyes, but your smell brings tears to them."

The soldier roared and tried to sweep Pall into a bear hug, a maneuver the smaller man eluded clumsily. Samuel looked doleful.

"A few weeks ago, you wouldn't have gotten away with that. Look at me. I'm just a shell of my former self."

"A shell that needs washing," Pall said in disgust.

"And a week of sleep. And something to eat." Samuel agreed good-naturedly. "But we're lucky we made it back in any shape."

"What happened? What kept you?" Pall demanded.

Samuel didn't answer. He called a halt in the lee of a church wall, where his men gratefully collapsed.

"Well, it's good news and bad, boys," he addressed them cheerfully. "The good news is we're home, and home in time for the celebration. The bad news is, by the looks of you, you'll sleep through it. I should take you back to headquarters for a regular mustering out, but I've no desire to herd you through this." He jerked his head at the crowds sweeping past them. "And you've no wish, I imagine, to walk any further than you have to. So get yourselves home."

His men mumbled their approval of this plan—the ones who weren't already asleep.

"And remember," Samuel lowered his voice. "We've just spent a few weeks on a topological survey. Nothing more. No late-night pillow talks with your sweethearts, now. The one who talks, answers to me."

His men grinned, saluted, and by ones and pairs vanished into the crowd leaving Samuel alone with Pall. For the first time, the captain's shoulders sagged with exhaustion.

"Well?" Pall asked impatiently. "I left a family dinner to come out here, and my fiancée is not happy."

"So you finally asked?"

Pall shook his head ruefully. "Asked? Alaina set the date and told me when to show up."

Samuel laughed. "She's a smart woman. And you're a lucky man." He swung two packs to the ground, the empty helmets ringing on the stones. "You know," he said, "it's a damn unfriendly place out there. Two men lost. Two good men."

"Citizens attacked you?" Pall asked doubtfully. "It's hard to believe with the peace talks going on and the delegation here in Ard Creggan."

"Yes," Samuel agreed, "it is damn hard to believe."

Pall looked around. "This is no place to talk. Can we meet later?"

Samuel snagged a sweet roll off a passing vendor's tray. Stuffing his mouth full, he squatted down, his back against a wall, within feet of the passing revelers.

"This is as good a place as any. And I have to report to the Concordia later. So it's now or never."

Pall look was pure exasperation. "You have no concept of security, have you?"

Samuel's guffaw competed with the festival din. "And who is going to overhear us in this?" he asked in good humor.

Pall was a stickler for rules and regulations, inordinately attached to process, but he was an invaluable acquaintance. Part of the Concordia administrative staff, he had the best contacts in the city for anything you might want—entertainment, goods, food, and information. If it could be bought, he could get it. Reluctantly, Pall squatted beside Samuel.

"So, tell me," he demanded.

"First, what have they done to Will since I've been gone?"

"What makes you think they've done anything to him," Pall asked, avoiding eye contact.

"I know the Concordia and Sinon Yar."

"He's a young fool. He got what he deserved."

"He has a fondness for the truth, that's all."

"Truth is no excuse. You make accusations, especially when they involve Sinon Yar, and you have to expect retaliation."

"What did they do to him, Pall?" Samuel repeated.

They closed down his newspaper for starters."

"And what else?"

"From what I hear, a year of exile, starting immediately after the festival. That's not common knowledge. Eon An had some support, but the most of the Ten Families caved to Sinon Yar's demands. Yar said his reputation had been damaged. He wanted imprisonment, but settled for exile. Considering everything, Will got off lightly. Give it a month. Maybe three. We'll start another paper. Different name. Same politics. When Will returns, he can ghost write all he wants. We'll get around the Concordia."

Samuel looked at the little man in amusement.

"We? Have you joined the ranks of ClearWorlders?"

"They're a bunch of raving dreamers. And if we're drawing up sides, I'd prefer to be on the one that's winning," Pall replied calmly. "But even I can't stomach Sinon Yar. He won't be happy until he takes over Ard Creggan. I won't look forward to that day. Well, what can you expect? He came up in the mines—a Citizen, they say. He still has the stink of hard labor on him. Now tell me what you found."

Samuel's expression was grim. "There's not much to tell. We found an encampment out beyond the rim. They weren't trying very hard to hide."

"Then Will was wrong. It is the Citizens, after all, who are preparing for a major offensive, not Sinon Yar and his followers."

"That's the question that kept us out there all this time. And I'm still not sure."

"Either they are Citizens or they aren't. What's the difficulty?"

"The difficulty is that I think someone may want us to think they're Citizens."

Pall raised an eyebrow. "And the point of that would be?"

"I don't know." Samuel idly tapped an empty helmet with his finger.

Pall eyed him in disbelief. "You think those are Publicans out there. And that they're Sinon Yar's men. Is there any proof?"

"Not a particle. Except what my eyes tell me. I know how Citizens train, and camp, and deploy. And I know the look of Publicans doing the same thing."

"This is nonsense." Pall snorted. "What reason would Publicans have to train outside the walls?" He jerked to his feet, "No, take my advice, Samuel. If you value your commission, you won't say anything like that to the Concordia. Give them your report and keep it simple. And I'll see you afterward. We have things to discuss. Like who is going to be my best man."

"I will buy the first round to celebrate," Samuel said amiably and watched through half-closed eyes as Pall left. He sat for a while longer thinking his own thoughts. A Madonna passed close by, saw the scowl on his face and turned away to find a more promising client. Samuel didn't even notice her. After a while, he rose, picked up the packs and shambled into the crowd.

CHAPTER THREE

At about the same time, a well-orchestrated frenzy of activity was reaching its peak in the Deich compound after nearly a week of intense preparation. An army of staff had cleaned and readied dozens of rooms, while in the kitchen below stairs ten chefs and their assistants chopped, stirred, seasoned and contrived as though their reputations depended upon the succession of dishes they turned out. Which it would. That evening, the Family Deich, as the leading family of Ard Creggan and the Concordia, would host the solstice celebration for the heads of the Ten Families.

The Deich compound was a warren of chambers, halls, passageways and hidden gardens. From the entry courtyard, wrought iron doors opened into a central hall with alabaster columns reaching up six stories to a glass ceiling and two massive chandeliers.

That evening, musicians would play in the hall, while the Ten Families and assorted distinguished Publicans dined in a banquet room so large it could comfortably seat two hundred. The massive table was already covered with yards of freshly ironed white linen. Down the center of the table sat a mechanical marvel, a wonderful silver device in the form of a tropical island dispensing condiments and, at the end of the meal, steaming hand towels.

A sparrow of a woman oversaw the preparations from her perch on a stool, and she missed nothing, neither the smallest fray in a dinner napkin hem, nor her grand niece sneaking through the hall on her way to her rooms.

"Zoë!" Aunt Livia shrilled over the din. Zoë caught a glimpse of Aka scurrying off.

He must have told Aunt about this afternoon's adventure.

Cursing under her breath, she dodged around a clutch of women carrying plates and serving dishes to reach her aunt. Obediently, she bent to kiss her cheek.

"Where have you been?" the old woman scolded, "Never mind. I can see you've been with Eon again. When will you learn? How did he look?"

"Who? Uncle Eon?"

"Yes, Eon An. Who did you think I meant? That Publican Donncha?"

Aka had been very talkative, indeed.

"Uncle Eon didn't have time to talk with me."

Her aunt eyed her suspiciously. "That's just as well. I shall need to see you later, in my rooms." She broke off to shriek at two servants cleaning the chandeliers. "Careful you idiots, that's crystal." She turned back to Zoë. "That's the trouble with help these days; they're all quite useless. You'll wear the green dress tonight, the one we had made up from your mother's silk. It will look best."

"Thank you, aunt. But I will wear my uniform and look very well in that."

"You'll do as you are told, girl," her aunt snapped. "I won't have you looking like some paramilitary fundamentalist at a family function. What did you buy?"

"Your solstice present, Aunt, which you can't see until later. And something for Father. If he ever comes home again." Too late, she realized her mistake in giving her aunt an opening to deliver her usual lecture on her father's character. Jomini may be the head of the Family, but he did as he pleased, and not what Family tradition demanded. Livia could not forgive him for that.

"I saw the Counselor this afternoon," she said, hoping to deflect her aunt's tirade. "Or some of his guards. They were rescuing the peace delegation."

Her aunt's displeasure deepened. "So Aka told me."

"Are we expecting the Citizen peace delegation tonight, Aunt?"

"Mixing Publicans and Citizens," Livia snapped, "brings trouble. Mark my words." She controlled herself with a visible effort. "Perhaps they will join us. I have my doubts. There's talk the delegation will be sent packing. They cause too much unrest in Ard Creggan. And I, for one, say good riddance." She frowned at Zoë. "And you will wear the dress because the occasion demands it."

Zoë didn't bother to argue. She had promised her father that much before he left on his latest trip. Livia disapproved of the peace talks—and Citizens—but publicly the Family took no sides. As was their tradition, the Family Deich kept to itself. They were privileged, wealthy, and blessed with a near-miraculous ability to avoid the difficulties and entanglements of the other Ten Families. Zoë looked up at the stone coat of arms over the hall's massive marble fireplace. There was their family coat of arms, with its motto, "From the Past, Against the Future, We Stand," surrounded by ten orbs, the keys of the Ten Families of Ard Creggan.

Although there's nothing key-like about them. They're just round things. Keys aren't round. And as mottos go, ours isn't very clear. Her father had once promised to tell her about the motto's origin, but he always seemed to be away, and when he was at home, there never was any time.

"Well, I'm less worried about the peace delegation, and more worried you'll wear yourself out before the solstice begins," Zoë ventured.

Her aunt ignored her in favor of a chef carrying a grotesquely-carved tureen. The pungent aroma that wafted from the pot suited its fantastic shape.

"On second thought, perhaps I should worry about the digestion of our guests."

Livia's smile was malicious, "Our own people will appreciate this dish as a time-honored tradition. The barbarians. . . ."

"The peace delegation, Aunt. You'll cause a diplomatic incident if you forget that tonight."

"Don't correct me, girl," her aunt snapped, "and don't interrupt."

Zoë murmured an insincere apology and, as yet another dish appeared for her aunt's sampling, she slipped away. She took the steps of the main staircase two at a time, but near the top of the second floor staircase, her aunt called up to her. She was to be in her study in an hour. On time. They had matters to discuss. Zoë rolled her eyes. Discussions with Aunt Livia, especially in her rooms, were never pleasant.

"She probably found out about my new glider. Now how do you suppose that happened?"

Six flights up, at the very top of the house, Zoë looked for peace in her own rooms. But again there was none. Inside the door she was grabbed, spun around, stripped of her tunic and herded toward a very hot bath. Zoë went quietly because resisting Noor was like a leaf resisting the wind.

The two made an interesting contrast. Zoë and Noor were of a same height, but that's where the similarities ended. Noor was a Saurillia, like an oversized, though upright sloth with claws and teeth of a length and viciousness to give impressionable children fits. Zoë was not prone to fits. But she also knew better than to provoke Noor when she was irritable. And at the moment she was very irritable.

"The most important evening of the year," she growled, *"and where are you? Not where you're supposed to be. Now you come home. Late. And dirty. I smell bad dirt on you."*

Bad dirt was Noor's expression for the archaeological digs. Saurillias did not like the ground, especially pits; they preferred high places, except when they were nesting.

"Eon An should not encourage you. It is a large waste of a man's time to dig holes in the ground. And you are most foolish to go down these holes."

Zoë let the reproaches rain down like the water washing away the city's dirt. She was thinking her own thoughts.

Noor's head appeared around the door. *This person you are thinking of is not worth your time.*

Zoë smiled. Noor had always known what was on her mind, for the simple reason that Saurillias were telepaths.

Noor could not read all minds or know what someone at a distance was thinking. And crowds tended to block or confuse her reading. But Noor's ability was quite good enough to make Zoë wish, on more than one occasion, for a human and less aware nursemaid—especially when she was planning some mischief. This time, however, telepathic abilities weren't necessary to read Noor's disapproval.

"It was a long time ago, Noor," Zoë replied mildly and allowed herself to be wrapped after the bath in a long robe. She padded into her dressing room, followed closely by Noor's thoughts.

Not so long that you have forgotten this Tiernan, this Citizen. Pah.

Noor had an aversion to Citizens. Zoë thought she might have been trapped by Citizens, but her life before she entered the House of Deich was completely unknown. She had appeared one day, shortly after Zoë's birth. Surprisingly, Aunt Livia raised no objections and Noor became, after Zoë mother's death, a guardian of sorts to the girl. Even now, with Zoë grown, she showed no sign of relinquishing her control. The Saurillia gingerly carried an emerald green dress from the wardrobe and laid it out on the bed. Zoë turned in surprise.

"Is this a conspiracy? I've never seen so much interest in what I wear."

Your aunt wishes you to appear at the winter solstice celebration appropriately dressed for a daughter of the Ten Families, Noor replied gruffly. *And if you wish to make your aunt truly angry, you will be late for your talk with her.*

Zoë looked at the clock. It lacked only five minutes until the hour. Quickly, she pulled on the clean tunic Noor held out, pulled a brush through her hair, and was on her way to her aunt's rooms.

The shadows in the compound were lengthening as Zoë paused outside her aunt's rooms to tie her hair back and straighten her tunic. She tapped lightly on the door and entered.

Her aunt favored a style in her personal quarters that Zoë always referred to as High Gloom. The dark, old furniture, carved in bizarre shapes had frightened her as a child. The only light in the room was thrown from the burning logs in the fireplace. It cast the family coat of arms, a gilded replica of the hall's plaque, into relief. Her aunt sat near the fire in a high-backed chair. In its hold she looked fragile. She seemed asleep, but a hand fluttered up to motion Zoë forward.

"We've been waiting for you, Zoë. Come here to me, please."

As she obeyed, a figure emerged from behind her aunt's chair.

"Are you sure I'm not interrupting, Aunt?" Zoë asked quickly to hide her surprise.

The third person in the room was none other than the Counselor, High Justice to Ard Creggan, and chief negotiator in the peace talks.He was a frequent guest in the Deich Family compound, where, intentionally or not, he had a disquieting effect. For days after one of his visits, her aunt would be withdrawn and easily tired. Zoë also noticed that her aunt invariably did what the Counselor wished.

Zoë wished he was gone.

"Yes, come closer, Zoë. Your aunt and I would like to speak with you."

Livia remained slumped in her chair with the Counselor beside her, his hand on her shoulder. She seemed to shrivel under this touch, a marked change from the forceful woman Zoë had left earlier. The Counselor was thin, almost elongated, with a head that looked too big for his body, delicate features, and clear blue eyes whose habitual expression seemed to be one of excessive innocence. But when he smiled at her, Zoë knew how a rat felt just before the snake swallowed it.

"We were just talking," the Counselor said, "about the winter solstice. And another of our old customs, the Gabhain. A very beautiful ceremony. So seldom seen these days. A pity. These traditions are so worth maintaining. I understand the Gabhain gown of the Family Deich is over 300 years old." His voice was silky and it set Zoe's teeth on edge.

"I'm interrupting, Aunt. I can come back."

"Ah, no, child," the Counselor said. "Our conversation concerns you most particularly. Come here, Zoë. Closer."

Zoë advanced into the room, keeping her aunt's chair between her and the Counselor. Her aunt looked up at her and a chill passed through Zoë. With an effort, Livia drew herself up in her chair.

"It is about your father," she said harshly. "Jomini is dead."

Zoë looked from the aunt to the Counselor. His eyes narrowed in annoyance.

"Thank you for your refreshing directness, Livia." He turned to Zoë. "I have received word that your father's ship went down some weeks ago near the Gurama Islands. Apparently, the vessel was not particularly seaworthy and there was a storm." He lowered his eyes. "There were no survivors. Your father's body, what was left of it, was recovered only yesterday."

There was a whirling noise in Zoe's head. "I don't believe it." Her voice was over-loud in her own ears. She concentrated on a square of tile near her left foot, the glaze was neatly swirled, round and round and. . . .

The Counselor delicately cleared his throat.

"We are indebted to Sinon Yar for the news of your father's death. He has many avenues of information."

"He has spies," Zoë snapped.

"In times of unrest, the information Lord Yar has generously provided has saved Publican lives," the Counselor replied calmly.

Zoë suddenly felt very tired. "It can't be true. Publican fleets don't go that far into Citizen waters."

"Jomini was not on a Publican ship," Livia said. She sagged, her eyes closed. The Counselor gently settled her back in the chair. Taking her wrist, he timed the pulse. At length, satisfied, he returned to Zoë. His eyes were tiny pricks of light in the dark room.

"It seems your father was on a Citizen warship, my dear. Dealing with the enemy."

Zoë felt the air around them go very still. She chose her next words carefully.

"My father would not deal with the enemy."

"Yes. So we told Sinon Yar. He wasn't convinced. In fact, he produced a few documents that make it impossible to refute the accusation that your father was providing information about mining operations to Citizens."

Silence fell. A burning log falling to embers in the fireplace sounded like an avalanche.

"He's trying to find out what I know," Zoë realized. *"What does he want?"*

The Counselor continued. "Sinon Yar is one of the most influential Publicans in Ard Creggan."

"Now," Zoë said with scorn. "I remember when Sinon Yar was a nobody trying to push his way into the Families. Money wouldn't do it, so he got himself adopted. Too bad his foster father didn't live long enough to enjoy his son's success."

The Counselor cleared his throat. "The Family Yar does not approach the prestige of the Family Deich. They only aspire."

"What does he want, Counselor?" Zoë asked, her voice flat.

"Sinon Yar is very generous. He will forget this information about your father's treason in exchange for one or two considerations.

"A bribe? Isn't he wealthy enough?"

The Counselor's face registered his disapproval.

"I wish you would take the larger view of this problem and think of your family."

"I am thinking of my family, Counselor. With his information about my father's so-called treason, Sinon Yar could make life very difficult for us. Legally, he could take our estate. And yet, he only wants a—what did you call it?—a consideration. Forgive me if, knowing Sinon Yar as I do, I am suspicious."

The Counselor walked away from the women to the fireplace. He held a long, thin hand to the fire's heat. Zoë almost imagined she could count each chalk-white bone through the pale skin. Finally, he asked, "Zoë, do you know what the Gabhain is?"

"It's a kind of alliance ceremony, isn't it?" Zoë answered shortly, irritated by the return to their previous conversation.

"Oh, it is much more than that." he said with an odd excitement, turning back to the women. "It's an alliance between the Families. These alliances can only be contracted now with the approval of the entire Concordia."

Zoë waited.

"As the price of his silence, Sinon Yar has made two requests. The first is that as a token, you give him the ring your mother brought from Gurama."

"My mother's ring?" Zoë asked, surprised. "Why?"

The Counselor allowed his annoyance to show. "I cannot say. Perhaps it holds some significance in Sinon Yar's mind. He was a great admirer of your late mother. Certainly, it is not what I would have expected him to request. To the House of Yar it can only be a bauble."

Zoë frowned. "Whatever his reasons, he can't have it"

"And why not?" the Counselor demanded.

"Because," Zoë's mind raced. "Because my father had the ring with him. So unless they recovered it with his body, Sinon Yar will have to look for it on the bottom of the Galena Sea. You said there was a second request?"

The Counselor pursed his dry lips. "I can't imagine the second request will any more to your liking. Sinon Yar of the House of Yar expects the pledge of the House of Deich in the Gabhain. And since you are the eldest daughter of the family you would be the token of this alliance, his ward, to be given in the Gabhain ceremony. "

It was so unexpected, Zoë laughed.

"Is he joking? Or is he really insane? Why would Sinon Yar want to ally himself to us?"

"I have no idea," the Counselor retorted. "Obviously, it cannot be because he's heard you're a dutiful daughter. However, it may be that although the family Yar is rich, and has achieved some popularity with the rabble, the Ten Families do not recognize his leadership. An alliance with the Deich family would change that."

"They hate him or they're afraid of him," Zoë said flatly. "If he thinks forcing an alliance will change that, he overestimates my charm. And, if I remember correctly, Sinon Yar has contracted alliances with at least three families. And somehow all his wards—collateral describes them better—came to unfortunate ends. Doesn't that make you wonder, Counselor?"

"Only about your selfishness, girl. I cannot believe you'd listen to unfounded rumor when your family's position hangs in the balance. You're behaving like a child," the Counselor snapped. "Your duty to your family requires it. It may only be a temporary wardship. Is this so hard?"

Zoë looked down at her aunt. "I am aware of my duty, Counselor," she said evenly. "You may tell Sinon Yar that I will accept the conditions. And I have one condition of my own."

The Counselor raised an exquisitely drawn eyebrow. "A condition? I doubt we are in any position to make conditions."

Zoë continued as though she hadn't heard him. "If Sinon Yar wants me in this alliance," she said, "it must be tonight, at the solstice. Or not at all." She turned on her heel and marched from the room.

The Counselor barely noticed her departure, busy turning over in his mind what needed to be done.

"It is unusual," he finally said to Livia. "And the preparations will be rushed. But we can dispense with most of the preliminary formalities. Yes, my dear, it may work."

Livia looked up, pleading in her eyes. The Counselor smiled and stroked her hair.

••••

Near the edge of Ard Creggan, overlooking the outermost wall of the city, a man trudged up the steps of the campanile. Dwarfing the Dome of the Basilica beside it, the bell tower was the tallest structure in the city. A glass eye poked from its roof, pointed at the rim of the solar system. Reaching the door to the topmost platform, Sensa Tri paused to get his breath. He was a frail man, with the off-color skin of a man with a capricious heart. The key shook in his hands. This worried him. His mind and his hands had to be steady tonight. The calibration must be precise. He'd searched his entire professional life for evidence of this strange body, not knowing if it was comet, or planet or star. The ancient text had given him the exact spot to watch. Tonight would be the first opportunity in hundreds of years to observe it.

Some two hours later the calculations were done, the massive telescope was in position, and preparations completed, the photographic plates ready. He was extraneous matter now. Automation would take care of everything. With regret he closed the door on the tower room, locked it, and started the long walk down. The Concordia couldn't be kept waiting.

And if a straight line had been drawn from the lens of Tri's telescope it would have intercepted, somewhere near the heart of the galaxy, an object. An object twisting slowly in the astral winds. Yet as the solstice celebration began in earnest in Ard Creggan, the object awoke. Spinning faster and faster on its axis, it began to emit a beam. And with each rotation, the beam swept further and further until it scanned Ard Creggan's home planet, like a lighthouse beacon calling the traveler home.

CHAPTER FOUR

As night approached, a man stood on a shadowed porch high on the wall of the Citizen delegation's quarters in Ard Creggan and watched the city grow bright with lights for the winter solstice celebration. His nose wrinkled. He never could get use to the smell, a mixture of coal dust, smelting fumes, and baking bread, with a touch of ozone that meant snow some time that night. It reminded him of something just at the tip of a memory. The memory stirred. He was standing on a dock on a rocky shore, looking out over water. Snow was in the air then, too. On the horizon were the dark humps of islands. One of them was Gurama, his destination and home for the next year. A ship would soon approach over the gray, cold sea. There was a group of boys and girls with him on the dock, barely in their teens. They didn't speak; as uncomfortable with each other as only awkward teenagers could be, who also were life-long enemies. Tiernan looked them over. He'd never been this close to Publicans before. *Effete*, he thought watching them shiver in the cold sea spray, *soft and useless*. Their stay on Gurama was supposed to be eight months in the latest peace initiative, a chance, or so the propaganda claimed, for young Publicans and Citizens to examine common ground.

It feels more like exile. Already, he missed his barracks, the routine of training.

But he had been ordered to cooperate, and cooperate he would. A fluttering in the corner of his eye caught his attention. Out on the black rocks that passed for a beach in this place, a scarlet mass billowed and snapped in the keen wind. It resolved into a figure at one of the many tidal pools that pocked the cracked rocks. Hopping across the rocks to get a closer look, he discovered it was a girl. A Publican.

I should have known. No self-respecting Citizen wears color like that.

She was inspecting a shallow crevice.

"Look at these," she said, pointing. "What are they?"

He squatted down beside her to get a closer look. In the water, a translucent sphere extended lacy tendrils.

"It's beautiful. So iridescent," she marveled. "Look how it pulses, like it's breathing."

Tiernan examined the blob in the water. "If one of those things touches you, you won't think it's so beautiful. It packs quite a sting."

She looked at him directly for the first time and smiled. She had the most beautiful green eyes. He blushed and pointed to what looked like a rock in the water.

"Now there's something that may not be beautiful, but is a lot more useful."

With his knife, he pried a lump from the rock's surface. "Cockles. They're good to eat."

"Can we eat them like that?" she asked turning the shell over in her hand to inspect it.

"You can. But I don't recommend it," he said, amused. "I imagine they'll keep until we get to the island."

She slipped the shell into a bag hanging from her waist and went back to exploring the pools. Her hair fell forward into her face and with an exasperated sigh she dragged it back with one hand. Tiernan silently offered a piece of twine from his pocket of gadgets. She took it with another smile that made his head whirl. She moved on to another pool. Tiernan trailed along, happy to explain the fissures in the rocks, or identify the wildflowers or the sea life all around them. He could answer a third of her questions, struggled for plausible explanations on another third, and admitted ignorance on the rest. Whatever he managed, she accepted; the rest they discussed, worked out the possibilities, and occasionally made up something so ludicrous they had to laugh. By the time the ship to Gurama nudged into dock, Tiernan was more than half in love with this curious Publican girl, Zoë. The memory ended, as a shadow passed.

A second man had come out on the porch and moved to the railing, unaware of his presence.

"What are you doing out here, Brian?" Tiernan asked.

The newcomer spun around.

"Well, I call this lucky. I've been looking all over for you."

The two men looked to be the same age. They were both medium height with the wiry look of men who've lived hard lives. But there was something restless in Brian's face, maybe it was the way his eyes darted from one thing to the next, never settling.

"It's colder than a witch's tit out here," Brian said, shivering, and spat over the porch railing. "That'll be frozen before it hits the ground." He grinned at Tiernan. "Is freezing out here one of those soletei exercises in character building?"

"I came out to clear my head."

"It's more likely you'll catch cold."

A rumbling came from somewhere in Ard Creggan's foundations and Brian clutched the railing his eyes widening. The swaying stopped.

"That was close," he muttered.

"Just another tremor," Tiernan said, looking out over the city. He noticed a sheen of sweat on Brian's face despite the cold. "They don't seem to worry the Publicans."

Brian snorted.

"This place is coming down around their ears and they keep digging away like there's no connection. While you were at the negotiations today, I got out to look around. This is some place."

"What did you see?"

"The foundries." Brian's low whistle was admiring. "You should see the size of one of those plants. They wouldn't let me see the actual smelting process, but it was still impressive. If we had half their technology we'd be doing more than carrying small arms. They're forging something now that makes their current guns look like toothpicks. I'll bet its range is over 150 miles."

"Makes you wonder about their commitment to peace talks, doesn't it?" Tiernan observed dryly.

This stirred Brian's memory. "Yes, well that's why I came to find you. We have a visitor."

"I thought all the Citizens were out celebrating the solstice," Tiernan said, letting the irritation rise in his voice.

"It's the Counselor," Brian said, then leaned against the railing and closed his eyes with a smile. Tiernan cursed fluently, thoroughly, and with considerable imagination. When he'd run dry, Brian opened his eyes and smiled in admiration.

"It's a pity you're wasting your time here on peace negotiations, Tiernan. You have untapped talents."

Despite himself, Tiernan laughed. "In the diplomatic corps, perhaps? Damn the talks. We've been at this three months. So far we've talked about entourage size, the number and height of seats, the table size, even the length of breaks in the talks. Nothing about peace."

"Not to mention the warm reception we're getting in this place," Brian added.

"Yes, I know. I was with the group that was attacked today," Tiernan scowled. "I start to think these talks are wasted effort."

Silence.

Tiernan searched his friend's face. "It's been a long time, Brian. I used to know what you were thinking."

Brian shifted uneasily. "Just wondering how long this will go on. I'm with you. I hate sitting here, showing our teeth to a lot of fat Publicans." He turned away. "The truth is, this place spooks me. It's all these walls." He looked out over Ard Creggan. "They press in on you."

Tiernan didn't mock him. "I feel it too. Don't worry. If we don't see results soon, we'll go home."

Wrapped in their own thoughts, the two men watched the lights below them. Tiernan broke the silence first.

"Brian?"

"I'm still here."

"You remember the Black Pagoda?"

"The Pagoda!" He burst out laughing. "I haven't thought of that place in ages. Remember that time we got into the sanctuary?"

"Yes, I do. And thanks to you, I spent a week picking quills out of my backside."

"Me! How was I to know they kept quillipeds in the sanctuary? What made you think about that?"

Tiernan's gaze slipped to a far off compound. "No particular reason. But if anything should happen, it might be a good place to meet."

"If you think that's putting my mind at ease, you're wrong. What are you up to, Tiernan?"

"Nothing. Yet. Just keep it in mind."

"How about this?" Brian shot back. "We get in trouble together. It'd be just like old times."

"Not this time. This isn't strictly delegation business."

Brian clapped his friend on the back.

"A woman, then. Good. I began to think you were becoming a monk. This is the Tiernan I remember."

"Have I changed so much?" Tiernan's tone was so grim, Brian's smile faded.

"No more than I have, my friend," he replied in a low voice. "I feel like a snake that's shed its skin one time too many. Too many changes in too little time. 'Til I'm not sure where I stand."

Tiernan threw an arm around his shoulders.

"We're a miserable pair. After this, we need an adventure. Just like the old days. Now, come with me so that I don't forget my manners when the Counselor asks for a change in wall color or a different centerpiece at our peace talks."

And despite the foreboding at least one of them felt, they laughed again and strolled back inside.

••••

Cities were strange places to Citizens. Early in the Sequential Wars, the Citizens dispersed to smaller, isolated settlements, finding that less was lost if Ard Creggan's guns found their range. So Citizen society was a world of towns and villages, connected by a network of small roads. It was a defense mechanism, as was the rise of the soletei, the Citizens' most effective weapon. Soletei were selected for their physical abilities, intelligence, and especially for their dedication to the Citizen cause. Even poorly armed, with sidearms and homemade rifles, they were a formidable defense against the Publican armies.

It was the dream of every Citizen boy to be a soletei, the pride of every Citizen family to have a son in their service.

Tiernan's father was a farmer who recognized his son's natural ability and a curiosity he knew would never be satisfied by a lifetime as a farmer. In the spring of Tiernan's eighth year, when the other boys went on to lessons in the agricultural schools, his father took him to the largest nearby town for the annual soletei selection by the Tribune.

In two weeks of rigorous mental and physical testing, Tiernan competed against other boys for a place among the soletei. The Tribune examiners were exacting. They weighed, judged, and ruthlessly eliminated. Tiernan succeeded where many others failed. And in succeeding, he left behind his familiar world of planting and harvesting, of his parents and the village. He joined other children like himself in a military school, where minds and bodies were given over to a single objective—learning the arts of war.

There were some Citizen leaders who doubted the wisdom of an elite soletei corp. But as long as the hostilities with Ard Creggan continued and the land needed defending, their critics kept their doubts to themselves. Time enough to reconsider if peace ever came again.

The Tribune itself had sent a reluctant Tiernan to these latest peace talks in Ard Creggan. He suspected success at the peace table could mean the end of the soletei.

Unemployment was not on his mind, however, as he accompanied Brian back into the hall. Donncha, as head of the Citizen delegation, was exchanging pleasantries with the Counselor, who was alone, without his usual phalanx of aides and assistants. The running joke among the Citizens was that truly important Publicans never slept alone; they had at least six aides to make sure they closed their eyes properly. It was a poor attempt at humor, but illustrative. Citizens were unaccustomed to pomp and contemptuous of Publican fanfare. They repeatedly frustrated Publican efforts to aggrandize the talks. In turn the Publicans were forever mixing up the Citizens, confused by their common dress, and lack of ceremony and titles. One Citizen was the same as the next to the Publicans. Fortunately, the Citizens didn't care.

Taking up a position near the door Tiernan waited, feeling the eyes of the other men on him. They were uneasy. Donncha listened while the Counselor prattled on about the weather, and the solstice, circling diplomatically until he finally reached the point he'd come to make.

"I am afraid I must apologize," the Counselor began, "for this afternoon's disturbance. Your safely is, of course, my first concern. And it grieves me that you were subjected to what I can only consider to be attacks by dangerous and decidedly outlaw elements within Ard Creggan. Please be assured that we have one of their number in detention and we will ferret out the rest of these criminals. There can be no place in our society for their kind."

Donncha's smile was genial. "We thank the Counselor for his concern. Fortunately none of our people were injured today. We also share your belief that the majority of Publicans support a peace effort."

"Yes, well, there we both may be mistaken," the Counselor murmured. "The Concordia of Families has decided that the time may not be ripe for a peace effort."

Donncha's polite expression didn't change by a hair. "In my own experience there have been a least a dozen different peace initiatives, Counselor. As you know, I have been involved in most of these negotiations. We are, of course, saddened at this decision of the Concordia," he said, diplomatically. "Perhaps we will be fortunate to live to the next initiative. In the meantime, are we allowed to leave Ard Creggan?"

The Counselor threw up his hands in dismay.

"As though I would leave you to find your way without assistance. My personal guards will be at your compound in three hours to escort you to our gates and out of Ard Creggan. Forgive the lateness of the hour and the suddenness of the departure. It might perhaps be safer for everyone. Nothing will be allowed to mar your final hours."

"Our final hours, Counselor?" Donncha echoed.

"Citizen, you mistake me," the Counselor said with matched politeness. "I meant, your final hours within our city."

Then it was all over except for the good-byes. As the door shut on the Counselor, Donncha turned to his men.

"You heard. Prepare your gear. We leave within the hour."

As the men scattered in all directions, Tiernan took Donncha aside.

"You're leaving without the Counselor's escort?" he asked quietly.

Donncha nodded. "Safer, I think. We'll be outside Ard Creggan's walls before the Counselor knows it. He may say he wants to protect us, but I would trust my own instinct and live to see another peace talk. Even if," he said with sudden exasperation, "it is another useless exercise."

Tiernan turned away to find Brian at his elbow. "Better get our things. Looks like we're going home sooner than expected."

"And you?" Brian asked. "What about that unfinished business?"

Tiernan grinned. "Just remember what I told you."

Moments later a figure slipped from the Citizen compound and out into Ard Creggan. A moment later, he was followed.

••••

From the main hall, the sounds of musicians tuning their instruments floated up to Zoë seated on her balcony. Below in the city, shriller sounds signaled the official start of the solstice. Even when Noor appeared beside her, Zoë continued to stare out over the Ard Creggan rooftops.

"It is too cold to be out here, little one. And it'll do no good to pout over this," Noor added.

"And little good to try to leave," Zoë retorted, "because I notice my door is locked. I imagine that was the Counselor's idea."

"Well, it wouldn't be the first time you'd gone missing when you were needed."

Zoë grinned and kicked at a loose tile. It was true enough. But Aunt always thought the servants helped her out of the compound. She looked to the compound's roof just a few feet above. Crossing the roof was simple enough and there were plenty of ways to get down the walls and out into the city—if you weren't afraid of heights. She had done so frequently. But not, she admitted, in a dress.

Tonight Zoë wore a gown cut from one of her mother's. Despite its hand-me-down status, it was elegant. It bared her shoulders and revealed the slender woman her everyday tunic managed to hide. Even her normally wild hair was neatly upswept—a trick that had taken all of Noor's dexterity. And tonight, too, she wore her mother's jewels; a necklace that was a confection of emeralds the color of her eyes.

She twisted in her seat to count up four bricks and over one, and pressed hard on the brick face. One end of the brick popped out revealing the recess behind it. From its interior she removed a small box. She opened it and carefully gathered up a loop of chain from which dangled a ring with a solitary unfaceted black stone set in a carved swirl of dull metal. As a child, Zoë remembered being afraid of the carving, a snake's coils wrapped around the stone, its fangs sunk into the sides, holding it fast.

Before her last illness, her mother had given it to her. In Zoë's hand it felt warm, with the weight of a living thing. Looking at it now, the ring reminded her somehow of Uncle Eon's wall. She tilted the band to read the script incised inside the band. *What Time Forgets Is At Hand.*

Noor joined her on the balcony, her soft question breaking into her thoughts, *"Are you certain, child? Your father is not dead?"*

Zoë scowled. "I don't know. I don't think so."

"The Counselor says it is so."

"I don't trust him, Noor. But I think father may be in trouble."

Noor nosed the ring on Zoë's finger, then dropped to all fours and sniffed the night air.

"There is something in the wind tonight."

"It's the solstice, Noor. You always say that at the solstice."

"No. More trouble. Men."

Zoë giggled. "And you always say that, too."

Noor looked into the girl's eyes. *"You will do this thing? Tonight?"*

Zoë cradled her nurse's head in her arms, and slipped the chain and its ring around Noor's neck. It disappeared into her fur.

"It's the only way, Noor. I need to find father. You're going to help me, aren't you?"

There was the sound of a key turning in the lock. Zoë quickly replaced the brick and re-entered her room. It was Aunt Livia, come to take her downstairs. The majority of guests would not arrive for a few hours, but the family and a hundred or so close friends were invited for an early dinner. She looked nothing like the exhausted old woman Zoë had left earlier that day. She looked determined, in-charge, the old Livia.

"Don't keep me waiting, Zoë. Our guests will begin arriving any minute," she said, looking her over carefully. "Very nice. I'm glad you decided," she added with a slight smile, "to take my suggestion to wear the green silk. You're not as striking as your mother was in her day. Still, you do the family credit."

"My mother was beautiful, wasn't she Aunt?"

They began the long walk down to the main hall, the older woman leaning on her niece's arm.

"Zora was an intelligent woman. A stupid woman is rarely beautiful. Or at least," Livia amended, "not beautiful for long."

In an odd day, this was strangest of all. Her aunt never talked about Zoë's mother.

"And she was born on Gurama?" Zoë asked, taking the opening presented.

Her aunt seemed to consider her words. "Gurama was her home for several years; she was educated there. We had expected you to complete your education there, too. It was unfortunate that the wars made that impossible. If you ask me, your own experience of the world has been far too insular, limited as it has been to this city. But your father was not receptive to my suggestions to broaden your education." She paused, hand to her forehead. "I still can't believe he is gone."

"Do you really need to stand in the receiving line, Aunt? It's tiring and I'm sure our guests would understand."

"We will receive our guests properly. We are the Family Deich," Livia snapped with a resumption of her old spirit. Her voice softened. "Listen to me now. We won't have time later to talk. When your mother married Jomini she made a great sacrifice. Like you are about to. You do this for the family. Remember that. The family, our past and our future, are all that matters. Trust me. But most of all, trust yourself."

Zoë nodded.

They walked the rest of the way down to dinner in silence.

••••

Some time after the door closed behind Zoë and her aunt, a shadow dropped from the roof to the balcony of the silent room. Another shadow followed a moment later.

"I'll go in alone," Tiernan whispered.

"I'm coming too," Brian retorted and held up a hand to forestall Tiernan's objection. "You need me. Two can search better than one."

"I don't know how I let you talk me into coming in the first place."

"You didn't, I just followed."

"I wish you could follow orders."

"If you're going to get personal, I can think of a few of your sins, too."

"Just look for a ring. Black stone. Snake head. It could be almost anywhere."

"Well, that narrows it down," Brian muttered as they stepped across the threshold.

They stood for a moment, blinking in the bright interior then Tiernan moved to listen at the hall door. He waved Brian silently into one of the adjoining rooms.

Alone, he looked around. It was a large open room with the steeply sloping ceiling of a garret, but it was unlike any attic he'd ever been in. The walls were lined in embroidered blue silk, a garden of flowers. A thick carpet with the same flowers covered the floor. It absorbed his footsteps. Alongside the double doors they'd come through, there were four long windows looking out over the rooftops of Ard Creggan. The room's furnishings were spare but well-made: a comfortable chair in front of a fireplace, several shelves filled with books, and a writing desk. The desk held papers, but nothing of particular interest to him, although it appeared Zoë did not pay her bills on time. He pulled out the drawers, deftly feeling for spring panels and latches to hiding holes. Nothing. He crossed to the chair and to the small table beside it. A robe lay across the chair and as he picked it up to go through the pockets, the movement released a scent. Years fell away with the perfume and he was again struggling to grasp the intricacies of Palmerian pentameter on Gurama. A girl made fun of his attempts, but spent long hours teaching him the beauties of a long-dead language. He'd forgotten the conjugation of the infinitive, but with the scent, the sound of her voice and her face came back as clearly as though he'd seen her yesterday.

Tiernan felt the hairs on the back of neck stand on end. He whirled around, and jerked back as claws cut the air inches from his nose.

CHAPTER FIVE

At times like this it is odd what goes through your mind. For Tiernan it was the memory of a reconnaissance detail, five years ago. It was autumn and a cold rain had fallen for days. In the woods, red and yellow leaves covered everything. The sodden leaves deadened sound—the sound of footsteps, the sound of their voices. They came across the first body half lying in a stream, one arm over his head as though thrown up in self-defense. They found the other bodies nearby, shapes they first thought were rotting logs under the leaf cover. It took the rest of the day to find them all, an entire troop cut to pieces by a lone Saurillia. Maybe they came too close to a den. It happened. Females are easily provoked when they are protecting young. Now, standing in Zoë's room, he observed with a certain detachment. *This is a female Saurillia. And she's between me and the way out.*

His sidearms had been confiscated when he entered the city. But he had a knife. It might work—if she stood quietly and agreed to be gutted. He wondered where Brian was.

If he comes in now, she'll attack. But with two of us, we might have a chance. A stray thought.

I had no idea Saurillias smelled so musky.

Of course he'd never been this close to a Saurillia before. Not a live one. He didn't know anyone who had—and lived. From below in the streets, the music of the winter solstice carried up to the open doors. He could hear laughter, a clatter of applause. Nearby, a clock struck the hour. Faster than he thought possible, she lunged. Instinctively he threw the robe over her head, hoping to blind her, as jaws snapped shut, pushing him back hard against the wall. Then nothing. The Saurillia settled back on her haunches, cradling the robe in her paws, watching him intently.

Out of the corner of his eye, he saw Brian come out of an inner room. The Saurillia growled, but didn't move. Behind her, Brian eased slowly toward the balcony. Tiernan took a tentative step.

She has such little black eyes. And such long claws.

He took another step. Brian had reached the balcony before him and was already gone. He'd almost decided to make a rush for it, when the Saurillia's head went up, listening intently to some faint sound. She dropped the tunic and rose on her hind legs, her eyes on the door. A long rumbling growl vibrated through the room. Tiernan reached the balcony in two strides and without looking back, swung himself up to the roof, clambered up to the nearest peak, and from there to the lee of a chimney where Brian was waiting. Tiernan was surprised to find his clothes soaked with sweat.

"That was some guard dog. Did you find anything?"

"Nothing. But I think," Brian said, as a whuffing sound drifted up from the room below, "the guard dog is laughing at us."

••••

They made a quick if shaky descent from the rooftop and soon were part of the revelers crowding Ard Creggan's streets.

Ard Creggan on solstice night was a confusion of people, smells and commotion. There were vendors selling pastries, whole roasted birds, live songbirds, candies, wine, children's toys and cheap jewelry. Street entertainers drew knots of people at every corner, making little eddies of turbulence in the human flow. The din was overwhelming and Tiernan wondered if Publicans weren't a little mad from the noise. He watched and so he saw what went unnoticed by the rest. "See those men?" he said to Brian in a low voice. "They're not here for the celebration. They're not even interested."

"How do you know?"

"Well, for one thing, they're sober."

Brian bent to strip a robe from a Publican sleeping it off in an alley. He slipped it over his Citizen uniform. Tiernan did the same, lifting a cloak hanging near the entrance to a bar. Now they blended easily into the crowd. The men they'd first noticed were being joined by others coming from the side streets. Tiernan broke into a drinking song and staggered into three of them, throwing his arms around the nearest man in drunken friendship. Without a word, they pushed him off and kept walking. Tiernan watched them go as Brian came up beside him.

"They're armed, beneath those robes."

"Why?"

Tiernan took his bearings. "Don't know. But they seem to be heading toward our delegation compound."

"Donncha must have everyone out by now," Brian said.

"You take the avenue to the left." Tiernan motioned down a side street running parallel to the road they were on. "It should bring you to the back of our compound, hopefully before our friends. If Donncha is still there, warn him. If he's not, go after him."

Brian gave him a sideways glance. "And you?"

Tiernan made a quick decision. There was risk in splitting up. "I'll follow them. Hurry, we don't have a lot of time. I'll see you at the Black Pagoda. And no following me this time."

Without giving Brian a chance to argue, Tiernan tugged the hood of the cloak forward over his face and moved off. He threaded his way through the crowds, keeping the men in sight.

His pursuit took him ever further from the center of town. Here there were fewer stalls, fewer celebrators. He tried to follow, yet appear to be just another drunken reveler. For a while it seemed they were bent on the delegation's compound, but a twisting side street turned them away into one of the poorer sections of Ard Creggan. A sign unfamiliar to Tiernan, an inverted V within a circle, appeared with increasing frequency on the sides of buildings, on shop signs, and burned into the doors of private homes.

Like a dog marking its territory.

Then he was alone in the street. Before his eyes, the men he had been following had simply vanished. More men approached. Quickly, he bent as though to refasten a boot buckle. They passed so close their capes swept his back and this time he kept a close eye on them. Within a few feet they came to a blank wall—and walked through it.

"So that's it."

As another group approached in the street, Tiernan fell in with them, his heart beating faster as they approached the wall—and walked through as though it wasn't there.

A magician's trick, Tiernan thought, *smoke and mirrors, but effective in a dark street.*

They were in a narrow alleyway. A quick glance upward showed him guards posted on the rooftops. He walked on. Unexpectedly, the alley emptied out into a cobblestone plaza, surrounded on all sides by high walls, similarly guarded. Opposite the alleyway, a massive bunker of a building loomed. A balcony high up on its façade looked out over the plaza. And from the balcony hung a banner with the same device he'd seen in the surrounding streets. Beneath the balcony, an arch framed a staircase. Tiernan hugged the sides of the plaza, making his way toward the arch. This was not easy because the plaza was filled with tight knots of six or eight men. By the odd groupings, and the suspicion with which they eyed each other, Tiernan guessed this was the first time all the groups had assembled.

"They know their own men, their own leader, but no one else. Like cells. There is safety for someone in this. It's just a matter of finding out who that someone is. And what they're up to."

He had nearly reached the arch when a guard clapped a hand on his shoulder.

"You!" the guard bellowed, a huge man with the scarred face of a professional fighter. Tiernan slipped a hand under his cape for his dagger.

"Here," the guard barked. "Give these out to the men. And see you change yours, too."

He dumped a pile of gray coats at Tiernan's feet and strode away. The soletei passed out the clothes, watching with growing comprehension as the Publicans shed their gaudy festival capes to become Citizens in gray. Holding the dwindling pile in front of his face, Tiernan worked his way back to the arch and its dark stairway. Safely in its shadows, he threw off his borrowed Publican cloak and became like the rest. The plaza ablaze with torch light thronged with an army of Citizen imposters. Now the guards were passing out short blades, ideal in hand-to-hand combat, and small firearms. He gladly took a handgun; it was better quality than any he'd find outside Ard Creggan. It would be useful.

"*They could fool me,*" thought Tiernan. "*It will take even less for the people of Ard Creggan to believe they've been attacked by Citizens.*"

The stairway corkscrewed its way to the upper floor of the building, a nerve-wracking climb because it was impossible to see who might be descending the stairs. Halfway up, a roar from a hundred throats flattened him against the wall. Then silence. In the sudden quiet, a man's voice was heard. Tiernan crept up the last few steps to where a heavy drape guarded the entry to the upper room. Beyond the curtain, a voice rose and fell with a hypnotic cadence.

"There is nothing greater than a man's love for his city," the voice said. "Our city is our home, our living, our very family. Here a Publican is born, grows to manhood, learns a Publican's skills, does a Publican's work."

Cautiously, Tiernan twitched the cloth to glimpse a room draped ceiling to floor with heavy tapestries. It was empty but anybody might come up the steps behind him. He slid into the space between wall and tapestry. A worn spot in the fabric became a strategic peephole and his eyes grew accustomed to the gloom. The voice continued.

"In time, a Publican hopes to see his children follow in his footsteps. And he is proud of this. Why? Because he is proud of his city, our Ard Creggan. All things begin and end with Ard Creggan. Where is he safe? Where can he look around himself and say 'Here, here I am among my own. Here is everything I believe in. Here is everything I cherish. Here is all that I hold dear.'"

A murmur of assent ran though the crowd. Through his peephole, Tiernan could see a broad-shouldered man on the balcony, his arms raised to the crowd.

His voice rose.

"Here we are free men. Free to earn our living. Free to make homes. Free to meet, to think as we wish. Free to be Publicans."

A great cheer went up and it was some moments before he could resume. By then his tone had changed.

"But for how much longer? Even now, the clock is ticking. And with each tick, your days as free Publicans are numbered. Even now the Concordia chips away at our freedoms."

A voice from the crowd, "We've had enough of wars. Let's have peace!" Many in the crowd murmured their agreement.

"The peace talks?"

There was contempt in the speaker's voice. "Yes, the peace talks will bring peace. And what else? What is the price of peace? The Concordia is strangely silent on that. Let me tell you how they plan to purchase peace. They will do it by selling our city."

An undercurrent ran through the crowd.

"Ard Creggan, our beautiful city. Sold by the Concordia, our city's so-called protector. Hear me. There is another side to these peace talks. Yes, hostilities will end. Citizens may even sell you cheaper bread. Think of that, Publicans, peace and a cheaper loaf of bread."

"Sounds good enough to me," a voice yelled. A ripple of laughter ran among the men.

"Yes, but what price will you pay? In return for cheap bread? Have you thought of that? I'll tell you. Ard Creggan will open its gates to these strangers. In return for peace, the Concordia plans to hand over Ard Creggan to our enemies."

An ominous silence hung over the crowd.

"Citizens, foreigners, will come, settle here, take jobs, take wives—our jobs, our women—and spawn. Our birthright is Ard Creggan and it is being sold. Even now the Concordia plans to share the secrets of our foundries with Citizens."

The voice sank.

"I don't begrudge these Citizens their lives. But let them live elsewhere. Look around you. Do we have the land, or the jobs, or the houses to take in these strangers? Strangers who are foreign to our ways. What will we do when we lose everything to them? We will be outnumbered. They will overwhelm us. We will forget who we are and what is ours. We are the rightful inhabitants of Ard Creggan, not these Citizens. Can we accept peace at this price? These peacemakers, the Concordia, are our enemies," the speaker shouted. "They have been bought and paid for by our enemies. We must reclaim our city before it's too late."

The men thundered their approval. They were Ard Creggan's poor, living just ahead of ruin, short of money, work, respect and, most of all, hope. He had picked away at the scab covering their fear. Now with his words he gave them hope, offering better days. Better days and the chance for revenge. Payback for the slights and inequities that are a poor man's inheritance. All they had to do was follow him. They caught his fervor. Tiernan could feel it, like a wind sweeping up from the plaza. Straining to see more, he caught a pinprick of light out of the corner of his eye. It came from the opposite wall. Were his eyes playing tricks? No: where the light had been there was now a deeper shadow, the shape of a man. Tiernan felt safely hidden. If, as he suspected, there was an entrance behind that tapestry, it might give him the escape route he needed. The shouting from the plaza was deafening now. The speaker turned abruptly from the balcony and re-entered the room. And Tiernan recognized him. For days on end during the peace talks, they'd sat across from each other. It was Sinon Yar who strode across the room, arms wide.

"You see how they love me," he said jovially. "They will follow me into hell itself."

As he spoke, the shadow Tiernan had detected earlier resolved itself into a familiar figure.

"Let us hope you are right, Sinon Yar," replied the Counselor.

CHAPTER SIX

"The lost soul follows the best marked path," Sinon Yar crowed. "Fools will do anything rather than lead themselves. It's the same in politics, war, even religion. Especially religion. Men are such pathetic fools."

"That's a poor picture of our fellow Publicans, Sinon Yar," the Counselor cautioned. "Be careful you don't underestimate them."

"I don't underestimate their worth, just their intelligence. They are afraid and fear makes them stupid and easy to control. The ones who don't fear, I buy. It's very simple."

"There is nothing simple about the disinformation we have engineered, my Lord Yar. My people have spent months spreading allegations, hinting at scandals, undermining the authority of the Concordia. We have both invested a great deal in this venture."

Sinon Yar smiled. "A good investment for control of Ard Creggan."

The Counselor added, "And for the good of the people, of course."

"Of course, Counselor, and for the good of Ard Creggan. Where I will be the one who determines what is good for us."

Far from taking offense, the Counselor seemed to find a certain satisfaction in Sinon Yar's words.

A manservant drew aside a curtain at the far end of the room and entered with a lamp. Through his peephole, Tiernan could see there were chairs and a table arranged at one end of the room. Sinon Yar threw himself into one of the chairs. The Counselor remained standing.

"So what news do you bring me? Will the Family Deich agree to the alliance?"

The Counselor did not reply at once, but looked thoughtful. "The aunt will comply."

"And the girl?" Yar demanded.

The Counselor allowed himself a slight smile. "The girl is a different story. She may do as she is bid. She may not. I have instructed her aunt to post guards. It will remain for you, with your considerable charms, to win her over."

Sinon Yar's eyes narrowed. He suspected he was being mocked, yet his immense self-importance could not quite accept that possibility.

"As you say. Once the alliance is official, it will not matter. With Jomini dead, I will become the head of the Family Deich. And at the Concordia's behest, I will sit at their head."

"Tell me, Lord Yar," the Counselor asked. "Why are you doing this?"

Sinon Yar studied the Counselor. "It's late in the day to ask for reasons, isn't it?"

"I am nearly convinced you have none."

"Besides greed, you mean? Do you see this as my power play, Counselor? One against the many. A grab for all the little brass rings."

"A cliché, my lord. But I must admit you have puzzled me."

Yar poured himself a drink from a bottle on the table.

"I almost think you mean to say, we have puzzled you. We as a species. Are you one of us, Counselor? Tell me, do you bleed like me?"

"I can assure you I do, in case you thought a demonstration was necessary," the Counselor replied calmly. "So I conclude you are prepared to take over Ard Creggan for humanitarian purposes."

Sinon Yar laughed again. "You have a way of making it sound foolish, but yes, if you need my motivation, that's good enough. From happy accidents come unexpected success. Ard Creggan is failing—economically, socially, and morally. It's like a great dying monster. With the exception of our high and mighty Families, the majority of people in Ard Creggan—if they are not already starving or homeless—live in fear they soon will be. Our mines are failing and our production is falling. Men are without jobs. Yesterday, a man came to me, a good man. He hadn't worked in six months. He asked me for money to feed his family. Isn't that a man's right? To feed his family? In my precinct, we found another man doing unspeakable things to children, and the children stayed because at least he fed them, gave them a roof over their heads. We dealt with him, outside a court of law. When matters are in such a state, laws are completely without meaning. We are our own law. And meanwhile, the Concordia and the Families take no action."

"The rule of law is a cumbersome process, my lord," the Counselor demurred.

"Small plans never won a war. No, this is no time for the niceties of a democracy, Counselor. And this is no time for peace." Sinon Yar glared at the Counselor. "If there is anyone who has the vision to change the present, then he has the moral imperative to do so. That is my duty, Counselor. I don't want to rule Ard Creggan to satisfy my vanity. Where Ard Creggan is concerned, I have no ego." Sinon Yar smiled. "But enough of my personal ideology, Counselor. You've ended the peace talks?"

"As you wished."

"And how will you explain this to the Concordia?"

"By telling them the Citizens broke off the talks. It will never occur to the members of the Concordia to doubt me."

Yar was pleased. "It should be entertaining to see their faces when my Citizens join the festivities tonight. After my men attack, the Families will be so frightened they will accede to my offer to take military control of Ard Creggan to guarantee their safety. I'll even be able to produce the bodies of real Citizens as proof."

"Yes. That is the plan, isn't it?" the Counselor said.

Sinon Yar shot him a suspicious look.

"Yes, that is the plan. But there could be a slight difficulty in that area. For you. Nothing you can't solve, of course. You are always so resourceful," he added smoothly.

The Counselor was unmoved.

"You're not curious in the least, Counselor?" Sinon Yar needled. "Something that might upset your plans?"

"Interesting," the Counselor murmured, "that you enjoy these little games. I suppose you are referring to the return of the reconnaissance unit."

"I am. Their captain knows about our little training ground. He will tell the Concordia tonight. He may ruin our plans."

"If we had prevented his surveillance, we would have only confirmed their suspicions. You must learn to take the longer view. And," the Counselor added, "to trust me."

Sinon Yar smirked. "Trust you, Counselor? Well, let us see how much we really trust each other. So far, your eminence has been a remarkably silent partner. Can you pull this fat out of the fire?"

The Counselor appeared lost in thought for a moment. "There is no fire," he said finally. Sinon Yar threw back his head and howled.

"When Captain Samuel stands up in front of the Concordia tonight and describes what he saw, there will be a fire all right. And it will start with the bonfire they light under me. And, I warn you, if I burn, you will burn with me."

"You worry over nothing," the Counselor replied.

"You mean he won't tell them he saw Publicans? Armed Publicans? Training outside the walls under the direction of the Counselor's own guards?"

"No."

"And why not?"

"Captain Samuel will never address the Concordia. I will see to that."

"In that case, I will not keep you," Sinon Yar said with an exaggerated politeness. "In fact, you're already late."

He waved his hand and the servant pulled back the stairway curtain. Sounds of preparation from the plaza carried up into the room. The Counselor hesitated, backing instead toward the wall from which he'd first appeared. Sinon Yar rose with unusual speed and cut off his retreat.

"Come, Counselor," he wheedled. "It would do my men a world of good to see you before their little adventure, don't you think?"

"I think it may prematurely compromise my position, my lord," the Counselor snapped.

Sinon Yar shrugged. "No more than I have compromised mine. Shouldn't we all be equally at risk, if we're to share equally in the rewards? As they say, a timid heart reaps only dreams."

Caught, the Counselor swept down the stairs followed by Yar. Tiernan could almost feel his anger as he left the room. *This Sinon Yar has nerve, if nothing else,* he admitted.

The room was empty. He might have seconds to find the hidden door the Counselor had used to enter Sinon Yar's compound. Feeling blindly in the dark, he ran his hands over the wall. He was lucky, his fumblings depressed something. A narrow slit in the wall slid back without a sound, and a wave of damp air from the passageway beyond washed over him. A lamp, obviously last used by the Counselor, hung in the passageway. As Tiernan lifted the lamp, it glowed into life. He stepped across the threshold and the wall, as though primed, slid shut behind him just as Sinon Yar returned to the room. An odor, perhaps a whiff of moldy air, stopped Yar. He swept aside the curtain where Tiernan had stood moments before and passed a hand over the smooth wall.

"May I help you, Lord Yar?" said a voice behind him. He let the curtain drop.

"It's nothing, Caleb," he said curtly, walking back to the table. "I've just finished with the Counselor."

His companion had the unhappy look of a fanatic. "Finished?" Caleb said acidly. "If he breathes, he is not finished."

"You give the old man too much credit," Sinon Yar said. "But never mind. Have you given the men their orders?"

"Yes, Lord Yar."

"And they know what they are to do?"

"Yes, my Lord. The first group of men will take the outer compound."

"That shouldn't require too much finesse. I've paid for the loyalties of most of the Deich guards. It will be like sweeping up bugs."

Sinon Yar slapped his great hands together with glee. Caleb's habitual expression of disapproval didn't alter. He continued. "There will be a small contingent of the family's personal guard in the north tower."

"Good. See to it they stay there. The last thing I need is some enthusiastic soldiers putting up real opposition. Now there's a little change in plan. You'll take a second group of men. I have some special work for them."

Caleb's gloominess increased minutely. "We are over-extended now, my Lord Yar. The men are not as well trained as I had hoped."

"Your concerns are duly noted, Caleb. The raw materials are to blame. Deeply flawed," Sinon Yar said tragically, "deeply."

Caleb cleared his throat. "Yes, my Lord. You have a list?"

With a smile, Sinon Yar whipped out a crumpled sheet from an inner pocket.

"You are perceptive, as usual."

He drew Caleb to him and they bent their heads over the scrap of paper.

"You see, there are only a few. These should be killed. Possibly in the uproar, but feel free to improvise."

Together the men walked to the top of the staircase.

"And, my friend," Sinon Yar whispered in Caleb's ear, "if one of your men finds himself with nothing to do. I would appreciate it deeply if you would rid me of the Deich girl. It seems my intended ward has a mind of her own. I do not care for independent women. But be sure to kill her after the ceremony and the alliance is finalized."

"Certainly, my lord," Caleb replied. For the first time, he allowed his face to relax, and the laugher of the two men echoed in the room.

••••

Only feet away, Tiernan was alone in a narrow vaulted passage that rambled on into darkness. The main passage turned and forked nearly every ten feet with offshoots meandering into the darkness. At intervals, as he picked his way, he could clearly hear voices and conversations. He was passing inside the walls of several large houses or compounds. He could hear the sounds of Publicans preparing meals, arguing, of children playing—all the noises of people going about the daily business of their lives. With such an ear to Ard Creggan, it was no wonder the Counselor knew every wish, every move. The passage ran on, subdivided, forked, joined with other passages. Exits, however, seemed to be well hidden and he was beginning to wonder if he would ever find his way out when he heard a great babble of voices. He followed the sound, twisting through the maze. At times the voices sounded as though they were just on the other side of the wall, then they'd fade unexpectedly. He'd try to retrace his steps but the voices seemed to shift their direction as well. He froze. Somewhere ahead he heard the dry sound of stone grating on stone. He shuttered his lantern and peered around the next corner.

Not far ahead, a light crossed a passage intersection. A hooded figure carrying a lantern like his paused before a wall and appeared to fumble with something at waist level. A section of the wall swung back and the figure walked through. Tiernan waited until the opening was completely closed before moving up to the wall. Once he knew where to look, it was easy to spot the panels marking exits. Triggering the release mechanism, however, was a trickier matter. He was feeling for the right pressure on the panel when a rumble came from somewhere down below. The floor shifted under his feet. Dust billowed up in the narrow passage. Tiernan was thrown against the near wall by the tremor's force. Then it was over. Choking in the sifting dust, he held up the lantern and for the first time noticed cracks zigzagging throughout the walls. They were many, and most of them very recent. Older ones were clogged with debris, while the more recent cracks' edges were still raw and sharp. The light also revealed a peephole on the wall at about eye level that Tiernan hadn't noticed before.

Looking through, he saw an immense room, a banquet table at which sat dozens of Publicans, with more arriving all the time, all eating, drinking, and by the noise level, all talking. Up and down the long table, guests were taking seats and joining in conversations, helping themselves from the variety of dishes and platters loading the table. It was their voices Tiernan had followed. The tremor hadn't interrupted them at all. In a corner, some servants swept up fallen plaster, but the banquet went on. Some of the faces were familiar. He searched for one in particular.

••••

In the Great Hall of the Deich family compound, Publican society was arriving for the banquet. They were the heads of the Ten Families and their wives, their closest advisors, a few influential guests, relatives—an intimate group of nearly two hundred or more. As the daughter of the house, Zoë stood with Livia in the main hall to receive their guests. Publicans never did anything quickly or on time. Indeed, an entrance was everything to a self-respecting Publican. Each household entourage arrived separately, entering the main hall to maximum fanfare. The competition was to see who could create the greatest stir and early arrivals were only to be pitied for the small audience. The height of headdresses, the wealth of furbelows, the cut of a costume, the addition of a sizable jewel, an exotic animal—even someone else's spouse—were designed to elicit a response, preferably an envious one.

Eon An entered the House of Deich on the arm of a woman equally notorious for her expensive habits and her affairs. Maigra was distantly connected to the House of An through a mother who was even less conventional and more profligate. Few in Ard Creggan, seeing her on Eon's arm, had expected the liaison with the much senior male to last. She had confounded them by remaining circumspect and at Eon's side for these many months. Eon, for one, looked pleased with himself. Maigra was more difficult to read. Zoë greeted them both with real pleasure. Maigra and Zoë had had their differences in the past. The woman was quick to take offense for any slight—real or imagined—and Zoe's aloofness had been frequently misinterpreted. Still, when in Eon's company, Maigra seemed gentler, less thin-skinned. One could almost think she was in love with this man nearly twice her age. Zoë only wondered, as she embraced Eon, how Maigra overlooked his considerable paunch and his haphazard dressing. Maigra was, as usual, fashionably thin and elegant.

"I felt a tremor as we entered, Livia," Eon said jovially. "Was that part of the evening's entertainment?"

Livia did not smile. The unexpected was neither appreciated nor encouraged.

"We do not let such things concern us, Eon. The House of Deich can sustain far worse and survive, I assure you. Our foundations are secure."

The twinkle in Eon's eye didn't fade. "Yes, Livia. But now the House of Deich can truly say they have moved the earth to entertain their guests." He passed on into the banquet room, laughing at his own wit.

More family heads with their retainers followed in a steady stream. Nearly all the heads of the Ten Families had, at one time or another, accepted the hospitality of the House of Deich. Even though he had not held a position in the Concordia for several years, Ben Jaro of the House of Cuig was included in the celebration because he was a favorite. Zoë and Jaro's son, who had died in the Sequential Wars, had been childhood playmates. Ben greeted her affectionately, but with tears in his eyes.

Five years, and still he mourns.

Zoë passed him along to her aunt without regret; it was not her fault his son was dead but Ben Jaro always made her feel guilty.

The Shockat and Huckat families arrived together. Aunt Livia was cordial, yet distant. Curnon of the Shockat and Leig of the Huckat were the closest to social pariahs the extremely tolerant Ard Creggan society could muster. They were bullies, opportunists, and smugglers of anything that would turn a profit. That alone would not have black-balled them in society, but they also were undereducated and ostentatiously wealthy. And while money would always buy access, it usually did not open the Deich House doors. Only the solstice and the Concordia could accomplish that.

"And on top of it all, they dress badly," Livia sniffed. Her greeting was polite. Their position demanded that much. But no more.

Zoë dreaded even this public contact. She had been the target of Leig's amorous intentions in the past and now he loomed over her, his bovine face contorted with what Zoë presumed to be a smile.

"It is a great happiness to be in the House of Deich," he simpered, in a high-pitched voice so much like a young girl's. "We hope our houses will be as one with the Solstice." He lurched forward with the obvious intention of embracing Zoë, changed his mind, muttered a cursory greeting to Livia and quickly lumbered off to the dining room.

"What was that all about?" Livia asked looking after him in amazement.

Zoë turned to greet another guest.

"Perhaps he was hungry."

Livia glanced down at her niece's fist, half hidden in the folds of her gown. The blade of an elegant stiletto glinted in the light. "I can't say I consider that appropriate evening wear, Zoë."

"No?" said Zoë idly, her eyes on the assembly. "You have no idea how hard it is to find something suitable. I thought I'd done rather well. It matches my dress."

"That is not what I meant," her aunt snapped back under her breath. "You do not need such protection in your own home. You will give me the weapon immediately."

Another guest approached, was greeted, and passed on.

"Well?" her aunt demanded again.

"I think, Aunt," Zoë replied placidly, "that I'll be better off with it. But to keep peace between us, here is the knife." It wasn't such a loss; she had another.

At that, the gong sounded announcing dinner. Immediately, the guests still in the main hall paraded into the banquet room and the massive doors swung shut behind them.

If the Ten Families had an official religion, it was the table. They wrote books on food, held festivals dedicated to it, idolized the chefs who could produce ever more delightful dishes, and even conducted contests to devise the most elaborate menus. Down the long candlelit table, the diners' faces were a study in anticipation and greed.

With the first course, the buzz of conversation rose from the table, a cloud of gossip, deal-making and socializing.

"They say the Legislature will adjourn early. . .

Nonsense. They're short votes on the housing bill. If they'd get rid of that damn immigration provision. . .

Immigrants! We're being overrun. This is our home for god's sake and who are they?

. . .I can't recall his name, but he did that fascinating one-man show on lethargy last season. .

Seasoning. That's all our men need. A little seasoning and they could take on any Citizen army in. . .

Livia's dinners, while never too audacious, produced a steady progression of taste sensations, one building upon another, ascending in flavor and climaxing at precisely the right gustatory moment.

He does conflict so well. But really, I get so tired of him working out his love life on stage. I mean his body of work. . .

. . . Was so outrageous. How can anyone afford to live these days? I'm tired of nothing. Nothing on the shelves. Nothing in the stores. And then the cost. . .

. . . A divorce right now will cost him his seat in the Concordia. He can't expect the family to put up with another. .

Even the most jaded palates found something to stir their taste buds. Tonight, a certain species of fish would be served. Unexceptional, except that this fish was at its sweetest only at the winter solstice, and then only when hand caught. Brought live to the table, its skin turned the colors of the rainbows as it died. It would be the dining coup of the season.

. . . Time has no meaning to them. I mean it's not that they're lazy exactly. They just run on their own time. They're not like us.

. . .. But why should we guarantee a house and a job to everyone, Publican or not? The families take care of their own and the rest. . well what do we owe. . .

. . . Skyrocketing. But my cook has a friend who has a friend who knows someone outside Ard Creggan. And they get us the most wonderful things. Fresh or nearly so, but cheaper than. . .

. . . Cutting the heart right out of our boys. Gutting the military budget. Doing away with compulsory service. We won't be ready for a dogfight . . .

. . . .Because I know they're fighting again. But men are all the same, aren't they. He goes on hoping when everyone in Ard Creggan knows . . ."

Zoë sat outside the ebb of conversation. Across the table, Maigra, with Eon beside her, was concentrating on her dinner. Eon was talking politics to his neighbor. On Zoe's left was an elderly, and very deaf distant cousin. On her right an empty chair for a late arrival. Zoë didn't mind. She preferred her own thoughts to the conversation around her. She had just made a complete circuit of her plate with her uneaten food for perhaps the tenth time when the vacant chair was pulled out and a familiar voice boomed, "If that's the face you show all your guests, cousin, I'm not surprised no one is sitting next to you."

Zoë turned with a relief, "Samuel!"

The captain sat down and intercepted a passing platter. "And how's the family doing tonight? I've missed them these many months."

"But you hate family affairs," she protested.

"Yes. I believe they are bad for the digestion. But what could I do? All the pretty women in the city were here. I had to come."

The last comment was for Maigra's benefit, who, Zoë thought, had the decency at least to see if Eon was occupied before giving her attention to Samuel. For several minutes the two carried on a spirited, if somewhat inane conversation—from Zoë's point of view.

When Samuel finally turned his attention back to his cousin, she whispered, "I hope you're not considering having an affair with Maigra, Samuel. I won't like it if you are . . .and neither will Aunt Livia."

"Ah, she's practically family." Samuel teased.

Zoë eyed him balefully. "Aren't you suppose to be on patrol somewhere?"

"I've just returned and, by the way, some of my squad are camped out in your west wing. I hope you don't mind.

"Not at all." said Zoë. "Twenty or thirty more can't possibly matter. Does Aunt know?"

"No. And I'd rather she didn't. As we know, Livia has never cared much for the military."

" I wonder she let you in with your uniform."

Samuel smiled sheepishly, "Well, the truth is she hasn't seen me yet."

At that moment Maigra leaned across the table. "Your cousin is monopolizing you, captain."

"My apologies, Maigra," he said easily, "Between such beautiful women I wish I could break in two to give you both my undivided attention."

Zoë made a rude noise, but Maigra preened. "I'm afraid it is your cousin who will be breaking hearts tonight. I hear rumors of an alliance. She'll be leaving the Deich household."

Samuel glanced uncertainly at Zoë. Fortunately, Maigra's attention was claimed by Eon and she turned away. Zoë carefully mashed a piece of fish.

"So, Zoë," Samuel began. "Who's the lucky man?"

She examined her plate. "Lord Yar. And it's not a wedding. It's an alliance. More like a wardship. Nothing more. Just politics. Nothing unusual."

"And would this alliance be happening soon?" he asked. Zoe could hear the suppressed edge in his voice.

She kept her eyes down, avoiding his gaze.

"Tonight," she said as lightly as she could manage.

Samuel picked up his glass of wine. "It seems I have been away too long," he said, considering its depths.

Down the long table, Livia rose from her seat, and signaled to the heads of the Ten Families. While the rest of the Publicans continued their meal, they would convene the Solstice Concordia. Samuel drained his glass and rose too. He bowed to Maigra.

"Madam, my apologies. The Concordia begins and I await their pleasure." As he bent to kiss Zoe's cheek, he whispered, "I will ask our aunt what is really going on, if you are so tongue-tied."

Zoë caught at his arm but he shook her off. He ambled down the long room, pausing occasionally to talk to friends at the table, while Zoë's attention was claimed by another relative. When she next looked, Samuel was gone.

••••

Samuel left the main hall and began to make his way through a series of covered walkways and alleys to the south side of the compound where the Concordia met. He could not attend the entire meeting. He would wait in an antechamber until the Concordia called for his report on the reconnaissance mission.

He was startled by the Counselor's sudden appearance, almost it seemed from the very walls of the passageway.

"Captain, I am pleased to see you are back. Do you have any news?"

Samuel gave the Counselor a brief nod. "I have a report to make to the Concordia."

"Yes, yes, I know that. And I am curious what that report will be."

"I plan to tell the Concordia that Publican militia are training outside Ard Creggan."

"Of course you will," the Counselor said easily. "And, if you are wondering, yes, I knew about the militia before you went on your little expedition."

Samuel bowed. "Since it was your guard training them, I assumed you knew. Did you think I would keep this bit of treachery quiet, even to protect Will?"

"I am not ready for the Concordia to know certain things."

"The Concordia is waiting for my report," Samuel repeated.

The Counselor smiled. "You are a remarkably noble man, Captain. Duty and damn the cost. Is that it?"

"From what I've heard, you've already made Will pay. Our deal is void."

"You might be surprised what still might happen to your friend. And what about you, Captain? Don't you have anything to   lose?"

"You do what you want. I'm done dealing." He turned his back on the Counselor and continued down the corridor. For the first time in two weeks, he felt a load fall away.

The Counselor watched him leave. He raised a finger. Two guards stepped from the shadows. The Counselor didn't look at them.

"Kill him. Quickly."

••••

Samuel knew they were coming. Two against one was fair enough odds; he wasn't worried. Ahead, the passage constricted down for several feet before opening up to a small courtyard. As he anticipated, that's where the attack came. He easily deflected the first rush. They'd assumed, as a guest at the solstice celebration, he would be unarmed, but he'd kept his dirk and an elegant walking stick that soon showed its functional side. It helped that his attackers were unprepared for a defense. In the tight space, one caught a blow on the neck, staggered and went down. The remaining attacker struggled on. They were evenly matched in size, both big men, both willing to see the fight through. One had to win, the other to die. The attacker, however, had a significant advantage. He carried a small blade, almost toy-like, but looks in this case could kill. Its hollow shaft was filled with Moonseed extract. A scratch froze the surrounding muscle for hours. A deep cut poisoned even the involuntary muscles, stopping the lungs and the heart. It acted so quickly a wounded man would suffocate before he bled to death.

The two men fought blindly in the dark passageway, fighting by instinct, anticipating a blow, and grappling with shadows. At least twice Samuel knew he'd struck home; the stones beneath their feet grew slippery with blood and his opponent's breath echoed hoarsely against the walls. His attacker lunged and at the same time Samuel, slashing upward with his dirk, felt the blade go deep, felt at the same time the flick of a blade point scratch across the back of his hand. The man's full weight bore Samuel down. Locked together they rolled out into a courtyard in a tangle of arms and legs. Samuel rolled free first, kicking away his opponent, who lay where he'd stopped. In his back, a knife. But not Samuel's dirk. A man walked from the passageway shadows, put a foot to the dead man's back and pulled the blade free. Samuel saw, rather than felt his grip on his own dirk loosen. The Moonseed was working fast. In a matter of moments his arm would be numb. He doubted if he could win a fight with this newcomer in the time left.

"Still," Samuel muttered. "I've been lucky so far." He heaved himself to his feet. "We're unusually busy this evening, friend. Did you come for some exercise?"

To his surprise, the man sheathed his knife.

"I don't think Zoë would thank me for killing one of her guests."

Samuel nudged the limp body at their feet. "Then I'll thank my cousin for her taste in friends. I'll thank you now."

The stranger bent to examine the body.

"I've never liked a dirty fight and I've no love for these." He plucked the blade from the dead man's hand, and smashed the hollow point on the stones.

Samuel sagged against a nearby wall and clutched his arm. His rescuer stepped over the body to examine his wound.

"Do you feel it yet?"

Samuel grimaced. "It's spreading, but I don't think it's deep. My men are on the other side of the compound. We have antitoxin."

"Then you'd better get going," he said, stepping back into the darkness of the passageway. "And when you get to your men, you might prepare them for some more exercise, as you call it. The evening isn't over yet. Can you make it to your men all right, Captain?"

"Yes. I think so. And where are you going?"

"I feel like dancing. Do you think the family will mind an uninvited guest?" The voice sounded further away now.

Samuel willed himself to stay conscious against the advancing poison. "Since you're doing favors for the family tonight, you might do the same for my cousin. There's an unhealthy alliance planned for her."

The voice came floating back to his ears.

"I'll do what I can. Just remember, you owe a Citizen your life."

CHAPTER SEVEN

In the south hall, beneath a ceiling decorated with ivory lunettes depicting the eighteen astrological signs, the family heads were quarreling, as usual. There were the heads of the families An, Dha, Tri, Cheithre, Cuig, Shockat, Huckat, Naoi. And at the head of the table, Livia of the Family Deich.

"Read the roll, Eon," Livia directed over the din.

Leig of the Huckat surged to his feet. "I protest. There can be no Concordia of the Families without the Counselor."

Livia rapped the table impatiently. When at last silence descended she spoke, "Runai of the Family Cuig. Is there a Rule of Procedure that states the Counselor must be present to convene a meeting of the Concordia?"

As parliamentarian, Runai's knowledge of the Concordia' arcane rules was legendary. He contemplated his folded hands for a long moment then pronounced.

"There is no such Rule of Procedure."

"Then we may call the roll. Unless there are further objections?" Livia looked around the assembly, daring anyone to raise their hand.

"My apologies to the Families," Curnon of the Shockat said softly from the far end of the table, "and to the great Family

Deich. But is seems that a roll call will hardly be necessary. Sinon Yar is conspicuous by his absence. And as Runai Cuig knows quite well, all the family heads must be present to convene a Concordia."

Livia waved aside the objection.

"Sinon Yar may be influential outside this room, Curnon. But he is not completely essential to our business tonight. Only three-fifths of the Family heads must be present to convene a Concordia. Even without Yar, we have enough family heads present."

"But all ten keys must be presented if a vote is to be taken." This time is was Runai Cuig, objecting.

Livia attempted conciliation. "I don't speak for the other Family heads but perhaps a simple showing of hands will suffice? We all want to rejoin the festivities as soon as possible."

Runai was not convinced.

"The whole point of the presentation is to establish each Family's possession of their key and its authenticity. We should not waive the presentation."

Livia let her displeasure show.

"I don't think anyone is in the mood for a formal presentation, Runai Cuig. Are we agreed?" She looked around the table. "Good. Now the first order of business. It has been proposed we lift the embargo on machinery and smelting technology and provide both for a price to Citizens."

"Who has proposed this insanity?"

It was Vanick Naoi. His family owned two of Ard Creggan's largest foundries.

"Why would we give our secrets away? And to our enemies," he demanded. "No, this is not open for discussion. I am amazed at you, Livia."

He mopped his forehead, clearly disturbed beyond words by the suggestion. Livia rapped the table to make her point.

"I must remind you, at the solstice, it is the right of any Family to bring any proposal to the attention of the Concordia. It is also custom that a single veto kills any proposal. Are you vetoing this proposal, Vanick Naoi?

"I most assuredly am," he huffed. "The idea!"

"My apologies, brother Naoi, for raising such an upsetting subject. We will move on."

Burgess Cheithre shot up.

"The next order of business should be the stability report. I demand that we hear the report before we begin any other business."

Around the table other heads nodded in agreement. Burgess continued.

"We commissioned the report. It is time we heard the results. I have shops in the affected areas. What is the delay?"

The Family Cheithre owned or had an interest in nearly every grocery and food market in Ard Creggan. Burgess, however, was a poor advertisement for his wares; he was toothpick thin, with a voice to match. Leig Huckat leaned across the table.

"You're an old woman, Cheithre. You're as safe in Ard Creggan as you are in bed. Safer, if I know your wife."

Cheithre looked at Leig like a rich man looks at an outstretched hand.

"Perhaps if the Family Huckat conducted legitimate business during normal hours," he sniffed, "they also would be concerned."

Leig glowered but Burgess rushed on. "In the last week, there have been more tremors. There were two this evening alone. My goods have been damaged. And now business suffers. I want to know what is being done."

"As we all know," Livia replied calmly, "a report was commissioned."

There were calls from around the table.

"Let us hear it."

"Yes, the report. What are you hiding?"

Again, Livia rapped the table for silence. "There is no question of hiding anything from the families. Sensa Tri are you prepared?"

Sensa Tri rose from his chair and bowed. Taking a pair of spectacles from his breast pocket he kept the Concordia waiting for a long moment while he consulted a sheaf of papers before him. Finally, he began.

"In the question of the tremors. The seismic readings we have taken show activity is increasing."

The hum of whispers threatened to drown him out. He stopped, adjusted his glasses, made a note in the margin of a paper until the undertone subsided.

"In the last month," he continued, "there has been a swarm of some 2,000 quakes and minor aftershocks. And they are strengthening in intensity."

Leig sneered. "Tremors. Little bitty tremors to scare all the little bitty men."

Tri continued unperturbed.

"Tremors, yes. But when combined with the other information we have gathered, quite disturbing. We expect the number of tremors to increase in number and intensity."

Curnan Shockat thumped the table.

"Less evasion, more directness, Sensa Tri. This isn't a damn scientific symposium."

"I am aware of my surroundings, Brother Shockat," Tri responded evenly. "The gravity of this information, if nothing else, is my reason for proceeding methodically."

Livia intervened. "We are grateful for the thoroughness of your study, Sensa Tri. But perhaps under the circumstances, we can afford to study the matter further, without taking immediate action."

"There is more," he offered.

"Then tell us, you fool," Curnon snarled from the end of the table.

Tri was unperturbed. "As we were conducting our investigations, we also examined the foundations of Ard Creggan in an attempt to ascertain the effect repeated tremors have had on its structural integrity. As you know, the rock is heavily mined."

The Family heads shifted in their seats. The mining operations were old news. Each Family was entitled to a share of the subterranean mines, extracting ore as needed to supply their factories. Most ore was found in the surrounding caldera, but the purest ore was still found in the city's main pillar.

Tri reacted for the first time during the meeting; he frowned. "What we found was most disturbing. Excavations in certain areas have not been performed to the usual standards."

Conversation stopped.

"In what way have they not followed standards?" Livia demanded in the silence.

Sensa Tri shifted through his papers to find a graph.

"The supports have been compromised in nearly 80 percent of the caverns under Ard Creggan. This, coupled with increased tremors, has seriously destabilized the city."

Around the table, the Family heads shifted uneasily. Their livelihoods depended on the ore, but the excavation standards protected their lives and homes. Beneath Ard Creggan, in hundreds of caverns, the number and size of supports and piers were carefully calculated to carry the load from above without danger of cave-ins. The temptation to take more ore out and leave less support was counter-balanced by the knowledge that greed could cause the collapse of the caves—and of Ard Creggan. In case self-preservation wasn't enough of a motivation, Ard Creggan's mining laws and regulations were strict. Transgressions carried the death penalty.

"Do we know who is responsible?" Livia asked.

Sensa Tri shook his head.

"At the moment, it is unclear. But we expect to have an answer within the week. There are some engineers who are proving surprisingly uncooperative."

"You will keep us informed," Livia directed. "When you have the responsible party or parties," she said sternly, looking around the table, "they will be prosecuted to the fullest, as the law allows. My recommendation would be to appoint a committee to study the integrity of the supports and to monitor any damage the tremors may have caused."

There were nods of assent around the table.

Livia continued. "Now let us tend to the next order of business. I understand we have Samuel Captain Deich waiting to give us his report on the recent reconnaissance mission."

Runai leaned forward and whispered in her ear.

"It seems that report will be delayed," Livia said, "at least until we can locate the Captain. The next matter of business concerns the House of Deich."

"Ah," Curnan observed, "one shoe drops."

Livia sat back in her chair as Runai took over the agenda.

"We will next discuss, for Concordia approval, an alliance between the House of Deich and the House of Yar. A daughter of the House of Deich would become ward to Sinon Yar, head of the Family Yar."

"And there's the other shoe," Curnan said derisively, "Livia, you're marrying after all these years?"

"Please wait to be recognized by the chair, if you. . ." Runai began, but Curnon was already on his feet.

"The chair be dammed!" he bellowed. "This alliance is political maneuvering. Maneuvering at our expense. Consolidate the power of Sinon Yar and the Family Deich, and they will do whatever they please in Ard Creggan."

Brian Dha cleared his throat loudly. A political ninny, Dha faithfully misread Ard Creggan's convoluted politics. But this time he was certain of his facts.

"This alliance," announced Dha, "is proposed by the Counselor himself. I know this to be fact." He looked around the table with a self-satisfied expression while a tangle of arguments erupted. Over them all, Curnan made himself heard.

"Then why isn't the Counselor here to tell us himself?" he demanded.

"Because, I was unavoidably delayed." It was the Counselor himself. He had entered the room unnoticed . Now he took a seat next to Livia.

"Has Captain Samuel's report caused this uproar?" he asked innocently.

"It would appear Captain Samuel also has been unavoidably detained," Livia replied. "The present discussion concerns the proposed Gabhain."

The Counselor said nothing. He folded his hands and waited. And the best representatives of Ard Creggan's Ten Families cowered and fell silent. Finally he spoke.

"Your objections, if there are any, are understandable. There is perhaps something of the political maneuvering in this union. I believe that is how you referred to it, Curnon."

His tone was genial enough, but down the table Curnan broke into a sweat.

"But, I ask you, can we afford to let this opportunity pass? It is no secret how Sinon Yar uses his influence with the rabble. He grows stronger every day. And with this strength he is more of a danger to us than any conspiracy you could imagine."

Heads began to nod in agreement.

"Wouldn't it be in the Families' own best interests to know what is in the mind of Sinon Yar?"

More heads bobbed in unison.

"And how better to do that than to enter his inner circle, so to speak. Perhaps we can influence him. For the better, we hope? But let us hear our sister Livia's views."

"It is my niece who will be ward to Sinon Yar. She is aware of the honor." Livia said without emotion. "She thinks only of the safety and security of Ard Creggan."

Down the length of the table heads nodded in unison, even if Curnan's agreement might have been reluctant. The Counselor looked around.

"And what of you, Eon An? You are unusually silent."

Eon started as though poked. "Ah, yes. So. Whatever the Concordia believes is right."

A flash of contempt crossed the Counselor's face.

"Does the alliance have the approval of the Concordia?" he asked the assembly.

The vote was swift and unanimous. Then they adjourned, glad to be free of what had become unpleasant business. There was the solstice to enjoy.

"You will excuse me, Livia." The Counselor also rose. "I have last minute preparations to oversee."

Eon watched him go. At the head of the table, Livia seemed lost in her own thoughts, looking up only when Eon stood over her chair.

"Livia," he said softly, "you can't do this. Not to Zoë."

Livia waved his protest aside.

"These are strange days, Eon. The unrest. The fevers. And the tremors. More of those every day, too. We're all frightened. Family is all that matters right now. Zoë knows her duty. Don't waste your pity on her."

She looked uncertainly at him, then continued, in a low voice.

"There's something more you should know, Eon. The Counselor brought word today, about Jomini. He's dead."

"Not Jomini," Eon whispered.

Livia absently shuffled the papers in front of her. "On a ship off the Gurama Islands. I'm afraid he compromised us badly before he died."

Eon said nothing more. He turned away. Leaving, he looked like the old man he was.

••••

Back in the Great Hall, dinner was over, and the music had begun. The guests danced languid, passionate steps below impassive faces. A slow turn, stop, a few gliding steps, hands clinging, arms intertwined, then feet flashing for a beat, slow once more, slow, slow, turn, reach, a final flurry, repeat. A dance so sorrowful, only movement made it bearable. Zoë stood on the edge watching until an arm encircled her waist and pulled her into the current. She went, feeling a weight lift even as she was drawn through the steps, leading, following, falling easily into the rhythm of a body, spinning, separating, joining, turning, turning, slow, slow. Again the long spin down the room, anticipating the movement, slow, step, slow. Stop. The music ended. Zoë opened her eyes.

"You still mess up the crossover."

"If you'd let me lead, I wouldn't," Tiernan replied. The music was beginning for another dance. "I need to talk with you, Zoë."

She smiled up at him, playful.

"To catch up on old times? This isn't the best time."

He caught her arm, holding her to him as the floor filled again with entwined couples.

"I know. You're marrying."

"How do you feel about that?" she asked lightly, but at that moment there was a disturbance at the main doors. She pulled away.

"What luck, you may be in time to meet my intended."

Tiernan scowled. "That's your husband to be?"

A strong wind gusted through the open doors, rattling the chandeliers overhead. Will entered the hall scattering guests before him. Zoë barely recognized him.

"Luminous," she thought. *"He looks like he's lit from inside"* But maybe it was only the reflection of the gold robe billowing and twisting around him in the wind.

"You celebrate, while others suffer. You ignore the pain you cause."

Will's voice was shrill, piercing the music, silencing the chatter. "You turn a blind eye to the evils that destroy Ard Creggan. But outside, Publicans, we are building a fire that will purify Ard Creggan. This is the pain made visible. Tonight you see the cost of your redemption. Tonight you will listen. I will make you listen."

His words were lost as the house guards hustled him from the main hall. Through the open doors, guests glimpsed a crowd gathering in the plaza outside, among them a grotesque mob of paper Publicans, larger than life, dipping and twirling around a bonfire. The effigies shot into the night sky, arcing gracefully down into the flames. The fire roared up. Through the drifting smoke, Sinon Yar entered the plaza surrounded by his retinue.

"Well, so much for the entertainment." Zoë said. "And here's the last of our guests to arrive, so I'll be leaving you now."

She headed for the main staircase with Tiernan close behind her. At the foot of the stairs she turned in exasperation. "You really won't give up on this, will you?"

"No," Tiernan say flatly, "I won't. We must talk, Zoë. Now."

"Look around you Tiernan, now would appear to be a very bad time," she hissed.

Out of the corner of her eye she saw guards moving to flank her on the steps. For their benefit she said loudly, "Thank you for the dance. I'll say good-bye now. Perhaps we can talk after the ceremony."

Tiernan bowed, looking anything but satisfied. Zoë's smile faded.

"I really wouldn't stay for the rest of the entertainment," she said for his ears only and was gone. The guards blocked his way. Tiernan could only follow her with his eyes, up each flight of stairs, until she reached the very top. He turned away and lost himself in the crowd.

••••

When Zoë finally reached the door to her rooms, her hand shook on the knob. Closing the door behind her didn't stop the shaking. Noor emerged from the bedroom carrying a voluminous robe stiff with embroidery and a heavy veil. "Is everything ready, Noor?"

"*Nearly. I've put your things . . .* "

A knock at the door and they froze as the door opened slowly. Zoë exhaled.

"Uncle Eon. How did you get up here?"

"The old-fashioned way," Eon said, sidling into the room. "I bribed the guards. You have some seriously irresponsible servants, my dear."

"Yes, Uncle. I'm not surprised. It's all right, Noor, you may go."

Bearing the Gabhain dress before her like some dead trophy, Noor waddled into the next room. Eon waited until they were alone before gently taking her hand.

"Zoë." He tried again, "Zoë." She nearly danced with impatience.

"Uncle Eon," she prompted him, "did you have something to ask me?"

The misery in his eyes made Zoë forget the ceremony and the people below.

"Your aunt told me," Eon said so low Zoë had to lean close to hear. "About Jomini." He groaned. "We were good friends and he was the best man I ever knew. I will miss him. Just as if I lost a part of me." His voice grew stronger. "But I know he would not approve of this alliance. You cannot leave the Family. So I come tonight to tell you not to do this."

Zoë avoided his eyes. "It's what I have to do, Uncle. You know that."

"Nonsense." Eon huffed. "All Sinon Yar has is speculation, innuendo. We have a voice in the Concordia. He can't touch the Family."

Zoë didn't share his certainty. "He will try," she said. "He will succeed. You know he will. Besides this is such a small thing for me to do. Don't worry." She bent to kiss his cheek. "You must promise me not to interfere."

"I can and I will stop this." Eon's voice broke.

"What are you going to do? Throw yourself between us?" Zoë teased, hoping to lighten his mood. Instead Eon brought out a small blue flask from an inner pocket.

"This is for you," he said.

"Poison? I hope it's for Sinon Yar, not me."

Eon shook his head. "Well, it would be a pleasure to poison him, I'm sure, but there would be hell to pay. No, it's for you."

"You want me to take poison?" Zoë handed the bottle back. "No, Uncle, thank you. It can't be that bad."

"You foolish child, it's not poison," he said exasperated. Well," he sighed, "What could I expect you to think. No, a few drops and it induces a condition something like the fevers. Take it now," he urged her. "By the time you get downstairs, you'll be in the advanced stages of delirium."

"And besides making me very unwell and ruining a good party, how will this help me?"

Eon smacked his forehead. "Have I ever met anyone so dense? They'll have to postpone the ceremony. And in a few days we'll announce you're dead."

"That might stop the ceremony," Zoë said bluntly, "although I have a feeling Sinon Yar would just prop me up and carry through."

Eon looked baffled.

"Never mind, Uncle. Besides, what do I do after we tell him I'm dead? I can't pretend to be dead for the rest of my life. Sinon Yar's spies are everywhere."

Eon faltered. "I don't have that completely figured out," he admitted sheepishly, "I thought maybe I could put you in one of the digs. One of the deeper ones. Until things quiet down. Or something," he said. "It's not perfect, Zoë, but it's the best I can do on short notice." Zoë kissed his cheek. "Thank you, Uncle. I appreciate the thought, I really do. But if it comes to choosing between being Sinon Yar's ward and living the rest of my life in one of your digs, I think I would rather you not interfere."

"But Zoë, you can't!"

She pushed him protesting to the door. "Yes, Uncle, I can. And I will. Now go downstairs before the guards forget how well bribed they are."

The door had no sooner shut behind Eon than Zoë was running to the inner room, stripping off her dress as she went.

"Hurry, Noor. We don't have much time. The escort will be here any minute."

"Then they shall wait," Noor's thought came back calmly.

Down in the main hall, the Counselor signaled an assistant, who began to ring a brass bell. It would ring nineteen times, eventually silencing the music and parting the dancers. The Publicans began to congregate at the far end of the Main Hall and Sinon Yar took his place at the Counselor's side. The Gabhain had begun.

As the guests moved toward the ceremony, the guards followed, abandoning the main staircase. Waiting for this moment, Tiernan slipped up the stairs, following in Zoe's footsteps, climbing upward to the top of the compound.

Standing next to the Counselor, Sinon Yar looked out over the crowd.

"Are all the family heads here, Counselor? I wouldn't want anyone to be missing from the celebration. I don't seem to see. . . no, there he is."

"All the family heads are in attendance," the Counselor said irritably.

"Oh, that's right." Sinon Yar mocked him, "You told them to be here. And here they are. Such mastery, Counselor. I envy you."

Sinon Yar shifted his gaze to the topmost staircase.

"Ah, and here is my ward coming to join us." At the top of the compound, a heavily robed figure and an honor guard were making their way down the stairs in stately procession. Far up on the stairs, out of view of the crowd below, Tiernan also saw the honor guard approaching with a heavily shrouded figure between them. He drew back into an alcove. There was no telling if Zoë could see him. He certainly couldn't discern even her shape in the stiff Gabhain dress and veil. They drew abreast, then slowly passed by. So close. Close enough to smell her perfume. Her perfume. He stopped, grinned, and without another look at the procession, made his way up the last flights of stairs as quickly as he could without drawing attention. If he was right, there was no time to lose.

••••

In the main hall, the Gabhain bell continued to ring until the honor guard and its charge reached the side of Sinon Yar. About the same time Tiernan ran out of stairs and was faced with a series of closed doors in a long hallway. He tried the first one. And then the second. As he opened the seventh door, he heard a new noise from the Main Hall, the sounds of excited voices, a shout, then more. Time was getting short.

"*This has to be it*," Tiernan thought as he approached double doors at the end of a long hall. He tried the handle. The door opened without a sound and he was inside with a backward look over his shoulder. The room was dark and a doubt crossed his mind. Was this the same room he'd been in earlier? Footsteps. He crouched behind the bulk of a chair and waited. The door to an inner room opened and a figure was silhouetted for a moment in the light. Then the light was extinguished as the figure moved into the room. Tiernan's eyes readjusted slowly to the dark. A few steps and his hands closed around a pliable bulk. Then he went down, kicked hard in his bad leg. The room lights came up.

"I knew I should have locked that damn door," a familiar voice said.

CHAPTER EIGHT

"And I told you we had to talk," Tiernan said between clenched teeth, rubbing the old wound and discovering he had a pack in his grasp, not a girl.

"Glad to. On the way out." Zoë reached for her pack. "Are you through manhandling this?"

He held the pack out of her reach. "First, we talk. And what's in this?" he asked.

"Talking is not necessary. I think what you want is on the table." She jerked her head in the direction of a small table in front of the fireplace. As she hefted the pack and headed for the balcony doors, Tiernan crossed to pick up a velvet case on the table. He opened it. Inside, an emerald necklace sparkled, the light playing in its depths. He tossed it aside and caught Zoë at the balcony, grabbing her arm so tightly she yelped, more from surprise than pain.

"That isn't what I was looking for. Where is it?" he demanded.

Zoë struggled to free herself. His grip tightened.

"Take off your gloves," Tiernan ordered. Zoë made a fist, scowling.

"Take off the gloves or I'll... ." He stopped. "You know, I'm sure your bridegroom would love to see you," he said. "Shall we get his attention?" They glared at each other, neither moving.

Into the standoff came a new sound from far below. In the Deich compound courtyard, the voices of the ClearWorlders gathered around the bonfire, rose in a great chant that carried up to the attic room. Then an abrupt silence that drew Zoë and Tiernan's attention downward, as it did the evening's guests who poured from the doors. In the silence, a blaze of yellow, walked from the crowd to stand before the bonfire. His words didn't carry to the balcony.

"Will," Zoë whispered. Foreboding like nausea rising up inside of her. She struggled against Tiernan's hold, feeling the pain in her arm.

"The ring," he repeated, unmoved. "The ring first."

"Please, Tiernan," Zoë pleaded, "Let me go. Please, before he .. ." a noise like a collective sigh went up from below. The two spots of yellow joined their colors, bled together, and became one. Will spread his arms wide in the heart of the fire. Zoë's blood pounded in her ears. The room swam.

Regaining consciousness, Zoë looked up into Tiernan's face and swung. He slipped the blow easily, his expression of grim intensity unaltered.

"Don't waste your time. You have some visitors. Not here," he said as she looked around wildly. "Downstairs. Right after . . . ." he paused. "Right after the fire, soldiers entered the compound. Were you expecting Citizens tonight?"

"Guests, yes," Zoë muttered, pushing Tiernan away and finding her feet.

"These Citizens weren't dressed for a dance. And they weren't any Citizens I knew." Far off, there were shrill screams. "I'm pretty certain," Tiernan continued as though deaf, "these guests were Sinon Yar's men. If we'd known you Publicans were just going to kill each other off, we wouldn't have spent so much time on peace talks."

Zoë tried to dodge around him. Tiernan pushed her back.

"Stay put. There's nothing you can do for them now."

She stared at him, trying hard to recognize the old Tiernan. "You're doing this for the Deich ring? My mother's ring?"

"It might be your mother's, I don't know. It has a black stone with a serpent's head."

"We buried her with it. Do you plan on digging her up?" she spat, chin up.

"You're lying," Tiernan said coldly. "I know you have it. You showed it to me once, on Gurama. You didn't bury it with her. Give it to me now and I leave. And you Publicans can get back to killing each other."

"So the great soletei is just a common thief."

He pulled his arm back to hit her and felt the prick of a knife in his ribs.

"Aunt Livia," Zoë said with relief.

"I thought you'd be gone by now, child."

Like some amateur, he thought, *I let her come up behind me.*

Livia jabbed him again. "Don't take it badly, Citizen. My niece can be very stubborn and very distracting."

"What's happening downstairs?" Zoë asked anxiously.

"Some unexpected guests. Guests like our intruder here."

"Then he was right. Citizens. Here."

"I can recognize a Publican when I see one. Their masquerade wouldn't fool a child. Sinon Yar is a fool. His so-called Citizens attacked while we were distracted by the fire. Then we were saved by more of Sinon Yar's men who conveniently killed the impostors. But not before Sinon Yar settled a few scores."

"Uncle Eon?"

"Yes, Eon. Most of the heads of the Families. Leig, Runai. And Sensa Tri." Her voice trailed off.

"But why? Why now?"

Tiernan snorted. "Why? I imagine what's left of the Families are falling over themselves by now. Sinon Yar is Ard Creggan's savior."

"Then Ard Creggan is lost," Livia said bluntly. He felt the knife's pressure relax as she crumpled to the floor behind him.

He was surprised at how weightless she was in his arms. His hand on her back came away wet. Blood.

Livia's eyes fluttered open. "That's the work of Sinon Yar's worm, Caleb. I never liked him. And," she added matter-of-factly, "it appears he cared even less for me."

"Child, you should have seen Sinon Yar's face when he lifted the veil. Noor was wonderful." Blood welled-up at the corner of her mouth. Tiernan shifted the pressure on the wound.

Zoe fell to her knees beside Livia. "She needs a doctor."

"Stop your fussing," Livia snapped, but weakly. To the last, she was in charge. Livia looked up into Tiernan's face.

"I hope he is more clever than he looks." A spasm of pain crossed her face. "You should be gone," she said weakly, yet she motioned Zoë closer.

"Remember our plan," Livia whispered in her ear. "The keys are on their way out of the city. They will find you, don't worry. Go to Gurama. He will take you there."

Zoë looked doubtfully at Tiernan. "Aunt, I don't think . . ."

Livia cut her off. "Don't worry. He will have to in the end. You'll see." A spasm contorted her face. Tiernan laid her down gently and yanked Zoë to her feet.

"What was she talking about? What keys? What about Gurama?"

Zoë wiped the tears from her face. "Shut-up. I can get us out of here. And I can get you your precious ring. I don't have it. But I know where it is. But you have to agree to help me."

"Help you?"

"Get me to Gurama. Get me to Gurama and the ring is yours."

Tiernan looked toward the hall door. "We can discuss the details later. Right now, if you know a way out of Ard Creggan, you'd better tell me, because by the sound of it, we'll have company any minute. They're probably Sinon Yar's men. And they're probably after you," he said. "But if they find me in their present mood, I don't think they'll wish me a happy solstice."

Zoë had to agree. "Take my pack and meet me on the balcony."

"What are you going to do?"

She moved away without looking down at her aunt's body. "I'm going to lock that damn door."

••••

They were up on the roof and moving fast over the peaks and flats when the doors to the room began to splinter. As they broke open, a deceptively small device detonated. The shock wave unbalanced Tiernan as he made the leap to a neighboring compound roof. "What was that?" he asked landing hard.

"That's my way of saying I don't like drop-in company," Zoë said without stopping. "Plus, I think another tremor. Hurry. It's just over the next roof."

"What is?"

"You'll see." She looked back. "By the way, I hope you're not afraid of heights."

Floors below, Sinon Yar surveyed the room's wreckage, then turned to the men who weren't lying dead or wounded.

"I have reason to believe the Lady Deich has been kidnapped. Her abductors are Citizens and they must still be in Ard Creggan. I want them found. Search everywhere. You men take the roof."

"The roof, Sinon Yar?" one soldier asked in disbelief.

Sinon Yar picked the soldier up by his collar and shook him until he went limp. Then he threw the body aside.

"Search everywhere," he barked as the rest of the men fled. "Find them!"

••••

"I think it'll take both of us," Zoë said. They had crossed he didn't know how many roofs to reach the edge of Ard Creggan, with Sinon Yar's men in pursuit, never far behind. Now, she was hauling the tarp off a glider perched like a metal dragonfly at a roof peak. She slid into the back cockpit. "Take the front seat. And don't touch anything."

Tiernan hesitated even as a steel dart shattered a chimney flue behind him.

"If you've got a better way down, I'm all ears," Zoë said strapping in. "But do it fast because company is coming." She pointed to soldiers crossing the roof below them.

He looked out over Ard Creggan. The glider was held at the pinnacle of a steep metal runway sloping down the roof's incline. The runway came to an abrupt end in fifty feet. The ground was, well, awfully far below. And closing in behind them, were Sinon Yar's men. Tiernan climbed aboard. It was a tight fit.

"What do you have in here?"

"Supplies," she snapped. She was fiddling with controls and Tiernan felt a gentle bump. "That's the release. Gravity will take us down the track."

The glider, freed from its anchor, inched forward slowly then built speed rapidly. Tiernan clutched the rim of his cockpit.

"Shouldn't we be going faster?" he yelled. On every side, small eruptions of tile and roof slate announced that Sinon Yar's men were approaching their target. The glider was moving, faster now. They were nearing the edge, when the roof began to rock. To their right, an entire building listed, and in an explosion of dust and groaning timbers, sank a dozen or more feet. Around them, more buildings—what seemed like entire compounds tilted and, as the glider rode the last dozen feet to launch, sank into billowing clouds of smoke and dust. The glider dropped off the edge of Ard Creggan.

They were plunging toward the rock-strewn caldera hundreds of feet below. For heart-pounding moments it seemed each boulder rushed up to meet them. Then they were rising, looping back up toward Ard Creggan, catching the thermal updrafts and rising, higher and higher. A parapet stone fell just feet from them.

"We're getting too close," he yelled but Zoë kept her course.

"We have to stay in close," she shouted. "The thermals are strongest here. If we don't ride these, we won't get enough altitude to make it out of the caldera."

She pointed to the horizon where the jagged edge of the extinct volcano met the sky. They were nearly on level with the compound roof tops again. In one whole city quadrant, buildings stood at crazy angles to each other, leaning into their neighbors as though seeking support. The clouds of dust were darkening into black smoke as flames sprouted from windows.

He twisted around to see Zoë's face against the moon-bright sky. She was looking for the Deich compound in the fires below but it was impossible to make out which sections of Ard Creggan were ablaze. The glider swung higher, climbing, until below them Ard Creggan was a fractured disc of light. Then the glider pointed out beyond the rim and the dark countryside ran on beneath them. Behind, Ard Creggan's beacon remained visible for miles, then it too was extinguished.

••••

The Counselor leaned forward in his chair, consulting a large topographical map spread out before him on the table. He drew a transparent hook of a finger diagonally across the terrain, then tapped his front teeth thoughtfully.

"If, as you say, they are going north, they may be headed toward Gurama. The girl may feel she will be safe there." He consulted the map again. "There are obstacles. It will be dangerous country for travelers. I am not entirely certain of the soletei's role in this. Deal with him as you think best. But be sure, the girl has the ring. Of course," the Counselor's smile was mocking, "she might give it to you. But I wouldn't count on that happening. She's not as gullible as I first thought. They fooled me, those two. To think it was in Ard Creggan all these years. I suspected the mother, but I thought she'd given it to Livia." The Counselor looked thoughtful. "I've entirely underestimated the family Deich," he said grimly. "The novelty is refreshing. But it won't happen a second time."

He looked to the end of the room where a figure stood in the shadows.

"Bring me the ring. I must have it by the summer solstice and at the place I've arranged." His eyes narrowed. "I trust it won't take that long."

"And our agreement?" The visitor's question was barely audible.

"You'll have everything you want. . .providing you bring me what I request."

When the door shut on his visitor, the Counselor finally allowed himself to slump deep into his chair. His eyes darted back to the map, Ard Creggan at his center.

"Very soon, I'll see the last of you. They won't expect that. Not after all these long years. They left me, but I survived. And now this. . . this imprisonment is nearly over."

He recalled that day. And the cold. Most of all the cold. No one heard him rail then. *I raised my fists against that death-black sky and cursed them. But they didn't hear me. They had gone.* There was just the roiling darkness overhead, and the cold. It crawled out from his bones, skittering over his skin, squeezing the heart thudding slower and slower in his chest. He pushed it down again, into its hiding place. A bead of sweat rolled down from his forehead, gathering speed, to splat on the map.

"They left me," he repeated aloud, drawing strength from the hate that surged up to take the place of the cold. "So long ago, it feels like someone else's life." His eyes focused again on the map. "And now you're coming back. No fear, I'll be ready. No tales will be told this time to keep me here. Those orbs, your eyes, my wardens, they won't tell you a thing. I'll be very sure of that. Just one little key to snuff them out."

A thought seemed to give him energy. He sat up straight.

"And when I return, I'll be master of these. . .these primitives. So much for the redemptive qualities of incarceration," he chuckled and a long sigh escaped him. "It will be good to stretch, to be my old self again. It has been so long. So long." He settled back, his eyes closing. "A little key. That's all it will take. The final piece. And I'll have it soon."

CHAPTER NINE

Zoë put the glider down miles inside Citizen territory.

"Help me unload, unless you're just along for the ride."

Tiernan took the pack she thrust at him.

"Half this stuff is useless."

"Then leave the useless, and take what you think we'll need. I suppose you've got everything you need in your coat pockets."

Since Tiernan had some fairly interesting items in his pockets, he ignored the comment.

"We might have stayed up for a few more hours if we'd tossed some of this junk."

"You never know when you'll need something," she shot back from the glider's depths.

Tiernan held up a bulky tank. "You thought you'd need a water purifier?"

"Actually, yes."

"I hate to think what you would have brought if you'd had a week to pack," he grumbled. "But at least you thought of food."

Zoë looked over her shoulder at the pile he was making. "Not the dried stuff. I brought that as a last resort."

Tiernan began stuffing two backpacks. "This is a last resort. We'll find some food along the way, but we can't waste time looking for it. It's just until we get to Bellery."

"And where are we from Bellery?"

Tiernan picked up a stick and drew a rectangle in the dirt. "Here is Ard Creggan." He pointed to the bottom left corner of the rectangle. He stabbed the top right corner. "And here is Bellery."

"And where are we now?"

Tiernan look doubtful. "From our flight path, I'd say we're somewhere in this area." He waved the stick toward the lower left quadrant, still too close, in his mind, to Ard Creggan. "My best guess is we're a few days, maybe five or six, depending on terrain, from the Moher Gulch."

"What's the Moher Gulch?"

Tiernan straightened. "More like where. It's between us and the Black Pagoda."

"And you mention this Black Pagoda because . . . ?"

Tiernan turned back to packing as Zoë studied the sketch.

"If we're going to make it to Bellery, we'll need a travel permit," he said. "We can get that at the Pagoda. I hope. Unfortunately, I have some history with the place." He looked up and grinned. "But, you've got an honest face. Maybe they'll give you the permit. If they don't lock you up first, for being a Publican." He laughed at Zoë's expression.

"I'm kidding. The seers run the Black Pagoda and they don't care where you come from. They'll take you in. Once we get to Bellery, I can arrange transportation to Gurama. The island isn't as easy to get to as it used to be."

"How long to get to Bellery?"

"It depends."

"On what?"

"On how lost we get," Tiernan said shortly. "And if we run into any trouble. There are a lot of mercenaries and warlords setting up shop between here and there."

"I thought Citizens controlled this part of the country?"

"And I thought the Publican spies knew everything," Tiernan retorted. "We'd better get going. We should put a few miles between us and the glider before we stop for the night."

They hid the glider in scrub as best they could, and started walking. It was rough country, more than hilly, not quite mountainous. A few twisted pines hung on between outcroppings of bare limestone. Camp that night was beneath a stone overhang. Tiernan wouldn't light a fire, so dinner was biscuits and dried meat. He took the first watch as Zoë crawled into her sleeping bag. He sat up watching the moonrise. When her breathing grew deep and regular, he rose and stood over her. He almost felt regret. Zoë's eyes opened.

"My turn to watch already?" She rolled out of her bag, the blade in her fist twinkling in the silver moonlight.

"You were talking in your sleep," Tiernan growled, turning away. "I'll wake you when it's your turn."

They walked half the next day without two words between them. Rain fell on and off through most of the morning. By noon, the land and the weather changed. The stunted pines had banded together and in the process recovered some of their stamina. Now, as they left the cover of trees and walked out onto a wide stone ledge overlooking a valley, the sun broke through in a clear, hard light. Three hundred feet straight down, still shrouded in mist, the valley stretched out to the north, a deeply green forest so thick it escaped out of the valley and up the far slopes and disappeared over the other side.

"Too bad you didn't pack some rope," Tiernan said idly, looking over the edge.

Zoë leaned out to scan the rock face.

"I'd say it's 300, 350 feet down," she said, "Good rock. "Done much climbing?"

"Enough," he replied, sitting down several feet from the edge. Well into their second day of walking, he was limping badly.

She was worried.

"I don't like to climb without protection," she said, dangling her legs over the edge, "but this should be okay, if we take it easy. You don't live in Ard Creggan without learning how to climb. And Noor likes to get out."

"Who's Noor?"

"My nanny, my guardian, my duenna, my whatever."

She lowered herself over the rock lip. "You met her. She said you were a good climber. No finesse, but fast."

Tiernan looked blank. "I don't remember any Noor."

"Sure you do. I hear she made quite an impression." Zoë's right toe found a hold in the rock as her left foot skated down feeling for the next. The next move took her below the ledge, out of sight. "And she swore you'd remember her," Zoë said. "She's about my height. Hairy. Really big claws."

"The Saurillia is yours?" For a moment he forgot the pain in his leg.

"Saurillias aren't pets." Zoë's voice drifted back.

He limped to the rock edge. She was already several feet below the rim and moving faster than he thought he could match. She reached a ledge and balanced there.

"Well," she called up, "Are you coming or do we renegotiate the deal?"

"What deal?" He looked for the first toehold, lowered himself down, seeking out the next.

"The one where you get me to Gurama and I give you the ring." Her voice carried up the rock face. "You know, you haven't told me why you want my ring."

"The original deal still stands," he called back, lost his balance for a fraction of a second and clutched the rock face.

Use your head. Slow down. She can use smaller holds.

And there was his damn leg. He couldn't trust his full weight on it for long. Looking for the next foothold, he called, "You won't make it to Gurama without me." But he wasn't so sure. He couldn't tell how far ahead she was. She might make it off the cliff face in time to put some distance between them. In the forest below, it wouldn't take much of a lead to lose him.

I can't match her for speed. Not with this leg. And tracking isn't my strong suit.

A unit of men made enough tracks for a blind man. But not one person, not through that deep forest. Not even in his dreams. And especially not, he realized, if she knew where she was going. It was his guess she had maps in her pack.

He would have kicked himself if he wasn't fairly certain he was going to fall and kill himself anyway. Still he was moving well, making progress. Then he came to a smooth plate of rock spreading out and down to a ledge maybe 80 feet below. A crack split the plate in a diagonal down to the ledge.

That's the way down.

He shifted his weight off his bad leg, took a deep breath, and made the first move. The fissure began wide enough to take a boot toe, and a place to jam his fingers. Five feet, then ten. The fissure was narrowing. He took more weight in his arms, feeling the pain in his leg, feeling the fissure's edge cut into his boot soles.

If sweat is some kind of an adhesive, I'll make it yet. Otherwise a weak breeze was going to pull him off the wall. Five more feet went like that. Then five more. He felt along the fissure, jammed his toe into a spot, put his weight on it. The foothold held, his knee failed, even as the handhold crumbed, and he was scrabbling for a hold, any hold, as the rock slid by, skinning face and hands as he built up speed, falling toward the ledge. Rock beats bone. He was going to hit hard, ankle-snapping hard. So hard he'd bounce straight down. Two hundred feet, at least.

The impact knocked the wind out of him. But it came in the middle of his back, a blow slamming him into the rock face inches from that bone-crushing ledge. Zoë took her arm out of his back. He exhaled with difficulty. "Thanks."

"It's easier from here on." She was already moving out along the ledge. "Take your time."

It wasn't easier, but he appreciated the lie. It took another hour to reach the bottom. When, finally, they sat at the foot of the cliff their backs against one of the rock slabs peeled off long ago and lying half-buried in moss, the tree's shadows were lengthening and the forest beyond was nearly black. It felt good to be sitting. He offered his water bottle to Zoë. She took a long drink and handed it back.

"Do we camp here for the night," she asked, "or walk in? There's still an hour or two of light left."

Gingerly, he stretched his bad leg. "This is a pretty good place to camp. We stay put. I'll make the fire."

"Fire? Meaning hot food?"

"I owe you that, at least. You get some firewood. I'll make camp." He watched the woods swallow her up then looked back up at the rock face. The rays of the sun caught the rock face high above him. He thought he could make out the ledge where Zoë had stopped his fall. Good rock. *Funny how that hold crumbled. Did she plan that?* She'd been ahead of him. And she had time. But she'd also caught him. His head hurt thinking about it.

Zoë walked until Tiernan was lost in the maze of tree trunks and undergrowth. She stood quietly, letting her mind go blank, slowing her breathing. There it was.

"I'm here little one. Should I come to you?"

A wave of relief flooded over Zoë. *"No, stay where you are, Noor. I'm so glad you're alright. Did you have trouble getting out of the city?"*

"They didn't stop me. They had more to think of than me."

Instantly, images flashed into her mind; Ard Creggan's towers toppling, Publicans fleeing from swaying buildings, everywhere clouds of dust and smoke. As quickly as the images came, they vanished. She swallowed hard.

"I set the glider down where we planned, but I wasn't sure you could keep up."

"I'm not so old I can't keep up with one girl and a lame man. He slows you down. You should leave him."

"Not yet, Noor. I need him. He's taking me to the Black Pagoda. He says we can get a travel permit there. Do you know this place?"

"Yes." Her thought came back, tinged with disgust. Zoë caught the impression of darkness, but this wasn't the time to ask about it. Tiernan would be wondering where she was with the firewood.

"I think it will be safer if you meet us at the Pagoda, Noor. Once I have the travel permit, I can leave him. Do you have my things?"

"The ring is safe, if that is what you're asking. I will meet you at the Pagoda. I'm tired now. And I have something I want to investigate before it grows dark."

"Investigate? Like what? Is it dangerous?"

"This is not your business. Go."

Zoë indignation at being brushed off subsided as Noor's thoughts faded away. They were replaced by an unfamiliar emptiness. She got busy finding wood for the fire, trying not to think of Ard Creggan and Aunt Livia. It would be a cold night despite the fire.

CHAPTER TEN

They walked for days. The landscape changed from the cool green of pine forest to dusty brown, rolling hills. They saw few fellow travelers, but plenty of half-deserted villages whose inhabitants, mainly women, children and old men, looked just barely able to feed themselves, much less offer hospitality to strangers. Zoë noticed that the fields they passed, waiting now for the spring planting, were unkempt with last season's weeds, shrunken patches of untilled ground. The livestock, what little there was of it, wandered on overgrazed pasture.

One night, they sheltered in an abandoned farmhouse where a painting of a hopeful looking young man and his bride still clung to a nail on the parlor wall. There was nothing else left to show a family had ever lived there. Even the wallboard had been stripped from the studs. The neighboring barn hadn't seen a harvest in so long Zoë gave up the search for enough hay to make a bed. She lay down in the front room of the empty farmhouse under the gaze of the bridal couple, shivering through most of the night, cold despite her blankets. Tiernan seemed impervious; he slept soundly. Before the sun rose, she was up collecting their gear. He stopped her before she could refill their canteens at the well.

"The water's no good," he said and pointed to a glyph of a carrion bird scrawled on the well cover. "They threw bodies down the well. That's the warning."

Zoë backed away from the well. "When? Was it the family?" What came to her mind was the bridal bouquet in the portrait. Star flowers.

"Could've been any time," he said tying his bedroll. "Could've been Citizens or Publicans. There may have been a battle over that hill sometime, a skirmish in that field months ago. Sometimes you can bury your dead, sometimes you're advancing—or retreating—too fast." His gaze was on the weed-filled field. "Sometimes you can't find a shovel or a hoe or even a stick to dig a grave. And you either leave them for the animals to get them, or you find something else."

He shouldered his pack. "We'd better get moving. I have water enough for both of us until we reach the river."

"What happens at the river?"

"At the river, hopefully, we hitch a ride." He started down the road with Zoë behind him. Neither of them looked back.

••••

It was just past mid-day and Tiernan looked like a man who had suffered much. The day was hot, their water was nearly gone, and the black flies were hungry. They crested yet another ridge, in an endless series of ridges. Plodding ahead of him, Zoë made the summit first. "There's a river down there!" she called.

"Wait for me," Tiernan growled, struggling up the last bit of hill. Below them a silver ribbon curled in-between the hills. He shielded his eyes against the sunlight. "You're right. It's a river."

"Is it our river?" Zoë asked hopefully. He rubbed a bleeding black fly bite on his ear and tried to relate the river to the map in his head.

"It might be. Probably. Now we just have to find a boat. There's not much regular traffic these days."

"That looks like a boat coming now." Zoë pointed out to their left where, from down river, a canal boat was turning the bend. Then she was scrambling down the other side of the hill. Tiernan sighed and followed. Whatever happened would be an improvement.

Riverside, they found a dock jutting out from the mud bank. A few passengers were waiting; a trapper carrying pelts, and a man and woman who might have been homesteaders. Tiernan exchanged nods with a dwarf carrying a pack nearly twice his size, while Zoë sat down to wait. The narrow canal boat sidled up into the shallows, and the purser ran out the gangplank.

"All aboard, Citizens. The *Princess Madja* will be traveling north, northwest, with stops along the way. All meals included, fresh linens, and your choice of seating at the captain's table. All cabins double occupancy, if you please, and mind the rats, they're part of the crew."

At the thought of a bed, Zoë perked up. Tiernan squashed that hope.

"He means we sleep on deck, and we eat what we catch. Listen," he took her aside, "it might be better if you don't talk. I mean, until we find out who's on board. If they know you're a Publican, it might not be safe."

With the other passengers already on board, the purser hurried them along. "Now or never, friends, now or never. Ah, sir, thank you sir, that will get you the luxury suite," he said as Tiernan slipped a few extra coins into his palm, then added in a low voice. "And Lady Deich, may I say it is a true pleasure to see you alive and well."

"Thank you, Motley," Zoë whispered back. "But what are you doing here?"

"So much for incognito," Tiernan muttered.

"Motley and I do business in Ard Creggan. Or at least we did. Have you taken up cruising, Motley?"

"Ah, Lady, not permanently, I hope," Motley said brightly. "I have, from time to time, used this vessel to transport goods. With the present situation in the city, I thought it might be uhmmm, politic to take a few months and develop new inventory."

"Sinon Yar?" Zoë hazarded.

"The Ten Families named him head of the Concordia the night of the great fire. With complete authority in Ard Creggan," Motley said. "It seemed like a good time to absent myself." He turned to Tiernan. "Confidentially, Lord Yar and I transacted some business not too long ago, and between us, I had the better of him in the deal. However, I have reason to believe he has neither forgotten nor forgiven the incident. I will conduct business elsewhere until memory again fails him. Until then, I wander."

Zoë patted his back. "We'll be back home some day, Motley."

"Without a doubt, Lady," he responded with a resumption of his old cheerfulness. "In the meantime, let me show you to your accommodations."

He brought them into the bow, tight against the wheelhouse. A tarpaulin stretched from handrail to wheelhouse provided some shelter.

"I'm sorry it's not better," Motley apologized, "but the main cabin has been reserved by a very important and unsociable guest." As they stowed their packs, Zoë noticed a half dozen rough-looking men lounging on deck. Tiernan noticed too.

"Mercenaries," he said quietly. "Are you expecting trouble, my friend?"

"Foresight," Motley said, tapping his forehead gravely. "Foresight and planning will let us all sleep well, I say. Now I must see to our departure, if you will excuse me."

In a few minutes, the boat was underway. Zoë sat under the tarp and watched the bustle. The dwarf pulled a flute from his pack, spread out a rug, and clapped twice. To Zoë's amazement, his pack began to writhe and a monkey emerged. He was dressed in a red suit embroidered in gold, with a tiny plumed hat between his paws. He ran the feather several times between his teeth to smooth it, then took a seat on the rug. The dwarf bowed to the monkey, the monkey bowed in return, then took up the flute and began to play as the dwarf vaulted and leapt. For several miles, as the ship traveled down the river and the sky darkened between the looming hills, the antics of the dwarf amused passengers and crew. At the performance conclusion the dwarf skipped through the applauding passengers, passing the hat, while the monkey sat on the rail and watched the shore. Tiernan crossed the deck to drop some money into the dwarf's hand, lingering in conversation. He returned with news.

"Our entertaining friend is called Chaff. He's on his way to Bellery. He says he came by Ard Creggan. All foreigners have been invited to leave. By his account, the city is half in ruins."

He broke off as Zoë put a finger to her lips and pulled him into the darkness under the tarp. Behind him, a shrouded figure rose like a wraith from the galley way. The figure turned blindly as though searching for someone or something, until a servant appeared to lead the figure back below.

"That's a seer," Zoë whispered. "What's she doing here?"

Tiernan didn't want Zoë to see how uneasy the seer's presence made him. "I thought they'd stopped. . . I mean, you don't see them much anymore. Not unless there's trouble at one of the temples. Anyway, there's a law against interfering with them, so I guess that means we're safe."

They ate their evening meal quickly. Then, with the rest of the passengers, spread out their bedrolls and prepared for sleep. Tiernan lay across the entrance to their tent, for all appearances sound asleep. Silence fell on the boat, with only the sounds of night hunters coming across the water. Zoë woke with a start, Livia's face fresh in her mind. She poked her head out from the tarp and, as she did, saw a small shadow slip from the dwarf's bedroll and disappear down the galleyway.

The next morning dawned cold. A boy came to their tent with mugs of hot tea laced with cardamom. Tiernan looked her over in the hard light.

"You look worn out. Are you going to be alright?"

She nodded and walked away from him to watch the passing landscape from the rail. She hadn't been out of Ard Creggan in years and everything was new and fascinating. The river, the trees, and the animals she could see on the near shore, the birds overhead—everything was a novelty. The dwarf was peeling fruit for breakfast. The monkey, after a bit of prodding, woke and accepted half a mango, spitting bits of stringy pulp over the rail.

They all spent the morning fishing off the sides and idly catching dragonflies. The shore slipped past, though at a slower rate than before. The river became quite shallow in parts and there was the danger of sandbars. At times they hugged the shoreline so closely it was possible to reach out and pluck leaves from the trees overhanging the river.

Tiernan began watching both sides of the river ahead. As the sun crawled up the hills to appear directly overhead, Motley joined the watch. Inside the wheelhouse, the navigator's face was tense.

"This would be a great place to waylay a canal boat," Tiernan observed idly.

"Indeed, sir, you are not the first to think that," Motley replied.

"You've had some experience, I gather."

"Enough, sir, to be suspicious and to come suitably prepared."

Behind him on the deck, Tiernan noted several of the mercenaries arming themselves. The navigator rapped on the wheelhouse window to get the purser's attention, then jabbed a finger at the river ahead. The banks of the river were drawing together with only a narrow strip of water between them.

"Can we make it through?" Tiernan asked.

"Certainly, sir. If we're allowed to, sir. We may certainly make it. But only if we're allowed to sir," Motley repeated genially and pulled a machete from his belt.

Tiernan kept a wary eye on the approaching inlet and another on Zoë. She was keeping to the tarp, but if there was an attack, that would be little protection. There was probably no point in ordering her below deck; she wouldn't go anyway. Besides, the seer was down there. He checked his sidearm.

They entered the inlet, a tunnel of trees arching over the water, with dense vegetation on both sides. There wasn't anything he could put his finger on, yet something was wrong. Ahead, the river widened out in bright sunlight. But they had a distance to go to reach it. The crew took up poles to push the ship along. A pole caught in the interlacing roots of trees, and the clatter made them all jerk around.

"We're as nervous as a flock of birds," Motley said. "But we'll soon be out of this."

Tiernan tensed. "The birds."

"But there are no birds, sir," Motley protested.

"That's right. We're in the middle of a swamp and there are no birds." He pounded on the wheelhouse window. "Back us up. Hurry. It's a trap."

The navigator looked blankly at Tiernan. The boat nosed out into the widening river.

"Oh, but sir, we're nearly out," Motley objected. "Maybe you're imagining..."

There was a shout and at stem and stern iron chains emerged dripping from the water to corral the boat. With shouts and hoots, a flatboat swarming with pirates emerged from out of a side canal. In the commotion, the monkey scrambled up into the tree canopy and was gone from sight. The rest of the boat's passengers, not quite so agile, looked to their captain. Motley turned expectantly to his mercenaries, who just grinned and waved back at their approaching comrades.

"So much for the power of adequate recompense," he said philosophically.

On the flatboat, a tall woman in soldier's leathers shouldered her way to the front. She looked over the ship and its crew but her gaze stopped at Tiernan. She smiled broadly.

"Damn if it's not true! You wait long enough, the world will pass by your door. And I've been waiting some time for you, my love. Valois!" she turned to a bearded man at her side, "I want you to meet Tiernan. My own betrothed."

Tiernan sighed. "Hello, Deidre."

CHAPTER ELEVEN

Zoë spent the rest of the day locked in an open-air pen with the other passengers. Tiernan disappeared with the pirates. At dusk, the guards likewise disappeared after feeding the passengers. They seemed unconcerned their prisoners might try to escape and, listening to the wild life around them, Zoë wasn't surprised. Unless you wanted to hazard the dark swamp, the only way out was back up a muddy path past some heavily guarded shacks. The docks, and their boat, lay beyond. She guessed they had already off-loaded the ship's cargo. Beside her, Motley pulled his collar up around his ears and found a comfortable spot.

"You should try to sleep, Lady. Tomorrow will be a busy day." He waved a hand nonchalantly. "Don't let these pirates concern you. They have what they want. As far as they know, none of us is worth anything in ransom, and the ship is worth more to them afloat. This is the fourth time I have run across this particular band of ruffians. You will see. They will release us in the morning and we will go our merry, though much poorer, way." He sighed and closed his eyes.

"It is admittedly a steep price to pay to conduct business, but it's better than taxes and tolls, I expect. And if you're worried about your friend, sleep is what you need. Your friend will either live or not. Staying awake won't change that."

Around them, the other passengers made similar preparations for sleep. Not only Tiernan was missing, Zoë noticed for the first time. The Seer and the dwarf were gone too. She pulled her jacket tight around her and shut her eyes.

••••

If possible, Tiernan was enjoying the evening even less than Zoë. After Deidre's men had stripped the boat of its valuables, they'd brought the cargo back to the warehouse, a pack rat's jumble of crates, barrels, and bales. A massive tree had grown up around the warehouse, its limbs ribbing the walls in a clutch that would eventually pop its catch like a glass balloon in a giant's hand. Inside, pirates jockeyed for places at the long tables, grabbing food off the platters coming in from the cooking fire pits outside. All of the men were drinking heavily and most were happily drunk. At the head table, their hostess sprawled in a chair, bottle in hand. Ignoring Valois, who was sulking next to her, Deidre motioned Tiernan to the chair on her right.

"So tell me, husband mine, what have you been doing with yourself?" Seeing him frown, Deidre was immediately contrite. "Oh, don't be that way, dear heart. Don't be embarrassed. I haven't embarrassed you have I? Oh, look at the cute little man. Isn't he precious."

The dwarf Chaff had appeared in the middle of the hall. Tiernan didn't recall seeing him enter, but there he was. And he was giving a performance. The uproar increased as the pirates around the hall drank deeper, sang louder, and swore longer.

"When did you start in this line of business, Deidre? Last I heard, you were guarding the trade routes, not raiding them."

"Yes, well, the pay was better on this side of the law." She took a long swig from her bottle and glanced at Valois. "And we needed a steady income."

"We are exercising our initiative, my dear," Valois interjected.

As Chaff somersaulted past, Valois took aim with an apple, then hooted loudly with the rest of the men when the fruit splattered on its target. Chaff rolled to a stop at their feet. Deidre scowled with the effort of thinking.

"He had a monkey last time. He was better with the monkey. You!" She kicked at the dwarf. "Where's your monkey?" Chaff picked a grape off her plate and balanced it on his nose, mute.

Tiernan looked into the bottom of his glass. "They ate it," he said.

"Who ate what?" Deidre demanded, diverted.

"The passengers. They wanted to know what monkey meat tasted like."

Chaff grinned, flipped the grape in the air, caught it in his mouth and walked off on his hands.

Tiernan refilled his glass. "Here's to piracy as political expression," he toasted.

Valois scowled. It appeared to be his favorite facial expression. "Improving the welfare of the people is always a political struggle. And we prefer to think of our business as a reapportionment of the wealth."

"So this pir. . .excuse me, reapportionment, eventually will benefit the common folk?"

"You're skeptical," Valois said almost agreeably. "It's understandable. The middle-class has always resisted reform. Unless it comes in the form of lower taxes."

"Is he calling me middle-class?" Tiernan asked, indignant. Deidre snickered.

"It's really a compliment, dear heart. Valois believes that society will improve only if the class system is eliminated. It has something to do with haves and have-nots. But mostly about making us all haves. . .or have-nots— lose track."

"I'm all for that," was Tiernan's affable reply.

Valois ignored them. "You don't believe the message because we're not starving or living in squalor."

"Speak for yourself, love," Deidre replied and took a long pull on her bottle.

"What I mean is, we are not your typical reformers. We don't look like failures."

"You're certainly not like any reformers I've met," Tiernan agreed as Deidre rolled her eyes in boredom. But Valois was insistent.

"Why do true reformers, even men of uncommon insight and ideas, fail?" he demanded.

"They're crackpots?" Tiernan volunteered. Deidre giggled.

"They were under-funded," Valois replied. "To be successful, reforms must be bankrolled."

"So this," Tiernan gestured to the cargo around them, "is your bankroll?"

Despite a suspicion he was being mocked, Valois answered, "Technically, yes. Although we prefer a slightly more liquid form."

"Cash," Deidre interjected. "We sell everything for cash."

"And the money goes for orphans and widows and the homeless?" Tiernan asked innocently. This time Valois heard the sarcasm. "Eventually," he bristled. "Right now, we are concentrating on amassing our capital. When the time comes, we'll be ready."

Tiernan refilled his cup. "And what will you be ready to do?"

"The basic things. Grassroots stuff. Small business loans. Some investment. We see ourselves more as social engineers. Our goal is to move the people toward economic self-sufficiency, with regulation of course." He slipped an arm around Deidre, but she threw him off irritably.

"Regulation by you?" Tiernan asked.

Valois glared at Deidre. "Of course. You can't just throw money at these people and expect them to go out and succeed. They'll need guidance, discipline, and oversight. We're talking about uneducated people here. People with a history of exploitation. The underprivileged poor. You can't change that over night. It wouldn't be good for them. No, we will help the people, but it must be on reasonable, gradual terms if it is to succeed. It will be up to us to show them the way."

Deidre stroked Tiernan's cheek. "Don't waste your breath. My husband is a born skeptic, Valois."

Valois drew a dagger from his sleeve and balanced the point on a finger.

"Then perhaps I should explain to him it isn't polite to disagree with your host."

Deidre threw a leg over the arm of her chair and belched.

"And perhaps I should explain to you that he can say or think whatever he pleases, while I'm around."

Valois rose abruptly, jabbing the knifepoint into the tabletop. It quivered there like an over-sharp exclamation point. "Then perhaps I should see to our business, my love, and leave you to your games."

Deidre said languidly. "If you're finally going anyway, my love, please check on our distinguished visitor."

Valois swung back to the table, and lowered his voice, "Deidre it's insane."

"Just check on things, darling," she interrupted him, "No need to tell the world what you're doing." She kissed her fingertips to him. Valois muttered something unintelligible and swept out.

Tiernan leaned over to replace her bottle with a full one. "He doesn't seem your type."

Deidre giggled, "He doesn't talk so much in bed."

"Ah, that explains it. Perhaps you should tell him I'm not your husband before he puts a knife in me."

"But you are my husband." Deidre insisted, laughing now.

"Deidre," Tiernan began patiently.

"But you are," she interrupted. "I take betrothals very seriously."

"As I recall, you were seven years old at the time."

"And you were eight or nine. Just before you went off to be play at soldier. I swore I would love you forever and I have."

"Your constancy is touching. I'm sure Valois is also very touched."

Deidre sat back and looked at him through half-shut eyes. "He's mad about me. And so he's mad about you. And now he's mad that I want to keep the seer."

Tiernan was genuinely amused this time. "You're kidding. You're holding the seer? He's right, Deidre, you are insane."

"No, but think about it." In the manner of drunks, she was eager to explain. "A seer could really come in handy in my business. They see the future. I could find out all sorts of things."

"What sorts of things?" Tiernan pressed. Deidre scowled, concentrating with effort, but the thought escaped her.

"All sorts," she finished lamely.

"Deidre, is nothing sacred to you?'"

She looked at him soulfully, one eye wandering slightly. "Yes," she said, "love." By the time they stopped laughing, she'd become maudlin.

"Poor Valois," she said mournfully. "I guess I'll have to make it up to him. I do love him, Tiernan, even if he's a lump, lump. . ."

"Lumpenproletariat?" Tiernan volunteered. "No, Deidre, Valois is trying very hard not to be a member of the lower class."

"I don't mind the bumpkin classes, do you?"

"I wouldn't want my sister to marry one, if that's what you mean," he said with a smile. "What happened, Deidre?"

"What do you mean?" Deidre picked up a bottle and slopped wine liberally over herself and the table. Tiernan watched her empty it.

"You were soletei."

The woman threw a bit of meat to a mutt foraging under the table. "I left."

"You don't just leave the soletei."

"I did. I wasn't brain dead like the rest of you." She shifted restlessly in her chair. "I'd suffered enough. The life, the message, everything. It was like a damn priesthood."

"They had plans for you."

"They had plans for all of us. That's what bothered me. They had plans, but they didn't trust us."

"That's not true," Tiernan said evenly. Deidre looked at him from under heavy eyelids.

"You've been away too long. Aren't you curious?"

"Curious about what?"

"How we knew you were on this particular river. On this boat."

"I didn't take it personally. I just assumed you robbed every boat that came through."

Deidre snorted.

"We waited. Just for you. Knew you were coming."

Tiernan tried to keep his interest from showing. She was very, very drunk, but not so drunk she didn't know what she was saying.

"You knew I'd be on the boat?"

"Yup. Listen," she grabbed his wrist and pulled him closer, her lips to his ear.

Tiernan waited, but all he heard was the sound of snoring. Deidre was out cold. Tiernan looked around the hall. Most of the pirates were in a similar state or succumbing fast. He slipped from his chair and out of the hall.

••••

At the prisoner enclosure, he scanned the yard.

"If you're looking for our friend, I'm afraid you're too late," a voice said. Tiernan looked down as a dark pile resolved itself into a figure.

"Where is she?"

Motley rose with difficulty, leaning against the pen fence. One side of his face was dirty and swelling. "They came for her not long ago. I did my best to dissuade them, but," he said, wincing, "they were not convinced."

Tiernan hesitated. The purser waved a hand. "Not to worry. Our visitors are not nearly as observant as I. They have no idea she is Lady Deich. No, I believe it was our dear hostess' consort who initiated this plan. And he is most certainly in the dark. A perpetual state, I'm afraid."

Tiernan reached through the fence to grip the man's shoulder. Motley winced at the pressure.

"Thank you for trying. I owe you."

Motley slid down again into a heap again. "I will take that into consideration when next we meet and no doubt double your fare, soletei."

In the dark, Tiernan picked his way across the uneven ground, hampered by what he'd thought was ground fog, but now realized was smoke. Tiernan left the enclosure behind heading for the knot of outbuildings they'd passed on the way to the warehouse. If Zoë was with Valois, he may have taken her there. From the top of his boot he drew Valois' dagger.

CHAPTER TWELVE

"Well, it's a pity you can't tell us what our friend's plans are."

Zoë, seated, her hands bound behind her back, glared at Valois. She hoped it spoke volumes. He tapped the side of her head with the back of his hand. It hurt.

"Just getting your attention," Valois said, his face so close she could smell the wine. "I don't like your friend. I'm not sure about you. But I definitely don't like your friend. And I think killing you might irritate him. What do you think? Would that be true?"

Zoë didn't blink; she was testing the knots tying her hands. Valois raised his hand again, but seemed to think better of it.

"You know," he said conversationally, "I am not a possessive man. In fact, I believe I am quite broad-minded. I would not normally object to your friend, Tiernan, if we had started out on equal footing." He contemplated his manicure. "Deidre could evaluate our rival charms and I feel confident that under those circumstances, she would make the correct choice."

"She appears to be an intelligent woman," Zoë said agreeably. "But you're leaving the two of them alone together for an awfully long time. Tiernan is pretty persuasive, when he wants to be."

Valois considered this. "I appreciate your concern. But I wonder how much of your concern is motivated by your own self-interest." He lifted her chin with the point of his knife. "I find self-interest so unattractive in a woman." He had, she noticed, piggy little eyes above the beard. "But by now my beloved is more than likely dead drunk. I defy anyone to make love to Deidre when she is in that state. She is more likely to kill, than kiss."

Zoë thought this was even more reason to find Tiernan, but she kept that thought to herself. She had her own problems.

"No," Valois continued. "The real predicament is that I am a man of high moral standards. You look surprised. You shouldn't be. Stealing a man's goods is one thing, but I draw the line at stealing a man's wife. So to keep everything morally correct, I'm afraid I will have to make a widow out of Deidre."

"Haven't you ever heard of divorce?"

"Too messy. You have all those ex's wandering around, turning up at holidays, making family get-togethers so uncomfortable. Besides, Deidre seems much too fond of her little hubby. No, I prefer my way. It's simple, final, and economical." He smiled. "Besides, I don't like this old flame, Soletei Tiernan. And I will enjoy killing him. But first, I will need to kill you."

"I can't think why you need to do that."

Valois looked annoyed. "I told you, it will irritate him."

"Not that much. We barely know each other. We were passengers on the same ship."

Valois cocked his head, considering her.

"You're a bad liar," he said finally. "I speak, of course, as a man in love, myself. I recognize the symptoms. And I sympathize completely. So I will give you a choice. Everyone should have a say in how they're going to die, don't you think? It was a poet who said something about the world ending in fire or ice or something. I've always liked that. Fire or ice." He walked across the room to a pile of bales and canisters against the wall.

"Now, here we have the makings of a fire. These bales of something. I'm assured they're go up in flames, provided they're doused with enough fuel. Some of the loot. Isn't it nice we've finally found a good use for them. Or we have ice." He grimaced. "Well, not ice precisely. It's a bit too warm today. So we'll be substituting water. Specifically, our swamp."

He looked almost apologetic. "Now, you may feel you'll have a fighting chance in choosing the swamp, but let me warn you. The appetite of our local fauna is notorious. You might say we have no garbage problems." He looked at her in anticipation. "So which shall it be?"

He bent over Zoë, his face coming close to hers. His breath reeked of wine. It was her good luck, and Valois' bad, that he hadn't tied her feet because there are times when a kick in the crotch says it all. Something about the way his eyes widened, whether in pain or surprise, was worth it—even when he left her there, the smoke curling across the floor from a pile of rags. A great number of flames shot up faster than she expected. One moment it was a pretty little fire, then it was skittering across the dry floorboards, snaking out hot, bright feelers. The shack was dry tinder, and there was a good breeze blowing in from the swamp. Zoë struggled against the knots, and felt them dig deeper. Through the cracks in the floorboards, she could see water below. She slid to the floor. *At least the air should be better down here for a while.* And while there was life, there was always luck.

From a comfortable distance, Valois watched the shack begin to burn. It was easy enough for Tiernan to come up behind him and put a blade to his ribs. Valois continued to watch the fire.

"Ah, the outraged husband arrives," he murmured. "Your timing, in this particular instance, is better than you can imagine."

"Where is she, Valois?"

"Deidre? In the warehouse, I suspect. Where you left her."

"Not Deidre. The woman."

Valois raised an eyebrow but kept his eyes on the shack where flames were licking the windows. "Deidre wouldn't appreciate the implication, soletei. I'm not sure I do myself. But I make allowances."

"I'm losing patience. Where's the woman from the boat, Valois? The sooner you tell me where she is, the sooner we'll be gone."

Valois looked honestly surprised.

"Were you leaving? So soon? If I'd known I would not have gone to all this trouble. But, then perhaps I would have anyway. I like fires. And I dislike you."

"Tell me where she is or you'll be breathing with one lung."

"No need to be violent," Valois protested, feeling the pressure of steel against his ribcage. "She's right here. In fact," he said, his eyes widening, "I'm a little surprised you haven't heard from her yet. It's such a good fire."

Tiernan shoved him away, and started toward the shack. Valois darted in front of him, a knife in his hand.

"Oh, I can't let you go in there, Deidre's dear. You might burn yourself. She'd be so upset if I let you do that. And you know the last thing I'd want to do is upset her." He lunged; Tiernan shied. He didn't have time for this.

"You two had so much to talk about," Valois hissed, looking for an opening, "Old times, and old friends."

He slashed down. This time the blade point ripped the front of Tiernan's coat. "Maybe, the two of you talked about me. Did you? And what did you say? Poor Valois. Poor, pathetic Valois. I don't know what to do with Valois. Is that what she said? Is it?" He lunged again, wildly. Tiernan stepped out to the side, slapped the knife hand down and away, his elbow arcing up to catch the bridge of Valois' nose, ramming the cartilage deep into his brain. Valois went down and didn't move.

"She said you talked too much," Tiernan said shortly, stepped over the dead man's body and was blown flat in the mud as the shack exploded.

CHAPTER THIRTEEN

An alarm had gone off somewhere, Tiernan didn't know where, shrilling on and on, until his head was full of the sound and all he wanted to do was make it stop. But it didn't stop, it went on shrieking. He wanted to wake up and turn it off, only he was having such a hard time getting up. Then he was back, in the cold mud, his head pounding, the heat from the fire scorching his skin, and still there was that damn siren. Only it wasn't an alarm. It was a human making that noise. *Zoë.* The fog in his head slowly cleared. He could see what, or rather who, was making the ungodly noise and it wasn't Zoë. It was Deidre. She'd found Valois. She was sprawled in the mud clutching his body, her hair a black veil over her face.

Some of the pirates were forming bucket brigades to put out the fires that were spreading to adjacent buildings, but it looked like a losing battle. The fire had turned a toehold into a death grip, and was working its way back through dozens of hovels to the main warehouse. The heat was like a impenetrable wall and the air burned to breathe it. Nothing but a downpour, or an act of god, would stop it now.

Now pirates were running across the clearing trying to get to the safety of the water, and carrying any bit of loot they could grab. One man clutched a gold mirror, the next a washtub full of silverware. Tiernan stood over the woman. "For god's sake, Deidre," he said touching her shoulder. "Leave him."

The keening cut off in mid-wail. She looked up and the madness in her face made Tiernan back away. She was on her feet with Valois' knife in her fist. He faced her, unarmed. The blade flashed out, missing him by a hair as he jumped back. He dodged another thrust, then another. She was backing him into the fire's path, back until the heat scorched his back and there was nowhere to go. She lunged. But the lunge turned to a stumble, the wild look to mild surprise, as Deidre pitched forward into his arms. He sank to his knees, cradling her, knowing she was dead before they reached the ground, the shaft of a crossbow dart protruding from her back. Across the clearing, a man bent to reload. Behind him, a dozen more soldiers formed ranks. Tiernan let Deidre slip and stood to meet the attack. He faced the new enemy with a peculiar indifference, almost a relief. An officer stepped forward from the line of archers. Even over the flames' roar, his order carried to Tiernan.

"We have no quarrel with you. Drop your weapon."

Tiernan looked down at Deidre's body in the dirt, felt the skin on his back pucker from the fire, and his grip tightened on the knife she'd held. The archers raised their crossbows as a veil of smoke drifted across the clearing. When it cleared, another figure stood in front of the line. He dropped the knife.

Zoë.

The archers surged past him, fanning out into the compound. Tiernan heard the cries of men dying in the fire, many of them with steel darts in their backs. But all he saw was Zoë.

"I thought you were dead."

"The feeling is mutual."

"Are you alright?"

She ruffled her hair. "I think I got singed a bit. Thank heavens this place is built on a swamp. How about you?"

He bent to straighten Deidre's body, smoothing her hair and closing her staring eyes. He didn't answer.

"Motley and the others are being moved to the docks," Zoë said, pulling him away. "We should join them."

Tiernan started off across the clearing without looking back. She pushed past him. "Come on. I know a shortcut."

At the clearing's edge she darted down a trail so overgrown, Tiernan wondered how she knew it was there, but he followed, stumbling after her. They were moving away from the encampment, leaving the fire and the heat and the slaughter behind. Then they were out in the open again. Across a clearing was the dock and the moored packet ship. And something else. Tiernan made a grab for Zoë and missed.

"Stay where you are," he hissed.

She spun around. Gathered on a spit of land around the barge's gangplank were some twenty osprits the size of horses, but with the heads and talons of birds of prey. Zoë looked from him to the osprits.

"What? The archers brought them. They're fine. Come on."

Heads were emerging from under the wings of several of the sleeping birds. They stretched their necks toward them, flapping stubby wings against the night air. Eyes the size of black dinner plates watched them, but outside of the rustling of their feathers, they were quiet. Tiernan didn't move. Zoë stopped, puzzled. Not for the first time, Tiernan wanted to strangle her; but he kept his voice calm.

"They're osprits. They hunt anything that moves."

Zoë looked doubtfully from him to the birds.

"Walk on," commanded a new voice. A tall figure stood on the deck of the packet boat. Tiernan recognized the seer.

"They won't harm you, as long as I'm here," she said. "Walk on."

Zoë started forward immediately, the flock parting before her as she bounded up the plank. He had no choice. A forest of cruel beaks waved over his head as he entered the flock. Something primitive went on behind those bottomless eyes. Maybe it was the remnants of a lizard ancestry, pressing hard to get out and eat something smaller on the food chain.

An osprit strutted into his path. He edged around it, moving slowly, trying to communicate a calmness he didn't feel. Another osprit dipped its head to Tiernan's level, opening its beak soundlessly at him. He reached the edge of the plank and his boots made the board thrum. A quiver ran along the board behind him. An osprit was on the plank. Tiernan gained the deck in another stride. The osprit raised a talon, uncertain, but a crashing in the swamp, perhaps a pirate trying to escape the slaughter, was too tempting. The head pivoted, zeroing in on the sound. Several of the osprits moved off toward the swamp, clicking their beaks in anticipation, hunting.

The seer and Zoë were below deck. The cabin was large and, Tiernan noted, a lot cleaner than the rest of the ship. A lantern stood on the table throwing a golden pool of light just short of where the seer sat, her hood drawn down over her face. In the shadows, Tiernan caught a movement of something black. It was the monkey, Bergerac, grinning at him from near the seer's feet.

To Tiernan's surprise, she looked young, nearly his own age, her face soft and curiously unlined. Looks were deceiving; Seers lived several hundred years, the aging process slowed to a crawl by the same force that gave them the power to see the future.

"I am Eleanor and a seer, as you no doubt know. I am bound by my society's rules, so anything you tell me must be kept in confidence. Zoë says you are on your way to Bellery." Her voice had an unusual timbre, it stirred Zoë's memory of something or someone.

"Yes, Seer. . . Eleanor. That is our plan," Tiernan responded formally

"And your plans remain unchanged?"

"The water route was the most direct and the easiest. But it seems we were expected."

"It would seem, then, that you need to alter your plans. You are welcome to join my party, if you'd like."

"You aren't continuing by river?"

"No, under the circumstances my own guard will escort me to the Black Pagoda."

"The Black Pagoda?" Zoë blurted. Tiernan shot her a warning look.

"I can't promise you your trip will be shorter if you join us," the Seer continued as though nothing had been said, "but it will be safer. At least until we reach the Pagoda. After that, you can join one of the caravans going to the coast."

Zoë brightened. "Great. So we'll go with you?"

The Seer continued to watch Tiernan.

"With all due respect, how do I know this isn't another trap?" he asked.

"You are very unusual, soletei. I have never known anyone to question a seer's intentions."

"Forgive me. I just don't know which side you're on."

"Seers avoid taking sides. Taking sides damages our credibility." She appeared to be weighing her words. "Contrary to what you may believe, soletei, seers do not know precisely what the future will bring. We only provide hints, call them foreshadowings, of the future. We tease out what is most probable from all the infinite possibilities. So I am unable to tell you if joining my party will be the best or the safest move."

Tiernan was still uncertain. "How did the soldiers find us in the middle of a swamp? Did you know what was going to happen?"

"Were you blind, soletei, or preoccupied? It didn't take a mind reader to see there would be trouble. I had my suspicions when we boarded. And more sense than our captain in trusting to mercenaries. But our rescue is partly due to our friend, Bergerac, here,"

She reached down to stroke the monkey, who to Tiernan's surprise submitted graciously.

"The guards were on their way to meet me. We would have been rescued earlier, but I understand Bergerac has a weakness for fiddlehead ferns and was delayed."

The monkey preserved a dignified silence at her feet while inspecting the tip of his tail.

"Besides, Zoë didn't need rescuing and neither did you. You were doing quite well on your own."

"I wasn't," Zoë said bluntly. "I was lost in the swamp and something was hunting me. Something very large, I think. Then I heard my name. Did you call me?"

Eleanor shifted in her chair. "There are many strange things in the swamp. You were fortunate to escape."

Tiernan agreed, "Very fortunate. That shack went up like a firebomb." He frowned at the memory. "I was sure you were in it."

"I was when the fire started. My luck, there wasn't a solid piece of wood in the place. But Valois didn't know that. He just tied me up and left me. If the floorboards hadn't been rotten, I'd still be there. Why can't we go with Eleanor? She's going to the Pagoda."

Tiernan turned back to the Seer. "My dilemma is that the Oracle at the Black Pagoda is no friend to soletei."

"You must have upset Michaela a great deal," she said as though discussing the weather.

"We may have. We've had troops in the region for a number of years."

"Ah, not your troops, soletei. You. I've heard a story about two young soldiers who were discovered in the novitiate quarters one night."

"You know how stories get started." Tiernan interrupted quickly, shooting a glance at Zoë. "It's been a long time since I've been to the Pagoda, Seer. And it is possible I may have met, I mean, Michaela could have. . ."

Eleanor took pity on him. "If you want to know what your reception would be at the Pagoda, let me ease your mind. The old Oracle is dying. I am on my way to replace her."

Tiernan turned the alternatives over in his mind, "In that case, we accept your offer. We will be happy to accompany you."

Zoë clearly favored this change in plans. "Good. I find it hard to believe Sinon Yar has tracked me down this fast," she prattled on, innocently. "But I guess anything is possible. I would feel a whole lot safer with your guards."

"Zoë," Tiernan growled.

The Seer hid a smile. "She's not telling me anything I don't already know. News of Ard Creggan travels fast. And it might be safer if you were to keep an open mind on what Sinon Yar is capable of doing."

"Is that a prophecy, Seer?" Tiernan asked without apparent humor.

"An observation. I know Sinon Yar. He has always been a presence in this country, although in recent years he has kept to Ard Creggan." She looked away into a dark corner of the room. "Years ago, he captured a Seer, a novice named Otsego. He attempted to break her for his own purposes. You see, he thought knowing the future would be extremely profitable."

She paused, as though the words were difficult.

"Osego was young, inexperienced. In the end, she felt the only way to escape was to kill herself. No one deserves to die in such despair."

She continued briskly. "We will travel together as far as the Black Pagoda. The soldiers should be returning, soletei. Perhaps you will go above deck and tell their captain I wish to speak with him."

Feeling dismissed, Tiernan went. Zoë curled up in a pillowed recess. "I hope we're not going anywhere tonight. I'm ready to sleep."

"In time, child. But tell me, first, do you have news of your Great Aunt."

"You know my Aunt Livia?"

"She is an old friend of the seers and has been of great help to   us."
"She's dead," Zoë said flatly. "It was Simon Yar. Or rather one of his men."

"Are you certain she is dead?"

Zoë thought on some level that was an odd question, but she answered as completely as she could. "She was dying when I had to leave her. She looked to me to be mortally wounded and I doubt anybody could have helped her."

Eleanor looked thoughtful. "And did she have any instructions for you. Anything she particularly wanted you to do or keep?"

Zoë hesitated, struggling with the desire to tell everything to Eleanor and have her help.

"No," she said flatly. "Nothing."

"Oh well," the Seer said lightly. "The truth has a way of revealing itself. For example, what are you doing with this soletei?"

"He's taking me to Gurama."

"Why do you want to go there?" Eleanor asked sharply.

"I was there when I was young and it's the only place outside of Ard Creggan I could think of to go. I hope it's the last place Sinon Yar would think to look for me. I should be safe there, if the Abbot lets me stay."

"That's true. It will be safe for now. Both Citizens and Publicans have respected the monks' neutrality. But if nothing else, Sinon Yar has a magnificent ego. Reports are he has already consolidated his power in Ard Creggan. He may pursue you, yes. Perhaps he has his reasons.'"

"I was just something he needed to get entry into the Concordia," Zoë said dryly. "I don't think he needs me now, but I can't be sure."

"And you are determined to go to Gurama?"

"Yes, please." Zoë's eyes were closing in sleep.

"I'm not certain this will solve anything," Eleanor said to herself, watching over the sleeping girl. "She is a complication. She and her soletei." Bergerac cocked his head and contemplated the sleeper. "Well, there's no point in thinking of that. She plays a part, but it is unclear if she is up to it. We shall have to wait and see."

The next morning they left as tendrils of mist and smoke rose from the swamp. In daylight, the compound's bloody squalor dampened their spirits. Even the giant osprits seemed anxious to leave. The fires had burnt out leaving behind the acrid smell of charred timber. Only the warehouse, by some fluke, was untouched. In the predawn, Tiernan laid Deidre's body on the trestle table still littered with the remains of the night's interrupted feast. As the sun edged over the horizon, he set the fire and watched until the warehouse was engulfed. Then, with the others, he mounted an osprit and rode north out of the camp, with the temple guards, Eleanor, Chaff with Bergerac, and Zoë.

CHAPTER FOURTEEN

The osprits easily picked their way through the swamp that gave way, by the end of the second day, to marsh. Then the marsh became woods, the woods thinned, and the clearings grew more frequent. On the morning of the third day, a downpour kept the osprits' wings folded over them, sheltering from the rain but holding in the reek of wet feathers. Just when Zoë was thinking it would be better to be wet, the rain stopped, the sun came out, and the wings folded back. Above them, a rainbow arched down into the next clearing. Tiernan nudged his mount off the path and into a grove of slender white trees. She followed. They moved between tree trunks like silver pillars stretching up into the a sky so blue it hurt to look. That was the day she thought of later, when she remembered their adventure.

Tiernan was cautious. Days had passed with no sign of pursuit. The Seer's own guard were professional soldiers; he couldn't fault them. Yet, he remained uneasy.

"Do you remember our first night on Gurama?" Zoë asked. They had made early camp and, as the day turned into a clear night, they ate their dinner around a rare fire. Tiernan smiled but continued to eat.

She turned to Eleanor. "We were part of a children's peace campaign, one of the last. They thought that by bringing the children of Publicans and Citizens together on Gurama, getting us early, so to speak, we'd have a chance at peace."

"And was it successful?"

Tiernan looked up from his plate. "War broke out."

"But we had a good time while it lasted," Zoë protested.

"Maybe you did," Tiernan said. "The monks liked you."

"Only because, unlike you, I paid attention. Oh admit it, we had fun. Remember the time we took that little sailboat, out? What was it called?"

"A ketch. And neither of us could sail."

"But it was such a beautiful day. And you wanted to go swimming."

"And you didn't tell me you couldn't swim."

Zoë grinned. "You wouldn't have let me come, if I'd told you." She turned back to Eleanor. "We used to have great adventures."

"Well, that was certainly an adventure," Tiernan snorted. "It was fine sailing out, but tide and wind were against us sailing back. It took us hours. It was past curfew and the abbot was ready to take our hides. But we were sunburned so badly, he just sent us to the infirmary. I don't think I've ever hurt so much in my life." Tiernan smiled to himself. "We must have driven the monks crazy."

"It couldn't have been easy for them," Zoë agreed. "They weren't prepared for a pack of children."

"We weren't that young," Tiernan said evenly. "I went from Gurama straight into combat. Many of the Citizens with us on Gurama were dead within the year."

Zoë stared into the fire and said nothing. Eleanor wrapped her robes tighter against the cool night air. "Perhaps we should turn in. We'll start early tomorrow morning. We need to be at the Inn of the Trident before nightfall."

Tiernan rose without a word and went off to his bedroll. Zoë departed in the opposite direction.

••••

Late the next afternoon, they came over a rise and saw smoke curling from the chimneys of a small village. The thatched roofs of two dozen or more whitewashed, improbably picturesque cottages lined up on either side of the main road, and at their midpoint a public house, a sign with a trident swinging over its door.

A rustle in the tree overhead and Bergerac dropped down to his shoulder. Accustomed to the monkey's sudden appearances, Tiernan offered him a biscuit he'd saved from breakfast. It was accepted with Bergerac's usual gravity.

"And where have you been, my little friend? You're out and about on your adventures a lot lately." Almost he swore Bergerac winked at him before leaping over to another mount. The osprits took his pounces in stride, allowing him to ride on their backs, but generally refusing to heed the little monkey when he pulled on the reins. They had their standards.

The captain of the guard, a soldier named Iler, kicked his mount into place next to Tiernan. "We'll be stopping in the village overnight," he said.

"Here?"

"You sound surprised, soletei. You have an objection?" Iler's tone was even, but his look was a challenge.

"No," Tiernan returned. "But you know we are being followed. Ever since we left the swamp."

The captain smiled. "I heard you soletei had eyes in the back of your head." He shifted in his saddle. "Did you also know we've had reports of Citizen troops crossing this part of the country? Almost like they're looking for someone."

Tiernan ignored the lure. "Then it wouldn't seem like the best time to announce our location by staying in a village."

"Those are the Seer's instructions," Iler said curtly. Tiernan would have liked to know what he was thinking. "You and the Lady Deich will join the Seer at the inn. My men will camp on the edge of town."

"I'll stay with you and the men."

"The Seer requested that you quarter at the inn," Iler replied and abruptly wheeled his mount to head down the line. Tiernan could hear him calling directions to the soldiers. Their small party still managed to crowd the inn's diminutive courtyard. The innkeeper, a bony man so colorless he looked bleached, greeted the Seer as though they were well acquainted, although Tiernan noted he was careful to show her the proper deference. Two children, a boy and a girl, trailed behind him, stopping round-eyed to stare at the osprits until a woman hurried out from the kitchen area to collect them, wiping her hands on her apron. Zoë and the woman exchanged a few words he couldn't catch. *Just some chitchat. The kitchen is probably in chaos with so many guests.*

As their mounts were led off to the stables, Eleanor took Tiernan and Zoë aside.

"Tonight, we will have guests for dinner," she said for their ears only. "I hope they will be able to arrange transport for you from Bellery to Gurama. I must ask you to be circumspect in your conversation both with them and the inn staff. There is no need to say you are anything more than pilgrims on your way to the Black Pagoda. Zoë, it might be better if you ate supper in your room. Your accent gives you away. They may wonder what a Publican is doing so far from Ard Creggan."

Tiernan tired to gauge Zoë's response to the Seer's directive. *"She's not pleased, but she's not objecting,"* he thought. *"Either she is behaving herself for Eleanor, or she is up to something."* He tended to believe the latter. It wasn't like Zoë to take kindly to being left out.

Their rooms in the back of the inn, strung out along a long hallway, overlooked a herb and vegetable garden. In the gathering dusk of a warm day, the spicy aromatics of spring flowers and mounds of silver herbs roiled through the open windows. Against the darkening sky, flocks of birds wheeled before coming to roost in the trees bracketing the inn, the air alive with their chattering.

On this way down to dinner, Tiernan tapped on Zoë's door. Earlier, while he was washing off the road dirt, he had heard her dinner being delivered. "Zoë?" He tapped a second time.

The silence went on just long enough to rouse his suspicions. The door opened a crack. Zoë peeked out.

"Do you want me to bring you anything?"

It sounded feeble even to his ears, but she just shook her head.

"No, I didn't realize I was so tired. I'm going to bed right after I eat."

"I'll stop up after dinner and tell you all about it."

"No, that's not necessary," Zoë said quickly. "I really want to get a good night's sleep in a real bed. I can hear about it tomorrow morning. Don't worry. I'll be fine."

She looked at Tiernan, waiting.

"OK, sleep well," he said, feeling awkward, as though something else should be said. "I'll see you in the morning."

"Yup. See you in the morning."

The door closed and Tiernan heard the creak of bedsprings. *She must really be tired. This hasn't been easy on her.* He went downstairs.

••••

Zoë sat on her bed, listening to the sound of Tiernan's receding footsteps. Then she forced herself to wait a bit longer. Finally, she felt sufficient time had passed. She moved to the window. By now, he should be at dinner with Eleanor and her guests. They'd both be busy for a while. She scanned the garden and outbuildings below. No one was around. The light was failing too; that was a help.

From the window ledge it was small matter to use the rough stonework to edge far enough to jump to a handy tree and from there scramble down into the garden. Just another shadow, she slipped from the inn compound and down a lane running parallel to the main road, hidden on either side by interlaced trees. It was slow going in the deeper dark of the lane. She had to be wary of tree roots tripping her up, while she kept an eye out for company. Still, she was taken by surprise when a shadow detached itself from a massive tree and uncloaked a lantern. The light partially blinded Zoë until it was turned to illuminate the woman who'd greeted Zoë in the courtyard that afternoon. She put a finger to her lips and signaled her to follow.

Not twenty feet down the footpath, they turned off onto a footpath that dead-ended at a jumble of boulders whose mass was only dimly felt in the darkness. To her right, Zoë heard the burble of flowing water. The light dipped as the woman stooped under a rock shelf and disappeared. Hesitating only a moment, Zoë followed. When she straightened up, she was in a cave, a shelter no larger than a few strides in any direction, lit by the lantern.

"You are from Ard Creggan?" her guide demanded immediately.

"Yes. I told you that at the inn." *What have I got myself into?* "You said you had news of Jomini."

"I do. Tell me, can I trust you?"

"What a foolish woman, to ask that now," Zoë thought. Instead, she said, "I've trusted you enough to meet you here. How do you know Jomini? And what couldn't you tell me at the inn?"

The woman held out her hand. A tiny silver pendant dangled from a chain looped through her fingers. "You recognize this?" she asked.

Zoë tried to swallow, but her mouth was dry. Of course she recognized the pendant immediately. It was her father's.

"Where did you get it?"

"First, tell me your family name."

Zoë squelched the voice of caution at the back of her mind. "I'm of the Family Deich."

The effect of her response was physical; the woman sagged. But her voice when she spoke again was filled with relief.

"I prayed someone would come. You are of the Family Deich, like Jomini?"

"Yes, I told you that," Zoë said impatiently. "Now tell me where you got his chain. Have you seen him?"

"Be praised. Tell, me how do you know him? Are you related, perhaps?"

"He is my father. Do you know where he is?"

The woman's delight at this information could not have been greater. "This is truly providential. Wondrous. Now I am certain I am doing the right thing. You have been sent, I know it."

Zoë interrupted her raptures. "Do you know where my father is?" she demanded.

"I am sorry," the woman said, trembling with excitement. "This must all seem very strange to you. It's just that we've been so worried. When the pendant arrived and there was no word, we didn't know what to think. We've just been waiting and waiting."

"We?"

An anxious look crossed the woman's face. She seemed to be considering both Zoë and some course of action. It didn't take long to come to a decision. With a dramatic flourish of her skirts, she stepped to one side. A child cowered behind her.

"This," the woman said dramatically, "is your sister. Livy"

••••

Back at the inn, the meal was over and the innkeeper was clearing the table. There were six for dinner: the Seer, Tiernan, and four men whose exact occupations had remained elusive throughout the meal. Conversation had ventured from the weather, to trade—a topic on which they seemed to be particularly knowledgeable—and on to politics. Tiernan would have guessed they were military men, or maybe ship's captains. Hard men accustomed to command.

Only when the innkeeper placed the bottle on the table and the door closed behind him, did they relax and push back their chairs. From her place at the head of the table, Eleanor nodded to Tiernan, who, before securing the door from the inside, checked the outside hallway for listeners. Still, it wasn't until the bottle had gone around twice, that the Seer rapped on the table.

"It is time to judge the authenticity of your wares, gentlemen. Please make your presentations."

As Tiernan watched with growing curiosity, each man produced from pockets, pouches, even a hat, cloth bags, each no bigger than a child's fist. Four bags. All eyes were on the Seer as from her sleeve she drew out a similar packet and placed it on the table. The occasional creak of a chair was the only sound in the room. As one, they loosened the drawstrings on the bags and tipped out the contents. Ten orbs, two from each bag, rolled to the center of the table, catching and reflecting the lamplight in a rainbow of colors, pastel yellow to deepest purple. Some unseen energy inhabited them. Each repelled the other, pushing and pulling, until all ten orbs settled into an eccentric glowing orbit on the table, revolving slowly.

"Gentlemen, the Keys of Ard Creggan," Eleanor said softly. "Thanks to you, they are assembled for the first time outside of the city. The risks you took to secure and deliver them will not be forgotten. Very soon I will be able to tell you why they were collected. For now, it is enough to say your actions will restore the balance and bring a lasting peace.

Heads nodded around the table. Balance was seldom a concern in a business deal. But peace was a different matter. War might be good for a few businessmen, but peace was profitable for them all.

••••

Zoë woke the next morning feeling as though she'd barely slept. Her mind was still running in circles. And she was tired of the circles. She had a sister. Her father had a second family. Her father had married. And didn't tell her. *I have a sister. And he didn't tell me.* She did the math for the hundredth time. She had been 13 when her mother died. That was 12 years ago. Livy was 12. *He certainly didn't wait long.* And he didn't tell her. *I have a sister.* Part of her was excited. Part of her wanted to throw up.

Livy.

"I was named after my Great Aunt," she'd said.

Her Great Aunt! *That's my Great Aunt. Not yours.* Zoë itched to know what her father had told Livy about his Ard Creggan family. It appeared to be a very lop-sided relationship; she'd never suspected her father had another family. *Of course, it does explain why he was gone so often.* And her father would have some explaining to do, when she found him. She pulled herself out of bed and dressed quickly. She needed to talk to Eleanor.

To her surprise, the Seer was already up and eating her morning meal in her room while sorting through what looked like a stack of messages. It had been a late night. Tiernan and Eleanor still hadn't come up from the dining room when Zoë had returned to her room and finally, near dawn, fell into a fitful sleep. But Eleanor looked refreshed, even buoyant. Zoë accepted the offer of a cup of tea but refused a muffin. Her stomach was tumbling. Without looking at the Seer she blurted, "Do you mind if someone joins us?

"For breakfast?" Eleanor asked. "Not at all. But ring the bell for more toast. Is it someone you've met here at the inn? I didn't think you'd had time to make friends."

Zoë had the feeling Eleanor knew all about her excursion last night.

"It's a girl. Her father is a Publican, her mother works here at the inn. Well, she used to work here. She died a few years ago. Her uncle and his wife keep the inn. They don't think it's safe for her here anymore. They want us—me—to take her to Ard Creggan."

"That might be difficult, under the circumstances," Eleanor said.

"Yes, I told them the city isn't the best place to be right now. That's why I thought she could come with us to Gurama. There was a school there, once. She'd be taken care of."

"That seems like a good idea, if she's indeed in danger here," Eleanor agreed. "and what does your sister think of this plan?"

Zoë blushed. "Does everyone except me know about her?"

Eleanor shrugged. "I suspected. I have visited this inn a number of times over the years. Your father was a frequent visitor and Livy is growing to look remarkably like him."

Zoë pulled Jomini's silver locket out from under her tunic. "She had this. It belongs to my father. She said it arrived several months ago with instructions to contact the Family Deich in Ard Creggan."

"I wonder how they planned to do that?" Eleanor mused. "It was certainly fortunate that we arrived when we did."

Zoë put her teacup down. "What was she like? Livy's mother."

"An innkeeper's daughter. A local midwife, with a reputation as something of a healer. That reputation, the help she gave to the people around here, protected her and Livy from reprisals."

"Reprisals?"

"Yes. Livy's father—your father—was a Publican, remember?"

Zoë paused. "How did she die?"

"There was an outbreak of fever. She was nursing the sick. She died."

"How old was Livy?"

"What is she, now? Fourteen? Then, she was nine, maybe ten. She's an odd little thing. So quiet. I don't think I've heard her say more than a dozen words. Her uncle and aunt have cared for her since her mother died." Eleanor smiled. "You've met Livy's Aunt Melinda?"

The look on Zoë's face was enough of an answer.

"Melinda should have gone on the stage. This inn is a little too humdrum for her."

"Was Livy's mother like her?" Zoë asked uneasily.

"No, Elena was quite different. I would describe her as a restful sort of woman. Not the adventurous type. I imagine the only risk she ever took was falling in love with your father."

"That worked out well," Zoë said dryly.

"Actually, I believe she was quite happy with the arrangement. At least she appeared to be. As was your father.

You probably don't want to hear that. Children often find it difficult to accept their parents' relationships. He must have been very lonely after your mother died."

"He had me and our family." Zoë knew she sounded petulant and didn't care.

Eleanor seemed about to say something, but then said, "Well, if nothing else, this changes your plans."

"How do you mean?"

"You have the pendant. Surely this means your father is dead. Have you ever known him to remove his pendant?"

"No," Zoë admitted reluctantly. "But that's not proof he's dead. It's just proof he sent a message to Livy."

Eleanor turned back to her correspondence. "Well, that is a discussion for another time. Livy is certainly welcome to join us. We'll be leaving soon. You should be getting ready."

They rode away from the inn in mid-morning, their departure creating nearly as much commotion as their arrival. The innkeeper saw them off, patting Livy awkwardly on the head, but managing to look more relieved than sad. Melinda cried, of course, which caused her two toddlers to wail, setting the osprits dancing nervously and making them even more difficult than usual to mount. Tiernan gained his saddle only after several tries. By then, he had no time to remark on Livy's presence. They were off.

For the rest of the day, Tiernan rode with the guards. Whenever he fell back, trying to talk with Zoë she kicked her mount into a bone-jarring trot that made even the simplest conversation impossible. He noted she also kept her distance from their new companion. And the girl didn't say a word to anyone. She wasn't bad looking, he decided. Not his taste, but attractive enough. In response to his casual chatter about the passing countryside, she only blushed and ducked her head. At dinner the first night, she ate quickly and went straight to her bedroll.

"Well she's not here to add to the conversation," Tiernan said, half-joking, to Zoë. "Is she running away from home?"

Zoë glared at him and flounced off to bed. At a loss, Tiernan turned to Eleanor, who took pity on him.

"The girl's name is Livy and she will be traveling with us," she said. "If you need to know more, you will have to ask Zoë. But," she cautioned, "you might wait a few days before you do." Tiernan addressed his dinner plate, certain, not for the first time, that the minds of females were unfathomable.

••••

They traveled for nearly a week and Livy never said a word the entire time. At first, Tiernan had thought she couldn't speak, which was preferable to thinking she wouldn't speak. But finally, even Zoë became concerned.

"Get her to talk," she told Tiernan over the dinner dishes one night. "It isn't normal for a girl her age to be this quiet. Get her to talk. She likes you."

"She likes me?" Tiernan said, amazed. "How can you tell?"

Zoë grimaced. "Don't be an idiot."

They'd camped by a small lake ringed by spruce trees. Tiernan wandered down to the shore to watch the stars come out in the night sky. Looking up at the navy blue bowl pricked with lights, he tried to identify the constellations forming overhead.

"Now, that should be the Stelae Constellation. I think," he muttered looking at a chain of bright stars to the south. "Or maybe that's the belt of …' He stopped, lost in the night sky.

"The Stelae Constellation is to the west," a firm voice said, quite close by, "about two fingers up from the horizon at sunset. And the Pich Belt won't be visible for another month."

Tiernan looked around for the voice and found Livy perched on a rocky outcropping.

"So how do you know so much about stars?"

She hunched her shoulders and retreated back into silence. He sat down on a nearby boulder and looked out over the lake.

"It's peaceful here," he said appreciatively. "There was a lake near where I grew up." He chuckled. "More like a pond, in comparison. I spent every summer there until I was nine. We built forts in the woods and swam all day. And at night we'd make fires on the shore. I remember I caught these turtles. They had yellow stripes. What do you call them?"

"A'jak." Livy said shyly.

Tiernan snapped his fingers. "That's it. And one summer this duckling followed us everywhere. He must have thought we were his flock. We called him Maddy."

"That's silly. Ducks don't have names."

"Sure they do. Madra vulgaris. That's the scientific name. Maddy for short."

Livy giggled. "What happened to him?"

"Winter came and he flew away," Tiernan recalled. "I wonder sometimes if he looked for us the next summer."

"Why, where did you go?"

"We went, I mean, I went to military school."

"You left your family? You were younger than me."

"That's the way they train some soldiers. We start young."

Livy stared at him as though turning some thought over in her mind. Even in the dark, Tiernan found her direct gaze disconcerting.

"You don't have a home anymore." It was a statement, not a question.

"Not really. It all changed after that."

"Did you mind?"

Tiernan considered, remembering the raw emotions of a nine-year-old cut loose from everything familiar. "Yeah, I minded," he said softly. He looked over at Livy. "Hey, wanna build a bonfire? Just for old-time's sake?"

Livy jumped down from the rock, and began gathering wood. She was smiling.

••••

On their last day before reaching the Black Pagoda, they made camp early. By now they'd set up camp so often, it was routine; everyone knew their tasks and went about their business without much talk. But they were tired of the road and looking forward to the end of their trip and the promise of hot baths and soft beds. Tiernan looked around the bustling camp and noted an absence. As usual, Livy had gone off by herself.

"What are you doing, brat?"

Livy gave him a fleeting smile and glanced around quickly to see if anyone was looking. "Watch this," she whispered. She held up a small glass ball, rolling it back and forth over her extended fingers several times before tossing it lightly up into the air. And it was gone.

Tiernan applauded. "Nice one. So where did it go?"

Livy grinned. "That would give the trick away." She produced the ball from under her jacket. "You're not supposed to know."

He tried to snatch the ball, but she was faster. It disappeared again. "You're getting better," he admitted. "I can't even tell how you do it anymore."

"Well, that's the point, isn't it?"

Tiernan noticed her eyes dart over to where Zoë was putting up her tent.

"You should show Zoë. She'd like it."

Livy eyes widened. "No. You promised."

He flicked a wayward strand of hair out of her eyes. "Relax runt, your secret is safe with me. After dinner we'll play a game of draughts, OK? I still have to win one."

She produced the orb, her attention once again on perfecting the sleight of hand. Tiernan walked over to help Zoë finished setting the pegs for her tent.

"She spends too much time alone," he grumbled. "Kids her age should be out running around. You should get her to do things with you."

She barely gave her half-sister a glance. "I don't know how to talk to children," she said dismissively. "I'm not even sure what they like to do. Besides, she likes your company better."

. "I play some games with her. I get her to laugh. It's nothing you can't do."

"Are you kidding? You're the only one she talks to."

"She's like any other kid," he replied. "And she's lonely. Besides, she's fun to talk to." Tiernan watched Zoë struggle with the tent. She was scowling. "Why don't you like her?" he asked abruptly.

"You mean, why don't I spoil her and treat her like a baby, like the rest of you?"

"No, why don't you like her? You never talk to her unless you have to. I've never seen you spend more than a minute alone with her."

"Well, maybe I have better things to do."

He snickered. "I can't believe it."

"Can't believe what?" she demanded, giving the last tent peg a whack.

"You're jealous of a little girl."

"You don't know what you're talking about," she snapped, stepped into her tent and yanked down the flap. In a thoughtful mood, Tiernan wandered off to see what was for dinner.

CHAPTER FIFTEEN

Approaching from in-country the temple rose up unexpectedly. Monolithic, sprawling, it was a mass of blackened stone tumbling across the plain toward a retreating sea. Teams of stone horses still strained to pull the sun's chariot, with wheels taller than six men and flanked by granite elephants the size of hills. Sailors had once navigated by the temple's pinnacle lanterns, but time and dirt had choked the flood plain and now the temple stood miles from shore. The Black Pagoda stood alone. The old Seer Michaela lived there now, surrounded by her entourage, visited by the infrequent traders or pilgrims' caravan.

The audience with Michaela began inauspiciously. She was asleep on a daybed in the cavernous audience hall. Snoring. Around her, a dozen attendants waited patiently in the gloom. Eleanor drew up a chair. Tiernan, Zoë and Livy took seats beside her.

"Is this necessary?" Tiernan whispered. "Can't you give us the travel permits?"

Eleanor shook her head. "Michaela specifically requested that the three of you be present. She must have her reasons."

"She looks ancient," Livy whispered.

"Michaela is over 495 years old," Eleanor said, matter-of-factly.

Livy goggled. "Will you live that long?"

"Possibly longer. Michaela didn't take the best care of herself. She is aging now only because she is losing her ability to see the future. It happens to us all, eventually. Nothing is permanent, not even the sight."

"What will happen to her then?" Zoë asked.

"When her sight fails completely, her life will be over. One day, perhaps soon, she will go to sleep and never wake up. It's supposed to be peaceful, a release. But she's fighting the end. That makes it painful for her."

The snoring broke off as Michaela shifted on her bed.

"Your guests are here, Michaela," Eleanor said loudly, "as you requested."

The old Seer's eyes opened. "I can hear you. Whispering. Plotting. Making your little plans. I can hear you just fine."

She propped herself up on one elbow, sending masses of chains, charms and amulets around her neck jingling. She was a wraith, skin and bones and a tangle of wild hair. She glared first at Zoë, then Livy, lastly a long look at Tiernan.

"Soletei," she spat. "I know you. You're a trouble-maker, you are. And now you want something. That'll be a cold day." She lay back. "I am shutting my eyes," she said wearily. "When I open them, please be gone."

Eleanor motioned to them to stay put.

"Oracle," Eleanor intoned, her voice echoing in the drafty hall.

Michaela opened an eye. "Oracle. Now I'm a damn oracle. You don't give up, do you?" She opened both eyes. "This wasn't my choice, you know. I wanted to marry a nice boy and settle down. Have a family." She pulled a cigarette from under a pillow and lit up. A blue cloud of smoke spiraled toward the ceiling.

"Of course," she inhaled deeply, the cigarette tip glowing red, "that wasn't to be." She puffed for a while in silence. Livy fidgeted and Zoë glared at her. Michaela lit a second cigarette from the butt of the first and continued.

"I could see where every relationship was going, you see," she said. "Two months, two years, twenty. I could see it all. I

157

kept waiting for the right one to come along." She sighed. "He never did. Of course, I knew that too. That's the worst of it."

"Oracle," Eleanor tried again.

"They're all gone now," Michaela continued, as though deaf. "I'm the only one who remembers. I'm the only one left. When I'm gone, it will be like all my years, all my past, didn't happen at all." She looked over at her visitors. "My advice to you is to hang the consequences and just do whatever it is you want. Knowing the future is no gift. Ask the girl."

"Who's she talking about?" Tiernan asked under his breath, but Michaela was swinging her legs over the side of the bed, her necklaces clashing and clinking together like hundreds of little bells. She motioned impatiently to Zoë and Livy. "Come here, you two." They cautiously approached the bed. She seized each by an arm pulling them closer. For a dying woman she was surprisingly strong. The odor of smoke, nicotine and something else—eucalyptus, Zoë decided—was overpowering. The old Seer cocked her head and for a long minute it was as though she was listening to something far away. They waited.

"I'm useless. I'm too old," she said bitterly, shoving them away. "It's there. I'm sure of it. But which one of you? I can't tell. It's all a jumble." She lay back down with a sigh. Her eyes refocused on Tiernan.

"You! I remember you. Oh, don't pretend, boy. That's the trouble with you military types. Too little imagination, too suspicious. Conspiracies. Enemies. Can't see what's under your own nose. Enemies are friends and it's any port in a storm. Batten the hatches. All hands. Loving hands at home. They'll turn on you in the end. No point in trying to change that. Won't come to anything though. Yes, that makes you think, doesn't it." Michaela scowled. "You think I'm raving. You don't understand any more than the rest of them. Ask me for the weather report. Study some entrails. Leave me alone."

She turned back to Zoë.

"And you. 'Where's my daddy?' Is that all you think about? Fire and water, girl, fire and into the water." She chuckled. "You're so close, you're walking in his footsteps. But when you find him, you'll just lose him again. Oh Judgment Day! Coming soon!" she sang, then fell to coughing. Attendants swarmed around her, offering a glass of water, pounding her back, fanning the air. Eleanor drew the three away from Michaela's bed.

"We're not going to get anything more out of her. I'm sorry."

Still, Zoë had hope. "She said I was close. That's good, isn't it? Tiernan? You look like you saw a ghost."

Michaela's mention of fire and water had come too close to the specifics of Jomini's death for Tiernan's comfort. Eleanor stopped at the hall entryway.

"I have to leave you for a while, but we'll have time to talk after dinner. I've made arrangements for you to stay within the main precinct of the temple tonight. Perhaps, in the meantime, you would like to visit the observatory, Tiernan. I believe you're expected. And perhaps you'll take Zoë and show her the solstice altar; it's on your way. Livy, there is a sizeable library that you might like to see. One of the novices can direct you." She stopped. "Whatever you choose to do, please do not go outside the temple walls after dark. I can guarantee your safety only here."

Michaela was passing them, a phalanx of attendants carrying her couch from the main hall. As she did, she growled, "Memories won't keep you warm, girl. And wishing won't make it so. Remember that." She fell back onto her pillows, her eyes closed, a butt clenched between her teeth as the procession left the hall. A tendril of smoke snaked up in her wake.

CHAPTER SIXTEEN

"Great place for an observatory, huh?" Tiernan was oddly excited, taking the steps two at a time, despite his bad leg.

"I guess," Zoë grunted, scrambling after him. They'd been climbing for a good twenty minutes, sometimes up twisting, tortuous interior staircases, more often scaling the pagoda's exterior stairways. Not just the view was breathtaking.

"How much further?" she panted, as he headed up yet another flight. "And why the hurry? It's a little early to look at stars."

"Early for star gazing. But almost late for tea," Tiernan said. "And Eleanor wanted me to show you the solstice altar first."

They had reached a terrace at the Pagoda's highest levels. Behind them, through an arch, another short flight of stone steps led up to an observatory, once its lighthouse. Before them, looking east, was the flat flood plain and, beyond, the ocean's silver glint. To the west and north swaths of green forest stretched to the mountains.

They'd disturbed two attendants praying before a rough boulder protruding from the center of the terrace. Now, as Tiernan and Zoë watched, one attendant ladled oil from a bucket over the rock, and stood back as the second attendant touched flame to the rock. A blue aura danced over the altar, quickly dying into sooty tendrils. The attendants bowed in unison and re-entered the Pagoda.

"This is an altar?" Zoë looked dubiously at the jagged rock.

"That's what they call it, but it's more like a star calendar. See, that point sticking up in the middle of the rock?" Tiernan said. "It's called the Tether. On the summer solstice it lines up with the Evening Star." Six quartz stones trailed in a line from the Tether, and at their tail, a trident etched into the stone. Even in the late afternoon light, the quartz glittered.

"The stones are the planets or stars, I forget which, and the rock itself is carved to mimic the mountain ranges."

Zoë looked off into the distance to the outline of the far mountains. She couldn't see the resemblance.

"But I've seen that symbol of the trident before," she said, trying to recall where. Memory failed and Tiernan was pulling her on, through the arch and up the adjacent flight of steps.

"Come on, I want to show you the observatory." At the top of the stairs, he knocked on a narrow wooden door. A voice from inside said in rapid fire, "Come in! Door's open. Watch the papers. Mind the cat. Take a seat, I'll be right down."

They'd entered on the bottom floor of the observatory, and Zoë was surprised at how spacious it was on the inside, a single octagonal room with a rudimentary staircase on the far wall leading to an upper floor. Or rather it would have been roomy if every surface hadn't been covered in papers and books, with more wedged into sagging shelves lining the walls. A mongrel assortment of chairs, some comfortably stuffed, others straight-backed, surrounded a table in the center of the room. The tabletop was likewise covered in drifts of papers, dirty plates, cups and saucers, and a large yellow cat, who rose and stretched at their entrance.

Footsteps overhead and in a moment a pair of stout legs appeared on the open stairs, followed by the rest of their host. He was just average height, a trim man with a neat graying beard. Winding his way through the piles of books on the floor, he kept a tray with a large tea pot, tea cups, and a plate of cookies in precarious balance.

"I hope you like this," he said, setting the tray down. "It's a bit smokier than I'm accustomed to, but I'm fresh out of green tea. We'll have to make do. Shoo, Nicodemus."

The cat moved as far as a chair and resumed his nap. Their host smiled. "My boy, you're looking well. City life must agree with you."

"It's good to see you again, Josepht," Tiernan said sliding into an empty chair. "Zoë, meet my father. I'm taking Zoë to Bellery. The seer is putting us up here for the night."

"Oh? So short a stay. I was hoping to see more of you. Well, it's good to have you here. Please try one of these, my dear."

She took one of the cookies from the plate Josepht offered.

"I bake them myself," he confessed. "I just throw whatever together and hope for the best. Sometimes they turn out well, sometimes they don't."

"They're delicious," Zoë said truthfully. "What are they filled with?"

"Why," Josepht said in amazement, "haven't you ever had carteen jam? I thought our children were raised on the stuff."

"Zoë is from Ard Creggan, father," Tiernan said in a low voice. Almost, she imagined, the cat stopped purring.

"Well," Josepht began awkwardly. "Well. And I thought Publicans had everything. Would you like another?" The cat resumed purring.

"Tiernan didn't tell me you were a scientist," Zoë said shyly. "I thought Citizens, I mean. . ." She stopped, lost in a gaffe.

"You thought I was a nice, hardworking farmer, like most Citizens," Josepht said kindly. "Well, I was. But I'm afraid my heart wasn't in it."

"We were the only farm house with an observatory," Tiernan explained. "Well, a telescope anyway."

Josepht chuckled in agreement. "Your poor mother would get so annoyed. She said I was more familiar with the stars than I was with my own fields. Now that may not sound so bad to you," he said as Zoë laughed, "but to a farmer, that's damning indeed." He smiled wistfully. "I miss that woman. She had a way with words." He brightened. "Of course after Tiernan went away, I had all this time on my hands."

"He sublet the farm," Tiernan said in exasperation.

"Pay no attention to the boy," Josepht winked at Zoë. "Mercenary. Just like his mother."

"Father, that was some of the best farmland in the township. You leased it out for a fraction of its value."

"And what I got was some peace from planting and harvesting year in and year out," his father retorted.

"One year," Tiernan said, turning to Zoë, "he forgot to bring in the hay."

"It was the year of the Regis Comet," Josepht said with dignity. "A magnificent opportunity to observe it at close range. The monograph I wrote was very well received."

"Yes, Father." Tiernan said dryly. "I'm sure it was. But we had to buy feed for the cows that winter."

Zoë smiled. "Was he always so practical?"

Josepht winked at her. "Always. Except when he was bringing home strays. He could not resist an orphan."

"Now Father," Tiernan growled. "Don't be telling stories."

"It's true. The house was a menagerie—lost dogs, baby birds, lame horses, I think there was a mouse or two."

"No," Tiernan protested. "Never mice. We had too many cats."

They laughed. "Those were good days, my boy," Josepht said, wiping his eyes. "But tell me, Zoë, Ard Creggan must have several excellent observatories."

Zoë blushed. "I think so, I mean, we do. At least one. I have an uncle who is an astronomer. I think he has published a few papers."

Josepht nodded eagerly. "That must be Publican Sensa Tri. I've always wanted to meet him. I've read several of his publications. And he's your uncle. What a coincidence."

"Coincidence?" Zoë asked, puzzled.

"Father," Tiernan murmured, as though in warning.

Josepht hurried on. "You know, Sensa Tri's calculations on the Regis Comet's trajectory, were nothing short of genius. They were quite invaluable to my observations. But I'm boring you. Nothing worse than an old man and his enthusiasms. Now tell me. What are you up to? You say you're on your way to Bellery?"

"Actually, we're on our way to Gurama," Zoë said.

Josepht sniffed. "That old rock. Why would anyone want to go there? Nothing but monks and rocks, and more rocks. Nasty, cold place. Of course it's perfectly isolated and as safe as solitary confinement. I spent a summer there once. Or was it a winter? It's so hard to tell the difference. I was using their archives. There was a very helpful monk, if I remember, Regid, or Regal, or Ralph, or something. Come to think of it, you were out there once, weren't you Tiernan? Long time ago. Something about a peace initiative. As I remember, you met some girl."

"Yes Father," Tiernan broke in. "What were you doing in the archives?"

"What? Well, they have a most comprehensive collection of astronomical charts. They must go back three hundred or four hundred years. Anyway, with their assistance I was able to verify that once every four hundred years or so there is a conjunction of the six planets in our system. According to my calculations the next will occur at the summer solstice."

"Um, that's very interesting," Zoë said cautiously. "Is it a portent?"

"A portent?" Josepht asked blankly. "Oh no. No portents. Just planets lining up. Gravitational pull might increase. High tides. Perhaps some weather anomalies. But outside of that, nothing unusual."

Tiernan and Zoë exchanged looks over their mugs.

"Nothing at all," Josepht continued, with barely suppressed glee. "Except for the new comet I've sighted."

"A new comet, Father? Congratulations! Do you get to name it?"

"Of course. I plan to name it after your mother. Floridana. But not until I'm certain it is a comet."

"Well, what else could it be? A moon?"

Josepht looked perplexed by the question. "Not a moon and its path isn't very comet-like, if you know what I mean. If it's in an elliptical orbit—and it would be a very large orbit—it might explain its rare appearance in our solar system. This much I do know. The archives on Gurama mention periodic sightings of an astral body over the millennium. But you know those old records. Everything is in terms of mythology and magical beings. There's no telling what actually happened. This time, I estimate it will pass very close to our own planet, so we'll finally get a good scientific accounting. Yes, most unique. Michaela has been most interested in my observations."

"The old Seer?" Tiernan asked.

"By your tone, you don't believe she could be interested in science. You don't know everything, my son," Josepht replied with some hauteur. "The Seer and I have been acquainted, professionally-speaking, for years. In fact, I dedicated my Regis paper to her. Yes, and she's made several contributions of her own to my mappings. She equipped this observatory herself. Of course, her health is failing now."

He suddenly looked concerned. "I hope the new Seer is interested in astronomy." He shrugged. "Well, no matter. Science will always find a way. If you give me a minute, you can take a look at the approaching conjunction of planets through my portable telescope. I'm afraid I have the main telescope already positioned to take a series of readings. Then I'm hoping to join you later for dinner."

Tiernan wasn't fooled. "You'll get busy, as usual, and forget all about dinner. Here, I brought you a present. A new lens." From his coat pocket he drew out a small velvet bundle and placed it in on the table. Zoë rose to gather up the dishes, but Josepht waved her off.

"No, my dear, don't bother. The dishes can wait." He opened the pouch like an excited child. "Yes, this is quite the lens. Give me a minute and perhaps I can show you." He stomped off up the stairs, lens in hand.

165

Tiernan had gone to stand in the open door, looking up at the darkening sky. Zoë joined him.

"Your father is a very interesting man." She was aware of Tiernan close beside her in the doorway and of a comfortable silence. Overhead the stars began to appear. Josepht's call interrupted their thoughts.

"Come up, you two. I can show you now."

On the top floor, the astronomer was bent over a spider of a telescope. A much larger version loomed over him, extending through a slit in the roof. "Do you remember our old telescope, Tiernan? I've made a few improvements. The seeing should be very good tonight. Very good."

"And the new lens?"

"Take a look. Yes, that was very thoughtful of you, my son. Imagine you remembering all this time that I needed that particular lens."

Tiernan bent over the eyepiece. "That's courtesy of Ard Creggan, father. I had their technicians grind it."

"Well, they do very nice work. Nice work, indeed. Do you see it, Tiernan? Here, let the girl have a look."

"What am I looking for?" Zoë asked as Josepht guided her to the eyepiece.

"Look for the six planets. They're nearly aligned. Well, we're standing on the sixth planet. So you're only seeing five. Here, perhaps if I adjust this."

Out of the darkness, a string of silver beads unexpectedly emerged. She looked up. "It's wonderful. It's so clear. It looks just like the stones on the solstice altar."

Josepht reclaimed the eyepiece. "That precise lineup hasn't been seen in several lifetimes. The planets won't be in conjunction again for, oh, another four hundred years. In fact, they'll be in exact alignment at the summer solstice. We're very lucky tonight. Very lucky. It's been overcast. I thought we wouldn't be able to see it. Very lucky."

"When will it pass, Father?"

Josepht looked as though he was doing some mental calculations, then: "I've plotted the orbit, but I still have some observations to make. Tonight's readings will give me a better idea. But here, my dear, perhaps you'd like another look." As Zoë bent over the telescope again, Josepht drew his son out of earshot.

"I don't want to guess, my boy. I might be wrong. And if I am, there will be unnecessary alarm."

"I need to know, Father."

Josepht ran his hand distractedly through his hair. "Well, that's the thing. Within its original orbit, it would not pass close to us at all."

Tiernan let out a sigh of relief. "So Jomini was wrong."

"Maybe. Sensa Tri's observations were practically prescient, so I'm quite sure, the comet, or whatever it is, will arrive at the summer solstice, just as the six planets complete their alignment. Quite spectacular. But it has been so erratic. A few nights ago, it appeared to change its orbit. Which I know is impossible. But if it stays on its present trajectory, it will come very, very close. As Jomini told us it would. I don't know how, but he knew. Poor Jomini. A brilliant man. So tragic."

"Father," Tiernan said in a low voice. "Zoë is his daughter."

The old man's eyes widened. "Oh dear. Oh, that's truly unfortunate," he said. "Does she know about your work with him?"

"No. And I don't want her to know just yet."

"You can't keep the truth from her forever, my boy. The truth has a way of wiggling its way out at the most inopportune moment. I learned that living with your mother. It might be better if she hears the whole story from you."

"I can't risk it yet, Father. When we get to Gurama, she'll understand."

"Well, then that's your business. But I must get back to my observations, if we want to be certain. Now Miss Zoë," he said returning to the telescope, "you've made an old man very happy, indulging me in my hobby. But don't let me keep you two any longer. I'll see you at dinner, perhaps. I have an hour or two of work up here. Lots to do. Take care going down." Engrossed in his work, he didn't even hear the door shut behind them.

••••

The fire was burning low in the grate. Tiernan and Zoë sat over the remains of their evening meal, staring into the flames, neither one doing much talking. The Seer had not joined them. Livy sat through supper with her nose buried in a book then excused herself. And Josepht couldn't be lured away from his observatory. So they were alone, just the two of them after so many weeks surrounded by others. From some closet or chest, the attendants had produced a dress for her of a bronze that shimmered in the firelight like a cloud at sunset. He liked it.

"She's a good kid, you know?" Tiernan said without preface.

Zoë refilled his glass. "Who?"

"You know who. Livy."

"She's not a kid."

"She's not like you, Zoë. She isn't..."

Zoë's quizzical expression told him he might be wandering into dangerous territory.

"She's in her own little world. She isn't like you," he finished lamely. "It's hard to believe you two are sisters," he admitted.

"So she told you?"

Something in Zoë's tone made him think this was unwelcome news. "I guess it's a relief to talk about it," she continued. "Now that you know, maybe you can help me decide what I'm going to do with her. I can't keep dragging her around the country. And I can't send her to Ard Creggan, not right now, anyway. Maybe she'd be better off here with the Seer."

"As a novice?" Tiernan looked appalled. "She's not cut out for this place either."

"You're probably right," Zoë chuckled. "Although I think Eleanor could handle her."

"What about you?" Tiernan asked, changing the subject. "What is your ambition in life? What are you going to do now?"

Neither had talked about Ard Creggan since the night of the fire. And since her options for the future appeared limited, she didn't want to go down that particular conversational path.

"I haven't thought about it," she lied. "And I could ask the same of you. What would you do if you couldn't be a soletei?"

It was his turn to dodge. "Can't we just sit and enjoy the moment?"

She put both elbows on the table, her chin in her hands. "No. You started this. Tell me. If all the wars were over tomorrow, what would you do?"

Tiernan looked blank. "I don't know. Not much call for a soletei caste if there's no one to fight, is there?"

"Well, I guess you could police or something," Zoë suggested helpfully. "People still need protection. I don't suppose that duty ever ends."

"Maybe I'd go back home," he offered.

"Back to the farm?" Zoë asked, doubtful. "Do you think you'd like farming?"

Tiernan looked as though that point was immaterial. "I guess so. Besides farming is the only other occupation I've ever known."

"You were eight years old the last time you were on a farm. What does an eight-year-old know about farming?" she demanded.

He saw her point. "OK, so it's not farming. What do you think I could do?"

"I think you'd be good at all sorts of things."

"Yes, but what?" Tiernan prompted, chuckling.

"Well, it wouldn't be an osprit wrangler. They didn't like you at all."

"Thank you, I didn't like them either. How about a glider pilot?"

It was her turn to laugh. "I saw you. You were white as a sheet when we flew my glider."

"It wasn't the flying, it was the pilot," he protested.

"Or you could be a diplomat, like my father," she suggested.

Tiernan looked away. "Zoë, there's something you should know," he began.

"It's just a silly game, Tiernan," she said, stopping him.

He sighed and closed his eyes, hearing the rustle of Zoë's dress. His heart pounded in his chest, so loudly, he wondered she couldn't hear it. He could smell her scent too, close by, the familiar perfume from all those years ago. Fingers stroked the hair from his brow, caressed his throat, moved across his chest. He felt her cheek soft against his. His fingers twined themselves in the loose tumble of her hair, and he pulled her lips down to meet his. It was better than his dreams. Much better.

The dining room door slammed back on its hinges and Tiernan was on his feet, putting Zoë behind him. To their mutual surprise, it was Brian in the doorway, Josepht pressing in behind him. "They're coming to arrest you, Tiernan," his friend said, without preamble,

"Citizens? Here?"

"Donncha," Brian said reluctantly. "Our own people. But there's a Tribune officer with the charges. You've got to leave. Now."

Tiernan took Zoë's hand. "Lady Deich, this is Brian Goodloe, my friend."

"Donncha wants to arrest you?" Zoë blurted. "Why?"

"That's an interesting question," Tiernan agreed.

"Orders," Brian said. "We were three days out of Ard Creggan when the courier caught up with us. He had Tribune orders to arrest any soletei. They even supplied a list. Your name was at the top. To his credit, Donncha wouldn't hear of it, at first. But there it was. Orders."

"There aren't many of us left," Tiernan said. "It shouldn't take long to round up all of us." They heard the bitterness in his voice.

Josepht broke in. "They say you've plotted against the state and the Tribune. You! Why, they may have us outnumbered, but I'll be damned if I let them take you, my boy."

Brian looked grave. "There's to be a fris."

"A fris?" Zoë looked around in confusion. "Somebody tell me what is going on."

"A fris," Brian said. "is how we Citizens deal with collaborators. I think the charge is something like, for supporting or in any way sustaining terrorists or terrorist organizations....or," he added, "for just showing too much interest in Publicans like you."

Brian and Zoë glared at each other.

"There's nothing we can do now," Tiernan said releasing her hand and walking over to stare into the fire. "Lady Deich, Zoë, it might be better if you found the Seer as quickly as possible. She may be able to offer you sanctuary. She has been a friend to my family."

"Even old friends turn on you," Josepht said, weariness in his voice.

Tiernan looked up. "What do you mean, Father?"

"I didn't want to worry you," Josepht said. He looked contritely at his son. "Our village turned me out months ago. They burned the observatory. Destroyed everything. I'm here because the old Seer was the only one who would take me in."

"We've had reports of attacks from all over the country," Brian broke in impatiently. "The Tribune encourages them. They call it an ideological purification or something like that. At first it was attacks on anyone suspected of dealing with Publicans. Now it's anyone connected with technology, even scientists like your father."

"I've spent my life protecting my people," Tiernan protested.

"They forget that," Brian said, his words were bitter. "All the Tribune remembers is how damn different you soletei are. They can't control you, and that means you're a threat. They aren't even bothering to bring some cases to trial. Just arrest and imprisonment. They're only holding a fris for you because of your standing with the men."

"I know, I'll go to the Seer," Josepht muttered. "She'll intervene. She'll have to. You wait and see." He darted off.

"We fought their wars," Tiernan said. "We died for them. We serve them."

"That was then. Now, the Tribunes say the soletei are a danger to the state."

"Deidre tried to warn me," Tiernan said. "I thought she was raving." He took a deep breath. "How much time do I have?"

"They've set up camp in the Pagoda's outside compound and Donncha has requested an interview with the Seer."

Zoë looked hopeful, but Brian dismissed this out of hand. "It's only a formality. They'll come for Tiernan with or without her permission. She won't jeopardize the temple's neutrality by resisting. Donncha plans to leave in the morning for Bellery with you as his prisoner."

Tiernan's grin was lopsided. "You see, Zoë. I told you I'd get to Bellery."

"You're not going with them?" she demanded. There was the sound of marching feet outside. But it was only the compound guards changing. With a nod, Brian slipped out to keep watch. Tiernan and Zoë were alone again, but there was an urgency in the air now.

"Listen, to me," he said. "It won't help my case if I'm arrested with you here. Get to the Seer. She may hide you."

Zoë looked at him as though he'd lost his mind. "You heard him. It's a witch hunt. You can't think they're going to give you a fair trial."

"Probably not. But I still have to go. It's our law and these are my people. I can't choose to obey only the laws that suit me."

"Then, I'm coming with you."

"If you go, it will be as a prisoner. I'd like to avoid that. You need to get to Gurama."

"But I can tell them the truth, Tiernan."

He gave her an odd look. "The truth. About what?"

"About why we were traveling together, about. . . ." Her voice trailed off.

"Yeah, you'll be a great witness. Besides, I don't think they're interested in the truth. No, I can find my way out of this, and if I can't, it would be easier for me if you weren't sitting in some prison cell." He paused as though trying to come to a decision. "Zoë, there are some things I haven't told you."

"It doesn't matter," she said quickly, but he stopped her.

"It does. I wanted you to hear this from me. Stop looking for your father. He's dead. No, let me finish. I know he's dead because I was there when he died. I wish I could explain everything but there's just no time." He had to hurry and the look in her eyes tore at him. "I'm sorry. I'm sorry I didn't tell you before this. I had my reasons. The important thing now is that you get to Gurama. That was Jomini's last wish. Everything you need to know is there." There was a disturbance at the outer door. Zoë stood mute. He almost wished she would scream at him, make some sound. They heard the inner compound gates bang and tramping footsteps.

"Sounds like my escort has arrived. Listen to me. Go to Gurama. Be safe."

He brushed her cheek with a finger, then turning on his heel he walked out to meet the guards. The door to the inner room muffled the words. Zoe could hear Donncha read the arrest warrant. She heard him give the command to take the prisoner into custody, then his voice raised again.

"Search the Pagoda for the Publican Deich. She is to be transported to Bellery for questioning."

"I won't get to Gurama after all," she thought, when something heavy hit her from behind and the room went black.

CHAPTER SEVENTEEN

Breathing hurt. There was an enormous weight on her chest. And it was very dark. There was a rumbling vibrating her chest. That, at least, was familiar.

"Noor!" she yelped, and got a mouthful of fur. The Saurillia rose to examine Zoë.

"Continue to struggle. It frightens the little men. They have run off, but they may return at any moment."

"I don't care. Get off me, I can't breathe. And stop chewing my foot. It tickles."

"I meant them to think," Noor said, *"that I was eating you and meant to kill them next. That part I most certainly meant. But they ran away."* She sounded disappointed.

Zoë crawled out from under Noor. "I'm very glad to see you," she said hugging as much of her Nurse as possible. "Have you come to rescue me?"

Noor regarded her reproachfully. *"You are a grown woman. You are perfectly capable of rescuing yourself. We said we were to meet here. I did exactly as we planned. Was that not right?"*

"Yes, yes, Noor, exactly right," Zoë reassured her. Her voice cracked. "I am so glad to see you. Did you have any trouble following us?"

Noor rose to full height and shook herself out like a dog. *"Citizens. They all smell like goats. They are very easy to follow. And from the treetops I kept an eye on you. But when you came to the water, I came ahead here. I did not like that particular water."*

Remembering the pirate camp, Zoë had to agree. Meanwhile, Noor was making for the door.

"Now would be a good time to leave," she was saying, *"I think the soldiers will come back, but they are afraid and are looking for others to give them courage. We will talk later. Come along. The Seer Eleanor is expecting us."*

The guards were indeed gone, at least for a moment. The two padded from shadow to doorway and down corridors within the Pagoda, Noor leading as though pulled in the right direction. They heard running footsteps, sometimes very close-by, sometimes echoing far off. That night, the Pagoda seemed to be filled with Citizen soldiers searching for the Lady Deich and the Saurillia. But possibly they could be forgiven for not hunting quite as hard for the Saurillia.

Noor and Zoë made their way ever deeper into the heart of the Pagoda, until Noor pushed Zoë before her into a long paneled room. Eleanor sat writing at a table and Chaff was there, as well as Bergerac, who appeared to be amusing Livy with tricks. From an alcove, a blue cloud of smoke ascended to the ceiling, announcing Michaela's presence. Josepht was huddled in a far corner, his hands moving in his lap as though explaining to someone unseen. Eleanor didn't look up at their entrance, but addressed them as though they were expected.

"Michaela has authorized a caravan visa for Chaff. It should get you safely to Bellery. A ship's captain there is in our pay. He will take you to Gurama without asking questions." She rolled the document tightly and handed it to Chaff.

"Officially, you will be part of Chaff's caravan. I suggest you contrive some believable reason to be traveling to Bellery."

Michaela's cackle floated out on a cumulus cloud of smoke. "Those Citizen troops are wandering in circles tonight. But they'll figure out you're still alive. What kind of trick will save you this time, girl?"

175

Eleanor ignored her. "Chaff, you will leave tonight. Livy will accompany you. Donncha doesn't know her and he won't stop her. The Lady Deich will join you in a few days." She smiled at the dwarf. "The less you know, the less you have to deny, my friend."

The dwarf bowed, winked at Zoë, and bounded off, followed more sedately by Bergerac. Zoë took his vacated seat next to Livy. Noor settled down on the floor next to her.

Eleanor turned to Zoë. "You will join Chaff outside the compound walls. You will take an alternate route I will show you and meet with the caravan outside the immediate range of Donncha's troop."

Zoë took a deep breath. "What will happen to Tiernan?"

"He'll be taken to Bellery where a trial will be held. And after a suitable demonstration of justice, I imagine he'll be exonerated. . .or executed."

Zoë's stomach heaved. "I'm not going without Tiernan."

Michaela snickered. "Love is always screwing up plans, eh Elly? She won't go without her man."

"He's not," Zoë began, but thought better of it.

Eleanor folded her hands in her lap and gave Zoë her full attention. "Tiernan has been arrested," she said as though addressing a child. "I cannot help him escape without jeopardizing the neutrality of the temple. That cannot happen. You are wanted by the Tribune. Unless you want to spend the foreseeable future in a prison cell, you must hide. Now, what is your objection?"

Zoë's eyes dropped before the Seer's calm gaze and Michaela let out a whoop. "The fool let the cat out of the bag, didn't he, girl?"

Eleanor looked displeased. "Zoë?"

"I just need to talk to Tiernan."

"You know that's not possible. Not without risk to us all. Besides, what could he say now that he couldn't have said in all the weeks you've been traveling together?"

Livy came to stand beside her sister. "Is it about my...about Jomini?" she asked in a small voice.

"I'm sorry, Livy," Zoë began.

"Is he alright?"

"Father. . . ." Zoë's voice broke. She started again. "Tiernan said he was with Jomini when he died."

"He's dead? How?" Livy's voice quavered.

"How did he die? I don't know. Tiernan was arrested before he could tell me. He told me to go to Gurama. He said everything I needed to know I'd find there."

"That was helpful of him," Eleanor said. "It is unfortunate he wasn't as forthcoming when he had more time to talk. But perhaps if he had spoken earlier you would not have listened. Tell me, why did he agree to take you to Gurama?"

Zoë blinked back tears. "For the ring. I told him I'd give him my mother's ring as soon as we reached Gurama."

"Well, there's one explanation. You wanted to find your father. He wanted the ring. If he'd told you your father was already dead, you wouldn't give him the ring. Very simple."

"Or the boy killed Jomini himself," Michaela said crossly from the shadows. "Wouldn't doubt he could do it."

Livy and Zoë glared at her.

"Not Tiernan." It was Josepht, roused by Michaela's accusation. "He'd never harm your father."

Zoë flushed; "I know he didn't, he couldn't have. . ." Her voice trailed off with her doubts.

Eleanor was more direct. "Michaela may be right. I imagine as a soletei he's done things he wouldn't tell his own father." She gave Josepht a questioning look. "Do either of you know him anymore? He was a child when he left you, Josepht, and it has been years since he was the boy you met, Zoë."

"The Tiernan I knew once wouldn't have hurt anyone," Zoë said flatly. "But he's a soletei, isn't he."

Eleanor looked bored. "Disillusionment is interesting only in the very young or the simple-minded," she said to no one in particular.

"He didn't kill my father." It was Livy, speaking so softly she might have been talking to herself.

"Like you'd know," Michaela scoffed. "You're a child."

Livy's eyes flashed. "I do know," she said loudly. "Because Tiernan brought me my father's pendant." She hurried on, as if afraid they'd stop her.

"I wasn't supposed to see him. He came one night, late, while I was in bed. I heard him and my uncle talking. I snuck down and saw Tiernan. They didn't see me. He brought my father's pendant and told my uncle I was to go to my family in Ard Creggan."

"Why didn't you tell me this before?" Zoë demanded.

"My uncle told me not to tell," Livy protested. "And Tiernan didn't say anything, so I didn't think I should either. It didn't hurt anyone."

Eleanor looked thoughtful. "Yes, Livy, I see your point. Your father's murderer is hardly likely to bring a keepsake to his daughter."

He forgot me, popped unbidden into Zoë's mind. *I'm his daughter.* She slipped Jomini's pendant from around her neck. It was heavy in her hand and unfamiliar. It didn't conjure her father's face, it didn't recall his voice. Michaela broke into her thoughts to wave at the door. "We're going to have company. So make yourself scarce, you two."

"Are you sure?" Eleanor asked. She listened intently.

"I'm dying, not dead," the old Seer snapped. "Donncha and two of his flat-footed ninnies. They'll be here in a few minutes. He thinks the little princess is here. Smart man."

"Where can we go?" Zoë looked around the room. There was one entrance and nowhere to hide except possibly in the small alcove with Michaela. Noor reared back combatively on her haunches.

"Don't get in a fuss," Michaela growled. "Think we're stupid?" She tottered, bent nearly double from the alcove, cigarette in hand. Scanning the wood floor, she wandered back and forth across the room, paused, stomped hard. A knob popped up from a floor board. "I can never remember where that damn cubbyhole is," she muttered, ambling back to her alcove. "Should put a marker on it or something."

"Thank you, Michaela, but that might defeat the purpose of a hiding hole," Eleanor said lightly. "If you would, Zoë, just lift up that trapdoor. I think there will be sufficient room for both you and Noor. You should probably hurry."

A few steps led down into a square dark crypt. Zoë peered down into the blackness. *I hope we don't have to stay in here very long.*

She started down.

Noor took persuading; it was a hole, after all. But very shortly, Zoë was crouched at the bottom with Noor whimpering softly beside her. The trapdoor closed over their heads. Almost immediately, there was a knock at the door. Overhead, Zoë heard footsteps, with an additional thump. Someone with a cane. Dust sifted down between the boards. Donncha.

"Good evening." Donncha bowed first to the alcove where Michaela was once again smoking up a storm and then to Eleanor. "I thought I should keep you informed of our progress. We are most grateful for your cooperation in the search." He walked into the center of the room, looked around, and nodded in greeting to Josepht. "My friend, my sympathy. I'm certain Tiernan will be exonerated. Please be assured I will do everything I can to prove his innocence. Ah, a novice?" He stopped before Livy. "You're very young to be considering a vocation, aren't you?"

Livy blushed.

"Our novices come to us at all ages, captain," Eleanor said curtly. "Not all of them will spend a lifetime with us. Did you say your search has been successful or are we to remain here all night?"

Donncha strolled over to inspect a wall hanging as though he had all night. "My apologies. But we've had reports of a Saurillia in the grounds. I have not sighted the animal myself, so I am personally doubtful, but you should perhaps take precautions. Wandering the halls might not be advisable." He poked under Michaela's bed with his cane.

"Can we help you look for something, Captain?" Eleanor asked.

"Oh, don't mind me." Something on the floor caught his eye. "Now what's that?" He turned to Livy. "Perhaps you'll get that for me, my child? I'm not as agile as I use to be. Would you pick that up, please?"

Livy obediently trotted over to where he pointed. A fine chain lay along a crack in the floorboards.

"What is it?" Donncha asked. "Perhaps you'd let me see."

Livy turned to Donncha. *He has kind eyes*, she thought. *He's a nice man.* She held out her hand to show him.

CHAPTER EIGHTEEN

Sinon Yar dismissed his secretary and the bodyguards. He pushed back from the desk, ignoring the piles of paperwork and walked to the window. Outside, the line of petitioners waiting for an audience, for a favor, for a decision, for a permit or one of a hundred irritations, stretched around the corner of the compound.

Following Sinon Yar's takeover of Ard Creggan, there had been some who had bided their time, hoping nothing would change except a random shuffling of titles and chains of authority. Some even welcomed the new Basillius, who began by declaring a referendum that elected him dictator for life in Ard Creggan's first and only landside election, the ballot boxes dutifully stuffed by his troops.

And who could blame them? Sinon Yar promised a proud new era; prosperity for all who joined him. Since he had already abolished the Concordia, and a wave of increasingly violent tremors had left half of Ard Creggan in ruins, he appeared to be the only reasonable hope.

The ClearWorlders were particularly enamored. In their view, he was the antithesis of the old regime, someone who could make change happen—their kind of change. In return for a few positions in the new administration, they threw him their support.

For a while, the city was an open experiment in the redistribution of wealth with stipends for the poor coming from heavy taxes laid on the rich. Then Yar opened the compounds of the Ten Families to squatters. That the best quarters went to Sinon Yar's minions was just happenstance.

But when the ClearWorlders, restless with the pace of reform, again began to agitate to close the mines, the crackdown was inevitable. It began with a small disturbance. The protestors were jailed. Then conspiracies were revealed and ringleaders arrested, which led to full scale purges. By then no one was safe. Whole sections of the city, suspected hotbeds of the insurgency, were cordoned off, shops and businesses slowly strangled of goods and customers. The homes of suspected resistors were razed, their families thrown into the streets. When the children stoned his troops in the streets, Yar shut the schools. The fledgling resistance movement was nearly doomed.

Except for those who went underground. The resistance went down deep into the maze of shafts and galleys tunneled out beneath Ard Creggan. The honeycomb of passages hid gangs of men who could evade Sinon Yar's patrols at will—providing they knew the old, hidden ways, the ways that maybe only an archaeologist who'd been digging in Ard Creggan for decades would know. Eon may have died in Sinon Yar's inaugural power grab, but his life's work found a new life and purpose.

"Captain, reporting in."

Samuel raised his eyes from the map spread out before him on a barrel head and adjusted the lamp. Its light flared outward into the gloom of the cave. He re-rolled the map tightly before addressing his lieutenant.

"How did it go, Pall?"

"Exceptional. I may be discovering talents I never knew I had."

"A talent for sabotage? How appropriate for an administrator. Do you think you'll be able to return to an honest life?"

Pall ginned. "Try me. I'll never complain about inventory reports again."

Samuel smiled. "Get some rest. We'll be moving again before dawn."

"What about you?"

"I have a visit to make, then I'll join you."

Samuel watched Pall hobble off, weaving through the men sprawled along the mine corridor who were sleeping or eating before the next strike up into the city. Like them, Pall lost everything by throwing in with the rebels; his home gone, his family—like so many others—refugees in the camps growing out beyond Ard Creggan's caldera.

"Did you tell him, Captain?"

Samuel looked down. One of the men from his old command was sharing his rations with a stray. The dogs sniffed out booby traps and mines.

"He'll find out, you know, Captain. If it was my girl, I'd rather hear it from you first."

There had been a sweep. Several suspected sympathizers with the insurgency had been detained, Pall's fiancé among them. It was rumored she had died the previous night in custody. Samuel shook his head. "Later. Let him get some sleep." He turned away abruptly and headed out into the maze of mineshafts and galleries. The soldier scratched the mutt's ears. "It won't come any easier, rested or tired," he said to no one.

••••

Several levels up from their makeshift quarters, Samuel touched a wall panel

and stepped into a basement room stacked to the ceiling with sacks and crates. A rat, disturbed, scurried away, leaving behind a pyramid of grain next to a split sack. Samuel took stock of his surroundings and estimated at least a month's worth of supplies for Ard Creggan's remaining inhabitants. Or a few days worth for the people in the camps. He leaned against a crate and waited. But not for long. A door opened, a streak of light shooting across the storage room to strike him. A figure silhouetted in the lamplight beckoned to him. By the time his eyes had grown accustomed to the light, he was being ushered into a strangely barren room of glaringly pale walls. At the end of the room, a female attendant pulled aside a curtain and motioned him inside. A sickly sweet odor filled his nostrils as he ducked behind the curtain. A chair sat beside a screen. He took it with relief, it had been a long day. From behind the screen, a voice asked, "How are you feeling today, Samuel?"

Despite himself, Samuel smiled. "Isn't that what I'm supposed to ask?"

A slight rasping noise was perhaps a chuckle. "I get tired of the same questions. I like to change things up. How are your intrepid insurgents doing?"

"Not so intrepid. But I think we're having an impact. Yar's troops think twice about showing their faces in the city unless they're in numbers. And we've disrupted the mining. I'm hoping that will be enough to make the Families negotiate."

"The Families are nothing; Sinon Yar is the only power now."

"Maybe not." Samuel said. "I came through the Old Market this morning."

A rustling of sheets. "Since you're here, I assume your timing was good."

"Better than some others," Samuel said. "Do you know how many were killed?"

A pause, then from behind the screen. "I was told twenty-five."

"That's a fair estimate. The woman who blew herself up killed some shopkeepers, and a number of women and children who were in the market. Is this a new tactic of yours?"

"Suicide is dramatic," the voice said softly.

"It's irrational," Samuel spit out the words.

The voice again, gentle, soothing. "It could be argued that the only rational response to Sinon Yar's persecution is to fight with any means at hand."

"These aren't soldiers being killed, these are our own people. They're civilians." Samuel stopped. Anger wouldn't help.

"Aren't you being naïve?" The voice grew stronger. "Shouldn't all citizens be part of the struggle regardless of age or sex? They stand to reap the benefits, after all. It seems to me that your rules of engagement are dangerously quaint."

Samuel shook his head, denying the words. "These bombings are terrorizing our people. They're leaving the city, moving out beyond the rim. I never thought I'd see it. Whole sectors of the city are abandoned. Even the scavengers know they're not coming back; they strip the houses within days."

"Change is always disruptive," the disembodied voice returned, "and painful. We will be a Republic again, not a dictatorship. Or whatever Sinon Yar is calling himself these days. Basillius, isn't it?"

Samuel's smile was twisted. "A Republic. Now who's being naïve. Ard Creggan was ruled by the Families; now it's ruled by Sinon Yar. Tell me how things have changed? Only the hand that holds the whip has changed." He caught himself again. His temper seemed to be on edge these days. "In a minute you'll have me advocating open government. For the people, by the people. We'd get even less done. No, I didn't come to argue politics with you."

"Then what did you come for, my friend?"

"I came to ask you to stop the suicide bombings."

Another pause that drew out so long Samuel wondered his listener had heard. Then finally, "The ClearWorlders are a humanitarian organization, Samuel. Not terrorists. We feed people; we give them medical supplies and shelter, no bombs. Just ask anyone."

"I know these are your people," Samuel insisted. "And Yar retaliates because of your. He's torturing our people to find who's behind the bombings."

"Then perhaps he will find me and your problems will be over. Besides, you continue your own attacks."

"Against military targets. Not civilians. Not against innocents."

"Innocents. Are any of us without some stain of sin? Isn't it worth the price, if in the end we have a better society? A new Ard Creggan. These are acceptable losses."

"Do you think there is some kind of economy to this kind of killing?" Samuel demanded bitterly. "Or do you want to be a martyr?"

The screen quivered, slowly drawn aside to reveal the figure behind it. "Look at me, Samuel. Do I look like a martyr to you?"

Samuel looked down at the twisted figure on the cot, the mask of shiny red scar tissue that was his face, the bandaged arms ending in stumps, his fingers burned to cinders in the pyre he'd walked into willingly enough on the winter solstice night. Dragged from the embers, he had lived. Like this.

"No, Will," Samuel said with regret. "You look like a victim. Like the rest of us."

CHAPTER NINETEEN

In another room, far from Ard Creggan, the only sound was the steady thump of Donncha's slow step and cane as he crossed the room to Livy. He inspected the chain briefly. "This would appear to be a Publican's pendant," he said. "In fact, I suspect it belongs to a member of the Deich Family."

"What?" Michaela asked from her alcove. "This fugitive of yours is shedding jewelry now." She cackled.

Donncha's smile was thin. "Where the pendant is, Lady Deich can't be too far away." He looked to Eleanor. "Perhaps you could explain how this came to be here, in this room?"

Eleanor put her pen down with a trace of annoyance. "I have no idea, Captain. Will you would allow me to see it?"

"Gladly." He dropped the chain into Livy's hand again. Her fist closed around it. "My dear, why don't you take this over to the Seer?"

The girl returned his smile and did as she was asked, offering it for Eleanor's scrutiny. She barely glanced at it. "I don't think it's a mystery who owns this chain," she said.

Donncha's smile widened. "I'm glad you are being reasonable. Now perhaps you'll hand her over to me."

Eleanor turned to the alcove. "If you wish. Michaela?" She held up the chain.

The old Seer's head emerged, her eyes narrowed and she ducked back into the darkness of the alcove. A cacophony of jingling and jangling followed until. . . . "Thief!" Michaela's screeched. "That miserable thief took my charm. It's mine! I'll tan that girl's hide. Just let me get my hands on you. You stole it! I can't believe it. You little whelp!"

There was much more. It took awhile to calm Michaela. Finally, when the cursing had subsided to a grumble, Eleanor turned to Livy. The girl's sheepish expression was enough of an admission.

"I took it." She looked in surprise from Eleanor to Donncha. "She had plenty. I didn't figure she'd miss one."

Eleanor sighed. "Obviously, we need to address some gaps in your education. Thievery is not encouraged among our novices."

Donncha reclaimed the chain. He cleared his throat.

"I was obviously mistaken," he said. "I am sorry to have disturbed you. If you'll excuse me, I need to check on the progress of the search." With his hand on the doorknob, he turned. "I will be sure to let you know when we find the Lady Deich."

As soon as he was gone, Eleanor locked the door.

"You can come out now, Zoë."

Even before the trapdoor was completely open, Noor was pushing Zoë aside in her rush to get out.

"What was that all about? " Zoë asked, dusting herself off. "All I could hear was Michaela swearing. What happened?"

Eleanor looked over at Livy and smiled. "It seems your sister has some talents."

"Give me my chain, you ungrateful whelp," Michaela screeched. Livy grudgingly handed it over.

"You stole?" Zoë demanded. "From the Seer? Eleanor, I am so sorry. Livy, apologize. Right now."

"There is no need," Eleanor began.

"There damn so is," Michaela interrupted.

"Hush. Her methods may be suspect, but she certainly saved you," Eleanor said calmly. "Tell them, Livy."

They all looked at the girl, who blushed in the sudden attention.

"You dropped my father's....your chain and pendant. Donncha saw it. I fooled him." Livy said.

Zoë's hand flew to her throat.

"That was careless of you, Zoë," Eleanor said, disapproval in her voice. "Fortunately, your sister was able to switch the pendants. How she did that, I cannot imagine." She winked at Livy. "A little magic, perhaps?"

"My mother said there was no such thing as magic," Livy replied. "But my father," she said with a sly smile, "taught me."

With a pang, Zoë remember Eon An's coin trick. *Jomini taught you.*

"I'm not really good," Livy said. "But I can do some things. Enough to fool that stupid man."

"Confused, perhaps, but not as stupid as you think," Eleanor said. "He had time to take a good look at your pendant. He's suspicious."

Zoë winced. "He knew Jomini. He must have seen him wear it."

"Livy saved us all a most uncomfortable moment," Eleanor agreed. "It would have been difficult to deny Lady Deich's presence if he had the pendant in hand. At the very least, they would have searched the room. As it is, your little subterfuge will buy us some time. But not much. We must get both of you away from the temple tonight. As we planned. Livy, you leave immediately with Chaff."

Livy started for the door. Zoë stopped her. "Thank you," she began. "I am. . . I am most grateful. Father would have been proud of you."

Livy's hug was fierce and unexpected, and although her sister returned it awkwardly, the young girl left with a smile in place of her usual scowl.

"She will be a great responsibility, I think," Eleanor said, returning to her paperwork. "She is impetuous, but very bright. She has great potential."

"If I see one more person with potential," Michaela's disembodied voice harrumphed, "I'm going to hurl. Potential. What's that supposed to mean?" Her head emerged from the smoke wreathing her alcove. "The wind is shifting," she said. "Smell it? It's swinging around to the west. Time for a change."

"Change, Michaela?" Eleanor asked with sudden attention. "Now?"

Michaela yawned. "Everything changes. But no need for worry yet." She lay back against her pillows, grinning. "The wind is shifting. Time doesn't matter. It all changes anyway. So says the prophecy."

"What prophecy?" Zoë asked.

Eleanor hesitated. "The seers recognize thousands of prophecies and innumerable portents. She could be talking about any one of them."

"You know the prophecy as well as I do, Elly," Michaela snapped. "'When in the west a second moon. . . .'"

"What's that about a second moon?" Josepht had come back to life. "What's that you said?"

"It's just nonsense," Eleanor said, curtly. "I could quote you a dozen like it. And they'll interpret it any way that suits them. They always do."

"Don't feel bad, Elly," Michaela consoled. "Not your fault Ard Creggan falls. Yar's an idiot."

"What?" Zoë asked blankly. "Ard Creggan falls?"

"Yes, but not while you're in it, so don't get worked up," Michaela said impatiently. "Tell her, Elly. You never know, it might help."

"I tell you, it's a waste of time." Eleanor paused. "Alright then, but quickly. We must leave soon."

In a quavering voice, Michaela began.

'When in the west a second moon,
makes six a string of pearls,
then nature bends,
and time's erased,
the final reckoning unfurls.'

"What about the moon?" Josepht pressed her. "You said a second moon, and a string of six. Now could those be planets? Or could it mean a comet?"

"Be careful what you read into it," Eleanor cautioned.

"Fine," Michaela said. "Then this prophecy means it's time for me to die."

"Not everything is about you."

"Aha!" Michaela crowed, "So you do know what it means."

Eleanor sniffed. "It's vague."

"It's in the Book of Documents. The Book cannot be wrong," Michaela said defiantly. "The reckoning is coming. Why else would you be here? Why else would you all be here?" Satisfied, she resumed smoking.

"We'll see," was all Eleanor said.

••••

The next few hours were an exhausting blur to Zoë. There were preparations to be made. She was shown a map and made to memorize the caravan's projected route, and the point where they were to rendezvous. Noor would accompany her. A knapsack was packed with enough provisions to last several days.

"She's the only protection I'll need," Zoë said when the Seer offered her the escort of her own archers. Besides, there was no point in involving the Black Pagoda more than necessary.

Finally, well past midnight, it was time to go. Opening the door, Eleanor glanced down the corridor to where one of Donncha's men stood guard. A Pagoda attendant darted from a cross corridor and, as they watched, the guard slowly slid down the wall into an untidy heap. He would awake with memories of pleasant dreams.

"Stay close," Eleanor whispered. "It is very easy to lose your way. And there is a great distance to cover before you are safe."

Down corridors, through so many galleries Zoë lost count, finally down a short passage between walls so close they leaned in to touch overhead, they came to the end of a passage. There was a low opening in the wall before them, so low, Zoë had to stoop. Noor sniffed the darkness inside. The memory of the hiding hole was still too fresh.

"This passage leads to the outside," the Seer whispered. "You will come out far from the temple, and well outside of the Citizens' perimeter guards. Take this lamp, but do not light it until I have closed the wall behind you and you are at the other end of the passage. Follow the blue blaze marks on the walls. They will guide you." She paused as though considering her words carefully.

"I'm sorry, child," Eleanor said. "These are difficult times and what I have to ask could endanger you even more."

"I think it's past time to worry about that," Zoë said ruefully.

Eleanor handed Zoë a lumpy bundle the span of two hands. "This must get to Gurama. Give it to the abbot. He'll know what to do with it."

Zoë pushed the package down inside her knapsack then strapped it to Noor's back. "That's as safe as it can get. What's inside?" she asked.

"It's probably better that you know very little about it. And, tell me truthfully, do you have your mother's ring?

Zoë didn't hesitate. "Yes. Noor brought it out of Ard Creggan. I have it."

Eleanor relief was apparent. "Don't show it to anyone. Keep it safe. Just remember, when the time comes, it will reveal its own truth."

••••

Bending low, Zoë and Noor entered the passage. The wall opening slid shut behind them. Immediately , the cold weight of the Pagoda's walls closed in. Noor whimpered. Zoë's hand scraped the rough-cut rock ceiling overhead, guiding her where her eyes couldn't see. Just when her legs and back were aching past endurance, her hand found the end of the passage roof. She straightened cautiously and lit the lamp. A yellow blossom of light erupted, casting a pool of light no further than her toes. Noor snorted.

"OK, we're going," Zoë, muttered. "Don't push."

What followed was food for an anxiety-stoked nightmare. At times, she was sure they'd lost the way, but couldn't remember any alternate turn they might have taken. Then she would rush ahead, her heart thumping, Noor treading on her heels, until another blue blaze on the wall reassured her they were on track. So it went for what felt like eternity, tripping over the uneven flooring, scraping hands on the rough rock. Noor whuffled anxiously down her neck, pushing her to go faster. Then, at the end of a long passage, the blue markers disappeared. They faced a blank wall. Zoë tried to keep her panic down.

"Okay, we'll have to go back and pick up the last marker, Noor. We must have gone wrong somewhere."

As she spoke the lamp flame flickered and died. The darkness was like a hood over her head. But even as she strained to see, a soft breeze touched her cheek. She turned toward it and moved forward blindly. A wall. Her hands skimmed the surface searching for a lever, a handle, anything to show the way. Noor, frantic now, pushed Zoë from behind. For a moment Zoë felt her nurse's weight flattening her, then the wall gave way! The false wall turned on its pivot and they pitched forward. Overhead a million pinpricks of light blinked in the night sky. They were outside.

They spent that night in a treetop nest Noor constructed. The Saurillia insisted on getting as far off the ground as possible. She smelled Citizens on the air. Besides, she was still muttering about nasty dark places, so nothing would do but to take to the trees.

"This isn't bad," Zoë said testing the branches, but Noor was already snoring. She settled into the curve of her sleeping nurse and looked up into the treetops. A breeze ruffled the leaves, rocking them gently. As exhausted as she felt, sleep would not come. She pulled the chain carrying her father's pendant out from under her shirt and slid the ring onto the chain with it. She sighed.

Noor groaned, "*You are keeping me awake.*"

"Sorry."

"*Do you wish to return?*"

"No."

"*Then you wish to go to Gurama?*"

"I don't know."

Noor opened her eyes. "*You must decide which distresses you most.*"

Zoë continued to stare into the dark.

"*You must decide,*" Noor said matter-of-factly, "*whether you truly believe this Tiernan would kill your father.*"

Zoë glared at her. "Why didn't he tell me? Father was dead and he knew."

"*Why ask me? I thought you knew this Citizen well.*"

"I never said I knew him well," Zoë retorted.

"*I was not the one kissing him.*" Noor growled and turned over.

"I was not kissing him," Zoë snapped. "I wasn't." Tears slid down her cheek.

"*The Seer Eleanor can block her thoughts from me.*"

Zoë wiped her tears and weighed this new piece of information.

"Is that unusual? Are all seers like that?"

Noor stirred. "*I don't know. But she kept even her smallest thoughts from me. I think she did this deliberately.*"

"Is she hiding something?"

Noor growled as though to say this was obvious.

Zoë opened the knapsack and pulled out the bundle Eleanor had given her. The knot securing the bundle bore a glyph, now glowing dully in the moonlight. She hefted the bundle speculatively.

"It's certainly heavier than it looks. Do you suppose we should open it?"

She slid a finger under the seal, exploring its strength even as Noor reared up, making a sound deep in her chest that set Zoë's teeth on edge.

"*Not to open. Not. Not here.*" The Saurillia's anxiety threatened to infect Zoë.

"Noor, be reasonable," she said, feeling the lumps within the packet. "It's not safe to carry something around, if we don't know what it is."

Noor whimpered as Zoë snapped the seal and untied the strings. Excitement tingled in the pit of her stomach. The packet was wrapped, layer upon layer, opening it was like peeling an onion. When the packet's contents were finally revealed, her breath caught. Ten orbs shimmered a dull rainbow in her lap. Noor sniffed them suspiciously. Zoë pushed her away.

"Stop it Noor. They're the Families' keys. I've never seen them all together." A flame within each, burned small and steady. She wanted to touch them. Hold them.

She brushed her hand softly over the spheres.

Without thinking, she touched the ring on its chain. A wave of sounds crashed over her. Singing, her mother, Jomini, Aunt Livia, at her 12th birthday party, Ard Creggan's bells, a school, children's voices, the yap of a puppy she'd had when she was four. More memories. Faster. A woman singing over a cradle. Faster, faster. A funeral dirge, a drum roll, a soldier. A fire. A great fire. Burning. Just as suddenly she was yanked back to the treetop. Noor stood over her growling, the ring in her jaws. Zoë blinked and looked at her empty hand, still dazed.

"What was that?"

"*Memories.*"

"I didn't recognize them. They were like. . . ."

"*Someone else's memories.*"

"Yes."

"*Your family. The Family Deich. Memories of generations.*"

"Could you see them too?"

"*Only what I could sense in your mind. They were not clear.*"

Zoë exhaled. "There was so much coming at me. It was one thing after another." Noor's windy snuffling let her know what she thought of this latest phenomenon.

"Did the orbs do that?"

"*It was the ring.*"

"Don't be silly, Noor. I've worn that ring hundreds of times and that's never happened before." She stopped and looked again at the orbs. "Of course, I've never had all the keys together like this. I doubt anyone has."

Zoë's hand shook as she rewrapped the stones. Only when she'd stuffed them back into the knapsack, out of sight, would Noor relinquish the ring. Zoë lay down and tried to quiet her mind. Her mother. Her father. Aunt Livia. *It was like they were here with me. Alive again.* When she finally slept, she dreamed of Ard Creggan.

The next thing she knew, it was first light.

CHAPTER TWENTY

"Yes, Caleb. What is it?"

The manservant seemed to materialize at Sinon Yar's elbow.

"There's been another disturbance, Basillius Yar. In the northeast quadrant."

Yar continued to watch the crowds milling in the plaza below his tower.

"What this time?"

"A suicide bomber."

"Another one?" He stifled a yawn.

"The second this week, Basillius."

"Have we found who is behind the bombings?"

"No, Basillius. There was nothing that could positively identify the bomber."

"And you've questioned anyone who might have information?"

Silence.

"Well?"

"We questioned several suspects."

Sinon Yar turned from the window to give the man his full attention. The servant took a step backward and averted his gaze.

"It is unlike you to be evasive, Caleb. I admit I'm curious. What did you find out?"

"Unfortunately, Basillius, the detainees were. . . unresponsive." The man cringed as the temperature of the room dropped several degrees. Yet Sinon Yar's voice was silky.

"Unresponsive? That was careless of you Caleb. I thought I had taught you better. Or perhaps you've failed to maintain the proper detachment. Are you becoming too involved in your work? Perhaps you need a reminder."

Caleb flinched and took a step backward, but at that moment the door flew open and the Counselor swept in followed by Sinon Yar's bodyguards, who seemed to be at a loss how to stop him. Yar barely glanced in his direction, his attention still on Caleb.

"I demand to know what you're going to do about this latest outrage," the Counselor began. His usually sallow cheeks glowed pink.

"Outrage, Counselor?" Yar flung back at him. "Are you referring to yesterday's sabotage in our metallurgy factory? Or the looting of our armory last week? Or perhaps you mean the bomb that went off outside the military barracks last night? And Caleb tells me there was a suicide bomber just this morning. So which outrage, Counselor? Please, be specific."

"We live in unsettled times, Basillius," the Counselor replied soothingly, for the first time giving him the self-conferred title. "Ard Creggan is not the place we once knew."

Yar stared coldly at the Counselor. "I assume you mean it has improved?"

"Of course," the Counselor replied without hesitation.

Sinon Yar turned back to the window. "Perhaps you might shed some light on the activities of the saboteurs. Perhaps tell me how they appear at will anywhere in my city, move about without anyone seeing them, how they know our plans as soon as we do."

The Counselor stiffened. "If you are insinuating I know anything about these

terrorists . . . ."

Yar smiled without humor. "There's not much you don't know, Counselor."

198

"Let me assure you then. . . ."

"Your assurances are unnecessary." Yar was rapidly losing interest. "I will, of course, give the looting the attention it deserves. Thank you for bringing it to my attention."

"There is another matter."

"And what would that be?" Yar replied with exaggerated politeness.

"Let me be frank," the Counselor began, eyeing Yar warily. "The people are leaving Ard Creggan. Not that it is any reflection on you, Basillius," he hurried to add as Sinon Yar's expression hardened. "So many have lost homes in the tremors, and they believe the city is unstable. I'm sure they are moving to the camps beyond the rim only until the tremors subside."

"I am aware of the rumors. To demonstrate there is no danger, I have persuaded the heads of the Ten Families to remain in Ard Creggan."

"I am impressed. I would not have thought it possible to keep the Families here."

Almost, Yar smirked. "They were easily convinced after I made it clear any Family head leaving the city forfeits all claims to the ore." A pause. "Were you thinking of leaving Ard Creggan, too, Counselor?"

"It may become necessary for me to see to certain matters." He looked pointedly at Yar's manservant.

"Caleb," Yar ordered. "Give us a few moments alone." When the door closed behind him, Yar swung back to the Counselor. "What have you learned?"

"Only that the soletei traveling with Lady Deich has been apprehended and is now in custody in Bellery."

"You were able to convince the Tribune to take action, I see. You have a very long reach, Counselor."

"I have a little influence, Basillius. And they were anxious to show their regard for Ard Creggan's new leader."

Yar glowered. "And the girl?"

"She has yet to be found."

"Then why are you wasting my time?" Yar snarled. "She must be returned to Ard Creggan and soon. Must I remind you of the prophecy?"

The Counselor bowed slightly. "Calm yourself, Basillius. There is every reason to believe she is somewhere in the vicinity of Bellery. I have people watching for her. She will be found." He watched Yar's expression closely. In another man, the look on Sinon Yar's face might have been fury; the Counselor knew it was fear.

"The prophecy says, 'the daughter's will'. She is that part of the prophecy and without her Ard Creggan will fall. I must not fall."

"Yes, Basillius, I understand. She will be returned." The Counselor's side-ways look at Sinon Yar was calculating, cautious. "You should rest, Basillius. You need all your strength in these difficult times."

Yar picked up a ceramic paperweight and crushed it into powder between his hands. He turned back to the window. "Send my man in to me when you leave, Counselor. And see that you bring me the news I want to hear. Soon."

When Caleb returned moments later, Yar was still by the window.

"Is he gone?"

"Yes, Basillius."

"Find out what our Counselor is up to. He isn't being completely open with me. And I am suspicious of his sources. For one so habituated to Ard Creggan, he has a remarkable reach. I trust you can ferret out the details."

"I will do my best, Basillius. Will there be anything else?"

Sinon Yar returned to stare out the window. Below in the plaza, a long line of supplicants waited.

"You know, Caleb, I thought being dictator for life would be more enjoyable."

"Yes, Basillius. There is an execution scheduled this afternoon," he added.

Sinon Yar looked hopeful. "Maybe that will lift my spirits. In the meantime let my wife know I expect her to join me for dinner tonight."

"The Lady Maigra is not in her chambers."

"Did you check the compound?"

"She is not in the compound."

"Now that's interesting. I wonder where my elusive bride has gone? Well, I'm sure she'll turn up. More time for me to catch up on my work. Who's next in line, Caleb?"

His manservant consulted a list. "Representatives of the ClearWorlders."

Yar looked faintly puzzled. "I thought I'd outlawed them."

"Yes, Basillius, you outlawed the political arm. This is the charitable works division."

"Is there a difference?"

Caleb's expression was impassive. "Their soup kitchens feed a great number of the homeless."

"They ladle out sedition with their soup. What do they want?"

"To distribute medical supplies to the rim camps."

Yar glowered. "You mean to the cowards who left. No, if the people in the camps need medical attention, let them to return to Ard Creggan. Next?"

"The head of the Family Cheithre."

"Burgess Cheithre? No, I remember, he is dead. I killed him myself. Who was next in line?"

"An uncle, Basillius. Quite old. In his nineties, I believe. The rest of the family left him behind when they moved to the rim camps."

"Leaving him the sole representative of the Family Cheithre. That was clever of them. And what does he want?"

"He would like to bury his nephew—outside the walls of Ard Creggan."

Yar's laugh rattled the windows. "I bet he would. The old fox. Well, tell him he has a choice. He can bury his nephew outside the walls of Ard Creggan and forfeit the family rights to the ore. Or he can bury him here in the city, keep his ore rights, and I'll deliver the eulogy myself." Yar yawned. "Tell the rest of the petitioners to come back after the execution. That might help them focus their requests."

"Yes, Basillius."

"And Caleb?"

"Yes, Basillius?"

"No more mistakes with the interrogations. Hasty steps delay the race. I dislike sloppy work and I would hate to lose you."

Caleb bowed. "No, Basillius."

••••

Samuel refolded his map, slipping it back into his jacket. He depressed a stone and a gap opened in the rough tunnel wall. He emerged into the courtyard of a deserted compound. Around him, the house windows were dark, except where bits of glass still clung to the frames, throwing back the light of a moon scuttling between clouds. He knew this house. Or what was left of it. The great central hall of the Deich compound lay around him in ruins, its six stories of alabaster columns cracked, its stairways drunkenly askew. The skeleton of a massive chandelier dangled from the center, its twin already lying in shards in the courtyard. Underfoot, fallen crystals glinted.

After the damp of the tunnels, even Ard Creggan's night air was sweet. But tonight there was a hint of perfume. "Maigra?" he whispered.

A shade detached itself from the deep shadows of the ruins that were once the Deich compound.

"How do you do that?"

He smiled. "I could find you in the dark."

An unladylike snort. "Not that you would." Maigra walked to the center of the courtyard and he thought, not for the first time, that she was an exceptionally beautiful woman.

"Now that's not fair. I've been busy," he protested.

"Yes, I've heard. Two warehouses this week alone. Sinon Yar wants to hang you all."

"I'm glad to hear we are having an effect."

"An effect? You're becoming an obsession." She laughed softly. Samuel liked the sound.

"When is the next sweep scheduled?"

"Tomorrow. Early morning. From the People's Square south through the Naoi Family compound."

"That's good. We'll be on the other side of the city when they sweep. Will Sinon Yar be with them?"

Maigra hesitation wasn't lost on him.

"Don't tell me you're feeling like the loyal wife," he teased.

Even in the moonlight, he could see her face change.

"I give you the information you need, Samuel. If he knew I was spying for you, he'd kill me." As he took her into his arms, she stiffened.

She's frightened, he thought. *Maigra is never frightened.*

CHAPTER TWENTY-ONE

Donncha pursued the Lady Deich. Citizen militia stopped and searched Chaff's caravan more than once. Fortunately, Noor sensed when the soldiers were near and swept Zoë up into the trees to hide until the searchers were satisfied and moved on. But that was just aggravating. Once they left the forest, they needed a better plan. And the plan, as Zoë presented it to Chaff, was to hide in plain sight—as a troupe of entertainers. It gave them the excuse they needed to travel through Citizen territory. No one would suspect a caravan of performers. Bergerac took some convincing; he didn't like touring. So the caravan became a traveling sideshow. Before they knew it, performers were joining them at nearly every town. Within weeks, they had a fire-eater, a contortionist, and a troupe of performing dogs, along with Chaff's juggling act. Zoë, or rather Esme, the Telepath, the headline act. It was all very theatrical. The curtain came up on a dark stage, with a single spot of light illuminating Zoë, who sat blindfolded—a blindfold that conveniently masked her identity. Noor sat in the wings, keeping her eyes open, and easily giving Zoë answers to questions offered by the audience.

When they weren't traveling between towns, mornings were generally given over to rehearsals and auditions. Zoë was continually amazed at how much hard work went into the light entertainment their little troupe provided. Auditioning local talent was one chore Zoë grudgingly undertook, with Chaff and Bergerac as her fellow judges. This morning, there was first a ventriloquist followed by a puppeteer. The ventriloquist had an unfortunate lisp; the puppeteer was amazingly clumsy.

"Anyone else, Chaff?" Zoë felt a headache gathering behind her eyes. "One more? Are they ready?"

The lights dimmed again to a spot at center stage. A pair of white gloves floated into the light, followed by a ghostly long-beaked bird, a mask.

"Clever," Zoë whispered. Just key lighting and a black costume, but effective. They could use a good Illusionist.

A plaintive piping accompanied a simple rope trick, followed by a covey of levitating cards and the unexpected appearance of a brilliant bouquet of flowers from a book. Easy enough tricks, fairly commonplace actually, but all imbued with a spectral air by the fantastical bird floating in the darkness. The lights narrowed to pins, picking out the disembodied hands cradling an ornate gilt box. The lid opened. The sulfur crest of a cockatoo erupted from the interior followed by a flutter of white wings. Before the bird could escape, the lid came down again. Once, twice, the hands dipped. On three, the box flew up in the air. The hands caught the box in its descent, twirled it around, tapped on the lid once, and flipped it open. Nothing.

The bird has flown.

"This one could be our headliner," Zoë whispered to Chaff, applauding. "The Great Esme has competition." As the lights came up, she walked down to the edge of the stage. The Illusionist was center stage, looking surprisingly small. The bird mask was disturbing even in the dim light.

"If you're interested, I think we could use your act. You earn a percentage of the gate, depending on how many shows you do, and we supply meals. What do you say?"

The glittering eyes in the mask reminded Zoë of the cockatoo's beady eyes. The Illusionist bowed formally and without a word marched off stage.

"Well, I'll take that as a yes," Zoë muttered.

She followed Chaff and Bergerac to find some lunch.

Maybe that's just carnival people. But those eyes. This Illusionist was a puzzle.

The tables in the kitchen tent were already crowded, a tangle of voices rising over the dishes. The food had improved as they moved out of the war-ravaged sections of the country. After weeks of potatoes and cabbage, and very little of those—despite Chaff's genius at finding food in the most unlikely places—they were enjoying an abundance. Bergerac hopped up beside her on the bench and offered a small covered basket. She opened the lid and smiled.

"They look delicious, Bergerac. She'll love them."

Livy entered the tent looking around for a seat. Bergerac scampered off with the basket as Zoë waved her over. She was flushed and out of breath.

"I'm just grabbing something quick. I promised to help Chaff this afternoon. Did you audition acts this morning?"

Zoë winced, guilty. "I'm sorry, did you want to sit in?"

Livy snagged a sandwich from a passing tray and squeezed in on the bench across from Zoë.

"No, I mean, I was thinking of an act, maybe."

"You want to perform?" Zoë didn't bother to hide her disapproval. "You know how I feel about performing in public."

"You do it." Livy's face turned sullen.

"Yes, but that doesn't mean I want you doing it. Aunt Livia would be furious if she knew either of us were performing. The Deich family doesn't entertain common people."

Livy put down her half-eaten sandwich. "But I'm not a Deich. Not really. So she couldn't say anything. Besides," she said, her eyes downcast, "she's dead."

Zoë ignored the last remark. "Your father was Jomini Deich. That makes you a Deich. We have standards."

Livy muttered something so low, Zoë couldn't catch it.

"What?"

"I said, you don't believe I'm a Deich," Livy repeated, just loud enough for her to hear.

"And you're talking nonsense," Zoë snapped. The girl's directness was disconcerting, especially when she hit so close to the truth. "You'd better get going. I'll see you tonight after the performance."

Livy was up, her lunch unfinished.

"Tonight." She hesitated. "Listen, Chaff may have found a wagon for me."

Zoë felt a twinge.

"I thought you liked living with Noor and me?"

Livy looked away. "It would be more room. I've got to go now."

"See you later?"

Livy nodded and dashed out.

••••

From Donncha's perch on the back bench in the uppermost gallery of the courtroom, he could only see the back of Tiernan's head as he sat at the defendant's table, and it was difficult to hear the responses of the witnesses called to testify. None of that bothered him. Most of the testimony was scripted and well rehearsed—and distributed in news sheets prior to each day of the trial. He'd even bought a few, at first. They helped him identify the people called to give information against the soletei, none of whom he recognized. Which was disconcerting because so many claimed to be Tiernan's comrades in Donncha's own company. *My memory must be failing me*, he thought, because there was only one other plausible explanation.

Weeks ago, he had received orders from the Tribune to abandon his search for the fugitive Lady Deich and report to offer his testimony at the trial of the Soletei Tiernan. He dutifully obeyed. His heart hadn't really been in the hunt anyway.

The lawyer appointed to represent Tiernan was a young man he'd seen only once before—on the Tribune staff. He asked Donncha a series of questions about his relationship with Tiernan, the soletei's mental state, and about anyone he may have contacted in Ard Creggan. But when he asked how long Tiernan had been spying for the Publicans, Donncha prepared himself for the worst. He wasn't disappointed.

"So Soletei Tiernan was frequently absent for long periods of time from the company while you were in Publican territory?

"How many times did he miss mandatory political education classes? You are saying you are uncertain of his politics?

"When did you first suspect his loyalties were with the Publicans?"

When he stepped down, Donncha knew that he had done more harm than good. Tiernan smiled at him, as though he understood. The testimony was drummed up, the witnesses suspect. The evidence mounted daily that Soletei Tiernan was a traitor. Even Tiernan's attorney took pains to distance himself from his client, telling the court, in his summing up, that he had taken the case on orders from the Tribune and against his better judgment. The jury began its deliberations. It didn't take a seer to predict the verdict.

"Captain?"

Donncha roused from his abstraction to greet Brian. He'd also been at the trial every day, sitting behind Tiernan, sometimes leaning forward to whisper to his friend, or pat his shoulder.

"Can we talk somewhere, Captain?"

They left the courthouse together, Donncha leaning heavily on his cane, ignoring Brian's offer of an arm. They walked to the park next door and a bench far from eavesdroppers.

"You've been a good friend to Tiernan. He must appreciate your loyalty," Donncha began, settling himself. It was a lovely afternoon, the sun was hot but a cool breeze was blowing that smelled of the sea.

Brian remained standing, glancing nervously at passersby who ventured too close.

"I don't believe the charges, nor do you. Everyone knows the Tribune is behind this. It's all just a witch hunt."

"You should be careful what you say, Brian," Donncha cautioned him mildly.

Brian shook his head. "They're not interested in me. But if Tiernan isn't careful he's going to hang." He sat down, leaning close to Donncha. "He could save himself."

"I think he sees the futility in any defense. It does appear to be a preordained verdict."

"But it doesn't have to be," Brian said impatiently. "Tiernan knows something that could be useful to the Tribune. Something that might change their minds, or at least win him some leniency."

"Then why doesn't he use this knowledge?" Donncha asked. "He certainly knows what will happen if they find him guilty."

"He doesn't care," Brian cried. "That's why I thought you could talk to him. Convince him."

"I take it you've tried?"

"Yes. But he won't listen to me. He might listen to you." He was back on his feet, shifting nervously from one foot to the other. "Just tell me you'll try, Captain. Talk to him. Before it's too late."

Donncha looked out over the park. On the far side was the stone wall of the Bellery's jail. From here, he could just see the top of the gallows they'd constructed to execute other soletei, those who hadn't had the dubious benefit of a trial.

"Tell me," he asked. "What does Tiernan know that would be so important the Tribune would be willing to take its collective boot off his neck?"

Ay the soldier's hesitation, Donncha sighed.

"Well, if you don't trust me, there's little point in involving myself."

"No, no, that's not it. It's just that. . . ." Brian seemed to be struggling with some decision. "Tiernan has the key to everything we need to know about Ard Creggan, its mining operations, the smelting process, the casting of the big guns. Everything."

"That is considerable information," Donncha agreed cautiously, "and quite valuable in the right hands. If we were able to manufacture long range guns like those in Ard Creggan, we could force Publicans to accept any terms we chose. Tell, me who did Tiernan get this information from?"

"From Jomini Lord Deich," Brian replied.

This bit of information seemed to impress Donncha.

"Ah, Lord Deich. Yes, he would be in a position to know." He paused. "But tell me, how do you know this? Lord Deich was never in Ard Creggan while we were there for the negotiations. Who is your source? Certainly not Tiernan."

"No. Not Tiernan," Brian said, looking like a mischievous boy. "Let's say that I made a new friend while I was in the city. A well-placed friend who would like to help Citizens."

"The Tribune would indeed spare the life of anyone—even an accused traitor like Tiernan—who could deliver Ard Creggan technology," Donncha said thoughtfully.

Brian grinned. "Ironic isn't it? The same Tribune that is trying to wipe-out technology in Citizen society, still wants what the Publicans know—as long as we can use it to destroy Ard Creggan."

Donncha weighed his next words carefully. "I agree. But I confess I'm still puzzled by Tiernan's reluctance to speak. This calls his allegiance into grave doubt."

"Tiernan is no traitor. He has too many principles. It's a real handicap for him."

"But if he has information that could help us . . . ."

There was a commotion at the courthouse. People were streaming up the steps. "The jury must be back," Brian muttered. "If he doesn't speak, he hangs. It's as simple as that." He looked down at Donncha. "Make him talk, Captain. Find out what Jomini Deich told him."

••••

That night, after the last performance, the wagon was more cramped than usual. Bergerac was hanging from the ceiling, trailing paper streamers across its length, while Zoë tried to make room for more chairs around the table. Chaff delivered a cake, then disappeared again with Bergerac to find more glasses. Zoë settled down to remove her stage makeup as Noor climbed up into her bunk at the far end of the wagon.

"*You've seen something.*" It wasn't a question.

Zoë continued to scrub her face. "I need to get ready, Noor. Livy will be here any moment."

Noor scratched herself thoughtfully. "*The child can wait. You've seen something that disturbs you.*"

Zoë scowled at her reflection in the mirror. "It's Livy's birthday. Let's not fight."

"*You should not use them, those orbs. They are bad.*"

"It's not bad to remember the past."

Noor huffed softly. "*It is not the past that's bad. It is that you are beginning to prefer it to the present. And now you have seen something that frightens you.*"

The first few times she looked into the Ard Creggan keys, there was a blur of faces, figures, a whiff of scent, flashes of light and sound. By concentrating, she learned to slow the sluice of images to a viewable speed, or to jump forward to a moment. Now, she could nearly always dive into the past and extract specific memories at will.

All the keys were accessible, to a degree. The Deich key, her own family's orb, was the most yielding, almost as if it recognized her. Unsurprisingly, the Shockat and Huckat orbs made her physically ill. What she saw of the past convinced her that Leig Huckat and Curnan Shockat were simply the last in a long line of miscreants. Discovering that one of her own long dead relatives had married into the Family Shockat was a seriously disquieting moment. But the last time she opened the keys, she had reached back as far as she could. And the tip of something cold, something malevolent, brushed by her in the darkness of the past.

"It's not so much what I saw. It was a feeling." She shivered. "I can't explain it."

"*What did you see before this feeling? Go there now. Let me see.*"

Unwillingly, Zoë threw her mind back. The memory was still fresh of that other black thing.

"*You don't need the ring, the key?*" Noor asked doubtfully.

"Sometimes. But not for the past I've already seen," Zoë murmured. "It leaves an impression." She mentally rifled through the memories, selecting the correct path and plunging down. "It was at the beginning. Back before the Families even."

"But that is not possible," Noor objected. *"The keys are the Families."*

The wagon interior was receding. She was falling softly through a miasma of sights and sounds, faces and voices spinning by. She was back at the beginning.

It was Ard Creggan, in shadow, before the mining, before the land had been stripped back in the hunt for ore. A clutch of thatched roofs huddled on a windswept plateau. Overhead, thunderheads piled up in a black mass, blotting out the light of day, sending a cold blast of air tearing at her clothes. Her fingertips tingled, like touching cold metal. A darkness crept up her wrist, pulling at her arm. She struggled against it, like a swimmer keeping her head above on-coming waves. She turned and looked into a face.

A warmth enveloped her and she was back in the caravan, Noor's massive paw on her chest, her black eyes looking into hers. Only when the blue had left Zoë's lips did Noor turn and clamber back up into her bed.

"You felt it?" Zoë asked, breathing hard.

"I felt you slipping away. If you had stayed longer, you might have died. The keys are dangerous. You should not use them."

Zoë paid no attention. "I can control them. At least tell me you saw the face?"

"Yes."

"It was the Counselor?"

"Yes."

"At the beginning," Zoë said. "And that coldness." She shivered, wondering.

"You are not the same," Noor repeated. *"You should stop."*

Zoë didn't respond. She needed a good memory to wash away the cold remnants. The sound of wind chimes.

"Zoë, stop wiggling. The hem will be all over the place."

She was eight. In the family's rooms, standing on a hassock, her mother kneeling in front of her, pins in her mouth, hemming her dress.

"I hate dresses."

Her mother put in the last pin and sat back on her heels to survey her work.

"You look very pretty."

"I look awful," the little girl pouted. "Everyone is going laugh at me."

Her mother looked up, amused.

"No, they won't. You know, you look just like I did at your age. Except I had braids."

She rose and kissed Zoë's cheek. "And I think you'll be prettier, too, when you grow up."

Zoë put her arms around her mother. "You smell like roses, Mama."

A knock on the door and she was back in the wagon. It was Chaff and Bergerac returning with the glassware.

"The child is coming."

Zoë darted over to extinguish the lantern. A step on the wagon ladder. In the narrow doorway there was Livy's silhouette against the caravan lights.

"Happy birthday!"

Zoë was nearly drowned out by Bergerac's screams and Chaff pounding on a tin pan. Even Noor rumbled. Then the cake, ablaze with candles, was produced and Livy hugged them all over and over. Zoë was glad they'd made a fuss.

Toasts were offered, cake was consumed. Chaff and Bergerac presented the birthday girl with a basket of strawberries, her favorite. Noor had made her a dress, which Zoë realized with a pang, made her look five years older and quite grown up. Finally, after multiple toasts were offered, several ridiculous games proposed and played, the party wound down. Chaff and Bergerac went off to their wagon, and Noor settled down in her bunk for the night. Zoë and Livy were left at the table, too full and contented to move.

"I bet you thought I wouldn't find out," Zoë teased.

The color drained from Livy's face.

Zoë reassured her. "Oh, don't worry. Noor told me. I'm glad she did. We couldn't miss your birthday."

Livy's face fell. "My birthday. Oh, I thought. . . ."

"So I didn't know what you'd like for your birthday," Zoë continued, so I decided to leave it up to you."

Her sister looked down at the table, playing with a fork. "Anything?"

"Sure," Zoe said, with a laugh. "Anything."

"Tell me about my father," Livy asked. "I didn't see much of him. I'd like to see what he was like when he was. . . .I mean."

Zoë's heart sank. It hadn't occurred to her that Livy would want to know about Jomini's life in Ard Creggan. She was conscious that a part of her wanted to keep that past her own. Still, Livy was Jomini's daughter, too. She took the Deich key from her pocket.

"I'll show you."

The orb twinkled on her open palm.

"It's called the Deich key. Each of the Ten Families has one. This is mine. . . our family's. Now, you'll have to trust me on this. Let yourself take in the images. They won't hurt you. And I'll be right here. Close your eyes, and try to clear your mind."

Zoë' covered Livy's hand with her own, then touched the ring hanging from a cord around her neck.

"Now, let's see if I can find it. I was about your age."

They were in the south hall of the Deich compound. The heads of all the Families, the entire Concordia, were gathered around the massive table. At the head of the table stood Jomini. Beside him, Eon An.

". . .presenting the gavel to you, Jomini, head of the Family Deich, a vote duly taken, selecting you as First Minister of the Concordia and of our city, Ard Creggan."

Zoë remembered this moment. Once again, there was the rush of love and pride she'd felt for her father. He was so handsome in the formal robes of his investiture. The Concordia was famous for its pomp and ceremony. Livy would be impressed to see Jomini like this. The applause was dying down; Jomini looked around; he smiled at his wife and daughter. Without warning, a rush of images.

What is happening? Her heart pounded. It was dark, the dark of a windowless room. She felt an indescribable sadness; her heart ached. She was weeping, tears running down her face. There was no will to even wipe them away. She recognized the figured carpet, the dark wood cabinets lining the walls with all the books. It was her father's study. A tap at the door and a voice. The sound of the voice only increased the pain. Zoë recognized that voice. It was her own.

They were back in the wagon.

"Why did it stop?" Livy shook Zoë's arm. "Make it work again."

Zoë slipped the Deich key back into her pocket, ignoring the pleading in Livy's eyes.

"That's enough for tonight," she said.

She felt drained, surprised by the unexpected shift in the key, unsettled by the raw emotion of the memory. But it was like a jolt of energy had hit Livy.

"What's the Concordia? And who was that little man with my father? Were you there?" She was full of questions.

"No more, Livy, please." Zoë pushed back from the table and stood, uncertainly. "I'm not feeling very well."

"Then let me try. I can do it."

"What makes you think you can?" Zoë asked, irritated. "You can't just wander around."

"But it's easy to direct it." Livy looked up, her eyes pleading. "Please, I want to see more."

"What do you mean? Did you direct it?"

Livy looked puzzled, as though it was obvious. "I just told it what I wanted to see," she said.

Zoë closed her eyes against a growing headache. "What did you want to see, Livy?"

"I wanted to see my father," she said, her lip beginning to quiver, her eyes filling with tears. "I wanted to see Jomini when he heard my mother was dead."

CHAPTER TWENTY-TWO

"What's my name?" shouted someone in the audience. After weeks of travel, the caravan had finally reached the outskirts of Bellery. In a park outside town, the caravan was entertaining the local populace with two shows daily. The Great Esme groaned inwardly at the question. There was always one.

"It's Tipset. But your brother always called you Tipset Topsal."

The audience roared. In Citizen slang, a tipset topsal was a clumsy drunk. The man shook his head in wonder and sat down, saying, "And him dead these 10 years."

Esme raised her voice.

"I believe the mayor of Bellery is with us tonight."

A dapper little man stood in the back.

"Mr. Mayor, you have a number of objects in your left pocket. Please, if you don't mind, I will tell you what they are."

To the crowd's delight, she described the contents of his pocket, right down to a stray shirt button.

"However," the Mayor objected, as the applause died away, "to be perfectly correct you've forgotten one thing."

Noor growled as the Great Esme regrouped to commune with the spirits.

"Yes. The spirits were reluctant to show me this item. Taking, shall we say, prophylactic precautions?"

The mayor seemed satisfied. He sat down amid general hooting and catcalls.

Later, in their wagon, Zoë scolded her nursemaid.

"Quit editing what you think I should know. You'll get us into trouble."

Noor climbed up into her bunk as Zoë stowed her costume, then started a fire in the little potbellied stove. In a moment, the wagon would be toasty. She put the kettle on.

"There are some things you should not know, even though, obviously, you do," Noor replied. *"And it puzzles me how you learn these things. I certainly never taught you. I suppose I must blame Aka. I suspect him of having many strange ideas. I believe he reads too much.*

It is also puzzling," the Saurillia continued, *"that this Mayor has a wife and also a woman called Naomi he has visited every Wednesday night for 20 years. They dance to old music together. And strangely enough his wife knows nothing about this other woman."*

"Now that's interesting," Zoë said, as she began to remove her stage make-up. "We might be able to use that. When is he coming?"

"Tonight. Soon."

The kettle was whistling. She filled a teapot and set out cups.

"Does the Mayor drink his tea black, Noor? Oh, it doesn't matter, we're out of milk anyway."

There was a knock and Chaff poked his head around the door.

"You have a visitor, Esme," he said and winked.

She took the hint, pulling the curtains across the bed where Noor was dozing, and turning the lamplight down to a dim glow. The door opened again to reveal the Mayor, hat in hand.

"Please pardon this intrusion, Miss er. . .Esme." The mayor bowed politely and mounted the few steps into the caravan. Zoë motioned him to a bench beside the stove.

"I'm happy to see you," she said politely. "Please have a seat. I hope you enjoyed the show."

Zoë wondered if this was a preliminary to being run out of town, not an uncommon occurrence in the world of traveling circuses and sideshows. The Mayor sat down with the air of a man whose mind was preoccupied.

"Yes, very nice. How did you know I took my tea black? Well, dear me, that's your line of business, isn't it. But let me come right to the point. I wonder if you might be in a position to give me some assistance?"

Esme waved a languid hand.

"I do not normally give private readings. There is so little point in reading someone's mind for them."

"The doctors might quibble with you," the Mayor demurred, "but I take your point. No, my request is related to official business. My name is Pieton and I have been mayor of Bellery for the last 20 years. Before that, I was the town judge for 15 years. But of course, you must know that," he continued, "because of your very remarkable abilities. I confess I attended your performance this evening to evaluate your skills. I was very impressed."

"You are here on official business." Zoë said, stalling. With her own exquisite timing, Noor was apparently napping.

"Official, yes and no."

A precise man, he searched for the right words. "In my experience, reading minds falls somewhere between levitation and religious statues that bleed. Even so, I hope you will consent to help me. You see, I have a man in custody. There has been an official prosecution of this man."

He stopped and his smile was sardonic.

"There's that word again, official. It keeps cropping up. You see, that's my problem. Everything about his prosecution has been very official. Very correct. The inquiry, the examination, the trial, the verdict and sentence were done exactly right."

"I can tell you are a man who values exactness, Mayor Pieton."

"I do. I value it a great deal. And in all my experience, this is the first occasion where everything went exactly right. Not a thing out of place. Textbook from start to finish. But you see," he leaned forward, "real life prosecutions aren't like that. Something or other unexpected will always come up. A good prosecutor plans for it. An experienced judge expects it."

"So much perfection troubles you?"

"Let me make myself clear. The Tribune has been meticulous in performing its duty over the last several weeks. They have held the fris, examined the evidence and found the soletei guilty."

"The soletei?" Zoë's voice broke, but if Pieton noticed, he didn't give a sign.

"Why the Tribune chose to prosecute this man, I don't know. And I don't care. They have their reasons. And they are welcome to purge any number of their own. But I dislike seeing my courts used to put an official seal on murder."

He stopped and collected himself.

"I apologize. I am not being very clear. I would like you to apply your skills to a question. One that has bothered me. The defendant didn't speak a word throughout the entire trial. He refused to cooperate with his attorney. Now, in itself, that's not unusual for soletei. They're a stubborn, close-mouthed group. I don't like them. But I have never willingly executed an innocent man."

"You say he was found guilty?" Zoe mind raced. *Tiernan . Execution?*

" I can arrange for a pass and you may interview the prisoner, alone," the Mayor said.

"You would do me a great favor if you would. I have tried to find out the real reason is for his prosecution. Why he is so determined to cooperate in his own death." He smiled slightly. "You see, I need to know for certain. I need you to tell me what is in this soldier's mind."

A wave of relief flooding through her. She'd see Tiernan. *I'll find a way to save him. I know I can.* Pieton cleared his throat. He was at the door, waiting.

"Oh, I'm sorry, Mayor. What?"

"I said, I must ask you to interview him immediately. Tonight."

"Tonight? Why?"

"Why, I thought you knew," he replied. "He will be executed tomorrow morning."

••••

"Noor help me. No, go get Chaff."

The door had no sooner closed on the Mayor, then Zoë was tearing around the caravan, trying to stuff everything she could lay her hands on in a bag. Noor rolled over and opened one eye.

"Noor!" Zoë screeched. "Get moving."

Noor opened the other eye.

"Where do you think we will go?"

Zoë cleared her dressing table in one sweep.

"To Gurama. Where's Chaff?"

"You are making too much noise," Noor grumbled. *"And Chaff is right behind you."*

Zoë turned around so quickly, she nearly fell over him.

"Chaff. Is the ship ready? We need to sail to Gurama as soon as possible."

Noor interrupted from her alcove.

"To change our departure now will raise suspicions. You will ruin everything."

Chaff's shrug indicated his indifference. "Tomorrow morning or the next. The captain is not paid to be particular."

"All this fuss just to rescue your soletei," Noor continued placidly.

"If I'm ever going to find out what happened to my father," Zoë said flatly. "I have to talk with Tiernan . I'm not saying we're going to rescue him."

Chaff's eyes widened.

"I can see what's in your heart, little one. Even if you can't. You will try to free him if you can. You will ruin everything."

"You don't know anything."

Noor slowly rose to her full height. Chaff wisely backed out the door as the Saurillia and Zoë locked eyes. The human's eyes dropped first.

"I make allowances because you're human and don't understand things very well," Noor growled. *"But even you cannot be this reckless."*

"Then you tell me what happened to my father."

"I can't see into that one's mind. He's not as open as the others. But one thing even he cannot hide. He loved Jomini."

"So, knowing that, do you think I should leave him to die? I'll never know the truth if he's dead." Zoë drew a deep breath. "Are you going to help me?"

Noor sank to her haunches with an audible groan. *"You will think of something on your own. You have the pass from the Mayor. That will be your entry. How you get out with him may take further planning . . . or luck."*

"Great. I can't believe I'm breaking people out of jail now. Well, get Chaff back in here. And Bergerac, too. You go to the ship with Chaff and wait for me. We will probably need to leave in a hurry."

All the time, Zoë had been collecting clothes from around the caravan, packing haphazardly. Now, pulling a chest out from under her bed, she flipped open the lid and dug into its depths, methodically at first, then frantically pawing through a riot of clothes and costumes. Finally, she rocked back on her heels.

"They're gone." She stared open-mouthed at the chest for a dull minute.

The Saurillia was silent. Zoë rounded on her.

"You know something, Noor. Where are the keys?"

"It was to be expected. She's just a child."

"Livy." Zoë fumed. "It's my own fault. I should never have shown her the Deich key. It was a mistake."

"She asked you many times to show her the memories. You refused."

"Yes, because I was wrong to show her the first time."

Noor snorted.

"You said yourself the keys were bad," Zoë reminded her nursemaid, even though saying it made her feel like a hypocrite. "I was just trying to protect her," she finished lamely.

Noor still didn't respond. But her black eyes were reproachful.

Zoë turned back to the chest. "Why am I worried? I mean, how far can she get? She doesn't have any money."

In the mound of clothes in the chest, a bit of white, a curve, caught her eye. She tugged it free. A white bird mask. Among the thoughts and emotions rushing through her mind, this latest revelation just managed to register. She waved the mask at Noor.

"Livy is the magician? The Illusionist? She's been working the show all this time? Were you going to tell me, or was this a little secret between the two of you? "

"You should not blame her. She wanted to be part. She wants to be part of your life."

"What part? My family? My father? She even has you wrapped around her little finger. She a lying little thief."

"She is your sister."

"She is not my real sister." Zoë spat out each word like separate hard things.

"She is your father's daughter. That cannot be changed."

"Why not? For all I know, my father has children all over the country."

Noor's low growl cut her off.

"You only have each other now. You must trust her."

"Trust her?" Zoë shot back angrily. "She stole the keys."

"You don't care about the keys. Only about the Deich key. You let a thing mean more to you than your own blood. I am glad it is gone."

"Yeah, well I'm going to get it back." Zoë stopped, suddenly aware of a problem. "I can't. Tiernan. I can't go."

Noor's thoughts came through clearly, but Zoë blocked them.

"You have to go after her, Noor. You must know where she is."

"Yes, I know."

"Then you find her and the keys. We need all of them on board the ship before we sail. That's dawn tomorrow."

"And bring her back?"

Zoë hesitated.

222

"If she wants to come back, bring her. I don't care," she said coldly and turned back to her packing. "But I need the key."

Zoë heard Noor leave without a word. Chaff returned to the suddenly empty caravan, Bergerac on his shoulder. It was time to make plans and no time to think of Noor or Livy.

Shortly before midnight, she slipped on the cape the Great Esme wore for her performances. Its volume would have hidden an arsenal if she'd been planning to assault the jail, but she had a different deliverance in mind.

"Come on, Bergerac. I'll need you with me tonight. Don't worry," she stroked the monkey's head as he climbed to her shoulder. "With luck, we'll be on our way to Gurama in a few hours. And if not, we'll be attending an execution.

CHAPTER TWENTY-THREE

"No visitors."

"Let me talk to your captain."

"He's gone. Come back tomorrow."

"I have a pass from the Mayor, signed by your captain, which says I can visit the prisoner. Tonight. And I'm in a hurry. So if I have to get your captain down here, I will. But you'll spend the rest of your career doing something worse that guarding this dump. If that's possible."

The guard looked up. He'd been late getting to his dinner. Too many disruptions. A man needs his dinner. The delay hadn't improved the food or his temper.

"Nobody gets in unless the Tribune approves."

Zoë thrust the pass at him.

"Also signed by Donncha. That cover it?"

The guard conceded the round and heaved himself to his feet. He unlocked the metal door behind him, and jabbed a finger down the corridor.

"Third cell from the end."

He went back to his dinner. Far down on the left of the cellblock, a solitary light shone through the door grate. Apparently, the soletei was the only prisoner in this wing of Bellery's jail tonight. Bergerac scampered ahead of her down the corridor. Jail seemed to be familiar territory to the monkey, which made her wonder how he and Chaff occupied their time when they weren't performing. Zoë took a deep breath and headed down the corridor, hugging the wall opposite the cells.

The jail sat just to the north of Bellery's heart, a street over from the cathedral and its landmark campanile and a quaint little square, where early on Tuesday and Saturday mornings, there was a farmers' market. The town's streets snaked away from the square, none wider than six men abreast, all of them meandering wildly through the city until they emptied into the busy harbor. Like most of the buildings in the town, the jail was brick and native sandstone, its exterior blocks rising upwards in grimy ranks until they topped out in tall iron spikes. It wasn't a big building for the simple reason that crime in Bellery was relatively amateurish and usually petty. The cells housed more drunks and small-time thieves than murderers. Anyone with a true talent for mischief was conscripted into the military and quickly found that their former peaceful, albeit dull, existence in Bellery was not such a bad thing.

••••

Tiernan finished the letter and addressed it to his father. Beside him on a tray were the remains of his last meal. The guard was late coming to pick it up. That was okay, he appreciated the extra time, and he'd eaten well. As a soletei, he was accustomed to facing the possibility of death. It didn't affect his appetite. Disconcerting to him was the certainty of death this time.

Tomorrow morning, first light, he was going to be executed. None of his military skills, no amount of expertise or planning would change that fact. And unlike the hundreds of times he'd faced his own mortality before a battle, this time he was preparing for it. He'd written to his father and disposed of his belongings, realizing he'd accumulated very little of value in his life. He thought about Deidre. She had tried to warn him. Then he thought about Zoë and reached for another sheet of paper. But the pen didn't want to move across the paper. To the one person he probably wanted to say the most, he couldn't find the words to say anything.

He wondered where she was, if she was safe. Knowing her, she was either on Gurama or trying to get there. She just never gave up. Anyway, it would be better for her there than in Ard Creggan. If the reports were true, Sinon Yar barely controlled a derelict city. Daily he was harassed by rebels who appeared out of nowhere and disappeared into nothing. The rebels didn't have the force to stage a major engagement, but the cumulative effect was a disruption of the mining and the commercial life of the city. There were whispers that Ard Creggan was finally vulnerable. The Tribune bided its time. For the first time in decades, there was talk of an assault on the city.

The Tribune. Reluctantly, Tiernan thought back on his trial. That had been an eye opener. The presumption of guilt in a fris was always strong, but he had been unprepared for the prosecution. The charge was collaborating with the enemy, but not once in the months leading up to, or during the weeks of the trial was testimony received on any of Tiernan's contacts with Jomini. At first he was mystified. Then it struck him. They simply didn't know. And of course it didn't matter, because the false evidence piled up against him was enough. Even Donncha testified against him. Not willingly, but the prosecutor managed to twist his well-intentioned testimony. In the end, his own lawyer, tired of being overruled and too frightened to defend a man targeted by the Tribune, gave up objecting to speculation, supposition, and suspect eyewitnesses. Tiernan almost felt sorry for him. Not that they had a lot to say to each other.

Tiernan couldn't defend himself. *The charge was true.* He had worked with the enemy. Worked with him, plotted with him, believed in him. And in the end, he had failed. *I did my best, I did my duty. Why wasn't it enough?*

The guard was at the door. "Visitor," he snarled.

"Open the door." He knew that voice. And its owner possibly was one of the last people he wanted to see right now.

"Can't open the door. Orders, sir."

"And I am ordering you to open the door. Do your duty, soldier." The tone was pleasant, even friendly, but it left the impression the guard would do anything exactly as he was told.

The cell door opened.

"Donncha." Tiernan stood by habit and caught himself halfway to a salute. *I'm a civilian now*, he thought. "I thought you would have had enough of me during the trial."

Donncha sat down at the end of the cot

"I find standing tiring these days. I must be getting old." He looked with interest at Tiernan's correspondence.

"Were you writing to your father?"

Tiernan scooped the papers together, tidying the pile. "Yes, I was writing to my father . . and some others. I didn't know how to get a letter to Josepht." His voice trailed off.

"I would be honored to see that your letter reaches your father. There are some things I'd like to discuss with him. I find fathers sometimes have useful insights into the behavior of their sons."

Tiernan stiffened. "I don't think he'd be of much help," he said cautiously. "We've lost touch in recent years."

Donncha frowned. "Now that's too bad. You see I was hoping to ask him what his son was doing fraternizing with Jomini Lord Deich."

The cellblock grew so quiet the water dripping from a faucet at the end of the corridor plinked loudly.

"If you knew, why didn't you say something during the trial?" .

Donncha gave him a knowing look. "They weren't interested in finding the truth and I wasn't interested in adding to the list of trumped up charges. Especially against someone I thought I knew very well."

"Sir." Tiernan started. Stopped. "Donncha," he began again. "I am a traitor."

"Yes, my boy," Donncha said lightly. "To some people, working with Jomini Deich might make you a traitor. But, I'm sure you had excellent reasons. And," he said, a wave of his hand taking in the cell, "I am here to listen to them. Believe me, I am most interested. I have had dealings with Lord Deich over the years and I have always considered him to be a most intelligent and perceptive man."

Tiernan blinked. Nothing in his soletei training prepared him for this bland acceptance of outlaw behavior.

"Donncha, it's treason to give assistance to Publicans."

"Yes, yes," his captain said impatiently. "I'm quite aware of the law. And while I, as a diplomat, might bend those laws when needed, you, as a soletei, are sworn to uphold them. For you, death is preferable to breaking the law. And yet you did. And you did it for a Publican. Your sworn enemy." He leaned forward. "Jomini must have made you a very compelling argument."

"If I tell you, you leave Josepht alone. No prosecution."

Donncha agreed. "Trust me. No harm will come to your father."

A smile flitted across the younger man's face. "Funny, that's what Jomini said to me, the first time I met him." He took a deep breath. "It began nearly five years ago. My father was sharing information on his sightings with one of Ard Creggan's astronomers. Their data showed a convergence of planets and a new body from outside our solar system. Estimates were that they all would align around the coming summer solstice."

"Fascinating for star gazers, yet hardly a temptation to commit treason."

Tiernan scowled, remembering. "Jomini said that in the historical records, the convergence always coincided with . . . an event." He stopped.

"What kind of event?"

"Scriptures called it the Judgment."

"Scriptures, heh? You surprise me, I didn't think you were a religious man."

"You know I'm not. And neither was Jomini. You say you knew him. Then you knew there was a quality about him." Tiernan reddened. "I don't know what it was. He made you believe in him."

Donncha nodded in agreement. "He was the one man, Publican or Citizen, whose word I took as fact." A silence.

"Months ago, while we were in Ard Creggan, I heard rumors he had died."

"He was killed on our way to Gurama," Tiernan continued, remembering that night. "There was someone there who knew where the Judgment would take place. Someone called the Stone Keeper."

Donncha looked puzzled. "I'm afraid I still don't understand. He lost his own life—and risked yours—for what? An astrological anomaly? Because of a few lines in some old books? What was this Judgment?"

"Jomini called it an epicenter, a confluence, although he said some scriptures interpreted it more as a cataclysm. He believed that at a single astronomical moment, when the planets align in a particular way, the past becomes malleable, time itself can be changed. Jomini said it was our last best hope for peace."

"I'm afraid I've heard that many times," Donncha said mildly. "And, as you know, I've been disappointed many times. Tell me, is this the knowledge your friend Brian believes you have that could destroy Ard Creggan?"

Tiernan looked troubled "I'm sorry he involved you, Donncha. Brian is following his own path. Not mine. He'd use anything he could to destroy Ard Creggan."

"There's talk of mounting an offensive soon against Ard Creggan. Brian may get his wish."

"Not so long as Ard Creggan's guns are pointed at our hearts. They'll win as long as they have their metal and their foundries." Tiernan leaned toward him, an intensity in his face that made his captain uneasy. "But what if we could go back. What if we could alter the balance, make all the wars, all the deaths," he snapped his fingers, "never happen."

Donncha looked tired. "You can't change the past, Tiernan. Let an old man assure of that."

"Jomini thought he could. We were looking for the key that could make it happen when he died."

"A key? "

"Yes, a key that changes the past and the future."

"Difficult to believe, but if true, an opportune tool. Do you know where it is?" The note of hope in Donncha's voice wasn't lost on him. Tiernan's shoulders slumped.

"We had hoped the Stone Keeper could tell us."

"I wish Jomini was still alive," Donncha said abruptly. "I don't have to tell you, my boy, what sort of state we are in. If the Tribune continues on its current path, I fear there will be another civil war—if we're not at war again with Ard Creggan before that. I'm worn out. I don't the heart to ask another generation to sacrifice their children for a cause even I'm unsure about. If this Judgment was really coming, if I could believe you, it would be our chance to set a new path. To change the balance. Recapture our past." He sighed. "We have so little time left."

With a pang, Tiernan remembered what the dawn would bring. He held out his father's letter to Donncha. "Please tell him, I … "

Donncha waved it aside. "If you could only show me some proof that what you say is true."

"Proof?" Tiernan looked around the cell. "If my father were here, he'd show you star charts. If Jomini were here, he'd tell you about the records and chronicles he found. It was enough to make them believe. And me, too."

Unexpectedly, he smiled. "When I die, you'll be the only one who knows about this. Find the key. Change our past, Donncha, or we're lost."

His captain regarded Tiernan for what felt like an eternity. His face didn't reveal a thing.

"I'm afraid this no job for an old man," he said with regret.

Tiernan's heart fell. He had hoped.

"So," Donncha continued, "I think you should complete this task yourself."

"But the Tribune," Tiernan stammered. "Their verdict."

"Was obviously delivered in the absence of compelling and exculpating evidence," Donncha interrupted. "My boy, I have spent most of my life pursuing one or another peace plan. That I have failed spectacularly is apparent to even me. I have reached the point where I am quite willing to grab at this slightest of straws. You are my straw, Tiernan, my last hope. A Publican must be at this so-called Judgment. You must do it."

Tiernan smiled wryly. "I'm glad to hear you say it, Donncha, but I can't just walk out of here."

"You can and you will. That is an order. I'm not quite certain how you'll obey it, but I imagine your visitor might be able to assist you."

"Tiernan?"

"Zoë?" He was at the door in a heartbeat, she was on the other side peering in.

"What are you doing here?" He was angry and wanted to hug her at the same time. "How did you get in?" He looked past her down the corridor, checking for the guard.

Zoë waved the pass. "With this. From the Mayor."

Bergerac leapt from her arms to the grille, slipping though the bars to perch on Tiernan's shoulder, chattering all the while.

"Shut-up, Bergerac," Tiernan ordered. "Why is the Mayor giving you passes to see me?"

"He seems to think the Tribune made a mockery of his courts. He doesn't like it. He wants me to find out if you're innocent."

"And how does he think you'll do that?"

She grinned. "I'm the Great Esme. I read minds. In a sideshow. Well, Noor does. I'm the front." She looked doubtful. "At least I think that's the word for it. I'm learning a lot. But sometimes this show business stuff is confusing."

Tiernan sighed. "He sent a mind-reader? He must be desperate."

"Maybe he just thinks you're innocent," she retorted. Tiernan turned slightly and Zoë ducked down below the grille. "Tiernan," she hissed. "There's someone in there with you."

"Of course there is, you silly woman. It's Donncha."

Zoë's eyes widened in alarm.

"Is that you, Lady Deich?" Donncha asked, as though they were meeting on the street instead of a jail cell. "How very odd. I looked for you all over the countryside, and the minute I sit down, there you are. I wish I could ask you to join us but the cell door is locked and opening it would require the guard."

"He's eating his dinner anyhow," she replied, uncertainly.

"Good. That will give us some time to plan. I imagine you're here to keep Tiernan from his appointment tomorrow morning?"

She stood on tiptoe to get a good look into the cell. "How did you know?" she demanded.

Donncha chuckled. "How did you like the Mayor, my dear? I hope his visit wasn't inconvenient."

"Not at all. He was very nice." A glimmer of light and a suspicion. "You knew he was at the caravan?"

"Oh, Pieton and I are old friends. Relations, really. He married my sister, a very worthy woman, but I always found her hard to live with. I wonder sometimes, how he does it. At any rate, it was his idea to invite the Great Esme. A very good disguise by the way. It fooled me completely."

"Not so completely," Zoë muttered.

Donncha joined Tiernan at the door. "Now that Lady Deich is here, you should be on your way."

"You want him to escape?" This was unexpected.

"Yes, and as quickly as possible. Tiernan, it would be best if you exchanged clothes with me. I think my coat and hat will be sufficient to fool the guards. Take my cane, too. And if we're to make this work," Donncha added cheerfully, "you must hit me."

Tiernan's scowled. "Sir, I will not strike you."

"No, he's right," Zoë agreed, too readily Tiernan thought. "Hit him. Otherwise, they'll think he let you escape."

Donncha, Zoë, even Bergerac looked expectantly at Tiernan, who glared back. "I cannot strike a man your age. I . . .I might hurt you," he finished lamely.

His captain waved his objection aside. "Well, that's the point, isn't it? Oh, don't worry about me, my boy. I practically have a glass jaw. Just a tap and I'll be out. Now be sure to wrap me up well in the blankets, I don't quite have your girth and we don't want the guard discovering me before you've had a chance to get well away. Well, come on!"

Tiernan rolled Donncha's limp body in his blankets and placed him on the cot in what he hoped was a comfortable position, his face to the cell wall. With luck the guard would think the prisoner was sleeping. He motioned to Zoë.

"Guard!" she called down the corridor. "Open the door. Immediately! The Captain wants to leave. Guard!" The scraping of a chair, a key in the door to the corridor, the guard's plodding tread down the corridor. He carefully moved Zoë back from the door, then looked into the cell. "You ready to come out?"

"Well, of course he is," Zoë giving him the full Lady Deich effect, hoping it would deflect his attention from Tiernan's masquerade. "And you've kept him waiting. Open the door and be careful not to let that prisoner out. He is a dangerous man."

"He's doing nobody harm, just lying there. There's no cause for alarm," the guard protested, but mildly. *She's trouble, this one. Excitable.* "If the gentleman wants to come out, he can. No hurry. And him with a bad leg, too. No reason to hurry and go on so. Quiet now or you'll wake him. Condemned men have a right to sleep. Hush now. Or I'll put you in with him and we'll see how you like that."

Zoë blushed and bit her lip. Tiernan, with Donncha's wide-brimmed hat pulled low over his face, and leaning on the cane, limped through the now open cell door.

"That's more like it." The guard was whispering now. "We'll let him have a good rest. Tomorrow's a big day. You've worn him out with all your jabbering. Time all his visitors were gone."

He herded them down the corridor, all the time motioning them to keep quiet. Before they knew it, Zoë and Tiernan were standing on the steps outside the jail, the guard gently closing the door behind them. It was nearly midnight. The outer yard, a dusty, brown expanse with its gallows, was before them, the gate at the other side of the yard. Four guards had the night watch.

"Now what's the plan to get out of here?" Tiernan said under his breath.

"Plan? I didn't think we'd get this far," Zoë confessed.

"Great. Are those all of the guards?"

"Not counting the one inside, just the four at the outer gate."

Tiernan looked incredulous. "Only four guards? I'm supposed to be a dangerous prisoner!"

Zoë rolled her eyes. "I don't suppose we could put Bergerac to work as a diversion?"

The monkey disappeared under Zoë's cloak at this suggestion.

"Alright then, the direct approach. No matter what happens, keep moving," Tiernan whispered, stepping off. "Don't stop when you get to the gate. Just keep walking." They were halfway across the yard and the guards hadn't even looked up. One even seemed asleep. If they had taken notice, they would have seen nothing suspicious in two visitors, one cloaked woman and a stooped man with a cane. Zoë began to think they were going to make it.

The outer gate was opening. *A visitor at this hour?* Zoë faltered. "Were you expecting any visitors?" she muttered. She plucked the hood of her cape forward to shadow her face.

"No, no one." Tiernan whispered. She would see that the visitor was a soldier. He had finished checking in and was walking across the yard toward them. Tiernan was walking slightly behind her. She looked to the gate. One of the guards half rose from his chair. Was he watching the visitor or them?

"Keep your head down," Tiernan hissed in her ear.

The visitor was just a few strides away. Zoë, peeking out from under her hood, could just see his legs approaching. Tiernan looked past the visitor to the guard at the gate. *He's standing. Is he reaching for his weapon?* He grasped Zoë's arm; an elderly man bent nearly double and leaning on his companion. The visitor continued past them without a word. As they walked through the gates, the sleepy guards barely grunted at them.

Outside in Bellery's streets, they walked quickly down the main street, then dodged into the first side street, expecting the alarm to be raised at any moment.

"If we keep moving," Tiernan whispered hoarsely. "We should have plenty of time to reach the harbor before dawn, even if there are patrols looking for us. The more ground we cover now, the better. Are we the only passengers?"

"Chaff should be on board, already. The rest of the caravan left the city hours ago."

"What caravan? And how did Chaff get involved in this? And where's Livy?"

"Eleanor arranged for us to travel with Chaff. With Donncha looking for us, it seemed like a good idea to disguise ourselves." She grinned. "We have a road show, a carnival. We make a fairly decent living. Six acts, and I have top billing," she finished, pleased with herself.

"Nothing improper, I hope," was all Tiernan said.

"Improper? You sound so old-fashioned, Tiernan," she said lightly. His grasp on her arm increased painfully. "We were a mind reading act and I kept my clothes on, if that's what you're wondering."

"No. I mean. . ." he released her arm. Zoë hurried to fill the strained silence. "The caravan should be a few hours west of the city by now. If the Tribune suspects the Great Esme helped free you, they'll waste a lot of time following them."

"Livy OK?"

"She's fine," Zoë said tersely. "Wherever she is."

Tiernan gave her a side-wise glance. "You don't know where she is?"

Her shrug was fierce. "She left. She didn't tell me where she was going."

"So you two had a fight and she ran away? She's a child, Zoë. You're the adult. Grow up!"

"And I can't believe you're lecturing me on my responsibilities at a time like this. She has you fooled, just like she fooled Noor."

"And as I've said before, I can't believe you're jealous of your little sister."

"Believe me she has grown up fast," Zoë retorted. "She stole something of mine and took off."

"Livy isn't a thief," Tiernan said curtly. "I think I know her that well."

"Do we have to talk about this now? You're upsetting Bergerac," Zoë snapped at him.   Bergerac hissed and jumped from Zoë to Tiernan and back again.

"You're right. This isn't the time."   Then, after a long pause. "When do we have to be at the ship?"

"By dawn."

"Could be a busy night. It looks like the night watch is out in force." Zoë kept walking.

Ahead of them in the main square, the patrols were starting their rounds, dispersing down the many alleys and streets radiating outward through the city. Tiernan pulled her back into the recess of a shop door.

"We can't afford to be stopped right now. Questions would be a little awkward for both of us."

"We don't have time to play hide and seek," Zoë retorted.

Tiernan looked down the street. A two-man patrol was getting close.

"What do you have on under that thing?" he asked abruptly.

Zoë opened her cloak. "My traveling clothes. Why?"

"Too bad. There goes plan A."

"What was Plan A?"

"Distract them. Now we're into Plan B."

"Wait a minute. You'd object to me parading half-naked in a road show, but not for some patrolmen?"

"I despair of your morals, girl, if you can't see the difference between making a spectacle of yourself and being a bit of a tactical distraction," Tiernan said severely.

Zoë ignored him.   "What's   the   plan   now?" "Scare the hell out of them. Give me your jacket. If they stop us, don't say a thing. Trust me."

"I don't have much of a choice, do?" she said, shivering in her blouse.

Tiernan grinned. "Not anymore." He peeled off his own shirt, put on her jacket, then stuffed the shirt down the back, giving him an impressive hump. Her cloak over his shoulders hid the rest, and Donncha's hat, pulled low, shadowed his face. In a last minute inspiration he added the protesting Bergerac, and before her eyes he twisted into a shapeless, seething lump. She suppressed a shudder.

"You there." A soldier approached them.

Zoë turned slowly as Tiernan emerged from the shadows beside her. She watched the soldier's face blanch. One minute he was all swagger, the next he'd turned white as a sheet and was backing away. In another minute he was walking fast in the opposite direction.

"Well, what got into him?" she wondered aloud. Tiernan chuckled, an unsettling sound coming from that deformed shape.

"A fairy tale, that's what. The witch, Mathilde. She lures men with a young girl, then cuts their hearts out. That's how Citizen parents scare little boys—and keep them from chasing girls."

Zoë briefly speculated why Citizen boys weren't encouraged to play with girls, but Tiernan already was moving off in a lurching trot down the dark street. She brought up the rear. For some reason, having that contorted figure following her, even if it was Tiernan, made her skin crawl.

The soldiers they came across must have felt the same; several passed quite close to them, but none seemed eager to stop them on a dark, deserted street. Still, they spent the rest of the night evading patrols, dodging down alleyways. Precious time was lost while a sentry posted at the harbor slid into sleep. They reached the ship as the sky was beginning to lighten, the captain pacing on deck as sailors readied the ship for departure. Zoë was half way up the gangway when she heard a voice call to her from the quay.

She froze, afraid to look back.

"Keep moving," Tiernan hissed in her ear. "Here, take Bergerac. I'll deal with this."

Reluctantly, she boarded as he turned back to the quay.

Bergerac disappeared into the ship's bowels, probably to find Chaff. She went below deck to a cabin to wait. It wasn't long before the ship creaked, and sounds of activity on deck told her they were under way. Still no Tiernan. She made for the deck

But someone was descending the ladder. Zoë fell back, then relaxed when she recognized the man.

"You're Tiernan's friend, Brian, from the Black Pagoda, isn't that right? Where is Tiernan?"

Brian smiled broadly. "Good morning, Lady Deich. And yes, everything is just fine. Tiernan's a little tied up at the moment. He asked that you make yourself comfortable."

She half smiled, uncertain. "Where is he? On deck?" She tried to move around him to the ladder; he blocked her path. "Probably better if you were to stay below deck for a while. Until we clear the harbor."

"That was you at the jail, when we were leaving!" Zoë blurted.

Brian mock-bowed. "Guilty. I was hoping to find you. I figured you'd show up, sooner or later. I watched for you at the trial, but you didn't come. I knew Donncha would flush you out."

"Donncha?" she asked, hoping she sounded clueless. Behind her back, she felt for the cabin door latch.

"That would be the old fool you left behind in the prison cell." His tone had changed. She took a step back into her cabin.

"You went to a lot of trouble to find me. Why?"

He smiled but it didn't reach his eyes.

"As we left Ard Creggan that last night, a mutual friend asked me to be sure something in your possession was safe." He took a step toward her.

"What are you talking about?" Her thoughts raced.

Where is Tiernan? Why doesn't he come?

Brian's smile creased into something ugly.

"I'm talking about a ring, like a snake with a black stone in its mouth. The Counselor said it was a family heirloom, so I figured you'd keep it with you. I'm right, aren't I? And please don't think Tiernan will appear and save you, Lady Deich. He won't be making this trip. If you want to live, you'll give me the ring. Now."

Reflexively, Zoë's hand went to the cord around her neck.

"Lose something? Or trying to fool me? Which is it?" He advanced. Zoë took another step back into the cramped cabin. There wasn't anywhere else to go. He was so close now, Zoë could smell something sour on him, an odor like an old fur coat.

"I sent it on ahead," she said as calmly as she could.

"Where?" he demanded. She didn't like the edge in his voice. Desperate men were unpredictable. "Where did you send it?"

"To Gurama. To the Abbot."

He struck her in his frustration. She could have slipped the blow easily enough, but she wanted him to believe her. It was the best lie she could think of at the moment.

"Abbot Rajid," she whispered, after he locked her in the cabin and went above deck again. "I hope you're ready for this."

CHAPTER TWENTY-FOUR

From the pier, Tiernan watched the ship leave the harbor. He didn't wave; he was tied to a piling. Or shout, as he was gagged, too. Zoë was on board with Brian Goodloe, a man he was going to kill if he ever saw him again. That possibility, however, seemed remote. It was only a matter of time before a patrol found him and returned him, late, for his own execution.

Of course he knew Brian had recognized him in the jail yard, and hadn't raised the alarm. He'd thought his old friend was helping him escape. So when he appeared on the dock, he had been glad to see him. Until Brian hit him from behind, and left him trussed up like a piece of meat.

It wasn't the betrayal so much, as it was the sucker punch.

Out of the corner of his eye, he glimpsed something dark darting up from underneath the dock. Probably rats. He shuddered. He hated rats. Something soft brushed his fingers, and he jerked. A slight vibration in the rope. If the rat started on his fingertips, he'd find a way to break its neck. He yanked hard. A yelp of pain.

"Hey! I'm trying to help."

"Livy?"

And there she was, peeping over his shoulder.

"You're just making the knots worse. Stop moving."

"And I'm glad to see you too," Tiernan said.

It took her a while. Brian was a professional after all and he'd meant the knots to hold. Then he was free. But still land-bound. He surveyed the boats tied up along the dock. Any one of them could sail to Gurama, but his sailing skills had not improved since the ill-fated voyage with Zoë years ago, and there would be heavy seas between Bellery and the island.

"I don't suppose you know how to sail?" Livy shook her head, clutching a bundle to her chest. He looked at her closely.

"Your sister said you ran away."

A tear slid down her check. Then another. Tiernan looked around. This was not the time.

"It's OK," he added, attempting to stop the tears. "She just sounds mad. She doesn't mean it."

Livy hiccupped. "Here." She held the bundle out to him, her face wet. "You take this back to Zoë. Tell her, tell her, I'm sorry." Her face crumpled as tears welled up again.

"You give it to her, when we see her," he said. "She's your sister. She'll understand."

Livy wiped her cheeks with a shaky hand. "No. You don't understand. It's my fault."

Tiernan pushed down his impatience. The ship, with Zoë and Brian on it, was sailing ever further away. And his chances of catching them were receding as well.

"What's your fault, Livy?"

"Noor. Noor's dead."

"Who's...?" he began, then remembered. "How?"

"Some men. Soldiers. I was coming back to the caravan outside Bellery. I heard them, so I hid. They were going through all the wagons. I didn't think they'd seen me. But one of them must have. He was coming to get me. And Noor..."

She buried her face in his chest.

"She tried to protect me. I ran. Noor told me to come here. I heard her, in my head."

He patted her back awkwardly. "She can do that. What happened then?"

"I've been waiting here on the dock. I hid when the patrols came through. I wanted to come out when I saw you and Zoë, but that man...."

"Brian? The man who tied me up? What about him?"

He could barely make out her muffled words. "He was there. He was one of the soldiers at the caravan."

Tiernan took her by the shoulders. "Are you sure, Livy?"

She stared back at him, mute. He turned away and started down the length of the wharf. Livy dashed after him.

"Where are we going?" she asked, catching up.

"We're going to Gurama. There's a man there I have to see. And very possibly kill."

"How are we going to get there?"

"A boat. If we can find one." Most of the working boats had put out to sea already, or weren't due back until mid-morning. A weather-beaten sailor in oilskins was sitting in his ketch, smoking a pipe and contemplating the sunrise. He nodded in greeting.

"Would you be that soletei officer they had on trial?" he asked.

"I am." No sense in denying it. Bellery was a small enough place.

"Thought so. You're looking for a boat?"

Livy slipped her hand into his and clung. Against his better judgment, Tiernan asked.

"Can you take the two of us?"

The sailor grunted and waved them aboard.

"She's hardly bigger than a mite. Barely counts."

Tiernan jumped down into the boat, settling Livy into the bow, then helped cast off the lines. In minutes they were heading out into the harbor.

"You might get into trouble for this," Tiernan said, taking a seat in the stern with the old man. The sailor adjusted the sail.

"My boy fought with you. Said you were a good man."

"What's your boy's name?"

"Henry. Henry Foxhall."

Tiernan looked away towards the horizon, where Zoë's ship was small and getting smaller.

"He was a good man, too."

The skipper tapped his pipe over the side. "That letter you wrote meant the world to his mother."

They sailed in silence until they were beyond the harbor. Tiernan pointed to the speck that was Zoë's ship.

"That ship is on its way to Gurama. I need to catch it. Can we do it?"

"Not a chance," the skipper said. He pulled on his pipe and blew a cloud of smoke.

Tiernan's heart sank.

"Waste of time to try," he continued. "See, they need to keep to deep water. We don't. We can take a direct line. I'll have you on Gurama and me halfway back to Bellery before they even touch shore. You might want to catch some sleep." He winked at Tiernan. "I don't suppose you got much rest last night, what with everything."

Tiernan smiled and went forward. Livy was already asleep under the tarp. He tucked in beside her, shifting around to get comfortable. A hard lump caught him in the back. He was still wearing Zoë's jacket. He examined the coat lining carefully. A small slit and a ring, its band in the shape of a writhing snake, fell into his palm. The rising sun struck glints off the glassy black stone.

Clever girl, he thought and slipped the ring into his pocket. Then he closed his eyes for some much needed sleep.

CHAPTER TWENTY-FIVE

The ketch sailed into a shallow cove on the mainland side of Gurama. There was a narrow ridge above the cove and Tiernan knew that the monastery's fields and barns began on the other side. The larger ship would have to dock on the far side of the island, facing the main gate of the monastery. As promised, they had arrived in plenty of time to watch Brian and a smaller figure disembark, accompanied by two heavily armed guards. Brian and Zoë disappeared inside the monastery, but their escort was turned back at the gate.

Livy shivered beside him in the early morning cold.

"Listen, runt, I'm going to leave you for awhile."

She clutched his sleeve, but he reassured her.

"It won't be for long. I just need to find a friend of mine. In the meantime, you're going to stay somewhere safe. I can't be worrying about you."

She followed him obediently and Tiernan wondered how long this newly penitent Livy would last. They made their way to the monastery's dairy. As a student, he'd spent many a predawn hour there tending to the milking before classes. The haymow would be a convenient place for Livy to hide. She scampered up the ladder and was hidden in a wink.

"You stay put until I come back," he whispered and was off.

Now, if he remembered rightly, there was a back stairway to the student dormitories. It was almost too easy to sneak in unseen while the monks were in the milking parlor.

Skirting the refectory where he knew the rest of the monks would be gathering for their first meal of the day, he passed down a long low corridor with pavers worn smooth over the centuries by countless feet. He paused at a flight of stairs. Footsteps. He hid in the darkness under the stairway.

Some monks were returning from morning prayers. Trailing behind them was a figure Tiernan recognized immediately. Abbot Rajid. Lost in thought, the Abbot was well up the stairs over Tiernan's hiding place before he paused. "Well, Tiernan," he addressed the shadows, "are you coming?"

He remembered the Abbot's chambers all too well. Students who were disciplinary problems became very familiar with the room.

"It's like old times seeing you here, Tiernan," the Abbot said, reading his mind. "I used to think you broke the rules just to visit."

Tiernan grinned. True, the Abbot had punished him, but just as often he'd given him a sympathetic ear.

"I'm afraid I'm in trouble again."

"You and the rest of our poor world. Why do you think I can help you?"

"Jomini was sure you could."

"Ah, Jomini. He wrote, months ago, to expect him. But then, nothing. I heard he had passed."

"He was killed, on his way to you."

Rajid sat down behind a desk loaded with papers and scrolls. His visitor took the chair across from him. "That is troubling. Do you know what purpose he had in mind coming here?"

"He believed there was someone here," Tiernan began, "who he called the Stone Keeper." Tiernan looked at the Abbot expectantly. He had half-hoped the name would produce the individual and his search would be over. He continued, less assured. "Jomini said this Stone Keeper knew where the Judgment would take place."

"The Judgment, my boy?" Rajid asked as though inquiring about the weather. "That sounds ominous. I don't recall anything about a Judgment."

Remembering his conversation with Donncha, Tiernan plunged on.

"Jomini called it a crossroads. A point in time when the past is open and can be changed. He said it was our last opportunity to right past wrongs. He said it was the last chance for a lasting peace."

"Tell me, did he use that specific phrase, 'right past wrongs?'" The Abbot asked, sharp enough to make Tiernan careful.

"I think so," he replied. "I'm not sure. It might have been something about righting wrongs. Does it make a difference?"

"Perhaps no difference at all. Please continue. What did he expect you to get from this Stone Keeper?"

"He said the Stone Keeper had a ring, and the ring was the key to the Judgment. I have the ring, but I need the Stone Keeper to tell me where the Judgment will take place. Jomini believed the map was here with the Stone Keeper."

"Yes, we'll get to that in a moment," the Abbot said genially. "Now, tell me more about this Judgment. What did Jomini tell you?"

Tiernan chose his next words with care. "He said some scriptures refer to the Judgment as a time of darkness and destruction. He didn't know what role the ring played —whether it forestalled or triggered the destruction."

"Knowing Jomini, it will become clear in time. My old friend was a very thorough man. Perhaps if I saw the ring?"

Tiernan held up the ring, the spine of a snake twined around the stone clenched in its jaws.

The Abbot regarded it thoughtfully. "So you've come back to us. I wondered where you'd gone to. This ring is well known to me. Did you know that together the moon and the snake make a glyph. I wonder?" He stared off into the middle distance for a moment then snapped back, a new energy in his voice. "Yes, that's it. Get that folio down for me, please."

From the top of a tall bookcase, at the Abbot's direction, Tiernan pulled down a dusty over-sized portfolio.

"I'd nearly forgotten about these," the monk said. "Their provenance was so uncertain they were withdrawn from our library. I kept them, well, because I have a problem throwing away books, as you can see. This is a codex with a bit of a twist. You'll see. Each symbol or glyph is linked to a prophecy. Some of them are quite puzzling. For example, here's one that talks about how a river will flow backward to its source. Don't ask me how that is even possible, but apparently it foretells a double lunar eclipse. And there's another one, even more perplexing, about showers of frogs. Oh, there are dozens. It makes for fascinating reading. Let me show you."

"I'm sorry," Tiernan interrupted, trying hard not to show his impatience. "We really don't have time. You may already have visitors who are looking for the same information I am."

"Yes, there is a stranger requesting an audience. He arrived this morning, with a young woman. He seeks what you do?"

"In a way, yes."

"And you want me to deny him that knowledge?"

"I do."

"Why?"

"Because he'll use it to harm others."

"And you won't?"

"No."

Rajid sighed. "It must be wonderful to be so sure of the consequences of your actions. I think that's a peculiarity of youth. But, as you say, this is no time for a philosophical discussion. Let us find the symbol first, and then determine our course of action."

The two heads bent over the book page after page. Finally, after what seemed half the book, Tiernan found the glyph and the prophecy associated with it.

"Read it aloud," the Abbot prompted.

Tiernan flushed. "It's in Mesarian."

"Yes, I know," the Abbot said calmly. "Let's see how well you remember your lessons. Begin, please."

He was 16 again and in class. He began, halting over the lines.

Years fall away,
The time repeats,
The stone keeper tells the tale.
He carries the key,
That frees the truth
When time and memory fail

"And then there's the glyph again. The snake with the circle. Except the stone is the circle on the ring." To his chagrin, he was sweating. "That doesn't make any sense. Did I translate it right.?

The Abbot glanced over the page. "Oh, you did an excellent job. The Stone Keeper tells the tale, eh? Well, I think it's time we consulted an expert."

"Someone here on Gurama?"

The Abbot smiled. "You might say that. Bring the lamp, if you please." He led Tiernan down several staircases and passageways until they arrived at the Abbey chapel. Behind the chapel altarpiece there was a simple gated door Tiernan had never noticed before. "Well, you didn't spend much time in the chapel when you were here," the Abbot said, applying a large key to a stiff lock. "Besides, I doubt if anything in here would have interested you then."

Behind the door, twelve stone steps led down, and the moist odor of dirt and decay rose to tickle Tiernan's nose. The Abbot raised the lamp. Long, narrow tunnels stretched away to all points of the compass, each tunnel wall punctuated from floor to ceiling by shallow alcoves. Here and there, the lamplight picked up the tea-brown gleam of a skull or bone. They were in the Abbey's catacombs. "Stay close," the Abbot cautioned, starting down one of a handful of identical passageways. "The tunnels can be very disorienting."

Several levels down and too many turns later, they stopped before a blue-black metal door without doorknob or keyhole.

"Tell me you have the key," Tiernan said.

The monk closed his eyes. "Not the kind of key you're thinking," he murmured. "Now be very quiet, while I concentrate. It's a little tricky."

Silent as a tomb, Tiernan thought looking back over his shoulder. In the lamplight, the Abbot appeared to be meditating, his eyes closed. The light from the lamp shimmered on the closed door. *Or did it?* Tiernan stepped back. A sinuous line thrashed just beneath the door's surface. And disappeared.

Abbot Rajid stood in the open doorway. "Coming?" They entered a circular chamber, ringed on three levels by vertical niches. The upper levels were empty, but on the bottom floor where they stood, each niche held a standing body robed in a monk's habit. Each stood, head bowed, hands crossed across pelvis, skin gleaming like brown leather.

Torches flared to life beside the niches.

Tiernan whistled low and soft. "What is this place?"

"A little reverence, Tiernan. You are in the presence of the past Abbots of Gurama."

Directly in front of them, a singular figure, nearly six-feet tall, faced them in a gold-leafed niche. Unlike those of his companions, his arms hung at his sides, the palm of one hand open to them, the other hand grasping a blade with a serrated edge, a glassy black shard. A terracotta medallion, heavily embossed, hung around his neck. From under his monk's hood, a thatch of still vibrant red hair framed the skull. But it was the eyes that made Tiernan shudder, staring eyes that seemed unchanged in death.

"Shouldn't his eyes be closed?"

"Usually, yes. But this is an unusual case. The incorruptibility of the body. Some of our order see it as a sign of his sanctity."

"He looks . . . alive."

The Abbot bowed deeply before the niche.

"Over 500 years ago, he was our Abbey's first Abbot. His name was Johan Pietra."

An inscription in gold outlined the niche. Tiernan read it aloud.

"He saw the great Mystery, he knew the Hidden:
He marked the Journey beyond the distant,
He held the knowledge of all Time.
He prepared the way to Judgment,
And opened the record of Stone."

"This is our expert?" Tiernan asked doubtfully.

"The codex was fairly straightforward. The prophecy said Stone Keeper. And this is Johan Pietra, otherwise known as Johan Stonekeeper."

Tiernan groaned. "I thought this would be a whole lot simpler."

The Abbot threw up his hands. "Questions are easy. Answers are much more difficult."

Tiernan edged closer to the mummy. "May I touch him?"

"My boy," the Abbot chuckled, "he's dead."

With those eyes on him, Tiernan had his doubts. "Why the spike? Is it a religious symbol or something?

"It's called Pietra's Thorn. According to legend he was never without it. What possible use it may have had, is anyone's guess. It is, you will notice, still razor sharp."

"Maybe it's the key in the prophecy," Tiernan muttered. "Unfortunately, we're looking for a map, not a key."

"Never reject knowledge, my boy."

Tiernan already was moving on. "Monk's robes. I don't imagine he'd keep a star map in his robe. So we're looking at the obvious. What is this?" He gingerly lifted the medallion. "It's heavier than it looks. Could this be a map? It has all these signs on it."

The Abbot looked doubtful. "Those are the signs of the zodiac. Johan Pietra was fascinated by the heavens. To be honest, I'm beginning to wonder how our Abbot Pietra is connected with this Judgment," he mused. "What was he up to all those centuries ago?" He stopped, listening. "We're going to have visitors. You young people are so impatient."

A wide-eyed monk stuck his head into the chamber, only to be yanked backwards. Brian entered, dragging Zoë with him.

"Sorry, Abbot, I got tired of waiting. I knew you'd understand. And one of your monks was kind enough to find you for us. Hey, Tiernan, I thought you'd be dead by now. Now don't get too excited, buddy." He made sure Tiernan saw the knife against Zoë's neck. "I will kill her if you get any closer. Abbot Rajid, you have something I need. A little something Lady Deich says she sent you. I just need to collect it and I'll be gone."

Tiernan shook his head. "You don't know what you're doing."

"I know which side I'm on, comrade. You, however, seem a little confused. Now move out into the middle of the room where I can keep an eye on you. That's right. Lady Deich, I've heard you're nothing but trouble. Let's prove them wrong. Ask your Abbot friend for the ring."

Tiernan looked at him impassively. "You're wasting your time, Brian."

Zoë gasped as the blade pressure on her neck increased. A red bead sprouted under the knifepoint.

"Maybe. But if you think I won't cut her throat, you're wrong. Of course, I don't need to kill her. I can carve her up a bit. She's pretty enough. But maybe if we took a little off here and here. . ."

"No! There must be no violence here," the Abbot protested and pointed to Tiernan . "He has the ring."

"That's the spirit," Brian said pleasantly. "Now buddy, if you'll just toss me the ring, the lady is all yours."

Tiernan didn't move. "Why are you doing this?"

"You want an explanation? I thought that would be obvious. My enemies' enemy is my friend. Isn't that the way it goes? You would be amazed at the number of people who want to get their hands on that ring of yours. Including your own Counselor, Lady. He's the one who set me on your track. And I win no matter who I give it to. Seems we're all after the same thing—the end of Ard Creggan and you Publicans."

Zoë flinched.

"Oh, you didn't know that, princess?" He whispered in her ear. "And you know what else, Lady? I came across that wet nurse of yours. And you know what I did?" He chuckled. "I killed her."

To Zoë's eyes the room seemed to expand and contract around her. The smell she'd caught on Brian, she placed it now. *Noor.*

Brian's voice in her ear. "I enjoyed killing that one. It took four of us, and we took our time, too. Ohhh, don't cry, Lady. And Tiernan, buddy, any closer and I promise I'll kill her, too."

"Brian, we don't have to do it this way," Tiernan said evenly.

"You're getting soft," Brian sneered. "Where's that tough-minded soletei? You never used to quibble over a massacre. We'll save thousands of our own people. And Publicans die. Win. Win."

"Do it, Tiernan," the Abbot interrupted. "Give him the ring. It is of no consequence." It was the voice of a headmaster to his student. The soletei's training struggled with his heart.

"Believe me," the Abbot insisted, "the ring is not important. Give it to him." In one motion, Tiernan pulled the ring from his pocket and threw it.

"No," Zoë whispered. The ring arced across the room toward Brian. For an instant, the gemstone glinted darkly in the torchlight, all eyes on it. Brian stepped wide of Zoë, his arm outstretched, reaching for the ring even as Pietra's spike coursed across the room speeding to the very center of his forehead, burying itself there. He didn't even quiver as he hit the floor.

Zoë stood open-mouthed. Walking stiffly, Tiernan crossed the room without giving her a glance to squat down beside Brian's body. From the dead man's curled fingers, he retrieved the ring. Gently, he drew down the lids over the staring eyes, laying his hand palm down on Brian's forehead, reciting the prayer for the dead under this breath. When he was done, he freed the spike with a quick tug and rose. "We'll bury him here on Gurama, if that's permitted. He has no family."

The Abbot nodded absent-mindedly, already returned to the study of his long-dead predecessor.

"Of course. In time. But time is not our friend right now. We must concentrate on the business at hand or it will be too late."

Zoë came to stand beside Tiernan; her hand seeking his. He didn't look at her, but his grip tightened on her hand.

"I was wondering," Rajid mused. "I was merely wondering how my predecessor became so knowledgeable about our current situation. He was a simple monk. He didn't travel. He wrote one book, the rules for our order. He was nothing except our first abbot. Don't mistake me. He was an exceptional religious leader. A moral man in a godless, unprincipled age. But, otherwise, completely ordinary."

Tiernan tried to focus on the Abbot's words.

"If he's so ordinary, how would he know enough to leave a map to the Judgment?"

"Perhaps you could tell us, my dear." To his surprise, the Abbot's question was directed at Zoë.

"Me?" She flushed and dropped Tiernan's hand. He felt the warm metal of the ring in his palm and clutched it.

Rajid's smile was knowing. "You've had both the ring and, if my sources are correct, the keys from Ard Creggan in your possession. Unless you have changed greatly since your time here, I imagine your curiosity got the better of you. Did you discover their secret?"

"What secret?" Tiernan demanded, looking from Zoë to the Abbot. In the silence, a tug of wills beneath the surface. Zoë gave in first.

"I meant to tell you. Just later. It didn't happen until after we left the Black Pagoda. I didn't think anyone else knew," she said looking at the Abbot.

"There was good reason for keeping the two parts separate. The ring here on Gurama, guarded by the monks. And the keys in Ard Creggan, under the protection of the Families. And it was a good arrangement until Jomini became, shall we say, acquisitive."

"My father? But the ring was my mother's."

Rajid's tone was nearly apologetic. "But you see, before it was your mother's, this ring was passed down to every Abbot of Gurama. You're looking at Johan Pietra's own ring."

"It can't be," Zoë protested. "My mother wore this ring for as long as I can remember."

"Zora, your mother...." Rajid began, then seemed to reconsider, and took a different tack. "Did you know she was a seer? Well, a novice. Still in training. She left Gurama without completing her studies. A pity. She showed real promise."

Mother a seer? Zoë had the sensation of walking down stairs and unexpectedly missing steps. The Abbot continued.

"She was raised here. But she met your father and renounced her vocation—ran away, really—to be with him in Ard Creggan. She took the ring."

Before Zoë could dispute this, he hurried on. "I don't blame her. It was probably at Jomini's instigation. As you know, he was obsessed with crystals, the Ard Creggan keys, all of them. The ring, with its provenance, would have been irresistible to him. Such a tantalizing piece of the puzzle. When did she give you the ring, Zoë?"

"The year I was here on Gurama," she said curtly. "She gave it to me before I left Ard Creggan. She told me to keep it hidden. To never tell anyone, not even Father, where it was. She made me swear."

"Well, you didn't keep that promise very well," Tiernan scoffed. "You showed me the ring two weeks after you got here. Come to think of it, you left before the end of term," Tiernan said. "I never knew why."

"My mother was dying. Not even the Counselor could save her." She drew a deep breath. "The point is she gave me the ring," she repeated stubbornly.

"And you never knew what it was capable of," the Abbot said, "until you had the keys. What did you see then?"

Zoë's expression grew distant, as though her thoughts were far away.

"You need the ring to access the keys of the Families, don't you Zoë?" the Abbot prodded. "Tell us what you saw."

She exhaled slowly. "People. Family. The Families. Ard Creggan's past," she said in a dreamy voice. "All of it. Back to the beginning."

"And what did you see at the beginning? Take us back to the beginning."

Her lips moved soundlessly, her eyes focused on a distant event. Painfully, the words stumbled out. "I was there. I saw. . ." She covered her ears at some unheard sound, cowering, terrified.

"Stop it!" Tiernan cried, but the Abbot held up a hand, silencing him. "This is no time to be emotional." Then whatever frightened her was gone. She straightened, her face oddly blank as though she was sleepwalking.

"Tell us, Zoë," he urged. "Tell me what you see."

She stumbled toward Johan Petra and stepped up into the niche. He towered a head above her, his leathern skin dark against her pallid face, the remnants of his red hair, so like hers. She stepped back down, the medallion that hung around his neck in her hand, the rotten leather throng breaking at the slight tug. The medallion slipped from her fingers to the floor, shattering, shards of fired clay skittering across the pavers. Zoe's smile, sweet and empty, crumpled with her to the floor. Tiernan barely caught her in time. Beside them, Rajid bent to pick something from the floor, brushing away crumbs of clay.

"What's happening to her?" Tiernan demanded, brushing the hair away from her face. Beneath his fingers, the blueness of her lips alarmed him..

"She'll return to us in a minute, don't worry," the Abbot said reassuringly. "Perhaps in the meantime, you'll find this interesting." He dangled the medallion before Tiernan. Except it wasn't the old medallion at all. The disk the Abbot held glowed gold. "Apparently, Johan Petra had his secrets. This disc was hidden inside his medallion."

Tiernan felt the shock of recognition. On one side of the medallion, seven quartz dots lined up with a gold bead, an arc intersecting the seventh dot. On the other, a trident below a fort on a cliff.

"I've seen this before," he stammered. "It's the alignment of the planets coming at this summer's solstice. It's like the one on the solstice altar at the Black Pagoda."

"How did she know the medallion was there?"

"I have my suspicions, but we shall have to ask Lady Deich when she wakes. Come now. It's time we left this tomb."

The Abbot was already on the way to the door. "Hurry, Tiernan. We have plans to make."

Tiernan lifted Zoë's limp body. "Where are we going?"

"For the moment, to my chambers. But you will need to leave Gurama quite soon. The summer solstice is nearly here."

"But we don't know where we're supposed to go," Tiernan protested.

"Don't worry, my boy," the Abbot said as he led the way, "Johan Pietra has already given us one clue. With his help, we shall find another. Hopefully, in time."

CHAPTER TWENTY-SIX

Back in his rooms, the Abbot pulled down volume after volume from the shelves, each more dusty than the last and increasingly brittle with age. Tiernan looked in disbelief at the growing stack of books, then around at the book-lined study. Zoë, although still unconscious, was on a couch in a corner. He was reassured by the faint color returning to her face.

"No, these won't do at all," Rajid muttered under his breath. "What we want is the original text." Tiernan jumped out of the way as a precariously balanced stack of books crashed down. "Never mind them," Rajid said dismissively. "They'll all this century. All subsequent interpretations of Abbot Pietra's book. We need something much older. I know I have it here someplace." He slid a gilded box from a bottom shelf. "Ah, here it is."

On the front panel of the box there was a blackened icon of a monk holding a spike in his right hand. Above his left hand's raised palm hovered a circle of orbs. A latch on the side released the lid. Inside lay a ream of loose parchment pages, their binding long since disintegrated. The Abbot sorted through them quickly. He ran his eye over each, then set it aside.

"Each edition should be the same as the last, but with each new edition, subtle changes crept in." He lifted another sheet.

"Each author reinterpreted the original, drew slightly different conclusions. We have the advantage of having the original, the actual words of Joann Pietra." Zoë stirred, opened her eyes and sat up.

"Ah, my dear. So glad you have rejoined us." Rajid indicated a growing pile of pages to his left. "Most of the book concerns the founding of this Abbey." He tapped a smaller pile to his right. "But in this early section, Johan Pietra describes something he called the Judgment. I thought I had remembered that correctly. One reads so much, it's difficult to keep it all clear sometimes. From what I can tell, this Judgment was an event he experienced first-hand. Here, I'll read you what he saw:

> *The skies roared with thunder and the earth heaved,*
> *Then came darkness and a stillness like death.*
> *Lightning smashed the ground and fires blazed out;*
> *Death fell from the skies.*
> *When the heat died and the fires went out,*
> *The plains had turned to ash.*

"That seems fairly clear. Earth heaving, lightning, fires, ash. Comprehensive death and destruction." Tiernan said with satisfaction. "Jomini said it might be like that."

"Don't be too quick to interpret this literally," Rajid reproved him. "There was a deplorable tendency toward drama in my predecessor's day. It certainly made for a more interesting read. What a simple monk may have observed as a cataclysm, we may see as a natural event—a meteor or an earthquake. Perhaps even the conquering of a people. Leave your mind open to the possibilities." He fished Johan Pietra's medallion from a pocket under his robes and held it up for both to see. "Now Tiernan, you say you've seen this alignment of planets before?"

"I told you, at the Black Pagoda. My father says this alignment will occur again at the summer solstice. At that time, all the planets in this system will align."

"May I see it please?" Zoë walked unsteadily to the table to inspect the medallion.

"There's a prophecy," she said, turning the medallion over.

"Which prophecy would that be?" Rajid asked absent-mindedly, engrossed again in his papers.

"The one the old Seer at the Black Pagoda told me before we left."

"Ah, Michaela." Rajid looked up with a warm smile. "How is she?"

"Dying, eventually. She said there was a prophecy, an old one. I thought she was raving.

When in the west a second moon,
makes six a string of pearls,
then natures blend,
and time's erased,
the final reckoning unfurls.

"So how do we interpret this one," Tiernan asked, "if we're not supposed to look at it literally?"

The Abbot chuckled. "It probably means exactly what it says. Although you may need to take some liberties with the moon part. Moons don't make a habit of just appearing out of nowhere, do they? Did Josepht say anything about a moon in the alignment?"

Tiernan scowled. "Not a moon. Nothing so big. But maybe a comet. He seemed pretty excited about it."

"Good. Good. Yes, that certainly could be the moon in the prophecy. So when the comet and the planets are in alignment, we can expect this final reckoning to occur. Nothing we didn't already know. But what happens next? That's the question."

"Time's erased?" Zoë said with a shudder. "Sounds horrible."

"Yes. But again, this could be a very unsophisticated society's take on unusual, but very natural events. Tell me Tiernan, did your father say the comet would pass close to us?

Tiernan's hesitation wasn't lost on the Abbot.

"Well, my boy?"

"The orbit has been erratic. There's no sure way of telling, but if it continued on its most recent path, it might not miss us at all. It might hit us. In fact, it most probably will."

A knock and Tiernan moved to cover the opening door. The Abbot looked up from his pages.

"Ah, an addition to our little group. Who is this?" Livy stood in the doorway looking scared and clutching a packet to her chest.

"Livy, I thought I told you to stay put." Tiernan's harsh greeting surprised Zoë nearly as much as the relief she felt at Livy's appearance, but she was across the room and hugging her half-sister in a minute, simultaneously delivering a lecture on personal responsibility, unexplained absences and the duties of family.

Livy extracted herself from Zoë's embrace and silently held out the packet.

Zoë gave her a quick kiss and a smile. "Thanks, love," she whispered. She gently laid the bundle on the table before the Abbot and untied the straps. With a single motion she flipped back the wrappings. From one of the pockets she nudged an orb free. Soon all ten orbs glinted in a rainbow on the table. They gazed at them mesmerized for a long moment.

"You're looking at the Keys of the Ten Families of Ard Creggan, Tiernan," the Abbot explained. "You should feel honored. Few people outside of the Concordia have ever seen all the Keys together."

"The Seer Eleanor told me about them," Tiernan said, hefting a grey orb. "But, if they're so special, why would the Families let them leave Ard Creggan?"

"In normal times, they would never have allowed it," Rajid conceded. "But the seers can be very persuasive. And for many families it was simply a matter of price. Yes, I know, they are all sadly lacking in an appreciation of tradition. I'd heard the orbs were smuggled out of the city the night of the first earthquake. And none too soon. Much of the city has collapsed since you left."

Ard Creggan. Zoe swayed and as Tiernan steadied her, he corralled a pale yellow orb rolling toward the table edge. The walls of the room disappeared. Images, faces sped through his mind, then a warmth spreading across his body, blooming into searing heat, eating into this flesh, hot tendrils snaking over his skin. He clawed at his face, his lungs on fire.

"Tiernan!" Zoë's face swam toward him, her voice snapping him back to the room.

"What happened?" he asked, his head still spinning. He looked down at the orb in his hand, the taste of metal in his mouth.

"What did you see?" the Abbot asked.

"Everything." Tiernan faltered. "A fire. Your city." He turned to Zoë. "I saw a crypt. There was a seal over the door, two hammers on a forge."

"The Family An," Zoë murmured. "Their compound is next to the Deich compound in Ard Creggan."

"I saw a man, a young man but with white hair. I remember him from the celebration that last night. The one they threw out." He shuddered. "The fire was all around me. . . I mean, him." He brushed at the memory of flames. Understanding dawned. "This is how you knew about the medallion. You saw it. Can anyone see things? The past?'

"I imagine it works," the Abbot said with some satisfaction, "only if a descendant who holds a special key opens the door. Tiernan, would you empty your pockets, please? Let's find that key."

Reluctantly, Tiernan disgorged his pockets. A ball of string, a pouch with a few coins, a pocketknife, a folded map, and finally a ring with a snake coiled around a black gem rolled out onto the table and glimmered in the lamplight.

The Abbot picked it up. "Ah, here it is. Our key to all the keys."

Tiernan turned on Zoë. "But why would it work for me? I'm not a Deich, I'm not even a Publican."

"You didn't have to be," the Abbot said. "You just had to touch one." He nodded at Zoë. "And of course, hold the ring."

"So we know the orbs, the keys, you call them, retain memories. As the scripture said, the record, or testimony would be carried in the stones. I believe," the Abbot finished on an oddly buoyant note, "you are looking at Ard Creggan's story, carved into stone. Not literally, of course, but collected within each orb."

"In Ard Creggan, we have a Feast Day of the Keys," Zoë began. "It celebrates when the Ten Families were given their orbs."

"Ah, local folklore. Always so fascinating. Are there any traditions of how the keys were presented. Perhaps this ship Abbot Pietra mentions.?"

Zoë shook her head. "No. It's just every year at the winter solstice. The children receive presents."

The Abbot was already shuffling through his stacks of pages, and keeping up a running commentary.

"Yes, yes, quite a common tradition. Nearly always a quaint figure. The personification of prosperity and plenty. Father Time. The New Year. The Gift Bringer. What you might call a quadripartite divinity presiding over the end of the old year." The Abbot stopped shuffling papers and looked up. "Do the Publicans have a particular name for him?"

"We call him Father Peter," Zoë said in a faint voice.

"Yes. Well. We probably should have anticipated that," Rajid said dryly. "Now, soletei are trained in memory skills, aren't they Tiernan? Perhaps you'll tell us what was written in Johan Pietra's niche."

With a weary sigh, Tiernan began to recite.

"He saw the great Mystery, he knew the Hidden:
He saw the Journey beyond the distant,
He held the knowledge of all Time.
He prepared the way to Judgment,
And opened the record of Stone."

"Very good," Rajid beamed. "A remarkable memory. They've trained you well. But although that is inscribed, this is what Abbot Pietra originally wrote." He read from a fragile parchment:

"I saw the great ship, I knew their purpose;
They held the memory of time.
They had journeyed from beyond the distant,
They had journeyed to pass judgment,
The witness would be carried in the stones.

"Of course, in the original Mesarian, it should be sung," Rajid admitted.

"That isn't much like the quote in his niche," Tiernan objected.

"As I said, each subsequent translation interpreted slightly differently what he originally wrote. By the time Johan Pietra's niche was painted, it had become something else altogether." He continued. "I believe Johan Pietra saw something all those centuries ago. He talks about a journey from a great distance to pass judgment. That has me puzzled. Well no matter. Let us continue. He calls it a great ship, but it may have been anything large and unusual in the sky, perhaps a star or a comet."

"Or an alignment of planets?" Tiernan suggested.

"Yes, it might have been. Although their powers of observing the heavens at that time would have been rudimentary at best. Still, six bright planets aligned in, what did the seer's prophecy call it? A string of pearls? A lovely image. It would have been noticeable. And from all reports our Johan Pietra had an absolute mania for star observation."

Tiernan picked up the ring.

"The witness would be carried in the stones. Does that mean the keys or this stone? It's just a stone, black stone. Snake thingy. In a circle."

"It's really not a circle," Zoë said from long familiarity. "It's like a moon. See, the stone placement inside the snake's mouth indicates the moon glyph. If it was zero it would be over its head."

An idea niggled at the back of her brain. "I've seen this before. Somewhere." She tried hard to recall, but it was all in fragments. The smell of dirt. Rough stone. "I think it was Uncle Eon's last excavation. It was the same day I left Ard Creggan. He was working in the dig. He rushed me out before I could . . ." she stopped, "No, I can't remember."

"Why not show me?" the Abbot suggested. "In the An stone. Eon An wouldn't have had time to register the day you visited as a memory in the key. So we need something earlier. Perhaps when he first found the site." He placed his hand lightly over Zoë's. "Whenever you're ready, my dear."

Of course, Zoë thought, *Eon An died that night.*

She touched the yellow An orb. *Will. Will.* An overwhelming, aching feeling of sadness, of anxiety washed through her. She pushed beyond, but it dragged on her, slowing her as she fell through the days. There, a marker to follow in memory, the scent of earth, of freshly turned soil. She was at the dig again. And she wasn't.

"Eon, it's nothing but mud down here. I'll get dirty."

"And no one will look lovelier than you, Maigra dear, if you do."

A woman giggled. Maigra? A different Maigra, warm, unguarded, with Eon An in the same grotto Zoë had visited that last day.

"Now here's what I told you about, the carvings. See?"

Zoë smelled the acrid stone, heard her uncle's familiar voice.

"Ten ships under sail below this sweep of six stars. And a seventh star arcing in toward them. And here's the moon glyph. What's interesting is that Sensi Tri believes this same celestial alignment will occur at the summer solstice. Isn't that fascinating?"

"Perhaps it's a portent."

"Oh, I wouldn't think so. See, the ships are in a harbor of some kind here, below a castle or fort. Ard Creggan is nowhere near a body of water like that, so I think we're safe."

But Zoë felt the tiny nugget of doubt in Eon's mind.

"Now this glyph is very interesting. Let's see if you've been paying attention. What does this mean?"

Maigra leaned in. Zoë could smell sandalwood and osmanthus on her skin.

"It looks like a trident with an arrow through the shaft." A puzzled scowl. "Is that the Goddess glyph?"

"Very good! I shall have to take you with me on all my digs. You will be quite helpful."

Maigra blushed and leaned against him. A warmth spread through Zoë.

"The trident is a common reference to the sky goddess," Eon continued. "She who brings life. In many cultures, there is a female figure who descends to the underworld to rescue a husband or a brother. Hmmmm." He was lost again in the carvings, grunting in response to Maigra's quick hug. He didn't notice when she wandered off to explore the rest of the grotto. Zoë felt the sick surge of fear when he looked up and didn't see her.

"Maigra where are you?"

She was there near the back of the cave and his fear was as piercing as a nail.

"Please my dear, come back."

Maigra turned unsteadily. Zoë's head ached and the grotto walls spun around her. She could feel Eon's heart pounding, his vision narrowing to see only the woman. He moved toward her, staggered, a wave of nausea washed over him.

"It's the gas," he gasped. "You must try. I can't help you. If both of us are affected, we'll never leave this place. You must come back. Try, my dear. Please."

Maigra slumped to her knees.

"Let me sit down for a moment, Eon. I feel so tired. That's not right, is it? I can't feel sick and sleepy at the same time. Maybe if I just lie down."

The urge to sleep was overwhelming.

Zoë felt Eon's need to rush, to pull her to safety, warring with the paralysis creeping up his legs, slowing his steps to a shuffle. By the time he reached her, he wouldn't have the strength to move again.

"No, stand up. You must come here, to me. Now. You will die . . . .very quickly, if you don't. Please, Maigra, please."

His pleas were a sob, tears streaming down his cheeks. The woman looked up through the fog rising before her eyes. His tears glittered from a great distance. Sheer will dragged her back from the darkness, feet encased in lead dragged her forward step by step. The last thing Zoë felt were Eon's arms around her. Darkness closed over her head.

The Abbot and Zoë were standing in his chambers, a faint nausea still clinging to them.

"What a lovely woman," the Abbot murmured. "Did she die?"

Zoë still felt lightheaded. "That must have happened before I visited the dig. Maigra was at dinner with us the night. . . the night I left Ard Creggan. Eon said some workers had gotten sick from gas in the grotto. He didn't say it had been Maigra."

"I gather that was your Uncle Eon An. The woman he called Maigra, I sensed a closeness there," the Abbot ventured. "Were they lovers?"

Zoë hesitated. "I thought so, once. But the feeling I got was so…"

"Avuncular?"

She reddened. "I thought she was using my uncle. Now I think she truly cared for him. Things aren't always what they seem, I guess."

"Yes, well, it has given us what I needed. Your uncle said the mark of the goddess was common. It may have been once, but signs of her worship have all but faded away. Except for a few places that I know of. Tell me, Tiernan, have you seen this symbol in your travels?" Rajid scrawled something on a scrap of paper and pushed it across to him.

Zoe looked over Tiernan's shoulder at the drawing of a trident. "That's carved on the Pagoda's Solstice Altar, remember?"

"And I've seen it on the Island of Bey, east of here," Tiernan added thoughtfully. "It's carved into a hillside."

"A drawing on a hillside?" Zoë asked. "Are you sure?"

"Don't be such a skeptic, my dear," the Abbot said. "Chalk deposits below the soil make the outline white. Tiernan, the hillside you mention wouldn't happen to be near a wall or a fortress, would it? In the grotto carving, the inscription shows ships gathered under a fortress."

"Then it's the Island of Bey for certain. That's Dun Nemed," Tiernan said grimly. "A fort on the coast of the Island of Bey, due east of here. Your father and I were going there next when our ship to Gurama was intercepted. Maybe they weren't stopping us from coming to Gurama after all. Maybe someone didn't want visitors on that island."

"Let's see what Johan Pietra has to say." The Abbot consulted a sheaf of papers again. "He's been fairly helpful so far. The inscription you read is part of a longer section. Listen to the remainder."

Ten times ten, doubled again.
The cycle turns to retribution's end.
Judgment sits when six align.
Gather ten keys and
One of line.
Seek the goddess
Kneel to her song.
Set memory free.
Release the wronged.

"That's something of a confirmation. The time when six align, points to the summer solstice alignment of the planets. *Judgment sits when six align.* Jomini referred to this judgment, you said Tiernan. *Gather ten keys* is obvious. *One of line* is less clear. But we'll come back to that. *Seek the goddess,* could mean the symbol of the goddess on the Island of Bey. Certainly, it must have been well known in Johan Petra's day. *Kneel to her song.* I confess I have no idea what that means."

"I'll just have to figure it out when I get there," Tiernan said.

The Abbot sat back in his chair, his eyes closed, whether in thought or in exhaustion, it was difficult to say.

Zoë, however, was seeing clearly.

"Tiernan, how did your father know about Sensi Tri's observations of the comet?"

"Maybe he read the journals." His tone told her not to push. She asked anyway.

"How long was my father working with your father, with Publicans?"

Something in Tiernan's face changed, as if a charade had ended. He looked relieved.

"A few years," he said, matter-of-factly. "He mainly worked through the academics, through Sensi Tri and my father."

"That was treason for a Publican. What was so important that my father would commit treason?"

"Why don't you look in the Deich key?"

"I never saw my father touch the Deich key, only my Aunt Livia. I always wondered why. He must have known the key would record his memories, expose what he was doing."

"I guess there's no harm in telling you now," Tiernan said with a shrug. "He called it the Judgment. I don't know how he learned about it. Something your mother told him or showed him. She had the sight. That's why he collected crystals. He thought he might find answers in them. It took him years to find out it was Johan Pietra's ring. This ring." He held it up. "This opened the keys. That was ironic." His laugh was hard. "To know what it could do, to search so long for it, to have it right under his nose. And then to have his wife, then his daughter hide it from him."

Zoë felt her face turn hot.

The soletei continued. "He believed you when you told him you didn't have it. He kept looking. When we were attacked that last time, he was on his way to Gurama. He thought your mother had sent it back here. I knew better. I knew you had it."

"You didn't tell him?"

Something changed in again behind Tiernan's eyes. "Jomini needed the ring for his reasons. I need it for my own."

He slid the Eon Family orb into the packet along with the others, refolded the cloth and tied it up. He pocketed the ring. He didn't look at either the Abbot or Zoë.

"You have to admit, it has worked out better than even your father could have planned. Thanks to you, I'll be at Dun Nemed at the right time with the ring and the keys." He made for the door. Zoë blocked his way.

"The keys stay here." She heard her voice unnaturally shrill. "And the ring, too. I brought them to Gurama for a reason. They'll be safe here. That's what my father wanted."

He smiled as though at a headstrong toddler.

"I don't care about keeping them safe. And neither did your father."

For the first time, he looked at her, and she didn't recognize him.

"Jomini didn't want to save us from some catastrophe. Oh, maybe he did in the beginning. In the end, he was so caught up in that fantasy. Now Donncha thinks it's our only chance for peace—or the end of Ard Creggan. In his mind, they're one and the same. They both were delusional."

"And you're not, Tiernan?" the Abbot asked mildly.

"I can't afford to have illusions, Abbot Rajid. If these times have taught me anything, it's to seize the opportunity and use it to my own advantage. I will use these," he tucked the packet under his arm, "any way I can to give my people an advantage."

"You're no better than Brian," Zoë said, her illusions shattering painfully.

"Now that's where you're wrong. He wanted the keys to learn Ard Creggan's secrets and destroy it. Just more war. We've had enough of that. I want change. And I can get that on Dun Nemed. With these." He patted the bundle of orbs. He raised the blade of Pietra's Thorn as Zoë took another step toward him.

"I couldn't let Brian kill you, Zoë," he said evenly, "until I had everything I needed. But there's nothing holding me back now, so be careful." He half-bowed to the Abbot. "Abbot Rajid, thank you for your help. I hope you understand why I'm doing this, but I understand if you won't be giving me your blessing."

"My boy, I understand better than you know," the monk said with a sigh. "And you are making a very serious error."

Tiernan's expression clearly said he didn't care. He turned to Livy.

"You'll come with me."

The girl looked from Tiernan to Zoë.

" 'One of line'," Zoe sneered. "Like the prophecy says, one of the Deich line. Did you plan to take her with you all along, Tiernan? Even back at the village?"

"I knew who she was when Jomini sent her the pendant. He meant her to be part of this." To Livy he said, "You're a Citizen, even if your father was a Publican. Think of your people now and your duty. After the solstice, you'll be free to go anywhere you want."

Zoë knew Livy was scared. And she knew Tiernan, at the moment, was capable of anything.

"Go with him, Livy. He won't hurt you as long as you do what he wants. Don't worry, I'll find you."

"Jomini would be proud," Tiernan mocked and Zoë's fingers itched to choke the words in his throat. "I'll be taking the ship and I wouldn't try to follow." He pushed Livy before him through the door.

As soon as the door shut, Zoë's legs trembled so badly she found a chair across from the Abbot and sat down.

The Abbott rose with a sigh. "You've had a shock, my dear. Something to drink might help." From behind a thick volume of ornithological plates he took a bottle. He didn't speak again until he placed a tumbler of amber liquid before her.

"It tastes like the something you'd scrape off the stove," he said, "but it does amazingly restore you. Try a sip."

He was right. It tasted like old leather and smoke, but it cleared her head.

"We have to go after them."

The Abbot poured himself a drink and sat down across from her.

"You will, but not tonight. We have a fishing boat that can take you to the Island of Bey and Dun Nemed tomorrow. If you leave at first light, you can be there by tomorrow afternoon, providing you have smooth sailing. That should get you there in plenty of time. I think you should be able to rescue Livy before the alignment occurs."

She put her drink down.

"He won't hurt Livy. He likes her."

The monk raised a quizzical eyebrow.

"And what does that have to do with anything? He may be less than happy when he finds out the keys won't work for her."

Zoë stared at him.

"The stones will work for her. She's a Deich. 'One of line,' remember? Besides, she's used the keys with me before."

"You've used them? Together? Ah, did you perhaps show her how to use the keys, as you did with me and Tiernan, by touching your mother's ring?"

"Yes, I think so, yes." Her head hurt. Suddenly, she was bone tired. "But what difference does it make? The prophecy says, One in line. She's Jomini's daughter. She's in the Deich line."

"Ah, that's the problem with jumping to conclusions about old prophecies," he confided. "Tiernan never really thought things through as a student. I'd thought he'd matured. No, my dear, it's not that either of you are Jomini's daughter. It's that you are your mother's daughter."

Zoë looked at her drink and decided it had the opposite effect of rendering clarity.

"What does my mother have to do with this?"

"Johan Pietra's own words, *One in line*. Remember them? He meant his own line. Johan Pietra's line through your mother. You are his heir."

Abbot Rajid pulled a cord hanging near his desk. Somewhere in the Abbey a bell rang.

"Now you'll want to get some sleep," he said to the speechless Zoë. "You'll be leaving early."

••••

Dawn was a long way off when Zoë said goodbye to the Abbot. From the window of his rooms, he followed her progress down to the wharf by the bobbing lanterns the monks carried. The Abbey's own small fishing boat stood ready for her to board. Rajid had spent most of the night searching his library for anything that might help her on Dun Nemed.

"I found very little, Lady Deich. I'm sorry to say."

Zoë stifled a yawn. She'd had only slightly more sleep than the Abbot. "I'm not worried. All I plan to do is get there, get Livy, and get back to Ard Creggan as quickly as I can."

"Back to the city? Do you think that's wise?"

She avoided his eyes. "Of course. I thought they'd be safe here. But now I know the keys are the Families. We can't rebuild Ard Creggan without them."

"Tell me. If you needed to destroy the keys, would you be able to?"

Her eyes widened in alarm. He hurried to reassure her. "I'm not certain you will need to, but the scriptures refer to the release of memories from the keys as a cathartic event. They don't speak of the keys surviving this. In fact the successful Judgment seems predicated on the keys being emptied and extinguished."

Zoë expression turned mulish. "No. I have to return them to Ard Creggan with their memories intact. They belong to the Families. We need them. They're our past. We're nothing without our past."

Rajid voice was gentle. "Zoë, the writings I consulted spoke about the power of the keys. They also have a subtle, compulsive effect."

"You sound like Noor. They're not evil."

"I didn't say they were evil." He felt her resistance. It was farther along than he had guessed. He plunged on regardless. There was so little time.

"You must be willing to sacrifice them, Zoë. What the Judgment is, whatever it is, will hang on you being willing to open the keys and empty them."

"You don't understand." Her protest was a wail. "The keys will bring them back to Ard Creggan. They'll be alive again. I can be with them."

"They're just memories, Zoë. They're not real. They're not alive."

"They're real. I can feel them."

"You don't need these orbs to remember them."

"Don't you see?" Zoë said, her voice rough with fear. "There isn't anyone left. They're all gone, my father, my mother, Aunt Livia, Noor. If no one else remembers, did they exist? What if I forget?"

"Zoë, there is much more at stake here."

"Not for me."

He let her go then. He had little hope.

"You give up too easily, my friend."

Abbot Rajid didn't turn from the window as Eleanor entered the study.

"Everything is falling into place," she reassured him as they watched the boat leave the dock. "The solstice approaches and the keys are on their way to Dun Nemed."

"Perhaps," he responded. "Nonetheless, I am worried. There are reports of the Counselor outside of Ard Creggan. He is an unknown factor. And the boy's actions were unexpected."

Eleanor's gaze seemed to be on something other than the little fishing boat nosing out into the sea.

"Leave the Counselor to his own fate. With Tiernan, we took a calculated risk. Just as giving Zoë the keys was a risk."

Rajid snorted.

"A risk? Her curiosity has always been her weakness."

"And Tiernan's need to protect has always been his," Eleanor replied.

"You knew he would take the keys," he said, turning to her in astonishment. "Why didn't you tell me?"

The seer's expression was almost smug.

"We anticipated only that he might take them. He has been taught to seize any chance. We knew his feelings for his people. His own history fighting Publicans. And his own impetuosity." A hint of a smile curled Eleanor's lip. "It didn't take a seer to see that given the opportunity, he would take the keys."

"You manipulated him. And me." Rajid was annoyed. "Why?"

"It's simple. We couldn't trust Zoë with the keys. She had become too attached. Perhaps it is in her blood. We weren't certain she would give up the keys. He will."

"He certainly gave Zoë up easily enough," the Abbot said bitterly. "I thought he loved her." Like most celibates, he was incurably romantic.

"If it's any consolation, he thought he loved her, too," Eleanor said, much too dismissively in Rajid's opinion. "Which do you suppose is stronger?" she asked. "The love for a person or the love of a dream?"

"Thanks to your machinations, Eleanor," the Abbot said, "we may find out."

He took himself off to bed then, and in his dreams a black cloud spread out across the land.

CHAPTER TWENTY-SEVEN

As Zoë sailed to Dun Nemed, the ship carrying Tiernan and Livy slipped into the harbor just below the fortress of Dun Nemed on the Island of Bey. Sunrise hadn't lightened the gloom. Dark clouds piled up overhead and the cold sweeping off the water had crept into Tiernan's bad leg. He hurt and it wasn't putting him in a good mood. Adding to his discomfort was the look in Livy's eyes.

It had been a difficult voyage for everyone. Once they'd sailed clear of Gurama, the ocean swells grew in size, sending waves crashing over the deck.

"Well," the captain said philosophically. "We'll not be worrying about pirates this trip. The canny ones will be in harbor and glad of it."

Restless, Tiernan took shelter in the wheelhouse, but the captain was too talkative to suit him. Not that he minded the company, but he had too few answers to match the captain's questions. He headed below deck.

It wasn't any quieter down below. Tiernan stuck his head in the galley. The cook looked up from balancing a pot of hot coffee and a pan of sausages. The smell was enticing, the room steamy, and it would have been good to put his leg up and have a hot cup or two. But not now. He continued down the passage, swaying heavily as the ship dipped and shuddered. The first cabin was obviously the crew's, the double tiers of bunks empty now, the bedclothes rumpled as if the men had just fallen out of their berths. Tiernan closed the door and continued down the passage. Two more doors, but a light under the door of only one. A shout from above deck carried to him; the storm was building. His footsteps, the opening of the cabin door, were lost in the ship's creaking and the wind's howl.

Livy sat on a bunk, clutching a basin, rocking with the ship's motion, the packet of keys beside her, unopened. As Tiernan entered, the smells of grease and fried sausage billowing in behind him. She retched and threw up. Tiernan quickly shut the door and retreated to the galley until they reached harbor. When they landed, the ship's captain had no time for lingering good-byes.

"There's no safety for us here," he told them, putting them ashore without ceremony. "We'll be sailing before this storm and hope it don't catch up with us. If you want my advice, find a well-built house as far from the coast as possible and bunker down. From the looks of it, this is a 100-year storm and we'll all be lucky to see the back of it."

The Island of Bey was nothing but hard rock and rockier soil. The fortress of Dun Nemed sat on the edge of a cliff that reared up from the ocean in a slab as smooth as black glass. On the land side of its walls, a maze of stone led down to the harbor and a cobblestone quay. Only a handful of fishermen lived on the island, their cottages cowering alongside the dock. On the steep hillside rising from behind the cottages to the outer walls of the ancient fort, the white lines of the Goddess' trident glowed in the storm's peculiar green light.

Livy appeared on deck, pale and shivering in the wind. The lure of solid ground had obviously roused her and she pushed past Tiernan in her hurry to get down the gangplank. Once on the cobblestones she looked around, misery etching her face.

"I want some tea," she whimpered.

Tiernan started up the narrow path to the fort. Fat drops of rain had started to fall.

"You should have eaten on the ship. There's no time now," he said without sympathy. "Come on."

Livy didn't moved, a mulish look on her face.

"I want a cup of tea," she repeated and sat down in the middle of the path.

"Get up, or I'll drag you," he ordered.

She sniffed, disconsolate, hauled herself up, but her knees buckled. She folded like a puppet whose strings had been cut. Tiernan was left with no choice than to pick her up and, cursing himself, the weather, and women, knock on the door of the only cottage with a visible light. Once they recovered from their surprise at having visitors, the fisherman and his wife took them in readily enough. The kettle already was steaming on the stove, and the woman clucked and fluttered about until the girl was tucked up next to the fire in the second-best quilt, a steaming mug in her hands, and the expectation of a coddled egg. Tiernan fumed and waited.

••••

In Ard Creggan, Sinon Yar stood at a tower window looking down on the deserted plaza below. He had nothing to do. The petitioners, the hangers-on, the sycophants and followers were gone. Dead or disillusioned. "Or dispossessed," he muttered, as the tower swayed ever so slightly in a tremor. Around the compound, buildings leaned into each other or sprawled from their foundations, testimony to the destructive power of the quakes. Ard Creggan was crumbling away.

His attention was taken by a lone figure crossing the plaza. Even at this distance Yar recognized Caleb's wraith-like figure. In recent months he had taken to wearing black, a very atypical color for a Publican.

My own High Executioner, Yar thought idly. *What shall we do when there's no one left to execute?*

From his vantage point in the tower, Yar saw a second figure in red approaching from the main gate. His rolling gait tickled Yar's memory; almost, he could place him. *Some administrative manager, perhaps. Nothing to manage here*, was Yar's sour thought. *He must want something.*

The visitor caught up with Caleb, leaning in as though to deliver a message for his ears alone. From above, the figures merged for the briefest of moments, the black enveloped by the red visitor's coat. As Sinon Yar watched, the black figure staggered back; fell to one knee. The other turned away abruptly, as though from a brief yet unpleasant conversation. He strolled from the compound. No one challenged him. There was no one left.

Sinon Yar turned to bark an order and caught himself. There were no soldiers outside the door, none down the hall. He remembered that. *Good plans are undone with too little anticipation.* He turned back to the window. Below in the plaza, Caleb was a dark, still comma in the dirt. A movement on the edge of the compound caught Yar's eye. A hooded figure slipped from a covered walkway. Yar's full attention now was on a furtive figure scurrying through the gate and out into the city. A note had appeared on his desk that morning. *Your wife is unfaithful.* He knew where Maigra was going. He was amazed how much that stung him. *A weak heart breaks a strong man.* Ard Creggan might be slipping from his grip. He couldn't stop that. But he could stop the woman.

Sinon Yar crossed to a wall-hanging, raised a fold, and stepped behind it. Pressure on a concealed panel opened a narrow passage. A dank breeze fluttered the tapestry and he walked through into darkness. Behind him, silence descended on the empty room. Down in the compound, the black comma added a dash of red.

••••

Zoë scanned the coastline of the Island of Bey as the fishing boat hit the top of a swell. The rain that threatened earlier was pelting down so hard the island was only a shadowy hump rising from the sea. Still, in the downpour, a light was visible at the top of the cliff. Someone was at Dun Nemed.

The captain and his crew didn't waste time. The fishing boat was secured and the sailors scattered among the low stone cottages, all of whose inhabitants appeared to be relatives or acquaintances. The captain stood in the sheltering doorway of one of the cottages with Zoë. Unlike the rest of his men, he didn't avoid her eye. He was a man with no illusions about his own short-comings.

"You're welcome to stay here," he said. "I'll take you back to Gurama when the storm is over. I think you've something you need to do up there." He jerked his head in the direction of Dun Nemed. "I'll tell you straight, neither I, nor any of these folk will have anything to do with it, or help you, if you go up there. You're on your own. I just thought you should know that. But like I said, if you're here when the storm clears, I'll take you wherever you want to go."

Zoë looked from the captain to the black mass that was Dun Nemed. She wanted desperately to stay there next to a warm fire. "I've got to go."

He nodded. "Then come in for a moment. My cousin Dio has news of your sister."

Inside, a round little woman left a sizzling pan on the stove, wiping her hands on her apron to greet them.

"I knew the minute I saw you, that you were kin," she began with a warm smile. "There's a great family resemblance between the two of you."

Zoë digested that observation with difficulty. "You saw Livy?"

"She was here with a man who limped. He made out he was her brother. But I didn't believe that. Oh, he was kind enough to her, but he didn't act like family, if you know what I mean."

"She was all right?" Zoë tried not to sound alarmed.

"Oh, she was fine when she left here. No, just soaked through, the poor thing. But we dried her out well enough, even though that awful man kept wanting to leave. I told him," she said with a combative look in her eye. "I wasn't going to see that child walk out of my house without something on her stomach, not while I had something to say about it. And her so sick from the sailing."

Zoë felt an odd sympathy for Tiernan, caught between two such determined females.

"They left together a few hours ago. She told me there'd be her sister coming after her who'd want to go to Dun Nemed. When I saw you, I was to give you this."

Dio pulled a carved box from her apron pocket and handed it to Livy.

"I have to say she's a clever little thing. She had me and the husband wondering with her magic tricks. I've never seen such nimble little fingers. I was tempted to count the silverware when she left," she chuckled. "Now what was it I was suppose to tell you? Sounds like a bit of nonsense. Knock once. Look twice. That was it." She smiled broadly.

"Did the man say anything?" Zoë asked.

"Oh yes," Dio said, giggling. "He made her show him what was in the box. And the little scamp did. Nothing!"

She hooted with laughter. Zoë smiled uncertainly. Dio mopped her eyes with a corner of her apron, still chuckling, and went back to her stove with the air of a woman who'd done a good job under difficult conditions.

The captain followed Zoë back outside.

"There's something else." He lowered his voice and closed the door behind them. "It wouldn't do to upset Dio. She's delicate, you know. But another ship put in here last night. And someone came ashore."

"Did anyone see who it was?"

He shook his head. "They keep their curtains and doors closed on the nights when this ship calls. But word is whoever it was went up to Dun Nemed. And didn't come down again."

Even in layers of oilskins and wool, Zoë shivered.

"The thing is, they don't care to find out. On the nights the fort sings, a ship puts in, a visitor goes up to Dun Nemed, stays for a few hours, then leaves. It's been going on for as long as they can remember."

Zoë wasn't sure she'd heard him right. "The fort sings?" The captain looked embarrassed.

"Well, that's what the locals call it. It's a humming more like. But on a night like this. . . ." He faced into the mounting wind. "On a night like this, it'll soon be like a pack of banshees wailing. You can hear it clear out to sea. No one goes up there then. Not any of us, anyway."

Zoë's mouth was suddenly dry.

"Thank you, captain. For everything." She shook his hand. "And I hope to see you again."

He watched her start up the path to Dun Nemed, reflecting on the strange ways of some people, then went back inside and enjoyed a large plate of bacon and eggs under the watchful eye of his favorite cousin.

•••

The rain sheeted down, sending cold fingers to search out every exposed piece of skin, blinding her as she trudged up the narrow stone path. The rutted paths that promised a direct line to the fort suddenly would veer off in an entirely different direction. She clutched her oilskins around her and counted. The key to finding your way through the maze, the captain had told her, was to take seven lefts. Seven lefts, he said, and you'll be at the entrance to Dun Nemed.

She was climbing now, slipping on uneven, rain-slicked stairs. From the sound, a low rumbling drone, she knew she was nearly to the fort. Over a tumbled outer wall of grey blocks, the remnants of a breach wall, through a narrow defile, and she was within Dun Nemed itself. Across a paved expanse, the fort's unassailable fourth side, the cliff edge, and beyond that the black heaving sea. *Has there ever been such a desolate place?* Zoë wondered.

A circular stone cairn squatted at the very center of the fort. In the driving rain, it was hard to see for certain, but standing stones appeared to parade around the inner perimeter of the fort, surrounding the cairn except for one truncated stone, a gaping hole in the circle.

She wedged herself between the nearest standing stone and the inner wall of the fort to get out of the howling wind. There was a new tone nearly too low to be heard vibrating deep in her chest, setting up sympathetic vibrations in her pocket. Zoë drew out the box Livy left for her. The illusionist's box hummed a discordant little tune in her hands but when she opened the lid there was nothing in it.

Now what did Dio say? Knock once, look twice. Well I've looked once already.

She closed the box again, rapped the lid, and opened the box a second time. Snuggled down in the bottom, a green orb glinted up at her.

That's my clever little sister, Zoë thought. *At least the Deich orb is safe. But what about the rest of the keys? Where are they?*

Zoë sagged against the hard stone, hunched under the pelting rain. A projection on the stone's face dug into her spine. Curious, she inspected the face. What the rain hid from her eyes, she felt with her fingertips, sweeping away dirt and lichens. There were glyphs cut into the stone face. Slowly at first, but with each line deciphered, her fingers sped on to the next.

Ten times ten, doubled again.
The cycle turns to retribution's end.
Judgment sits when six align.
Gather ten keys and
One of line.
Seek the goddess
Kneel to her song.
Set memory free.
Make known the wrong

That's not quite right. Zoë tried to remember the script in Johan Pietra's book. *But which part is wrong?* Feeling down the face of the stone, her fingers found a shallow niche in the stone's base and above the niche the glyph for the Huckat Family. *Each standing stone must correspond to a Family.* In a flash of lightning she saw the orb nestled in the niche.

And that's another thing that's not right.

••••

Sinon Yar was not amused. An intermittent drizzle soaked him within minutes of leaving the warren of passages snaking through the cracked walls and compounds of Ard Creggan. Ahead of him, a show of lamplight warned that Maigra was slowly picking her way through the rubble-filled streets.

He vaguely recognized the neighborhood as being near the old Deich Compound. To his left was the great plaza, the scorch marks still visible from the bonfire that had blackened its pavers the night of the solstice. Beyond that, the great double doors to the Deich House sagged on their hinges, above them a multitude of blank, black windows, as though the house itself had shut its eyes to the ruin.

The night clouds thinned, passing away from the face of a full moon. The broken stones around him sprang into sharp relief. Glints of light ricocheted from the glass shards still clinging to the window mullions. Sinon Yar blinked. Thousands of eyes blinked back.

Ahead, the light disappeared. He hurried forward rounding the corner of a building, into an alley. No light. The alley was dark, deserted.

Once again, the clouds parted. Moonlight showed him a ladder descending into a pit. Two more feet and he would have fallen down. Sinon Yar was not surprised at his luck; he took it for granted. Maigra had taken that route. He knew it. He climbed down.

From along the black tunnel, he imagined he could hear voices; a woman's low murmur, a man's deeper reply.

At least they're still talking, he thought coldly. *Even Maigra isn't so degenerate she'd make love in this pit.*

If someone had suggested he loved his new wife, he would have ridiculed such a notion. A blow had been dealt to Sinon Yar's vanity by his own wife. In his experience, an unprecedented blow. He needed to discover this man who she preferred. Over him.

"*Not that it matters.*"

He crept farther down the passage.

••••

A warm light grew brighter at the end of the passage. The passage was so narrow, its rock slab walls leaned in to touch, barely an arm's length overhead. Here and there niches no wider than the span of a man's hands held ashes. Tiernan felt sure a few also held bones. He strained to hear any sounds above the storm outside.

At least here, I can't hear that damned droning. It's getting worse by the minute.

He thought of Livy alone out there.

There's no telling who, or what, is in here. I'll look things over and then, if it's safe, I'll get her. By the sounds of things, she's almost done.

He judged this only by the swelling harmonics outside, a shift from non-descript drone to a minor key.

Livy was out there. *You have a job to do. Do it.*

On first entering Dun Nemed, he'd seen the tactical advantage in building a fort with an unassailable fourth wall. But there was no military advantage in the standing stones ringing the fort's interior walls. If anything, they interfered with the line of fire. It had taken Livy to see their purpose.

"There are ten stones," she said pointing out the obvious. "And there are ten keys." He inspected the nearest stone face, not sure what he was looking for.

"There's a glyph halfway up the stone."

The rivulets of rainwater streaming down the stones actually helped outline the symbol.

"You see?" he said, shouting over the wind and the keening of the stones. "See? There's an Ard Creggan Family name. Each standing stone must correspond to one of the keys."

What was the inscription? Gather ten keys and one of line. Seek the goddess, His heart was pounding.

"Right. We're above the Goddess' mark of the trident. But what do we do with the keys?"

Livy found a crevice in the wall out of the rain and crawled in. She pulled her hood up over her head and sulked. Around them, the stones thrummed deeply in the wind, the chord discordant and swelling.

Kneel to her song.

He knelt before the stone. In a flash of lightning, he saw it, a niche a few inches from the base.

"We need to match the keys to the glyphs."

Set memory free, release the wronged.

Livy covered her ears with her hands.

"I want to go," she cried. "It hurts."

Tiernan pulled her hands down and pointed to the stone heap in the center of the fort. In the lee of the cairn, unexpectedly, a door.

"Put the keys in the right niches and you can go in there." He pointed at the door. "It should be dry."

She looked at him, resentment in her eyes. "How do I know which stones go where?"

He threw down the packet with the orbs on the pavers, pulled the ring from his pocket and slipped it onto his finger.

"Take my hand. Touch each of the keys. You'll be able to open them and see which Family key each one is, just like Zoë did. Match them to the glyphs on the stone. I'll be right back."

Livy's eyes widened. "I'm not staying here alone."

He grabbed her arm, harder than he meant to. But he was too driven now to let up.

"Figure out the keys first," he barked.

It took her longer than he expected to identify each of the keys. It wasn't like when Zoë had opened the Family An key with him. He didn't get a slew of memories. He put this down to Livy's inexperience. Yet he suspected her of drawing out the process to delay him. Finally it was done. By then, both of them were soaked again and cold.

"Now place the keys where they belong," he shouted. "I'll come back for you." The clash around them had intensified.

"Don't enter the cairn without me. Remember that. Don't come after me." He scowled. "I mean it, Livy."

She pulled away from his grip, glaring at him. But she nodded assent.

The last he saw, she was running between the standing stones delivering the keys to their niches in the blowing rain. He turned to the cairn door. He'd seen a tear of light escape from between the rock walls of the cairn as they entered the fortress. Someone was in there. Livy might be safer in the storm.

A curtain hung at the end of a short passageway, light and the sweet smell of burning peat spilling between the panels. Cautiously, he parted the curtain and stepped down into a circular chamber. A sarcophagus occupied most of the middle of the room. Across from the door, a man sat on a bench before a fireplace. It was who occupied the bench that made Tiernan blink.

"Come in, Tiernan ," the Counselor said cordially, as though he were sitting safe in Ard Creggan. He took a sip from a steaming mug in his hands. "Perhaps you would like something warm to drink?"

CHAPTER TWENTY-EIGHT

To test the depth of a man's resolve, first kill what he loves. The proverb came to mind as Maigra shivered in the excavation's cold damp, the mud sucking at the soles of her shoes. A light ahead. Pavers underfoot now. There was the arch at the entrance to the grotto. The stone snakeheads in the keystone looked down with indifference. *Eon, it's nothing but mud down here. I'll get dirty. And no one will look lovelier than you, Maigra dear, if you do.*

A familiar voice. "You're crying, Maigra. An attack of remorse? Or does getting dirty make you weep?"

She didn't bother to wipe her checks. "The last time I was here, was with your father. I'm not ashamed to cry for him, Will. At least I mourned."

If the twisted ruin that was Will An's face couldn't show emotion, his voice made up for it in its bitterness.

"For all of what? Two weeks. Three? How is married life? Enjoying yourself as the wife of the mighty Basillius?"

She stifled the irritation at the resumption of a too familiar argument. "Is this why you asked me to meet you here? This place can't be good for you. Where are your nurses?"

Will half reclined in a chair, his head lolling weakly to one side. A lamp sat beside him on an upended crate. It was the light that had guided Maigra. Deep in their sockets, his eyes glittered feverishly.

"The whole of Ard Creggan is unhealthy at the moment. I sent them away."

Maigra's suspicions quivered.

"What are you up to, Will?"

"Just a friendly chat. Tying up loose ends. That's all. Come closer, Maigra."

With an effort he extended a bandaged stump. She ignored the gesture. What could one man like Will do? She looked around the grotto. It was bare except for the clutter left behind by the workmen: a tarp, a few shovels. The hand picks used to clean the carvings lay close to the wall where they'd been dropped in mid-excavation.

"Your ClearWorlders have been busy. Ard Creggan is nearly deserted, thanks to them. Are there many left still willing to blow themselves up?"

"There are always volunteers who want to change the world—no matter the cost."

A coughing fit threw him sidewise in his chair. She didn't move to help him. Slowly, painfully, he righted himself. Maigra made a tentative thrust.

"They'll come back, you know. Back to Ard Creggan. You can't keep the Families away forever. Ard Creggan is home. This is where we belong. You can't change that."

It was pure provocation. To her surprise, he agreed.

"You are right. I think Ard Creggan is like a magnet drawing the Families back. Back to their old ways, back to their old lives. To the old world. That's why it has to change."

"Change?" Maigra spat. "If there's anything we don't need, it's more change."

"Do you hear something?" Will interrupted, his eyes on the grotto entrance. "No? I thought I heard someone coming."

The woman looked down the long passageway, then quickly back at Will.

"Who? Who are you expecting?"

"Who? Perhaps your husband. Sinon Yar. Wouldn't you be glad to see him?"

His tone was innocent. Maigra wasn't fooled.

"I'd be delighted," she said dryly. "But my husband doesn't follow me around."

"Perhaps if I asked him to come. Perhaps if I told him his beloved wife was meeting her lover."

She watched him closely.

"So? Please don't be offended, Will. But when he sees you, he'll know that's a lie."

It was hard to gauge Will's reaction by the mask that was his face.

"Oh, I know that. So I invited Samuel too. He should be here any minute. You were the perfect bait for both men. You should be flattered, dear."

She was at Will's side, her hand gripping his arm. He groaned in pain.

"Why would you do this? They'll kill each other," she hissed. "Samuel is your friend."

"My cause demanded it," Will said without emotion, his eyes on the grotto entrance. "Sacrifices must be made. I expect them to meet. I hope they kill each other. The old order destroys itself."

Maigra's thoughts raced ahead, looking for a way to turn Will's plan.

"And what if Yar survives? He could. He could rebuild Ard Creggan. He's determined to see the city survive. Or Samuel. He could kill Yar. He's killed before. He'll win."

He looked up at her, his serenity only adding to her distress.

"And that is why my people are waiting in the mines below us. Thanks to my father's maps, I know the weakest spots. If those points fail simultaneously, as I plan they will, in a very short time, all this," his head rolled side to side , "will be gone. Ard Creggan falls."

She turned away from him, trying to think, but nothing seemed to penetrate the fear rising inside her. Unseeing, she steadied herself against the all, feeling the warmth of the great snake coiled in the wall beneath her hand. *Eon. What do I do? Tell me, please.*

"Will," she whispered. "Please. Let me warn Samuel. Let him live."

He didn't respond. It was hard to say if he even heard her. His eyes saw something more than her and the grotto. Now Maigra could hear footsteps approaching along the long passageway. Blindly, her fingers traced the relief of the trident above the snake's head. *The sky goddess, Maigra. She who descends into the underworld. To rescue a husband. Or a brother.* At her feet, the workman's tools, a chisel.

Will barely noticed when she stood over him. He hardly moved when the chisel's blade plunged into his chest, found his heart. Just a long slow breath from his lips and she was alone, listening for footsteps.

••••

"Tiernan, isn't it? I was expecting your associate, Brian Goodloe, but I imagine you'll do. We met during the peace talks. A waste of time, don't you agree? Well, we won't need to worry about them anymore," the Counselor said. He appeared to be in a very good humor. Tiernan didn't know what to say.

"Forgive me. This must be a little confusing. You are in possession, I expect, of the ring and—by the sounds outside—of the keys of Ard Creggan?

"You knew I'd bring them?" Tiernan stammered.

"Well, if not you, then Brian Goodloe or Jomini Deich, or someone else who believed all those prophecies Johan Petra and his minions salted scriptures with for centuries. They were determined the keys would be here at the right time. They should be pleased with themselves." He scowled. "But the ring, the key to all the keys, proved elusive. I wasted too much time looking for it. It only made sense to enlist additional help. Ah, I see you also have the Thorn."

Tiernan's hand went reflexively to his belt where he'd tucked Johan Pietra's spike. The spike's unnatural coldness reassured him.

"You must indulge me. The last time I saw that particular weapon, my son was forging it. It brings back so many tender memories."

"Abbot Pietra? Your son?" Tiernan blurted. The Counselor allowed his amusement to show.

"How undiplomatic of you, soletei. Yes, Johan Pietra was my son. Of course, when I last saw him and the Thorn, he was far from holy. In fact, I think it was his life up to that point that decided him on repentance. I tried to dissuade him. But like all men in whom morality blooms late, he was inflexible. He felt he must atone."

"For his father?"

"Me?" The Counselor seemed genuinely surprised by the accusation. "I made Ard Creggan a power. I gave them metallurgy, taught them everything I knew about commerce. I made Publicans wealthy. For me, it was business. My son never understood. He said he was going to spend the rest of his life attempting to atone for my so-called sins." He paused to chuckle. "By founding a monastic order. Imagine. Vows of poverty, chastity, and obedience. What a waste. I miss him, you know. He was one of the few people I could confide in. Perhaps that was a mistake. They say you should never make your child your friend."

His hand fluttered as though brushing the past aside. With a sigh, the memory expired.

"Well, I hope he was happy in his new life. But we're off topic. I assume you know what will occur this evening?"

"Jomini told me everything." The smoke from the fire wreathed his head and Tiernan's eyelids grew heavy. *Why was the Counselor smiling?*

"Jomini. My dear delusional friend, seeing mystical omens in the entrails of ducks and chasing crystals. No, I think he told you what he believed to be the truth, soletei. The reality is much more interesting. We're both here for the final reckoning, aren't we? When the six planets align and a second moon is sighted in the east."

Tiernan interrupted impatiently. "I know the prophecy. Let's see how well you remember." He began. "I saw the great ship, I knew their purpose. They held the memory of time. They had journeyed from beyond the distant. They had journeyed to pass judgment."

The old man raised a hand to stop the recitation. "It's easy to remember when it's your own past—even when it was so very long ago. Yes, I saw your so-called great ship. It left me here."

There was still venom beneath the words.

"They left me here, with good reason. I committed an unforgivable sin. Punishment was required. Retribution. This," he gestured broadly and Tiernan knew he meant the world beyond Dun Nemed, "this was my punishment and my prison. Today is my reckoning, my Judgment. The day the keys tell all. And when they do, I'll either be freed, or," his face darkening at the thought, "I'll be condemned to continued imprisonment in this hellhole. My fate hangs in the balance. Quite literally, in your hands."

"Set memory free, release the wronged," came to Tiernan's mind. Had he said that aloud?

"Yes, that's right," the Counselor said quickly. "You are remarkably well informed." He watched Tiernan closely. "Perhaps Jomini is to be congratulated after all. You've come all this way, through so many difficulties, because Jomini Lord Deich told you this day would be what? What did he promise you?"

Tiernan flushed in the heat of the fire that didn't seem to touch the Counselor. "Jomini said it was a time to change the past. *But whose past?*"

"You'd like to have a hand in deciding that, wouldn't you, soletei. Think before you commit yourself. What else did you learn on Gurama? I assume that's where you or Jomini discovered my son's writings. Johan wrote it all down as I related it to him. *The skies roared with thunder and the earth heaved, Then came darkness and a stillness like death.* Sounds remarkably like what is happening outside these walls doesn't it."

"Death fell from the skies," Tiernan muttered remembering past battles. "I've seen that. Ard Creggan's guns have a long reach."

"You're skipped a few lines, but the essence is intact," the Counselor said dryly. "The rest goes, *When the heat died and the fires went out. The plains had turned to ash."* He stared into the mid-distance. "No matter what you might think, soletei, you haven't seen destruction on that level. Let me tell you, they are unforgiving and remorseless. They are concerned with one thing only. My punishment. And my redemption. I was placed here to accomplish a specific task. You may hate the Publicans and Ard Creggan, but my sentence was to advance that society. I have accomplished that. I only hope it has been enough. And only the keys will tell them if my time here has been productive."

"Why should I care?"

The Counselor bowed his head. "Ah yes. You want to change the past. But let me convince you that you should care more about my future. What happens if I fail and remain imprisoned here?"

"I tell you, I don't care if you're freed or jailed." Tiernan said irritably.

The Counselor sighed. "Yes, we've established that. But you must realize, if I stay here I will continue to help the Publicans. And up to this point, that has meant Citizens have suffered. Let me confess that it took very little to persuade the Concordia there were no alternatives to war with your people. And if I suggested that poisoning the land might weaken Citizen resistance, well, they were all too willing to do their worst. So Publicans win. You lose." The Counselor leaned forward in his chair. "Wouldn't you like to change that?"

Tiernan eyed him, suspicious. "If your release is based on how much you've made Ard Creggan hated and feared, you shouldn't have any worries. You'll be freed."

"True," the Counselor conceded. "But my jailers are particular. They expected me to accomplish all this without, shall we say, reverting to my old ways. I found that very difficult to do. A man's nature is what it is." He smiled apologetically.

Light glimmered through the fog that was permeating Tiernan's brain.

"You're afraid of what the keys will tell them. You don't want them to open the keys." Confusion overtook him again. It was so difficult to think with the smoke and the cairn's wall pressing in. He couldn't breathe. "The keys are already in the stones." He shook his head trying to clear it. "You can't stop them." The Counselor's smile turned cold.

"They may be in place, but only one thing opens them. And you have it."

The black stone winked on Tiernan's hand.

"Only that the ring can open the keys." The Counselor's repeated. His words echoed strangely in Tiernan's head. "I imagine the Deich girl showed you how to open them."

Tiernan looked down at the ring as though it might have something to tell him. "She's outside. Waiting for me." He felt strangely weightless. He slid the ring off his finger and held it up to the lamplight.

"The Stone Breaker," he mumbled.

The Counselor brightened. "Ah," he purred. "I knew we'd understand each other."

••••

The storm had intensified and with it the painful keening of the standing stones. Zoë scuttled between the megaliths, feeling half-blind down their sides to interpret the glyphs. None of the orbs were in their right niches.

It's like whoever placed these couldn't tell which was which. The last megalith stood at the very edge of the cliff. As she reached it, a squall knocked her off her feet, rolling her across the wet pavers. She clawed desperately at the slick stone. Her left foot kicked out into empty air. Three-hundred feet below, the black depths sent up a icy plume to slap at her.

She was yanked into a profound silence.

CHAPTER TWENTY-NINE

The voices had stopped. The silence spurred Sinon Yar on. In his imagination, the silence could mean only one thing and he was determined to surprise Maigra in her lover's arms. He imagined her horror, the look on her face. And her lover.

I'll kill him with my bare hands. She won't be able to stop me. I'll break his neck. I'll break his neck in front of her. She can beg. I'll deal with her.

He ran the last few yards to the grotto arch. The twining snakes overhead opened their jaws in frozen terror.

The light that guided his way through the passage blinded him now at the grotto entrance. He lunged forward.

Where are you, Maigra?

And there she was, tenderly tucking a coverlet around a man whose scarred face glinted in the light. He sniggered. Maigra turned her back on Will to face her husband.

"This isn't what you think," she began, but he waved her explanation aside, giddy with his discovery.

"My dear," he said, laughing. "I thought many things. But this," he pointed at Will, "this I never imagined." His relief embarrassed him; but he was well on his way to believing he'd never thought her unfaithful.

"So you've taken up nursing on the side? I find that commendable. But I can't say much for your bedside manner. This is a terrible place to minister to the sick. Who is this poor soul?"

Maigra looked down at Will's body.

"Would you believe he's the one who's plotted against you all these months with his suicide bombers and raids?"

"Him?" Sinon Yar looked incredulous. Then angry. "He's the one? He's can't even sit up. What do you mean, he's the one?"

Maigra touched Will's shoulder. "He is . . was," she amended, "the son of Eon An. You killed his father. He led the ClearWorlders. It was the ClearWorlders who were his arms and legs."

He was still suspicious. "How do you know that?"

"Because he told me. Before I killed him."

She held the chisel up for him to see its whole bloodied length. Instinctively, Yar took a step back and made a mental note that his wife would soon vanish into Ard Creggan's prisons. *You could never be too careful.*

"It might have been more prudent for one of my people to interrogate him, my dear. They are more skilled at getting information out of people."

Maigra's eyes widened. She flew into his arms, scanning his face.

"But that's the reason I had to do it. To kill him. They're coming here. It was all a trap."

"Who's coming? Where?" Yar looked over his shoulder.

"Here. His followers. The ClearWorlders. He knew you'd come and he planned to trap you and kill you."

Yar's chest puffed up.

"You underestimate me, my dear wife. I can beat any number of them."

"You don't understand." Maigra's words tumbled over themselves. "They'll be armed. And there'll be so many of them. They'll kill you." She buried her face in his chest. "I couldn't bear that."

Yar looked uneasily around the grotto.

"Is there another way out?"

"No. Just back along the passageway. Wait," she froze, straining to hear something. "Is that them coming?"

Yar's face went white. He pushed her away.

"You stupid woman. This is your fault. If he'd been alive, I could have used him as a hostage. Now what do I do?"

Maigra sagged, despair crumpling her face.

"I didn't think of that. I'm sorry. Please, please forgive me. But. . . yes," her eyes widened, "there is a way out."

"What are you talking about," Yar snarled.

"Look. That tarp. Hide under it at the back of the cave. They'll never look there."

"You fool." He'd had just about enough of her. "They'll search after they find him." He jabbed viciously at Will's body. Maigra's smile trembled through tears.

"Not if they find me here. Next to him. And if I say you just laughed when you saw the note he sent and knew it was a trap, and that you're not coming. Maybe if I tell them the truth, they won't search."

"What truth?" Yar asked with half a mind; he was wondering if the tarp would be big enough to cover him.

"If I tell them I killed Will."

"They'll kill you," he said, without caring.

She threw herself at him again, wrapping her arms around him and pressing her body tight to his, sobbing.

"I don't care. I'll do anything to save you. But hurry, I'm sure they're coming now. Promise me you won't come out until they're gone."

Down the passage, small noises echoed. Someone was approaching. Without hesitation, Yar accepted her sacrifice. He tore the tarp from the pile of tools and ran to the back of the grotto. Maigra watched him disappear under its folds, a second, larger heap added to the other piles of equipment in the grotto. Unremarkable.

The grotto was silent again.

Carefully, Maigra wiped the tears from her face.

••••

"The Stone Breaker." Tiernan's memory coughed up the name. "That's what the monks called your son."

The Counselor seemed genuinely amused. "Well, that's one of the perks of starting your own religion. The Stone Breaker. I did not give Johan credit for so much perception. He knew the power of the ring. As you do."

Tiernan looked down at the ring. "I told someone once that all my military training taught me was the value of seizing the advantage. So what is the advantage to me if I break the ring stone and keep your past secret?"

The Counselor watched him.

"Tell me what you want, soletei," he purred. "Ard Creggan at your feet? Wealth?"

"Can you give me those things?" Tiernan asked.

The old man laughed softly.

"I could. I've done more for others. You remind me of a young man I know in Ard Creggan. He leads an interesting group of people who desire change so badly, they are willing to die for it. It helps, of course, that they have lost everything. A man at the bottom of a well grabs any rope thrown to him. What rope may I throw to you, soletei?"

"You're a prisoner yourself. How can you help me?"

"Why, I can change the future. Your future. That's what you want, isn't it?

"A chance for a future," Tiernan amended. "That would be enough."

The Counselor's smile mocked him.

"I've already provided for your future. For every year that I have been imprisoned, I have sent out of Ard Creggan a sliver of a share, a negligible portion of the metal they produced. Decade after decade, ships brought it here to Dun Nemed. It is piled around you now, part of the very fortifications, the walls all over this island. After Ard Creggan falls, there will be no more ore, no more smelting. The man who possesses Dun Nemed controls all the ore left on this world. He can make the future whatever he likes. I give it to you."

"I am no merchant," Tiernan scoffed. "What would I do with it?"

The Counselor opened his arms wide.

"Use your imagination, soletei. You can do anything you want. You will hold a monopoly—after Ard Creggan falls. I recommend keeping prices high. Your reserves won't last forever. But they'll last long enough. And I'll give you the technology to fashion any weapons you'd want. "

"And Ard Creggan? You talk as though it has already fallen."

"As we speak, yet another native son's desire for change is reordering the future—and removing the last of the city's underpinnings. I can guarantee the city will be a pile of rubble before this night is over. Your competition gone. You face a very interesting future, soletei. In a way, I envy you."

Tiernan barely saw the right for the possibilities leaping into this mind.

"Your keepers won't like that."

"No, they will not," the Counselor admitted. "But then, they don't have to find out."

Tiernan nodded, this time in agreement.

"What do I do? How do I stop the keys from opening?"

The Counselor looked surprised.

"It's simple. A blow from the Thorn should do it. It's made from Ard Creggan metal. Nothing harder. It should break the gemstone. You should hurry, however."

Tiernan slipped the ring from his hand.

"Do it quickly," the Counselor urged him. "The storm is very near its peak. My jailers are not known for their patience and they barely know their own strength. I don't blame them. I am impatient to leave this place, too. They won't wait forever. Ard Creggan is falling. Break the ring. Save us both."

Tiernan laid the ring on the tomb's stone lid. He raised the spike. A single blow smashed the stone into black shards. He felt like a man waking.

The Counselor turned his head, listening. To a silence. There was no sound of the storm outside. He stood and stretched. To Tiernan's amazement, he rose a much younger man, the years fallen away. "There, that's about right," he said. He looked down at the sarcophagus and ran his hand slowly along its length. "Well, my dear, our last meeting. I have enjoyed our conversations all these decades." On his way out, he brushed past Tiernan without giving him a glance.

••••

For the second time that night, a man entered the grotto and halted inside the entrance. Samuel saw at once Will was dead. The upper half of the blanket covering his thin body was stained dark red. His head flopped forward at an unnatural angle, as though he was hearing the confession of the woman sitting beside him, Maigra's bowed head touching his arm.

Samuel felt an unexpected pity—for both of them— but not surprise. The message he'd received earlier that day had not fooled him. "Come to me, quickly, my love. He knows everything. I'll wait for you in the grotto."

Maigra wasn't his lover. She was their spy in Sinon Yar's household. She gave him information, not her body. But only the two of them knew the truth. Obviously, it was a trap. Samuel came anyway. Because he wouldn't desert Maigra, no matter the risk.

And he wouldn't judge her now.

Samuel heard a sound, between a groan and an exhalation coming from the back of the cave where a tarp covered some digging equipment. Maigra heard it too. She half rose, sat down again, her fists clenched in her lap, her eyes on the grotto floor. Samuel moved towards the tarp.

"Leave it," she said roughly. He barely recognized her voice. The face she turned to him was not Maigra's, not the old Maigra. It was as though every pain, every bit of grief that she'd suppressed all these long months finally had been allowed to leave its mark on her face. He looked away to the heap at the back of the grotto. A hand extended from underneath the tarp, with thick fingers that had once raked the ground, as though trying to crawl.

"Who is it, Maigra?"

She closed her eyes. "A man. No one important. His wife killed him." She said it so artlessly, he was sure he'd heard wrong. "You see, the gas accumulates back there in the cave. It kills in minutes. It took a bit longer with him. But he's dead."

"Sinon Yar?"

"Yes, I told you." Maigra scowled as though he was simpleminded. "Eon brought me here when he first found the grotto." She looked over at the lifeless heap.

"If Eon hadn't risked his life, I would have died." She turned around to look at the wall carvings, the great snake undulating above Will's body. "Did you know this was his greatest discovery, this grotto. He'd been looking for decades. And he'd nearly given up hope. One day, he just happened upon it. I think that's the happiest I've ever seen him."

A distant rumble and the room rocked. A second shock, followed by a third. Part of the back wall fell in, burying the first and last Basillius of Ard Creggan. Dust choked the air. Samuel stumbled to Maigra.

"We have to get out of here. Before the tunnel collapses."

"Will says all of Ard Creggan will fall. He's made sure of it. The end of the old order. The end of Ard Creggan. He wanted to kill you too." She smiled and the sight frightened Samuel more than her pain. "I couldn't let him hurt you, Samuel." She touched his cheek.

Another wrenching noise from deep below. Dirt and stone rained from the ceiling. Samuel pulled her to her feet but she slipped from his grasp and backed toward Will.

"Maigra, please."

She sat down beside Will's chair. "I'll wait here for Eon. He'll be back."

"He's dead, Maigra." She winced. A crack lengthened in the ceiling. Any moment it would come down on them. "He's dead," Samuel repeated.

Her mouth twisted.

"I killed Will. He was Eon's son and I killed him."

He desperately wanted to find the right words. "Will was behind the bombings. Innocent people died because of him. He wasn't blameless."

Maigra looked at him with gentle pity. "I didn't kill him for any of those reasons. It might have made it easier if I had. But I didn't." She paused. "He was my half-brother."

Samuel stared at her. "Then Eon...."

She nodded. "It was our secret. I made him promise he wouldn't tell. I didn't want Eon hurt. People would have talked. It would have interfered with his work."

"Did Will know?"

"I don't think so." She looked up at Samuel." Do you think Eon will forgive me for killing my brother? His son?"

A rumbling, growing louder by the moment, choked off Samuel's reply. This time he didn't wait. He pulled Maigra up and dragged her down the passageway. A dense cloud of dust billowed out as more of the grotto collapsed behind them. They made it to the foot of the ladder. He looked up, panting. The opening above glowed red. What was left of Ard Creggan was burning. What now? The ladder. *Will couldn't have come down that ladder.*

Maigra smoothed her dress, looking around as though surprised to be there. "Eon will think we've left him. We should go back."

"Yes. That's right," Samuel agreed. "We need to go back. Eon will use the other entrance to the grotto, won't he? Where's the entrance, Maigra? Did Eon show you?"

She smiled. "Of course he did, silly."

Back down the tunnel, just inside the entrance, she froze. Will lay under the writhing coils of the carved stone snake, as water streamed into the grotto from the broken wall. The fallen stone exposed a narrow corridor behind, its arches marching away into darkness.

"Eon said there had to be a way for the priests to get in without being seen," Maigra whispered.

Samuel pulled her into the corridor, picking up the lamp that somehow had escaped the stone fall. She resisted only as long as Will's body was visible, looking back until a turn in the alley cut the grotto from view. Successive shocks sent them careening into the walls, clambering over fallen stones. The slabs overhead stolidly resisted the pull of the disintegrating rock around them. Samuel knew they wouldn't for long. They ran when they could, crawled when they had to, sometimes through narrow gaps of rubble. The passage seemed to go on endlessly. Side alleys tempted them, but they kept to the main passage. The heat was stifling at times when the passage led upwards, near to the surface where Ard Creggan was its own funeral pyre. Then the path sloped downward, steeply downward, for a long while. The air grew cooler, damp. The rumblings grew more distant. Finally their lamp shone on a massive wooden door, banded with rusty iron. There was no retracing their steps. If the door didn't open, they would die here at the bottom of Ard Creggan.

Samuel took a deep breath and pushed hard against the door. The wood panels fell to splinters, rotten. Outside, the stars beyond the rim winked.

"Time opens all doors," Maigra said softly and walked out into the cool predawn.

CHAPTER THIRTY

The storm still raged. Rain lashed the island, the late afternoon sky as dull and dark as slate. The wind wailed through every crick and cranny of the stone fort's walls.

Silence enveloped her.

Am I dead?

"Are you alright, Zoë?"

She sat up. Livy threw her arms around her, knocking her flat again.

Zoë hugged her with one eye on the edge of the cliff; it was too close. Then she looked around in disbelief. The sisters sat just inside the circumference of the standing stones. Beyond them, the elements still hurled themselves at Dun Nemed. Inside the megaliths, silence and calm reigned. From each of the standing stones, blue-green columns of light spiraled up into the sky, undiminished by the storm, penetrating the black, boiling clouds overhead, holding back the tempest.

"I was behind that one." Livy pointed at a megalith nearest the cairn, "when it lit up. I came out, saw you, and they've been like that ever since. It's sort of eerie."

Yes, Zoë thought, it was, at the very least, eerie.

"Where's Tiernan?"

"He's in there." She pointed at the cairn. "He told me to stay out here and do my job."

"He would," Zoë said tartly.

At that moment, the door to the cairn opened. The Counselor emerged, followed by Tiernan. Zoë blinked. The desiccated old man was gone, the years dissolved. He was as young as the soletei.

"Ah, Lady Deich. And this must be who?" The Counselor peered at Livy who shrank behind her sister. "By the looks of her, another Deich brat. How nice, a family reunion. Well you're both a long way from home. Have you come to say farewell?"

"I'm here to reclaim the keys of Ard Creggan."

"How melodramatic. But patience. The keys will be yours in a moment."

"He says this Judgment is his jailers, his people," Tiernan corrected himself, looking sideways at the Counselor, "come to take him home. It's the end of his time here. He'll be gone. Just like Johan Pietra's book said, 'Release the wronged'."

"I don't care about him. I want the keys."

"Oh, my dear. You are too late. I'm afraid Ard Creggan is dust. Your cousin Will was extremely industrious, for all his limitations. He's brought the city down around his head by now. Admittedly, with a little assistance from the maps I made sure he found, but he chose his own path."

She felt the anger rising inside her. "If Ard Creggan is gone, it's because of you. Nothing happened in that city, without you knowing about it. Nothing. So open the keys. Let your jailers know what you've really been doing. Let them judge if you deserve to be set free."

"Yes," he said, unruffled. "Let them judge." The Counselor's smile was suddenly malevolent. "But first, why don't you ask your soletei what he's done with the only way to open them?"

A shiver of cold misgiving passed through Zoë. She looked to Tiernan standing dumbly at the Counselor's side.

"We made a bargain, didn't we Tiernan. Do you know what his half of the bargain was?"

The Counselor held out his hand. On his open palm, lay the gold snake band, a bent gaping mouth where the stone once sat.

"The soletei had his price," the Counselor smirked. "Publicans up, Citizens down. He sold you out, Lady Deich."

His laugh was caustic. "I spent centuries looking for that cursed ring, the key. And thanks to your father, it and your mother simply dropped into my lap."

Zoë's stomach felt like she'd been kicked. "You killed my mother."

The Counselor was taken aback.

"On the contrary. I was your mother's most attentive physician in her last illness. I had no desire for Zora die before she told me where to find the ring. Believe me, no one was more distraught. I'd had such hopes. No indeed. I didn't kill your mother." He paused. "But I would have, if she had given me the ring."

The Counselor looked around him at the lights blazing upward, the tempest beyond. "You know, your father would have given anything to stand where you are right now, on the verge of meeting my keepers. How rich. He was in pursuit of a Judgment that was totally meaningless, a fairy tale. He was so willing to believe in a fantasy, as though that would cure all his world's ills."

He stretched as though he'd been cramped for too long..

"I've always found that men with altruistic goals are easily manipulated. All I've ever wanted to do is destroy things. But the keys restrained me. That's the one disservice my dear son did me. He made the Families guardians of their keys. Told them all sorts of horrible things would happen if they didn't safeguard them."

"Well, he was right. I imagine he got nervous when he learned what I was really like. If the stones recorded the Family memories, maybe he felt I would behave myself. It slowed me down a bit, I'll admit. I could have been much worse. But I managed. Forgive me. I seem to be very talkative this evening. It's such a relief to talk freely after several hundred years.

"You know, my jailers hid the key stone in the ring for good reason. All those memories locked away. If I was to avoid judgment, it had to be destroyed. It was just luck that my simple-minded son would find it on Gurama. And hide it from me all these centuries."

He gestured to the columns of light around him.

"Now they will review the keys. But it's all just a meaningless rush of impressions without the ring's keystone. I'll be released for lack of evidence." He laughed. His mood was growing increasingly jovial. "You lose Lady Deich. The ring is dust. You can't expose my record. The books are closed."

He laughed again, delighted with himself, and hopped onto the truncated base that interrupted the ring of megaliths. He looked up expectantly.

"It only remains for my jailers to arrive at a decision, which," he paused to listen, "they should do at any moment. Ah, yes, they have."

The same blue-green glow emitted by the standing stones, washed over him and launched skyward. His image wavered, like a mirage seen through waves of rising heat.

"I mean to keep our bargain, soletei, to a point. Providing you can turn a profit before I return. Because I plan to return. This time I won't have the keys to keep me in line. I plan to strip this world. There's the metal I've stockpiled. Did you think I would just give that up? That's valuable on any world. And your oceans. Water is priceless. And much more. I've been cataloguing your assets for ages. You people may be good for something yet. Oh yes, I plan to be very busy after I have my freedom."

The Counselor was fading, stretching, disintegrating into motes of light.

"I can't tell you how sick I am of you all," his voice floated back to them. "You are boring, simple-minded and willfully ignorant. I've spent centuries among you and I'm still appalled at how little your minds comprehend."

And he was gone.

Tiernan slumped to his knees, his face ashen. Livy clung to Zoë, crying.

The keys still hummed in their niches. The blue-green columns still stood around them. But already their force was weakening. A fat raindrop struck Zoë 's cheek, a gust of wind ruffled her hair.

"You have to do something," Livy wailed.

Tiernan struggled to his feet, his eyes anguished. She heard his thoughts clearly.

I've done this. He'll come back. Everything will be so much worse. I should have died first.

Another voice slid into her consciousness.

"The cycle turns to retribution's end. Judgment sits when six align. Gather ten keys and one of line."

One of line. Her hand touched the Deich key still in her pocket. A rush of memories.

Jomini, a child, reaching up to take his father's hand, the feel of his dry callused palm, her mother's arms around her reading a book aloud, the shockwave resonating in his chest from an artillery attack, the cries of dying men, a baby wailing, her mother handing her a blood soaked bandage. Their memories were there now, Tiernan's and Livy's memories of war. It wasn't just Publican memories in the keys anymore. It takes more than one person's memory to give the true story. *Open the record of stone.*

Zoë's heart pounded so hard she thought it must break. She'd never really needed the ring.

I'm one of his line. I've done it before. I can open the keys. Set memory free.

She looked quickly around the circle. The light columns had shrunk nearly to the tops of the standing stones. There wasn't much time.

"Livy, help me. Get all the keys and bring them to me."

The girl turned a tear-stained face to her.

"Move!"

Livy ran.

The first standing stone. The glyph: *Huckat.* Livy raced back with a handful of orbs, dropped them and ran for more. *Where was the Huckat key? There.* On to the next standing stone. Naoi. She scanned the keys, picking out the Naoi key. An. Dha.

Tri. Shockat. Cheithre. Matching glyph to key. Yar. Cuig. And finally, the Deich orb.

She ran back to the stump so recently occupied by the Counselor. Tiernan had not moved; Livy whimpered and clung to her arm. Zoë gave her a hug and gently pushed her away. There wasn't a lot of time.

"Stay with Tiernan. He'll take care of you. Don't worry."

Zoë stepped up onto the base.

A tingling maybe. Am I too late? Then there it was, imperceptible at first, a low hum, building again.

To Tiernan and Livy the sounds clashed and rang against each other, a cacophony of noise, painful to hear. Zoë heard something quite different. A run of notes rose around her from the keys now in their proper order. She could distinguish each one individually. Each note a memory, each line a history. They blended, weaving multiple harmonic overtones. The standing stones were singing.

One of line. Seek the goddess. Kneel to her song. Set memory free.

Zoë genuflected and let the memories wash through her, a living conduit as the keys emptied their now ordered memories, like a overfilled lake that finds a tiny crack in the dam wall, the trickle widening the gap, becoming a torrent, until the entire dam gives way.

He should have tried to stop her. He didn't. And perhaps, in his heart, he knew this was the only way. Livy, too frightened to move, didn't fully realize what was happening, even when Zoë, like the Counselor, became the insubstantial thing of dust and light motes, dispersing gently in the updraft, disappearing before their eyes. Almost, he imagined the phantom raised a hand in farewell. The ear-rending din trailed off. The storm vanished, the clouds parted. The orbs, still in their niches, were as clear as the moonlight that poured down on them in Dun Nemed.

••••

Livy refused to leave Dun Nemed, beating at Tiernan when he tried to drag her away. He could have forced her. But he didn't have the heart. Not anymore. She stayed five days. Five days waiting for Zoë to return, as though she'd just gone out for a walk and would be back any minute. Because for Livy to believe otherwise would leave her alone again.

Tiernan knew waiting was useless. If you had asked him how he knew, he would not have given a coherent answer. Perhaps it had been Zoë's face just before she disappeared. Her eyes were on something else, something of infinite interest. She was curious. She didn't look back.

When they finally sailed from the Island of Bey, it was with the assurances of Dio and the others that any unusual sounds or sightings in Dun Nemed would be reported to Gurama. But no word ever came to Livy. She began her schooling at the monastery and waited.

The Counselor's promise to return and plunder Gurama seemed less certain with every day, every year that passed. Whatever Zoë had unleashed in those final moments must have been enough to convince his keepers. Whether he was imprisoned on yet another unfortunate world, or if his punishment was more final, was anyone's guess. He was gone. And so was Zoë.

Within weeks, word reached them that Ard Creggan was gone too. The city collapsed in on itself during a night of violent quakes that ignited a conflagration so intense the massive guns at its pinnacle shattered like glass.

The surviving Publicans, living in squalor in their camps beyond the rim watched their city burn. They turned then to follow one of the few resistance leaders to make it out of the city alive. Tiernan even heard talk that Publicans were farming. Such a thing amazed him.

Peace even descended on the Citizens. The Tribune, suddenly deprived of its chief adversary, squabbled within its ranks and, for a time, consumed itself in an orgy of doctrinal purges. The old men who remained were too weak to stop the new guard who thought more of business and less of the party line. Everywhere, it seemed, the old order was being overturned.

In the long years to come, Tiernan would remember a conversation one late night, a conversation about what he would do when the wars were over. He bided his time. He was still soletei. They would need him again one day.

CODA

Zoë opened her eyes to a brilliant blue sky and whitecaps stretching out into the distance. Seagulls wheeled overhead, raucous. A white triangular sail on the horizon sped to a far away port. She turned in-island. The grey stones of Dun Nemed's windswept expanse radiated warmth in the sunlight. Swallows dove and darted between the standing stones and out over the green island. Grass crept between the broken pavers and green shrubs heavy with purple flowers poured over the inner walls. The massive stones of the cairn were tangled in vines, the door hung loose on its hinges.

I've been gone longer than I expected.

She looked down. At the foot of the pedestal, the sea breeze plucked at the browning petals of a floral wreath and swirled them away across the pavers. She smiled. It was a beautiful day after all, the sun warm on her back.

I wonder if that boat captain will still take me anywhere I want to go?

She stepped down.

ABOUT THE AUTHOR

K. E. Redmond is a writer living and working in Washington, DC, who also dabbles in whitewater kayaking, the martial arts, violin, and photography.

www.ingramcontent.com/pod-product-compliance
Lightning Source LLC
Chambersburg PA
CBHW071246170626
46809CB00001B/89